"We shouldn't be seen together any more than necessary," Natalie said.

"Why not? We've shared a breathing apparatus, a fishing boat and a taxi."

"Still. If there's a chance of me being taken rather than one of the other girls, I'd rather it was me."

Duff touched her cheek. "Again, they might not take you. Since we returned to the cave and those thugs fired at us, I'd say there is a strong possibility they'd shoot you rather than take you as a hostage."

"How else am I supposed to find where they hid my sister? I can almost bet they won't tell us if we ask."

"Then we have to find a way to follow them to where they are hiding your sister and the other girls."

"The longer she's missing—"

"We'll find her." Duff tipped her chin upward and lowered his lips to hers. "I promise."

NAVY SEAL
SURVIVAL

BY
ELLE JAMES

First Published in Great Britain 2016
By Mills & Boon, an imprint of HarperCollins*Publishers*
1 London Bridge Street, London, SE1 9GF

© 2016 Mary Jernigan

ISBN: 978-0-263-91897-7

46-0316

Our policy is to use papers that are natural, renewable and recyclable products and made from wood grown in sustainable forests. The logging and manufacturing processes conform to the legal environmental regulations of the country of origin.

Printed and bound in Spain
by CPI, Barcelona

Elle James, a *New York Times* bestselling author, started writing when her sister challenged her to write a romance novel. She has managed a full-time job and raised three wonderful children, and she and her husband even tried ranching exotic birds (ostriches, emus and rheas). Ask her, and she'll tell you what it's like to go toe-to-toe with an angry 350-pound bird! Elle loves to hear from fans at ellejames@earthlink.net or www.ellejames.com.

This book is dedicated to all those men and
women who serve in the armed forces protecting
our country and our way of life.
Thank you for your dedication and service.

Chapter One

"This is the life." Dutton "Duff" Calloway stretched out on the lounge chair beside the pool and closed his eyes.

Sawyer handed Duff a chilled and fruity Pain Killer drink before easing into the chair beside him. "I'm surprised all four of us were granted leave at the same time." He pulled the colorful miniature umbrella out of a chunk of pineapple and dropped it on the end table between them.

Duff downed a third of the drink. Normally he preferred an ice-cold beer. But the combination of orange juice, pineapple and whatever else went into the icy concoction was refreshing and helped add to the sense of relaxation he'd hoped to find in Cancun, Mexico. "I didn't look that gift horse in the mouth. I took the leave and ran."

"Flew," Sawyer corrected. "Yeah, I wasn't questioning our luck, either."

Duff shaded his eyes and stared past the palm trees to the beach beyond. "Where do you suppose Quentin and Montana got off to?"

"They said something about reserving a diving excursion for tomorrow. I told them to sign us up while they were at it."

Duff closed his eyes and soaked in the warm rays of sunshine. "Sounds good. After our last mission to clean up that terrorist training camp in Honduras, I'm satisfied to just be a bum and let the hotel staff and excursion coordinators do all the work."

Sawyer crossed his hands behind his head and leaned back, grinning. "Yeah. This is the life."

Duff's grin matched Sawyer's. "No boss, no guns, no terrorists. Just me, my friends and this..." He lifted the Pain Killer. "Now all we need is a good beer."

"And women," Sawyer added.

Silently, Duff agreed. How many months had it been since he'd been with one? He sighed. Too many to count.

A giggle sounded at the opposite end of the pool and the tittering of female voices drifted through the balmy air.

Sawyer leaned his head up. "Speak of the devils."

Life couldn't get more perfect. Duff swallowed more of the fruity drink.

The gaggle of young ladies appeared to be college-aged, all wearing bikinis and makeup, and carrying beach bags filled with towels and sunscreen.

Duff sighed. "Too young."

"Hey. We're not old men, yet." Sawyer sat up and studied the women as they strolled past their lounge chairs, headed for the beach. "Oh, wait. You are an old man at the ripe old age of thirty."

"That's right. And twenty-year-old, vapor-headed women don't do it for me. I like mine more mature."

"Here you go." Sawyer chuckled. "Mature women, three o'clock."

Two women who couldn't be a day under fifty strolled by.

Instead of grousing over a missed nap, he rose and followed Sawyer out to the beach. If he had to be awake, he might as well enjoy the scenery on the beach. Sawyer was sure to strike out with the blonde, and Duff would ask her if she'd like to have drinks later.

The worst she could do was say no.

NATALIE LAYNE STEPPED onto the Cancun beach, her toes curling into the warm, white sand. She'd followed her sister's footsteps as closely as possible without having her sister there to guide her. A week ago Melody had come to the resort with her Kappa Delta sorority sisters. Six young women with nothing but fun in the sun on their minds.

As Melody's only living relative, Natalie had asked her younger sister to report in each day. Melody had happily complied, texting each evening, letting Natalie know she was okay and having a great time. Until the fourth day.

Natalie's chest tightened. She hadn't received the call until late that night when a heavily accented voice came over the line announcing, "We are most sorry to report that your sister, Melody Layne, disappeared on a dive this afternoon at approximately three o'clock."

Having lost their parents two years before to a ten-car pileup on Interstate 10, Natalie hadn't been able to grasp what the man was saying.

Her sister? Disappeared? "What do you mean *disappeared*?"

"She was diving with a boat operated by Scuba Cancun. When she didn't come up with the others, the dive boat operator searched but could not find her."

A hundred questions had raced through her head as

she'd held the phone to her ear. "What else has been done to find my sister?" she'd asked, her voice sounding as if it came from someone else down a long tunnel.

Her sister. Gone.

Natalie had given up the highly volatile and extremely rewarding career she loved as a special agent to return to New Orleans to see her sister through high school graduation and the start of college. Someone had to be there for her after their parents died.

Now this.

No way.

Natalie had taken the information from the Cancun police officer and hung up. Stunned and numb, she'd turned to her computer. She'd been leery of her sister traveling to Mexico. The endless reports of corruption in the Mexican government and law enforcement had been enough to convince Natalie it had been a bad idea.

Melody had insisted Cancun was insulated from the corruption and had its own security to protect the thriving tourist industry.

At the time Melody was making arrangements to go, Natalie should have put her foot down. Not that it would have done any good.

Melody had a mind of her own and the money their parents had left. She had reached the age of majority and could make reservations without her sister's consent. And she had.

That gut feeling had proved right.

Within minutes of receiving the call, Natalie had hit the number for her former employer, Royce Fontaine, and asked for help.

As the head of the Stealth Operations Specialists, he could help her as no one else could.

"Natalie, are you ready to come back to work for us?" He'd chuckled. "Travel journalism too tame?"

"Royce, I need your help."

The laughter ceased. "Name it. We're here for you."

She'd explained the situation and paused for him to digest the information.

"I'll run a scan on the area to see if there are any other occurrences of missing women," Royce told her. "You're right to be suspicious."

"Let me know what you find. In the meantime, I'm headed to Cancun."

"Will do," Royce said. "I'll send Lance Johnson out on the private jet with the equipment you'll need to keep you wired so that we can find you if you run into difficulty."

"Thanks, Royce. I knew I could count on you."

"Anytime. I had Lance lined up to take on another mission tomorrow, but I can take it myself."

"I hate to pull you from other important assignments—"

"Nat, we're talking about your sister. Family comes first. That's why I'm sending Lance. Technically he's as good as Geek and a better shot if you need backup."

"Good." Natalie's mind had already been five steps ahead, working through everything she had to accomplish before leaving for Mexico. "I don't expect any cooperation from the Mexican government or police."

"Look, why don't you fly in the corporate jet with Lance? It'll save you time and money."

"I don't know. I'm thinking I need to perform this mission undercover. I might get more answers that way."

"Fair enough. But you'll get there faster on the SOS plane than flying commercial. I can have Lance dropped at a different airport. He'll meet up with you later. That way you arrive separately."

"Agreed. As long as I'm in Cancun by tomorrow."

"You will be."

While Natalie packed for Cancun, she went through her text messages and photos from Melody, searching for clues. Her mind played through many scenarios for what might have happened to her sister, each one worse than the last.

When her cell phone rang she was so deep into her thoughts, she jumped.

"It's not good, I'm afraid," Royce said without a greeting.

Natalie's heart plummeted into her belly. "What did you find?"

"In the past two days three young women under the age of twenty-five have disappeared from the Cancun resort area and Riviera Cancun."

"Why hasn't it been in the news?"

"All three were from different countries—Sweden, Australia and now the U.S. To each country, it was a solitary incident. The Mexican government isn't advertising this as a serial event. Contacts in Cancun say they're treating two of them as individual unfortunate incidents."

Rage shot through Natalie. "Bull! Three women? Did they all disappear diving?"

"Two diving. The third? They claim the young woman wandered off and probably fell into an abandoned underground tunnel associated with the Mayan ruins located at Chichén Itzá, a little over an hour outside Cancun."

Natalie couldn't believe in this day and age any country would give up that soon. But then Mexico had its share of internal issues. The police force could be run by the local drug cartel. They might not have an interest in finding the women. "Did the authorities even *try* to find the women?"

"My contact said they gave it a perfunctory look and abandoned the search when it grew dark. If you go—"

"There's no *if*," Natalie said. "I'm going."

"Of course." Royce continued. "You have your extra passports, yes?"

"I do."

"Pick one that's foreign, but not Australia or Sweden. And stay blonde. The three women thus far were all blonde."

"Nice to know."

"I had Geek run a background check on their families. They were from rather small families who have little money to pay ransom, much less to pursue lengthy litigation or to hire private investigators to search for their daughters."

Natalie's jaw hardened. The women were targeted for their blond hair, youth and their family's lack of financial backing.

"So what you're telling me is that you don't think they were snatched for ransom."

"No." Royce's single word in that flat tone said it all.

If the women had been kidnapped, their captors weren't going to bargain to give them back. They would be sold or drugged and forced into the sex trade.

Forcing the emotion out of her heart, Natalie said, "The sooner we find them the better off they'll be."

"Right." Royce gave her the details about meeting Lance at the New Orleans airport the following morning.

Once she ended the call, she sat back, tapping her bare toe, while she sifted through her passports. Part of her old life as an agent, the passports were vital to getting around the world without raising suspicion. Though she'd given up her job as an agent, Natalie had been hesitant to destroy the passports. Now she was glad she hadn't.

Picking the United Kingdom passport, she stared at the image inside. The likeness was still valid: blond hair, blue eyes. And the woman in the photo looked like her with shorter hair. Hell, it was her, three years ago when she'd been active as an agent, sent all over the U.S. and other countries to do what the CIA, FBI or Interpol either couldn't do or hadn't successfully managed to accomplish.

The passport would serve its purpose to get her past authorities and establish her as a young, single woman of limited assets and family connections on vacation in Cancun.

With the backing of her old team, she made hotel reservations for the same resort where Melody and her friends had stayed, using her UK alias, Natalia Scranton, age twenty-three.

Sleep had been impossible, but she'd tried anyway, keeping her cell phone on the pillow beside her in case, by some miracle, Melody was able to text her.

The next day she'd met Lance at the airport and climbed aboard the SOS private plane. Once the plane took off, Lance came at her with a loaded syringe.

Natalie held up her hand. "Stop."

"You need to be tagged with a tracking device. Should whoever took the other girls manage to snag you, we'll need to follow you to wherever they've taken you and the others."

"Yeah, but why the syringe? Can't I keep a tag in my pocket?"

"That would be fine if you were wearing clothing with pockets at all times. I suspect, since we'll be at a resort, you will be wearing a bathing suit."

"I could sew the device into the suit."

"Will you sew one into every item of clothing you could possibly wear?"

Natalie frowned. "Maybe. I've just never liked the idea of being tracked all the time, by anybody."

"In this case, it's for your protection."

"Okay, but put it somewhere I can dig it out if I decide I don't like it anymore."

"Sure. Where would you like it?"

"Between my toes." She lifted the hem of her sundress and held out her leg.

Lance injected the tracking microchip and sat back in his seat with a hand-held device. He hit the on switch and waited. "There." He pointed to the dot on the screen. "There you are. Now, if you're swimming, scuba diving or taking a shower naked, we'll be able to find you."

Natalie snorted. "Nice to know I'll have company in the shower."

Lance grinned and opened an aluminum suitcase. From it, he selected what appeared to be a tiny hearing aid and handed it to her. "You remember how these work?"

"Yeah, yeah. Let's get to the good stuff." She leaned toward the suitcase and plucked out an H&K .40-caliber pistol and several boxes of rounds. "I prefer the stopping power of a .45 caliber or 9 mm, but the smaller weapon will be easier to hide."

"Exactly." He handed her a set of throwing knives similar to the ones she had locked in her safe at home in New Orleans.

Natalie ran her hand over the handles, wishing she had time to practice throwing. These, too, she had given up when she'd decided to retire from SOS operations. How would she explain to Melody the need to have her own set of knives, especially when she was terrible in the kitchen?

Melody had no idea what Natalie had done before she'd returned home to New Orleans to be there for her after their parents died. Her sister thought she had given up the boring desk job in D.C., the first job she'd taken when she'd finished college.

That seemed such a long time ago.

Loaded with all the equipment and weaponry she could easily hide in her suitcases, in the room or on her person, Natalie arrived at the hotel, smiling like a young single woman on vacation, ready to soak up the sun and play in the sand.

She greeted the desk clerk in an English accent she'd perfected when Royce had assigned her to a case in Oxford, England. Despite staying there, she was so busy working the case, she didn't have time to play tourist and get to know the area. She asked for a room on the same floor as the one her sister had shared with her three girlfriends from college. Hopefully she'd find out more by hanging out with them at the bar, if they hadn't already gone home, frightened by the loss of their roommate.

As soon as she unpacked her suitcase and stowed her weapons in the room's lockbox, she stripped out of her sundress and pulled on the sexy swimsuit her sister had insisted she buy. She had, against her better judgment. Whatever made Melody happy made Natalie happy.

In what little there was of the black suit, Natalie had to agree with Lance and the subcutaneous injection of the tracking device. Anything other than her body beneath the suit would have stood out.

Dressed for the beach and hanging out with young people, Natalie grabbed a beach towel and sunglasses and headed down to the lobby. She passed through the lobby and out to the pool area, checking out all of the people she passed, wondering if one of them was behind her sister's disappearance. None of the young women looked anything like those in Melody's selfies.

Once out on the beach, she noted someone changing the yellow flag to red, indicating it was dangerous to swim.

Mothers herded children out of the shallows and teens frowned and complained as they slogged through the water to shore. A group of young women in colorful bikinis stood in water up to their waists, taking pictures of each other. The man hoisting the red flag, waved for them to return to shore, yelling something about riptides.

Natalie glanced farther down the shoreline, thankful for her sunglasses. The white sand was bright behind her lenses, but without the glasses the beach would be blinding.

Sand crunched beside her and a shadow crossed over her face.

Natalie tensed.

"Looking for someone?" a deep male voice asked.

She turned toward the man wearing nothing but black swim trunks and a smile. And, good Lord, he didn't need anything else. Suntanned and tattooed, his body was magnificent, his white teeth shining in his tanned cheeks. Dark hair, dark eyes and a friendly face topped him off.

"Not particularly," she answered, remembering to use the proper British accent before promptly turning the other way.

"Name's Sawyer," he said. "Me and my buddies just got here today."

"That's lovely." As handsome and well-muscled as the man was, he wasn't in Natalie's plan. She was there for her sister, not to flirt with muscle-bound men in sexy black swim trunks.

"Bug off, Sawyer," another voice said from behind Natalie and she spun to face an even taller man with jet-black hair and a jaw that looked hard enough to crack walnuts.

She tipped her sunglasses down, curious about the true color of his eyes. Her heart fluttered as the deep green orbs stared down into hers and took her breath away.

No. She didn't have time for the sudden tug of attraction. If she knew for certain where her sister was and that she was all right, Natalie might consider flirting with this incredibly handsome man with the tribal tattoos on his shoulders.

"Excuse us," he said. "It's been a while since we've been around a beautiful woman."

"No need to explain." *Just leave.*

A shout rose up, drawing those startlingly green eyes

away from Natalie and to a couple of splashing figures farther out than was safe. Both figures appeared to be women, one closer in than the other. The woman furthest out seemed to be moving out to sea despite her attempt to swim ashore.

Mr. Green Eyes left her and jogged toward the water, the one called Sawyer on his heels.

Natalie hurried after the two.

"Looks like the current is dragging them out," Sawyer said.

The man with the green eyes didn't respond; he raced toward the water without slowing. He charged in up to his knees and dived into the surf.

His friend dived in after him. Soon both men cleaved through the water.

No matter how strong they could swim, the current had a way of doing its own thing.

Sawyer stopped at the first woman, while Mr. Green Eyes continued out to the other.

A teen stood at the water's edge, watching the event unfold, a surfboard clutched under one arm. Natalie altered her direction and ran toward him. "Mind if I borrow this?"

He passed it to her without question.

Natalie ran toward the water.

By the time she slid onto the board, Sawyer was on his way back to shore with the first girl. Green Eyes had reached the other.

The poor woman was so frightened she clung to him, climbing up his body to get farther out of the water.

They were so far out, Natalie wasn't certain she'd get there before the two went under, but she had to try. The lifeguard wasn't far behind her. Between the three of them, they should be able to help the woman.

As she neared, Green Eyes was attempting to untangle the woman's arms from around his neck. The more he tried, the more desperate the woman became.

Then Green Eyes went under.

The woman clinging to him went down with him, but immediately let go and struggled to the surface.

Natalie paddled faster, searching the water for the man who'd disappeared. *Come up Green Eyes*, she prayed. Come up!

Chapter Two

Duff should have stayed at the pool with the kids. Now he was in over his head in the ocean, with a dangerous riptide and a panicked woman climbing all over him.

So much for relaxing.

When he'd had his fill of water up the nose, he dived down. The woman who'd clung to him despite all his reassurances that she'd be all right, let go and fought her way to the surface.

Duff stayed down long enough to circle the woman and come up beneath her. She slapped at the water, her strength waning.

Grabbing the woman by the ankles, Duff yanked her down, climbed up her back and secured an arm over her shoulder and diagonally down to her waist. Then he surfaced, leaning her back so that she faced the sky, her arms and legs batting at the water like a puppy learning to swim.

"Damn it, woman. Stop struggling," Duff bellowed.

"Way to make a frightened victim less scared," a female voice said from behind him.

He glanced over his shoulder into the blue eyes of the woman in the black swimsuit he and Sawyer had been talking to before they'd gone for a swim. "What are you doing out here?" Duff demanded. "Didn't you see the red flag?"

"I did. But I thought you might need something more than your muscles to get the woman to shore. The current is too strong to get her back on your own."

Duff treaded water with his one arm, his other clamped tightly around the woman, holding her head above water.

"What's your name?" the woman on the surfboard asked the one in the water.

"Lisa," she responded weakly.

"I'll bet you're tired."

The woman in Duff's arms nodded.

"My name is Natalia," the blonde said. "And this is…?" She raised her brows, giving Duff a pointed look.

"Duff," he said.

"And the lifeguard is here, as well," Natalia said.

Duff glanced behind Natalia at a young man barely out of his teens paddling toward them on a surfboard.

"Lisa, do you want to go back with me, or the lifeguard?"

Lisa gulped and answered, "You."

Natalia nodded. "Good. I think Duff can help you climb up on this board. Would you like that?"

Lisa nodded though her hands tightened on Duff's arm.

Natalia held out a hand and smiled encouragingly. "Take my hand, Lisa. The man behind you will help you onto the board and stay right beside you all the way back to shore. Won't you?" Natalia prompted Duff.

"I will." Between them, they hoisted the woman onto the board.

Duff took a moment to breathe normally before starting back to shore.

Natalia had Lisa lie on her stomach and then she did the same, lying over the woman's back. She started paddling. "Paddle, Lisa. The more you paddle, the faster we get to shore."

Lisa paddled, weakly flailing her arms, her face turned toward the shore.

Duff circled behind them and pushed the surfboard. With all three of them working it and cutting at an angle, they eventually made it to the beach, the lifeguard following. A group of young women met them, helped Lisa out of the water and enveloped her in a half dozen hugs.

Duff stood beside Natalia, propping the surfboard in the sand. "Thanks."

She responded in her pretty English accent without looking up. "You're quite welcome."

Duff held out a hand. "Name's Duff."

Natalia glanced at his hand and hesitated. Finally she shook it. "I'm Natalia. Lisa was lucky you were on the beach today."

He shrugged. "I'm glad I could help. Look, we didn't get much of a start back there. Would you like to have dinner with me tonight?"

She didn't even bat an eyelash before responding. "No, thank you."

"Duff!" Sawyer approached, his arm around a woman wrapped in a beach towel. "Glad you made it back to shore. Wouldn't be the same diving without you tomorrow."

Duff snorted. "Nice to know you missed me."

Lisa broke free of her group of friends and wrapped

her arms around Duff's neck. "Thank you so much for saving my life. I hate to think what would have happened if you hadn't gotten to me when you did."

"I'm sure someone else would have helped."

Lisa turned to Natalia and hugged her, too. "You two are my heroes. After the horrible past two days, I needed you."

Natalia hugged the woman. "Horrible? Did you get caught in the current yesterday?"

Lisa shook her head, her eyes tearing. "No, I lost one of my sisters." The rest of the young women gathered around her, all hugging each other.

"What do you mean?" Natalia asked.

Lisa sniffed. "We were on a diving excursion. She was my dive buddy. I turned away for a moment to see a moray eel in the coral. When I turned back, she was gone."

Natalia's face paled.

"Are you telling me she wasn't found?" Duff asked.

Lisa and her friends all shook their heads as one.

Natalia reached for Lisa's hands, her own shaking slightly. "What a horrible experience."

"If we could have a do-over, we never would have gone diving." Lisa dashed away a tear. "Melody was one of the nicest people I know."

"Didn't the dive master look for her?" Natalia asked.

A brunette in a pale pink bikini nodded. "He spent the next two hours searching."

A sandy-blonde added, "They radioed to shore and the shore patrol came out and helped in the search."

"Nothing." Lisa sniffed again. "I don't know why we came out to the beach today. I don't think I'll ever go in the water again."

The young lady wrapped in the towel, standing in the circle of Sawyer's arm, stepped away from him and slipped an arm around Lisa. "We can't leave Cancun until our scheduled flights. Lisa and I thought we'd look around in the water, even though Melody disappeared a long way from here. We kind of hoped the current would have carried her back this way. That's why we were out so far."

"It was stupid," Lisa said.

"At least you two are okay," Duff said.

Natalia nodded. "You should go back to your rooms and rest."

Lisa and her friends thanked them again and left the beach to return to the resort hotel.

"Wow, what rotten luck," Sawyer said. "To lose your friend and almost lose your life all in the space of two days. Not my idea of a great vacation."

"If you'll excuse me, I think I'll go lie down, as well," Natalia said.

"If you won't have dinner with me," Duff persisted, "will you let me buy you a drink later?"

She gave him a half smile. "We'll see."

He watched as the gorgeous blonde left, walking up the beach in her sexy black swimsuit, her long hair drying in soft curls around her shoulders. Beautiful and strong. What other woman would have jumped in to help in such a dangerous situation?

Sawyer made a diving motion with his hand followed by the sound of an explosion. "Turned you down, did she?"

Duff nodded, his gaze on the sway of Natalia's hips. "The battle's not over."

His friend clapped his hand onto Duff's shoulder.

"That's my man. We're on vacation here. What's a vacation without a beautiful woman to keep you company?"

Indeed. And Natalia had captured his interest in more ways than one.

He headed back to the hotel, Sawyer walking alongside him. "Didn't you say Quentin and Montana were looking into a diving excursion?"

Sawyer nodded. "I hope it wasn't with the crew who lost the girl yesterday."

Duff almost hoped they went with the same crew and to the same spot where the girl disappeared. Something wasn't right about losing a diver and not finding anything to indicate what had happened.

NATALIE HURRIED BACK to the hotel, grateful she and the two muscular men had been there to help save Lisa and her friend from the strong current. Not only was she glad the girls were still alive, she was also happy it had served as an introduction to hang out with them without arousing suspicion. She'd make it a point to find them at dinner or at the bar that evening. Perhaps someone had seen something they didn't realize might be a clue to what had happened to Melody.

Deep inside, Natalie believed her sister was alive. Finding her would be the challenge.

She stopped at the excursion planner's desk and asked about dive trips for the next day. She let the planner, Maria Sanchez, go through the different options and dive companies. When Maria didn't mention Scuba Cancun, Natalie made it a point to ask.

"Friends of mine came last month and went on a dive with Scuba Cancun. They said if I came to Cancun, I had to book with them. Do you book trips with them?"

Natalie blinked her eyes, trying for young, sweet and innocent, when all she wanted to do was to jerk the binder out of the lovely Maria's hands and make her own arrangements.

"Yes, we do book Scuba Cancun, but the last time I looked, they were full for tomorrow. Let me check and see if they've had any cancellations." She clicked her keyboard and stared at the screen, her brows puckered. Then they smoothed and she smiled up at Natalie. "You're in luck. They have one space available for tomorrow morning. Would you like me to book it?"

Natalie let go of the breath she'd been holding and nodded. "Yes, please."

If she thought it would do any good, she'd run around asking questions and demanding answers. But if there was a chance Melody had been kidnapped in some elaborate scheme to smuggle women into the sex trade, the people she wanted answers from would be highly unlikely to talk about anything to do with the missing college coed.

No, she'd have to keep her connection with Melody under wraps. Perhaps her blond hair and English accent would help set her up as the next target. The quickest way to find the kidnap victims might be to become one herself.

On her way through the lobby to the elevator, she made it a point to say hello to the front desk clerk, the bellboys and the concierge. If any one of them was involved in whatever might be going on, she wanted them to consider her as their next target.

On the way up to her room she noted the camera in the top corner of the elevator car. As she stepped out of the elevator onto her floor, she spotted one of the girls from the beach sliding her card into the door lock and hurried toward her. "I'm so very glad I caught you. I'm Natalia, from the beach." She held out her hand.

"Oh, yes. Thank you for saving my friends." She took Natalie's hand. "I'm Kylie."

"Are Lisa and her friend doing all right?" Natalie asked.

The pretty blonde smiled and nodded. "Lisa and Jodie are sleeping. Their parents were able to book them on a flight back to the States tomorrow morning. I wish the rest of us could have gotten on board, but the flight was full."

"I hope they have a safe flight back. Are you all going to dinner later? My roommate was supposed to come with me on this holiday, but her aunt died and she had to cancel at the last minute. I would love to have someone to eat with."

Kylie's brows rose. "You mean you're not with the hunky guys?"

Natalie smiled. "I only wish. They are kind of dreamy, don't you think?"

"Oh, yeah." The younger woman sighed. "They're just what I imagined finding here. If only things had worked out differently. Since Melody disappeared, none of us can think of anything else. The vacation is ruined and we're all ready to be home with our families."

"I can imagine. Nothing's worse than losing someone you're that close to." Natalie bit down on her tongue to keep from adding "Especially when she's your only living relative whom you love dearly."

"As for dinner…we will probably go down around eight. Since it's Lisa and Jodie's last night here, we'll end up at the bar for one last round before the group disperses. You're welcome to join us. I'm sure the others will agree."

"Thank you. I'm glad I won't have to sit awkwardly by myself." Natalie waved her hand. "See you around eight, then." She turned and walked toward the door next to Kylie's and let herself into her room.

First thing, she checked the disposable cell phone she'd purchased at the airport for any messages from Lance. She'd texted him as soon as she'd pulled it from the plastic packaging so he'd have her number.

Since her eventful walk on the beach, he'd had time to arrive and text her with his bungalow number.

With a couple hours to spare, Natalie figured she might as well check in with the agent.

Slipping a long, flowing skirt over her swimsuit, she plunked a floppy hat onto her head and left her room. Rather than take the elevator, she opted for the stairs, checking the locations of all the security cameras. She wondered if Lance could get into the security system and review footage from the night before last to see if it showed them potential suspects that could have been stalking the young women.

Lance had rented a bungalow on the resort property, giving him a little more privacy than a hotel room. He could set up his equipment and not worry too much about being bothered.

Natalie took a roundabout route, looking for security cameras strategically placed. Outside the hotel, the cameras were directed toward common areas and the hotel itself. The bungalows seemed to be more private.

Strolling along a pebbled concrete path as if she hadn't a care in the world, Natalie eventually arrived at the correct bungalow with its Do Not Disturb sign hanging on the door handle. A quick glance around assured her she was alone. She knocked softly.

A moment later Lance opened the door. "I was wondering when you'd stop by. I see you've already been in the water based on where the tracker located you." He jerked his head and stepped to the side. "Come in."

Natalie slipped inside. "Have you hacked into the police data files?"

"I'd love to say yes but, one, I just set up my system. And two, the local authorities' system isn't that sophisticated. I'm not even certain they keep data on computers."

"What about the hotel security system?" Natalie asked.

Lance crossed to the small desk located against one wall. "Working on that now." He sat in the chair and opened his laptop. On the screen was a map of Cancun, the resort pinpointed by a bold green dot.

"I see you're keeping up with me." Natalie was at once reassured and disturbed by being followed so closely. If it weren't for the nature of the case, she would never have let anyone inject a tracking device beneath her skin. Though she had confidence in her ability to defend herself, she knew her limits. Being drugged or outnumbered could reduce her abilities to nil. In that case, she'd be happy to have Lance track her and provide backup if or when she went missing.

"When you get into the hotel security camera files, check the bar, lobby and restaurants where Melody was to see if there are any suspicious characters paying a little too much attention to her. Royce gave you the picture of Melody, didn't he?"

"Got it. I'll let you know if I find anything."

"I'll be in the restaurant and bar tonight if you can get into the security system by then."

"I should be able to pull up the online system. I can keep an eye on you, if you'd like."

"Whatever." Natalie shrugged, staring at the green dot on the screen. "You already have me on the tracking system."

"True."

"Do one more favor for me, will you?" Natalie asked.

"Shoot."

"I met a couple of guys on the beach today. Both had tattoos and were well built. Check them out. I'd almost bet they're military, based on their bearing. They said they only got in today, but that could have been a line. Both hit on me."

Lance grinned. "If the rest of that swimsuit is as revealing as the top, I don't blame them."

Natalie frowned. "Find out who they are and when they arrived. They were certainly big enough to carry off a female with one hand tied behind their backs."

"Will do."

"Thanks. I'd better get back so I can be ready in time for dinner. If you find anything, I want to know ASAP."

Lance saluted. "Yes, ma'am."

With an hour to get ready, Natalie hurried back to her hotel room and hit the shower. Something didn't feel right about getting dressed up for dinner when her sister could be in some kind of hell, praying for someone to rescue her.

Rinsed and scrubbed free of the sticky salt water, Natalie toweled dry and then ran a blow dryer over hair, pulling the curl out. Applying the flat iron, she erased all the curl and left her hair hanging long down to her waist, the way college girls wore it. Normally, Natalie would have worn her hair pulled back in a ponytail. Her hair was long, but only because she was too lazy to go to the hairdresser on a regular basis.

Once she finished her hair, she applied makeup, another ritual she'd avoided over the past two years. With the intention of being the next blonde to be nabbed, she gave herself smoky eyes with a combination of blue and charcoal eye shadow topped with a thin stroke of black eyeliner and mascara.

Satisfied with the result, Natalie dressed in a short, soft blue dress with narrow spaghetti straps. The dress was another one of Melody's choices. Natalie hadn't worn it out of sheer modesty. The hem barely covered her bottom, revealing every inch of her long legs. The thin straps and form-fit of the garment meant thong panties and no bra.

Feeling as close to naked as one could be in a dress, Natalie slipped her feet into strappy silver stilettoes. Grabbing the matching silver clutch, she slipped money, her passport and one of the knives inside. At the last minute she flipped the switch on the earbud and stuck it in her left ear.

"Hey, Lance."

"I'm here, sweetheart."

"Don't call me sweetheart."

"You got it, babe."

Not in the mood to argue, she let his teasing slide. "Anything?"

"Your guys are two of the four who arrived today. I traced them all the way back to the plane they flew in on. Dutton Calloway, Sawyer Houston, Benjamin

Raines and Quentin Lovett. Their plane originated from New Orleans. Probably legit."

"Thanks."

"Do you want me to dig deeper?"

"Yeah, just in case they're buyers for the kidnapped women."

"Got it.

"And…Lance?"

"Yes, babe?"

"Remind me to punch you later."

A chuckle sounded in her ear.

"Will do."

"In the meantime don't talk to me unless I talk to you first or you find something major. I can barely think in my own head without a man in it, too."

She stepped into the corridor at the same time as Melody's friends.

"Oh, good." Lisa met her at the elevator. "We were just about to knock on your door."

"Thank you for letting me tag along." Natalie entered the elevator, followed by Melody's friends.

Natalie wasn't worried she might look too much like Melody that the girls would recognize her. The only picture her sister always carried with her was one of the two of them with their parents six years ago. Natalie had sported a short bob back then, her hair several shades lighter than now. And she was six inches taller than her younger sister's five feet, two inches.

"Have you heard anything from the police about your friend?" Natalie asked.

"No, but the Cancun police stopped by again to ask more questions." Lisa shook her head. "It's not like I had anything new to say. Melody was there. Then she wasn't."

Natalie's heart contracted and her eyes stung. The only way she could keep tears from falling was to remind herself that Melody was alive, waiting for her big sister to find her.

Dinner was a somber affair. Melody's friends spoke to one another in subdued tones, each quietly introspective after the past two days' trauma.

"Are you ready to go back to our rooms?" Lisa asked.

"No. We can't leave without drinking a toast to Melody," Kylie said. "Come on. One last drink before Lisa and Jodie take off in the morning. It'll be the last legal drink for them until next year when they turn twenty-one."

"Y'all go on without me. I don't feel much like partying," Jodie said.

"You have to come. We're going to drink to Melody. It wouldn't be the same without you." Lisa and Kylie each grabbed one of the girl's arms and marched her out to the cabana where reggae music was in full swing and a few couples moved to the beat on the dance floor.

Natalie followed the girls to the bar beneath a thatched-roofed cabana strung with twinkle lights.

They all ordered strawberry margaritas and stood around a table, no one making a move to take a seat.

"Melody's favorite," Lisa said, her voice cracking as she lifted her glass rimmed with sugar. "To Melody. I hope she's found safe and returned home."

Kylie's eyes filled with tears as she lifted her glass with the others.

Fighting her own tears, Natalie raised her glass. "To Melody," she whispered. *I will find you and bring you home.*

Chapter Three

Duff spotted her as soon as she stepped out of the hotel into the cabana bar.

She tagged along behind the group of young women they'd met on the beach following the rescue. They ordered sugar-laced strawberry margaritas, each with a colorful umbrella perched on the rims of their glasses. As one, they lifted their drinks in a toast.

Natalia sipped the sugary concoction and winced.

Duff almost laughed. A gut feeling told him she wasn't into fruity mixed drinks.

She set the drink on the table and glanced around the outdoor bar as though looking for something or someone. Maybe a rescue from the drink.

Duff strode to the bar and ordered two long-neck beers. Once served, he slipped up behind Natalia. "Looking for someone?"

She turned, the corners of her lips rising. "Not really."

Duff nodded in greeting to the other women at the table before turning his attention to Natalia.

She stared down at his hands, her brows cocked. "Are you a two-fisted drinker?"

"No, I kind of hoped you would prefer beer to whatever that is you're drinking."

Natalie crossed her arms over her chest. "Do I look like a beer drinker?" Her lips quirked again.

Duff chuckled. "Not really but, like I said, I hope you are."

She relaxed and held out her hand. "Actually, I don't really like sweet, fruity drinks."

"Thank goodness." He handed her one of the ice-cold bottles. "I was afraid I'd end up drinking both. Alone."

"Glad to help my fellow rescuer out." She tipped the bottle back and drank a long swallow before glancing up into Duff's eyes. "You don't take no for an answer often, do you?"

"I'm persistent. When I want something, I go after it and stay after it until I get it."

She snorted softly. "A prize to be won?"

"No, a challenge to be met." He lifted his bottle and tapped it against hers. "Anything worth having is worth fighting for."

"Like?"

"Freedom. The lives of your friends and family..." His voice deepened. "The love of a woman..."

She blinked, her smile spreading. "Wow, are you always this smooth with the ladies?"

Duff grinned. "Heard that on a movie. That's the first opportunity I've had to use it." He set his bottle on the table and took hers from her hand and placed it beside his. "Come on. Let's dance." He slipped his arm around her waist.

She hesitated. "And if I don't want to?"

"You do," he said. The fact she hadn't told him to bug off already gave him hope.

"Cocky much?" she asked.

"Only when I'm sure of myself."

"Which is often, I take it."

Despite his arrogance—or maybe because of it—she allowed him to lead her onto the dance floor. An up-beat reggae tune had some couples leaving and others stepping up the pace.

Once on the dance floor Natalie tilted her head to the side. "Sorry, but I don't know how to dance to this music. I tend to be all left feet."

"Then you haven't had the right partner." He swung her away from him and then pulled her into the curve of his arms, her back against his chest, his lips beside her ear. "Just relax. I'll do all the work."

The warmth of Natalia's hand in his and the way she wore that incredibly sexy blue dress, made Duff's insides curl and his body heat.

He twirled her beneath his arm and back to face him, his hips moving to the rhythm, his feet keeping the beat, urging her to follow.

The more he moved with her, his hand resting on the small of her back, the more her body relaxed. By the end of the song, she could anticipate his moves as if they'd danced together for years and she fit perfectly against him. Her long legs and lithe, athletic body felt right in his arms.

When the music switched to a slow, sensuous rhythm, Duff pulled her against him.

For a brief moment her body stiffened and then melted against him, her hand resting against his chest. He liked how warm and firm it felt there. Yeah, he could get used to this woman.

"So, what brings you to Cancun?" he asked, his lips

so close to her ear he wanted to nibble the pretty earlobe. In her heels, she still wasn't as tall as he was, but she was close.

His arms around her tightened and Duff leaned his cheek against her hair. "I'm sorry. Was my question too personal?"

She glanced up at him as if realizing for the first time that she was dancing with him. Her brow furrowed. "What was it you asked?"

Her question hit him in the ego. He'd have to make a better impression to keep her attention. "What brings you to Cancun?"

"I'm on holiday," she said with a smile.

"Alone?" he asked.

"I wasn't supposed to be, but that is the way of it. My friend's aunt died and she had to cancel at the last minute to attend the funeral."

"I'm sorry for her loss." He pulled Natalia close to his body and swayed to the music, his hips rubbing against hers, causing an instantaneous reaction. His trousers tightened and he wished they were somewhere more private—like his bedroom.

Natalia leaned into him, her fingers curling into his shirt, her nails scraping his chest.

Duff swallowed a groan rising up from his lungs. She was doing crazy things to him without even trying.

Natalia smiled up into his face. "What about you? Why did you come to Cancun?"

"Same. Vacation. Long overdue."

"Tough job?" she asked.

He snorted. "At times." He didn't talk much about his work, except to his Special Boat Team 22 team-mates. Most SEAL assignments required top-secret clearance. Information about those operations was only shared with people cleared for that particular mission. He found himself wanting to tell Natalia all about it. But he couldn't.

The music ended and she stepped away. "Thank you for the dance." She turned to walk away.

Not wanting the night to end yet, Duff caught her hand. "Will you dance with me again?"

She lifted one shoulder. "Maybe, but for now, I'm going to visit with my new friends."

And that was it. Natalia walked away, leaving Duff standing in the middle of the dance floor.

She returned to the group of young women and took up a position on the periphery, her gaze scanning the room again and again.

Duff frowned. What was she looking for?

A hand containing a chilled bottle touched his arm. "You look like you could use this."

Sawyer handed him the cold beer and took a drink of his. "So, what's the story?"

"What story?" Duff tipped his bottle and drank a long swig of the cool liquid.

"You came, you danced and she walked away. Now she's dancing with another guy." Sawyer jerked his head toward Natalia, who was walking toward the dance floor with a different man.

Duff's jaw tightened. So it wasn't her new friends she wanted to hang out with. Natalia wanted to dance with another man.

"Did you say something to make her mad?" Sawyer persisted.

"I don't think so."

His friend shook his head. "This is a first. I haven't

known a single female to turn down the Duff's incredible charm."

"Shut up, Sawyer."

Sawyer gave him an innocent grin. "Just saying."

So, Natalia wasn't interested. He should move on and find another willing female to spend time with. Unfortunately none of them appealed to him like Natalia.

She danced with a couple of different guys before Duff had had enough. He pushed away from the bar and announced to his friends, "I'm hitting the rack."

"Me, too." Montana stood, stretched and draped an arm over Duff's shoulders. "We're on for scuba at zero-eight-hundred."

"Should be fun," Quentin added.

"What's fun about scuba without blowing something up?" Sawyer asked.

Duff shook his head. "See you guys in the morning."

Sawyer leaned toward Quentin and Montana and said loud enough for Duff to hear, "He's just sore about being shot down by the pretty blonde."

Montana laughed. "Is that it? Duff's giving up?"

Quentin shook his head. "Never thought I'd see the day."

Duff left the cabana without waiting for his friends. As he entered the hotel, he glanced back at Natalia, dancing with yet another man.

He shrugged and turned away.

Who needed a female complication, anyway?

Focus on Melody.

Natalie smiled and laughed at each of her dance partners' jokes and acted as if she cared. If someone was after young blonde women, she needed to be seen and considered. Dancing with several men put her out in the middle of view as a single white female. She had to take advantage of it, even though she'd rather be dancing with Duff. For some reason the tough-looking man with a smattering of tattoos across his shoulders and back made her feel more feminine than any other man she'd ever been around.

When she'd been with the SOS, she'd felt as if she'd had to prove herself equal if not better than her male counterparts. Most of the men and the women who worked for Royce Fontaine were prior military, secret service or FBI. Natalie had been working as a boring desk jockey with a natural ability to shoot straight and true every time.

Her love of shooting had come about when she'd moved to Washington, D.C., and realized just how dangerous the city could be for a single woman.

She'd gone to the range to learn how to fire the .40-caliber pistol she'd purchased to protect herself. After firing a few times she discovered she was good and had tried other weapons the range had in stock. Soon she was an expert shot with every weapon the range had to offer, and salesmen were asking her to test and demonstrate their new releases. When she wasn't working, she was at the range.

Natalie had landed the SOS job when she'd run into Fontaine at the range. He'd been there at the request of the salesman. Royce had watched her fire several of the new weapons the salesman had brought along that day. When she'd finished firing, she'd given her feedback and turned to find the SOS boss staring at her with a smile.

That had been the beginning of the job she'd grown

to love, utilizing her skill with guns and her love of adventure. She'd become a Stealth Operations Specialist, one of the only agents who'd never served in combat or law enforcement.

Royce had set her up to go through a special three-month training program similar to infantry basic training only with mercenary soldiers. They'd cut her no slack and expected her to play rough, despite being a female. She'd come through, scoring the highest on weapons qualification, even on the live-fire courses and urban terrain exercises. She had a sixth sense for when to shoot and when not to shoot.

She'd been an operative for two full years before her parents were killed in an automobile crash, right before her younger sister's high school graduation.

Natalie'd had no other choice. Family came first, and you didn't give up on them.

As she danced she watched the bar. Several men stood out to her. Of course Duff and his friends, who'd arrived the same day as she, because of their obvious physical fitness and laid-back charm. Natalie sensed no threat from them. The bartender was a compact man with dark hair and darker eyes. He served drinks quickly, without talking, and the wait staff seemed a little intimidated by him.

Then there were the two Hispanic men who'd sat at a table in the corner, drinking Coronas and watching Melody's friends and her as she danced with a sandy-blond-haired playboy from New Jersey.

To Natalie every man in the place was under suspicion until she proved his innocence. And all bore watching.

When Duff and his friends left, Natalie felt her energy leave with them. Melody's friends didn't have the heart to stay and party when two of them would leave the next day and Melody remained missing.

"We're calling it a night," Lisa said. "I hope you have a better vacation here than we did." She hugged Natalie. "Please be careful."

"Thank you." Natalie hugged the other woman, as if by so doing, she was a little closer to her sister.

They rode up the elevator together and parted ways in the hallway of their floor.

A soon as Natalie entered her room, she tapped her earbud. "Anything?" she asked Lance.

"Got into the security videos. I've spent the past three hours going through all the footage."

"And?"

"I ruled out the hallway. The lobby had several characters I found lurking in the outdoor cabana. Could you slip away for a few minutes to check out the faces, or do you want me to try to send snapshots to your cell phone?"

"I don't want any hackers to intercept the messages. I'll be there in five minutes."

"Wear the earbud in case you run into any trouble on the grounds."

"Will do." She slipped out of the blue dress and stilettoes and into a long casual dress and flat sandals. If someone asked her where she was going, her answer would be for a walk on the beach. She took the stairs down to ground level and walked out the back door of the hotel. The pool was lit and glowed a soft ocean-blue, the water rippled by the salty breeze.

Natalie schooled her pace to take it slow, like a person on vacation enjoying the night air, not like a woman on a mission to save her sister. When the path curved toward the bungalows, she veered in the opposite direction and took a more direct route to the beach. If someone followed her, she didn't want him or her to discover her repeated visits to the bungalow where Lance worked.

By the time she reached the bungalow ten minutes had passed and the wind had picked up, whipping her long hair around her shoulders and across her eyes.

Lance opened the door as soon as Natalie knocked.

She slipped inside and crossed to the computer screen. The video had been paused on two dark-haired men sitting in the corner of the cabana. "I saw these two tonight. Same table, same corner of the cabana."

"Happen to get their names?"

Natalie shook her head. "No. They stayed at the table the entire time."

Lance fast-forwarded the video, stopping on an image of Melody and a man dancing.

Her heart came to a hard stop in her chest and Natalie sucked in her breath. Her gaze caught on Melody, laughing, dancing and flirting. She was so happy and carefree.

When her heart started pumping again, it raced, anger pushing blood through it faster and faster.

Natalie leaned toward the screen, trying to see the man with her, only getting the back of his head. "Can you see his face anywhere in the video?"

Lance shook his head. "No matter how many times I replay, I can't get a clear shot of his facial features."

"Melody is five feet two inches tall and, based on what she's wearing, she's probably got on at least three-inch heels, making her five feet five. He's at least another five to six inches taller than her. That would put

him right around six feet tall. And he has dark hair."
She straightened. "Anything else?"

"Several men in the lobby of the hotel. Some of them with women who appeared to be girlfriends or wives. Others were alone." He clicked on the touch pad and another view popped up on the screen. "This is the lobby."

Lance took her through several minutes of video he'd tagged as potential. When they were done, Natalie didn't feel any closer to finding her sister than before. "Tomorrow morning, I'm scheduled to go on the dive boat Melody and her friends sailed with."

Lance's brows dipped. "Stay with your dive buddy in case you run into trouble."

She snorted. "What are the chances the people who took Melody will hit the same dive boat two times in a single week?"

"Slim to none. If these creeps are smart enough to kidnap three women without raising a red flag with the local authorities, they won't go after someone on that dive boat."

Natalie sighed. "I know it's a reach, but maybe I'll get some information out of the crew. Perhaps one of them is in cahoots with the operation."

Lance clicked another button on the computer and a GPS tracker screen appeared. "Either way, I've got you covered. Get some sleep tonight and be careful down there tomorrow."

"I don't hold out hope on sleep." Natalie crossed to the door. "I can only imagine what Melody is going through."

"Yeah, it's gotta be tough when it's your sister. She's not my sister, and I can hardly wait to catch the bastards."

Natalie smiled. "Thanks for your help, Lance. It's nice to know SOS is backing me."

"We miss having you around. Nobody quite equals our best sharpshooter."

Warmth stole through her. They might not be blood relatives, but the members of the SOS team had been like family.

She opened the door and checked to make certain the coast was clear. A light breeze stirred the air. The moon shone bright through the gently undulating palm fronds, stirring shadows. But nothing else moved.

Natalie left the bungalow and headed toward the beach.

She passed another bungalow and was about to cut across to the more direct path leading through some bougainvillea bushes when the snap of a twig sounded behind her.

She spun, ready to face an attacker. Again, nothing moved in the shadows except the shadows themselves.

A shiver rippled across her skin in the balmy night air. Rather than cut through the thick bushes, she continued on the pebbled concrete path toward the beach. Once on the sand, she'd be in the open. Unless whoever was following her had a gun and planned to shoot her, she'd have half a chance at defending herself.

Natalie picked up the pace, stretching her long legs, trying to put distance between her and whoever or whatever was following her. By now she heard footsteps behind her.

Whenever she turned, she saw nothing. Trained to survive in hand-to-hand combat, she knew her limitations. She was better with a gun. A large man could subdue her, if he knew what he was doing.

Once out in the open, she could face her adversary head-on. No more hiding in the shadows. By the time she burst out of the palm tree shadows onto the beach, she'd gone past powerwalking, skipped jogging and was running all-out.

She turned to look over her shoulder and ran into a solid wall. Arms wrapped around her, holding her so tightly she couldn't move.

She tried to scream but a hand clamped over her mouth.

Chapter Four

Duff wasn't ready to call it a night. Though tired from traveling, his thoughts spun, going over and over the dance with the beautiful Natalia. She'd been in a hurry to end their time together but then made time to dance with other men. Not that Duff had any right to tell her who she could or couldn't dance with. Heck, he'd only just met the woman. Okay, so they'd survived a riptide together, but that didn't mean they were a couple.

Too wound up to lie down in his cabin, Duff had headed for the beach. The sound of the ocean washing up on the sand soothing him like nothing else.

He'd walked a mile along the beach and back, finally ready to call it a night when a woman burst out of the shadows. Still hurtling forward, she'd spun to look behind her, unaware of Duff on the sand. When she hit him in the chest, he reached an arm around her middle and clamped the other one over her mouth, sure she'd scream at being caught.

Not in the mood to fend off questions by anyone wandering past, Duff held on.

Her elbow jabbed backward, slamming into his ribs.

Duff grunted but maintained his hold. "I'm not going to hurt you."

She squirmed against him, her body slim and curvy beneath his hands.

"I'll let go of you if you promise not to scream," he said. "Do you?"

She stopped moving and nodded.

Duff released her and stepped backward.

The woman flung herself out of his reach and spun to face him.

Her wild-eyed stare registered with Duff. "Natalia?"

"Yes, it's me." She shot a glance toward the path leading to the resort. "Are you by yourself?"

"Yes." His gaze followed hers. "Why?"

"You weren't expecting anyone, were you?"

"No." He stepped up beside her.

Natalia was breathing hard, her fists clenched, her knees bent, ready for fight or flight.

"What's wrong?" Duff asked.

She stared into the shadows for a long moment before her body relaxed. "Nothing."

"Are you sure?"

When she stepped closer and stared back the way she'd come, Duff could tell she'd been frightened by something.

He eased an arm around her waist and pulled her against him, still staring at the path leading toward the resort. A strong desire to protect this woman washed over him and he found his free hand curling into a tight knot. "Did someone try to hurt you?"

"No." She leaned into him for a moment. "I think I got spooked by the shadows."

The warmth of her body next to his reminded him of why he was out walking along the beach. Natalia stirred him as no woman had in a while. Back-to-back

missions left little time to develop relationships. Not
that he had any intention of starting anything lasting.
He was on vacation. A lighthearted fling might be the
only thing he could engage in. Then she'd go back to
her life and he'd go back to his. If she was even willing
to consider a fling.

Natalia pushed away from his side and stood in front
of him. "I'd better get back to my room."

As she turned to walk away Duff realized he didn't
want her to go. He reached for her hand and snagged
it. "Don't go."

She paused, her brows pulling together. "It's late."

He tipped his head toward the sky. "Going in now
would waste all those stars."

She lifted her chin, her hair cascading down her
back. "They are beautiful."

"Gorgeous," he agreed, although he wasn't looking
at the sky. He was staring at the woman in front of him.
"Walk with me."

She hesitated for a moment, her gaze slipping to the
path from which she'd emerged. Natalia sighed. "Okay."

As they fell in step Duff maintained his grip on her
hand. Before they'd gone too far, Natalia slipped out of
her sandals and looped them over her fingers. Her toes
dug into the sand. "Never could wear shoes in the sand."

"Me neither." He lifted a foot, exposing his own bare
feet. "I feel more at home by the sea than anywhere else.
What about you? Where's home for you?"

She hesitated and then answered, "Oxford."

"I had the opportunity to visit Oxford two years ago."
Natalia stiffened beside him. "Did you?"

"I had a three-day layover while the plane we were

traveling on was being repaired. I managed to get a little R & R in. I spent an entire day in Oxford."

"That's great." Her fingers tightened in his.

"What's your favorite place in Oxford?"

She stepped toward the water until the waves gently caressed her toes. "I don't know. They're all pretty great."

Her vague answer set off a sharp nudge of suspicion. He changed tactics and fed her a lie to see if she'd fall for it. "I loved visiting the Angels Church and the Old Fort Museum."

"Yeah. The Angels Church is pretty," Natalia said.

Duff stood beside her, his feet sinking into the wet sand. She'd just fallen for his lie. He'd bet she'd never been to Oxford and that she wasn't even English. Too many times she'd slipped up and lost the English accent. Why would she put up a front with him?

That she was hiding something didn't make him want to ditch her. Instead it intrigued him even more. He played her game, letting her think he fell for her line of bull. If it was an act of self-preservation, she might open up to him if she learned to trust him.

With the urge to smile tugging at his lips, he went along with her charade. "My favorite is the Bridge of Sighs. There's something hopelessly romantic about the name and the beauty of the bridge itself." The bridge in Oxford was one of the most beautiful bridges he'd seen in all of his travels.

Natalia tilted her head to stare up at Duff, her lips twitching on the corners. "I would never have taken you for a romantic."

He puffed out his chest. "I can be as romantic as the next guy." Even though he killed terrorists as part of his job. Perhaps that was what kept him grounded. He noticed the beauty all around him, even in the worst places he'd been.

And the woman in front of him was truly beautiful with her blond hair and perfect figure. So what if she was lying? What did it matter? He wasn't planning on marrying her. As long as he kept a close eye on his wallet and made sure she wasn't hiding a knife beneath her skirt, he would be all right.

"I really should get back to the hotel," she said. When she tried to step away, the sand and sea kept her feet anchored. She lifted one foot, took a single step and the other foot refused to break the suction of the sand. Natalia—if that was her real name—teetered to one side and almost fell.

Duff swooped in and caught her in his arms, crushing her to his chest. "Are you all right?"

"Of course. I'm perfectly fine." She laid her hands on his chest but she didn't push against him. Her fingers curled into his shirt, her gaze focusing on the material bunched in her fist.

Duff might have been all right if Natalia had been old and ugly. But her beautiful body pressed against his length, her hips brushing his, was almost his undoing.

Her breathing grew shallow and rapid. "I really should go," she whispered with less conviction.

"You really should stay. The weatherman said there'd be a meteor shower in—" he glanced down at his watch "—twenty minutes."

"No, that wouldn't be advisable. I have a lot to do tomorrow. I need sleep." She didn't make a move to leave.

Raising his hand, Duff touched her cheek. "Stars weren't meant to be viewed alone."

"You have your buddies."

He chuckled. "Wouldn't be the same." Duff lowered his head. "There's something about a beautiful woman, a starlit night and the sound of the waves lapping the shore…"

"There's that poet again…" As Duff closed in on her lips, Natalia lifted her chin.

Their mouths joined, sending a spark of electricity shooting through Duff, the charge spreading throughout his body, culminating in his groin.

He deepened the kiss, sliding his tongue along the seam of her lips until they parted, opening to him.

Duff slid his hand down her neck, over her shoulder and around to the small of her back. At the same time his tongue slipped between her teeth and caressed hers in a long, slow glide.

The slender fingers lying against his chest climbed up around his neck and threaded through his hair. A soft moan rose up her throat, the breath it escaped on filling his mouth, warm and sexy.

When at last he lifted his head, he stared down into Natalia's eyes. "You bewitch me." He brushed a loose strand of hair behind her ears. "When can I see you again?"

She blinked, her glazed eyes seeming to focus at last. "I… I'm sorry…this shouldn't have happened. I have to go."

Though he wanted to take the kiss to the next level, he figured he would be pushing her too fast. If she didn't trust him enough to let him know who she really was, she certainly wouldn't trust him enough to make love to him.

He would make love to her before he left Cancun and she'd want to as badly as he wanted to.

She stepped away, but not before he captured her hand in his. "At least let me walk you back to the resort."

Her gaze darted toward the path she'd emerged on. "Okay."

With her hand in his, Duff walked her to the main hotel. Once they reached the entrance, she stopped. "You don't have to take me farther. I can manage on my own."

He tugged on her hand, pulling her up against him. "Will I see you tomorrow?"

Natalia shook her head. "I don't know."

"I'll find you."

"Really, I… We…shouldn't."

"You're probably right." He smiled and touched her cheek with the backs of his knuckles. "But I can't seem to resist." Duff bent and stole a kiss, intending a swift brushing of his lips. As soon as his mouth touched hers, he couldn't hold back. He circled his arms around her and crushed her to him, taking her mouth and her tongue in a soul-satisfying kiss.

When he let go, she swayed and touched her fingers to her lips. "Good night," she muttered and ran into the building.

NATALIE JABBED HER finger at the elevator button, her vision blurred, her limbs trembling and her lips tingling from Duff's kiss.

What was she thinking? She wasn't in Cancun to make love to a stranger. She was there to find her missing sister. If she hadn't run into Duff on the beach, whoever had been following her on the shadowy path might have caught up with her, revealing himself. Damn. It might have been her only chance to connect with one of the persons responsible for taking her sister.

The elevator door slid open and she stepped in. She punched the number for her floor and watched as the door slid closed.

A hand jutted through, stopping the door before it could close all the way.

Natalie's heart leaped into her throat. For a brief moment she thought it might be Duff, following her into the elevator for another of those earth-moving kisses.

A man—not Duff—stepped in.

Trained to observe, Natalie noted he was tall with dark hair, dark eyes and swarthy skin. He wore a white guayabera shirt, unbuttoned at the neck, with a gold chain around his throat. Dark trousers and polished black shoes completed his outfit. By the lay of the fabric of his trousers, she'd guess they were expensive and the thick gold ring on his right hand with the flashing white diamond marked him as a man with money.

She moved to the corner of the elevator.

The man started to touch a button on the elevator and dropped his hand without selecting a floor. The doors closed and the elevator rose.

A trickle of apprehension rippled through her. As far as Natalie was concerned, any man or woman at the resort could have had something to do with Melody's disappearance. Her gut instinct was to tackle the man and hold a gun to his head. But she couldn't do that to everyone she met. She'd be hauled off, thrown into a Mexican jail and left to rot.

Natalie knew that the sooner she found her sister the better. Time allowed the abductors the opportunity to move her to an undisclosed location or to sell her to the highest bidder, shipping her to who knew where.

On the edge, with every instinct telling her to slam the man against the elevator wall, Natalie clenched her fists and waited for the car to reach her floor.

The ping of the elevator bell announced their arrival. She was curious to see if the man got off the elevator or rode it up farther. Natalie stepped out and turned the opposite direction of her room, watching the elevator door in her peripheral vision.

The man's gaze remained on her as he leaned forward and punched a button. The doors slid closed and Natalie let go of the breath she'd been holding.

So he wasn't getting off at her floor or planning to attack her. It paid to be suspicious, but was she getting paranoid?

She stood for a moment in the hallway, watching the display above the closed elevator. The number changed from the eight to nine and paused.

What did that prove? Only that the man might have gotten off one floor above hers.

Shrugging, Natalie pulled her key card from her pocket and walked to her door.

The day had been long and she was tired. Her thoughts returned to her sister. Deep in her heart, Natalie knew her sister hadn't drowned or been eaten by a shark. She wouldn't give up until she either found Melody alive or... She gulped. Or she found her body.

STRIPPING OUT OF her clothes, Natalie stepped into the shower and let the water run over her face and hair. The warm liquid caressed her skin, trickling down her body, over her breasts and lower to the juncture of her thighs. If her sister wasn't in danger, if Natalie was really there on vacation, she'd have stayed longer on the beach, kissing Duff. She might even have spent the night making love to him. She wasn't a prude and she recognized chemistry when it hit her square in the chest. Or rather, when she hit him square in the chest.

Butterflies fluttered against the lining of her belly. Duff was a temptation she could ill afford.

Turning the warm water to cold, she forced back the desire stirring inside and concentrated on her next steps.

Natalie climbed into the luxurious bed and laid her head on the pillow, wondering where Melody was sleeping. With her sister missing, Natalie didn't expect to sleep at all. But once she closed her eyes, the exhaustion of worry dragged her into a deep, dream-filled sleep.

Throughout the night she suffered through nightmares of bad guys taking girls from their beds and herding them through the jungle. She also dreamed of Duff lying on the sand beside her, leaning up on one elbow to stare down at her. Then he was kissing her, nudging her legs apart with his knee. He lowered himself over her and thrust deep inside her.

Natalie woke with a start to the sound of her phone's alarm ringing in her ear. What she thought would be a sleepless night had passed and another day had begun.

She had to find Melody. She rose with renewed purpose, slipping into a bright pink bikini, sure to draw attention to her and her near-naked body. Hopefully the attention of whoever had targeted Melody. Setting herself up as bait seemed to be the only way she could lure Melody's captors out into the open.

A small group of young men and women gathered in

the hotel lobby, wearing swimsuits and carrying bags with towels and sunscreen.

A young woman with brown hair and brown eyes waved a clipboard above her head. "All those going on the Scuba Cancun dive excursion, if you've already checked in with me, please make your way to the bus outside. We leave in two minutes."

Natalie gave the woman her name.

"You're good to go. Find a seat on the bus."

With a quick glance around the lobby, Natalie hurried outside to the waiting bus. Once seated, she leaned forward, pretending to dig in her bag. She tapped the earbud in her ear. "Going silent as soon as we board the boat," she whispered.

"Roger," Lance responded. "Sure you don't want me out there as backup?"

"No. I can handle this."

"I have you on my GPS tracking screen. Be careful out there."

"Will do."

"Is this seat taken?" a deep, sexy voice asked.

Natalie jerked her head up and crashed into a strong, hard chin. "Oh!"

Duff Calloway clapped a hand to his jaw. "Sorry. I didn't mean to startle you."

"I'm the one who's sorry." She scooted over, allowing him to take the seat beside her. "I hope I didn't break anything. I've been known to be hardheaded."

Duff slid onto the seat, his thigh bumping against hers. "I've been hit harder in a barroom fight." He worked his jaw back and forth and then grinned. "I didn't expect to see you on this dive."

She shrugged. "Seemed like the thing to do in Cancun. My coworkers back home recommended the diving here."

"Have you dived before or is this your first time?"

"I have a couple of times," Natalie responded.

"Sounds like you and this guy have met before," Lance said softly into Natalie's ear. "If you want me to run a more thorough check on him, I can."

With one man in her ear and the other pressing against her leg, Natalie predicted this situation could get out of hand quickly. "So," she said. "What does Duff stand for?"

The man beside her smiled. "Dutton Calloway. Duff is the nickname my team calls me."

Lance chuckled in her ear. "I'll dig a little deeper into his background."

"Team?" Natalie turned toward him. "What kind of team?"

He glanced away. "Just the guys I work with."

Interesting. Natalie narrowed her eyes. "What kind of work do you and your team do?"

"We're kind of a search-and-rescue crew."

Natalie's eyes widened. "Like in the case of natural disasters?"

He shrugged. "Something like that."

"I bet it can be dangerous."

"You have no idea."

The bus lurched forward on its way to the dock and the boat waiting to take them out to the dive location.

"What about you?" Duff started. "You mentioned your coworkers. What do you do for a living?"

She smiled and glanced out the window. "I freelance as a journalist."

"Interesting." He tapped a finger to his chin. "What do you write about?"

She grinned. "Travel, people and places."

"I imagine you've been to more exotic places than Cancun?"

She nodded. "On occasion."

"Do you do much diving off the coast of Britain?" he asked.

"Not so much. The water is cooler and pretty choppy. I prefer to dive in warmer climates."

"You are an intriguing woman." Duff said. "And here we are."

All too soon the bus pulled to a stop at the marina where they boarded the boat that would take them to the reefs.

"Everybody choose a dive buddy," the excursion leader announced. "And remember, this person will remain with you at all times. If anything goes wrong during the dive, your buddy is there to ensure you get out of the water safely."

Duff grabbed Natalie's hand. "Got mine!" he said out loud, raising Natalie's hand into the air.

"Some wingman," Sawyer groused and glanced around for a dive buddy.

Natalie leaned closer to Duff. "What if I didn't want to be your dive buddy?"

"But you do, don't you?" He winked. "I promise not to make any moves on you while we're under water."

Natalie laughed. "I'm betting you have moves under water as well on dry land."

He tilted his head. "Guilty. I like to think variety is the spice of life, and live accordingly."

"You're hopeless."

The captain guided the boat out of the slip and into open water. Natalie excused herself, claiming she needed to stow her bag. Once separated from Duff, she made her way around the boat, identifying the two dive masters, the first mate and the captain. All were Latino men under the age of thirty, except the captain, who appeared to be an American ex-patriot in his late forties. Nothing in their faces indicated they were involved in a human trafficking operation. Hell, what did a human trafficker look like, anyway? But that didn't take them off Natalie's suspect list. She'd keep a close eye on them.

Duff had joined his friends at the front of the craft, staring out to sea, talking and laughing.

The crew was too busy opening boxes of equipment and checking the tanks and regulators to answer questions. The best Natalie could do was to introduce herself, which forced them to supply their names. She'd repeat them so that Lance would hear them clearly over the roar of the engine.

Using her cell, she snapped pictures of the boat, the passengers and the crew under the pretext of being an excited tourist on a fun excursion. When she had the pictures she needed, she shot them to Lance back at the hotel. He'd run them through facial recognition scans. Maybe he'd find someone with a record for abducting women.

By the time she was satisfied with her covert observations, she ditched the earbud into her bag, joined the guests on the deck and found her dive buddy.

While the dive master instructed the less proficient members of the excursion, Natalie grabbed a buoyancy control device—BCD—and a regulator and tank, slipping the straps over her shoulder. Then she selected a mask, snorkel and fins and sat on a bench to slip her feet into the fins.

Duff had his equipment on and tested well before Natalie. He held his fins in his hands and stood beside the men she'd seen him with the night before.

"Hey, Duff." The man with the black hair and brown eyes backhanded Duff in the belly. "You gonna introduce us to your dive partner?"

"Why would I do that?" Duff stepped between him and Natalie. "You'll just try to convince her to trade."

"Got that right. She'd be trading up." The man stepped around Duff and held out his hand. "Name's Sawyer. And you are?"

Before Natalie could reply, another man as tall as Duff with brown hair and green eyes shoved Sawyer aside. "You are beautiful. I'm Ben Raines, but you can call me Montana."

Once again, before she could reach out to take the man's hand, yet another man with black hair and blue eyes stepped in front of Montana. "Quentin Lovett at your service. Let's say you and me ditch these morons and team up."

Natalie laughed, her gaze searching for and finding Duff's.

His brows were angled toward his nose as he pushed through the hulking men. "Natalia and I are dive buddies. I suggest you find one of your own."

Natalie smiled at the men. "You're very flattering and it's nice to meet you, but Duff's right—we're dive partners."

"Lucky dog." Quentin groused good-naturedly. "If

she'd met me first, she'd know the difference between bottom skimming and quality."

The boat slowed to a stop and Guillermo, the dive master, directed their attention to the safety briefing. Once they had all been checked, one of the crew members went in first. The remaining passengers could either roll or step off the platform at the rear of the boat.

Natalie waddled to the edge, shoved her regulator into her mouth and breathed in. Good so far.

Duff stepped up beside her, took her hand and nodded. "On three." He put his regulator in his mouth, then raised one finger at time.

Natalie counted. "One...two...three."

Together they stepped off the platform and sank into the crystal-clear water.

The initial shock of breathing under water passed quickly and she settled into an easy breathing rhythm.

Duff fluttered his fins, pushing away from the boat.

Natalie followed to allow the others the space to enter without hitting them.

The dive master was the last into the water. He swam to the front of the group and led the pairs of divers, pointing out a sea turtle or an array of different kinds of coral clinging to rocks and crevices. The group stretched out along a rocky outcropping, following the master, moving slowly and scattering wide to see everything the ocean floor had to offer in the way of sea flora and fauna.

Natalie let the others pass her, stopping to admire a blue starfish clinging to the rocky ocean floor.

Duff swam ahead of her, glancing back every once in a while, giving her the hand signal for everything is okay. She nodded and returned the same.

The rest of the group had disappeared around the side

of an underwater cliff. Natalie eased along the rocky outcropping, admiring the colorful coral while searching for places a person could hide, jump out, drag a woman into a cave or crevice and effectively remove her without being seen by other divers or the crew in the boat above.

She passed a small cave, stopped and turned around. Was it just a cave or did it go all the way through the rocks to an opening on the other side? Natalie looked over her shoulder for Duff.

She could see the tips of his fins as he rounded the corner of the outcropping, swimming away from her.

If the cave was a tunnel, this would be a good place to snatch a woman and pull her away from the others, especially if she was lagging behind her partner.

Natalie's pulse quickened and she fluttered her fins, sending her toward the cave. She hadn't gone two feet into it before she could see it was a dead end.

A moray eel poked his head out of a hole, seeming to glare at her.

She swam out of his home and caught up with Duff around the outcropping only to find another shallow cave. After exploring it and finding it to be another dead end with a resident octopus, she began to despair. Where along this tour had her sister disappeared?

Ahead, the group passed through a narrow gap between two stony projections. By the time Duff and Natalie caught up, they'd move through what appeared to be a labyrinth of huge rocks and boulders. If the person in the rear didn't stay right with the ones in front, he could easily lose his way.

Natalie's gut clenched. This could be it. Her sister could have gotten lost in the maze of rocks on the ocean floor. Perhaps the authorities were correct in assuming she had drowned. She could have gone into a cave, gotten caught in the rocks and couldn't get out. If her partner had lost track of her, she wouldn't have known where to look.

Her heart sinking, Natalie didn't see the cave to her right until something snagged her regulator hose and yanked hard. The regulator popped out of her mouth, leaving her without the air she needed to breathe.

Panic threatened to set in. Natalie forced herself to be calm and reached over her shoulder, sweeping her arm to catch the hose and bring the regulator back to her mouth. Only the hose wasn't within reach. An arm slipped around her and unbuckled the straps holding her BCD and tank and yanked them from her shoulders.

That panic she'd held at bay set in.

Chapter Five

Duff stayed close to Natalia, keeping her in his peripheral vision up until that last huge boulder. When she didn't follow right behind him, he waited a second, then turned and retraced his path looking for her.

At first he didn't see any sign of Natalia or her equipment. Had she gotten lost in the maze in such a short amount of time? He'd seen her maybe fifteen seconds ago. She couldn't have gotten too far. Staying close to the last place he'd seen her, he checked behind one rock after another. Then he saw it lying half-buried in the sand. A single black fin.

His heart raced and he spun, searching all directions. A group of fish shot out of a large crevice in the rocks and skimmed past him as if hurrying away from a predator.

Surely, Natalia hadn't gone into the narrow gap between the rocks without her partner. She or her apparatus could get hung up. Without the assistance of a dive buddy, she could be stuck there until found or—

Duff kicked hard, sending his body flying through the water toward the crevice. At the entrance he pulled a knife from a scabbard on his leg, carved an X into the rock and then swam through. Once past the entrance, the gaps between the rocks widened, making it easier to maneuver.

He slashed an X on the rocks as he passed, marking his way back.

Something smooth and shiny caught his attention. As he neared, he could make out the metal around a regulator gauge and the bulk of a BCD and tank resting on the ocean floor.

He looked up, hoping to see Natalia at the surface, thirty feet above. She wasn't there. His heart racing, Duff hurried through the rocks. Where the hell was she?

Movement ahead made him kick harder. As he neared a large boulder, he saw fins kicking and flailing, the smooth, pale legs attached could be none other than Natalia's.

When he was close enough he could see that a man had hold of her around the neck and was feeding her a regulator. He had her arms wrapped in what appeared to be weight belts, her wrists secured behind her.

Anger spiked, sending a surge of adrenaline through Duff. He raced for the attacker, holding his knife in front of him. He'd kill the bastard if he hurt one hair on Natalia's head.

Natalia's attacker must have seen Duff. He shoved Natalia toward him and kicked away from them.

Duff wanted to chase after the man, but Natalia was without air and, carrying the weight of the belts, wouldn't be able to surface easily. Duff couldn't abandon her, nor did he want to.

She struggled, kicking her feet, trying to turn her body toward the surface. Without her arms to balance, she spun in a circle, sinking toward the ocean floor.

Duff grabbed her from behind and held her against

him. She fought, twisting her body in a frantic attempt to get free.

Finally, Duff spun her to face him, pulled the regulator from his mouth and shoved it toward hers.

She stopped struggling and opened her mouth, accepted the regulator, blew out the water and sucked in a deep breath.

Duff turned her, slipped his knife between her wrists and sliced through the heavy weaving of the weight belt material, taking several passes before he freed her hands.

When she was free, she grabbed hold of his BCD and anchored herself with him. Natalia took another deep breath and handed the regulator to him.

They buddy-breathed for a couple more minutes until she was once again calm.

Duff pointed to her apparatus and they swam together toward the pile of equipment resting on the sandy bottom. Together, they managed to get her back into her gear, tested the regulator and checked the gauges.

When he was certain she was okay, he pointed back the way they'd come, indicating she should go first.

Natalia swam ahead, looking back every few seconds as if she was afraid he'd disappear.

Following the marks on the rocks, he got her back through the maze. Sawyer, Quentin and Montana were swimming in a circle, looking for him. Soon the dive master and the rest of the group filled the narrow clearing.

Guillermo motioned for all to follow and they fell into a tighter string, moving through the rocks and out into the open. A shadow floated over them, indicating the location of the boat. One by one, they surfaced and waited their turn to climb aboard the boat.

Duff surfaced a second before Natalia.

When she came up, she spit her regulator out of her mouth and gulped in fresh air. She glared across at him. "Why the hell did you do that?"

He frowned. "What do you mean? I saved your life."

"I wasn't dying."

"If that man had his way, he'd have killed you."

"What's going on?" Sawyer swam up to them. "Why were you two so far back?"

"Someone attacked Natalia." Duff shook his head. "And for some insane reason, she didn't want to be rescued." He glared back at her. "Maybe you can explain."

"I didn't want you to rescue me. He was keeping me alive. I wanted him to *take* me."

"Are you out of your mind?" Duff bellowed.

"Shh." Natalie pressed a finger to her lips and glanced around. "I don't want everyone under the sun hearing you."

"What's wrong?" Montana swam up to them.

"Yeah." Quentin joined them, treading water. "What's with the pissing contest? They're waiting for us to get in the boat."

Natalia locked gazes with Duff. "Please, just keep this to yourself."

"Keep what?" Quentin asked.

Montana frowned. "Do you mind giving us a clue?"

Duff held up a hand. "All right. We'll save the question-and-answer session for later. After we get to shore."

"Okay." Natalia chewed her lip. "How do I know I can trust you and your friends?"

His lips twitched. "You don't."

"Hey." Montana splashed water at Duff. "We're the good guys."

Without releasing the lock on their gazes, Duff responded, "Just hold your thoughts until we get back."

Sawyer nodded. "You got it, Duff." He turned and headed toward the dive boat, followed by Montana and Quentin.

"When we get back—"

"I know. I owe you an explanation. It'll have to wait until we're on land." Natalia kicked her feet, aiming for the boat.

Duff fluttered his fins, sending him cleaving through the water, catching up to her quickly. While she climbed out of the water, he held her fins. She reached for them and took his, too.

Once on the boat, Duff helped Natalia out of her apparatus and set it aside. He wanted to get to the bottom of whatever craziness she had in mind.

The ride back stretched for what seemed like an hour when in fact it was fewer than thirty minutes. The passengers compared experiences of what they'd seen or encountered on the reef tour. All except Natalia.

She stood alone at the rear of the boat, staring back at where they'd been retrieved. She'd slipped a cotton sundress over her swimsuit, but the breeze from the moving craft plastered it against her curves, outlining her incredible form beneath. Her brows pinched in the middle, a faraway, melancholy look made her appear even more distant. She ignored the lively chatter of the other divers, her back to them, cut off from the normal excitement of having been on some of the most incredible reefs off the coast of Mexico.

After a few minutes the rest of the passengers grew quiet, their sunburned faces staring out over the water.

No matter how hard Duff tried, he couldn't make sense of Natalia's desire to be captured by a stranger and her refusal to bring the attack to the attention of the crew.

Duff paced the length of the boat until they pulled up to the dock and off-loaded passengers. He refused to let Natalia get away without cluing him in on her unbelievable statement.

NATALIE SPENT THE remainder of the excursion staring out at the ocean, wondering if what had almost happened to her was the exact scenario Melody had been subjected to. If so, she would have been just as helpless to free herself from her captor. Thirty feet beneath the surface, without air, she would have been forced to rely on her captor's regulator until they surfaced. But where?

Her gaze took in the shoreline, memorizing every detail she could. As soon as she could, she'd rent a boat and return. Perhaps she'd find the spot the attackers had been waiting. Maybe finding the location would shed light on who they were and ultimately lead her to her sister.

One thing the attack had proved was that her gut had been right. Melody was alive. She hadn't been swept away by a current and lost at sea. Someone had taken her, most likely from the same location.

As soon as the boat docked, Natalie was the first passenger off. She hurried down the wooden boardwalk, searching for a boat to rent. Where the excursion boats were moored, the vessels were large, designed to take numerous passengers to parasail, fish or dive. Farther along the marina area, Natalie spotted individual boats, smaller than the rest. She turned to the left and headed for them.

"Hey." A hand clamped on her arm. "Not so fast."

She stared down at the hand on her arm and then up into Duff's face. "Let go of me."

His three friends stood behind him, all muscular, some tattooed, each ready to champion their friend's cause.

Duff's jaw tightened. "You owe us an explanation."

"I told you. I didn't want your help."

"Woman, you're not making sense." Duff gripped both of her arms, frowning down at her, his brow furrowed. "A man tries to abduct you and, when I try to help, you tell me to butt out. I don't get it. Why would you want to be abducted?"

She glanced around, noting one of the deckhands from their dive boat holding a cell phone to his ear, staring at her.

Natalie grabbed Duff's arm and dragged him away from the boat and the prying eyes. His friends followed.

Once she had him out of earshot, she leaned close. "I wanted him to take me to where he hides the women."

Duff shook his head. "What women?"

With a sigh, she stared into his eyes and dropped any hint of an English accent. "The women who've disappeared from this area over the past few days. One of them was my younger sister. Melody."

Duff's eyes flared, his lips pressing into a thin line. "When?"

"Two days ago. She disappeared on the same dive boat. I'm betting in the same manner in which I would have disappeared if you hadn't been so heroic and saved me." She squared her shoulders. "Now, if you'll let me by, I need to rent a boat."

Duff shook his head, his body blocking her way. "Why are you renting a boat?"

"I have to go back to see if I can find where my attacker surfaced."

Again the big man shook his head. "You can't. We were among huge rocks that protruded above the surface. A boat would be smashed against those rocks."

"If they got in there, I can get in there," she returned.

"You're not going alone." Duff glanced over his shoulder at his buddies. "Right?"

"We're with you," Sawyer said.

"Whatever it is you have in mind," Quentin agreed. Montana nodded.

"I can't go boating with four big guys. I came here hoping to put myself up as a target for whoever is abducting women. If I'm seen with four hulking men, they'll look for easier prey." Natalie snorted. "Then again, after Duff rescued me on the dive, my gig might be up anyway."

Duff chuckled. "And here I thought I was helping. You really think we're hulking?"

Natalia rolled her eyes. "That's all you got out of what I just told you?"

He held out his hand. "Let me make it up to you. We'll go out on a boat to see if we can find the pickup point." He gave his friends a look. "Just the two of us."

"Hey." Sawyer frowned. "I was almost beginning to think this vacation was getting interesting."

"You three can split up and follow the crew members of the boat." Duff gave them a stern look. "And don't make it obvious. And, for the love of Mike, don't beat the crap out of one of them for the information."

Quentin shook his head. "You're taking the fun out of it, dude."

Duff grabbed her hand. "Come on, we'll make this look like a date. Just me and you."

Natalie wasn't sure she liked the idea of being alone with the man. "How do I know you're not involved in this abduction operation?"

Sawyer barked out a laugh. "Duff doesn't need to abduct women, they usually come to him willingly."

Quentin added, "In droves."

Duff shrugged. "We weren't here two days ago. You can check our flight records. We arrived yesterday."

"And before that?" she asked.

He shook his head. "Sorry, can't divulge that information. We were conducting black ops."

Natalie's belly tightened. "What do you mean? Secret operations?"

Sawyer leaned close. "We're Navy SEALs. Our missions are classified." He winked.

Duff shoved him away from Natalie. "You guys better go. Some of the crew members are leaving the boat now."

Sawyer, Quentin and Montana spun and hurried away.

Natalie glanced up at Duff. "And I'm supposed to feel safe with you just because you say you're a Navy SEAL?" She tilted her head to the side, studying him. "You could be feeding me a line."

"Take it or leave it." He held out his hand. "Right now we need to secure a boat and get back out to where we were diving. Something else that might be of interest to you, but might mean nothing, is that I saw a fin in the maze of rocks. I thought it was yours, but you managed to come back with both of yours."

Natalie's breath caught and held for a moment then she released it. "It could have been Melody's." She took his hand. "Let's go."

Farther along the marina they found a man willing to let them rent his small fishing boat for a crazy amount. Natalie didn't care. Melody was in danger. The sooner they found her the better.

Duff insisted on paying, then handed her into the boat. "Wear your life jacket," he ordered.

Natalie bristled but didn't argue. She buckled herself into the jacket and settled back in her seat.

The boat owner untied the mooring line and waved as Duff shifted the throttle forward and they eased out of the marina. As soon as the craft cleared the no-wake zone, Duff shoved the throttle forward and they sped out into the open water, bouncing over the waves toward the island reefs and the area where they'd been scuba diving.

Duff seemed competent and confident at the helm. Natalie was a trained agent, but she'd never had the opportunity to handle a boat in a lake, much less on the open ocean where the stretch of water was so vast a person could easily get lost.

"Where did you learn to handle a boat?" she asked.

"I grew up on a ranch." His lips twitched.

She shook her head. "Seriously. What did you ranch? Fish?"

He glanced in her direction, a twinkle in his eyes. "I grew up on a ranch near Port Aransas, Texas. When we weren't taking care of cattle, we were fishing. My dad taught us how to ride horses and fish before we were three years old. Mom cringed and let him. With four boys to look out for, she couldn't tell him no."

"No sisters?"

Duff shook his head. "No. Mom was outnumbered from the get-go."

"Why didn't you stay and ranch?"

"My older brother followed in my father's footsteps. My younger brothers and I all joined the military."

"All Navy SEALs?" Natalie asked.

"No. My brother Jack joined the army and went into the Special Forces. Gabe joined the air force and flies F-16s."

"So, you're really a Navy SEAL?" Natalie stared at his arms and the tattoos laced across his shoulders and back.

"I am."

"And you're on vacation, not some operation you can't tell me about or you'd have to kill me?"

He grinned. "We're really on vacation."

"Lucky you to run into me." She stared ahead.

"And the English accent?" Duff prompted.

"Completely fake."

"The name?"

"Close. Instead of Natalia, I'm just plain Natalie."

Duff's lips quirked on the corners and he stared across at her, as if assessing her. "I think it fits you better."

His smile warmed her insides. "I thought it would throw off the abductors long enough to think I'd make a good target."

Duff frowned. "Why would you set yourself up as a target? What makes you think you'd have a better chance of escaping once they had you?"

She didn't answer right away. Still unsure whether to trust him, Natalie didn't want to reveal she had a GPS tracking device embedded beneath her skin. It would lead to a lot more questions and answers she wasn't ready to give.

She glanced at the island shoreline, recognizing the shape and features. "We're getting close."

The coastline grew unfriendly and rockier.

"There." Natalie pointed to the rock formations jutting out of the water.

"Looks like the location." Duff slowed the boat and made a wide sweep around the rocky shoreline. Waves lapped at the jagged pillars, making it very dangerous for a small boat to weave between them. Anyone who tried would smash against the rocks and sink.

"Look." Duff pointed toward an opening nearer the shore protected from the waves by a long barrier of boulders. He eased the little fishing boat into the opening to find a small lagoon on the other side leading into a hidden cave.

Natalie stood, holding on to the windshield. "Damn. It's a perfect location for hiding prisoners."

"Surely the locals know about it."

"That makes me wonder why the authorities hadn't found it when they were searching for my sister." Her eyes narrowed. "Unless the investigator was in on this whole abduction deal from the start."

Natalie glanced around the sandy shore on the edges leading into the cave. She didn't see any footprints, but the tide had risen, sweeping across the sand in gentle waves.

Duff pulled the throttle back to the idle position near the entrance to the cave. "We don't know what we'll find in the cave. Whoever attacked you could be in there."

"Then let's go in," Natalie said.

He shook his head. "What if they're armed?"

Natalie's lips pressed together. "I'll take my chances. I need answers. If we could get hold of at least one of the people involved, I'd be that much closer to finding my sister."

He touched her arm. "And if they shoot you before you get your answers, who will save your sister?"

Her fingers clenched into fists. "We won't know if they're even in there if we don't go in and find out."

Duff backed the boat away from cave entrance and shifted it into idle. Then he stepped away from the steering wheel. "It's yours."

She frowned. "What are you going to do?"

He winked. "I'm going for a swim."

"What?" Natalie stepped behind the steering wheel. "What if you don't come back out?"

"Give me fifteen minutes. If I'm not back by then, go to my friends and let them know what happened. Don't come in after me. Someone needs to stay with the boat."

"But—"

"I'll be all right." He slipped off the end of the boat, dropping silently into the water. He swam toward the cave entrance, his arms cutting through the water with smooth, even strokes.

Natalie held her breath, her heart pounding.

When Duff reached the cave entrance, he dived beneath the surface and disappeared.

Chapter Six

Duff swam beneath the surface until the water darkened, past the point where sunlight streamed through the cave entrance. He eased to the surface enough to bring his eyes and nose out of the water and stared around the small cave, waiting for his vision to adjust to the darkness.

Nothing moved and he couldn't see any boats tethered to the rocks. The cave was empty.

At the far end of it he found a rocky ledge large enough to hold several people. A railroad spike had been driven into it as a possible place to tie off a boat while a diver slipped away to perform nefarious tasks.

Duff pulled himself up onto the ledge where he found a discarded soda can and a few candy wrappers. They might be able to lift fingerprints if he could get the items back to the boat without destroying the prints. Lifting them carefully so as not to leave his own prints, he stuffed them into his pocket. Though, being in Mexico, if the perpetrator was Mexican, they probably didn't have fingerprint databases like the ones in the States. Still, any evidence might be of use.

He glanced around the rest of the cave. No other landing point existed, just the ledge. He scoured it for any other evidence and turned to leave when he noticed a small gold chain protruding from a rocky crevice. He hooked his finger through it and eased it out.

At the end of the chain was a gold pendant in the shape of a dove.

Duff slipped the necklace into his other pocket. After another quick look around, he swam back to the cave entrance.

When he emerged, Natalie eased the boat forward. "I thought you'd never come back out."

When he stood beside her, he pulled the items from his pocket, laying the can and candy wrapper on a seat. "I'm hoping we can lift prints from these." He reached into his other pocket, dragged out the chain and held it up. "Do you recognize this?"

Her face blanched and her eyes swam with unshed tears. Natalie took the necklace from him, nodding. "I gave this necklace to Melody when our parents died. She never took it off."

"Maybe she left it as a sign."

Natalie slipped the chain over her head and settled it around her neck. "She's alive. We just have to find her."

Duff's heart squeezed at the ready tears filling Natalie's eyes. He pulled her into his arms and held her.

She rested her fingers against his chest, her body shaking. "She's the only family I have left."

"We'll find her," he said, smoothing his hand over her long, blond hair.

For an extended moment he stood in the gently rocking boat, Natalie held close in his arms.

When she straightened and pushed away from him, he brushed a strand of her hair behind her ear. "We'll find her."

"I hope so." She sniffed. "Before it's too late."

"I'll help in any way I can." Duff took over at the helm, easing the boat through the narrow channel and back into the open. As they cleared the watery field of rocks, Duff took in a deep breath and let it out. Though protected from the waves while navigating the secret entrance, there could have been underwater hazards he didn't know about. Having emerged unscathed was a huge relief.

He dragged in another breath, turned toward the mainland and shoved the throttle forward.

The roar of the engine masked any other sound. Something hit the windshield so hard and fast it left a round hole and cracks spreading out like a spider's web.

Damn, it was a bullet hole.

"Get down!" Duff yelled and ducked low in the boat, only raising his head high enough to see over the dash.

Natalie slipped out of her seat onto the floor of the boat and glanced to the rear. "We have a tail."

Another bullet shot through the glass right where Duff's head had been a moment before.

He swerved and shifted the throttle all the way down, running the engine wide-open.

"They're catching us," Natalie yelled over the sound of the engine.

Duff couldn't make the boat go any faster. The best he could do was to escape and evade being killed. He chanced a glance to the rear. As Natalie had said, their pursuer was quickly catching up to them in a newer, higher-speed vessel. They'd be on them in seconds.

Natalie crawled forward into the front of the boat.

Duff didn't know what she was doing but at least she was getting farther away from the approaching shooter.

She dug in one of the storage wells and pulled out an

anchor. Carrying the anchor, she worked her way toward him. "Let them catch up. I have an idea."

He had an inkling of what her plan might be, but it would be dangerous. Hell, it couldn't be any more dangerous than being on a slow boat, unarmed and pursued by a speedboat with men shooting at them.

When the other vessel had nearly caught up with them Duff pulled back hard on the throttle, bringing it to the neutral position. The fishing boat slowed immediately.

The other boat, so close behind them, swerved to miss hitting them. The shooter was too busy holding on to aim. They slid past, barely missing the fishing boat.

Natalie lunged to her feet, slung the anchor into the back of the other boat and ducked back down.

Duff shoved the throttle forward and turned sharply away from the speedboat.

Natalie had secured the anchor line to a cleat on the side of their fishing boat. When the line played out completely, it snapped tightly and yanked both boats hard.

The other driver was already turning toward them so quickly the boat tipped up on one side. The pull from the anchor dragged the speedboat over even farther, flipping it upside down.

Duff stopped immediately and backed up enough that Natalie was able to untie the line from the cleat.

Free of the other boat, Duff drove off.

"Wait!" Natalie yelled. "We should go rescue one of them. They'll know where Melody is."

"Or they'll have another boat full of shooters on their way. Or their weapons will fire fine wet. We need to get the hell out of here."

"We can't just leave them. They might be our only chance to interrogate."

Duff turned the boat around and slid up close to the capsized craft. One man floated facedown in the water, unmoving. Another cried out and swam toward their little fishing boat.

Already, Natalie was leaning toward the man as he came up along the starboard side.

"Take the helm," Duff commanded.

Natalie glanced up.

"I can get him on board quicker." Duff left the steering wheel and passed Natalie as she took his seat.

Duff reached for the hand of the survivor.

The man's fingers curled around his and Duff dragged him up the side of the boat. He almost had him over the lip when a shot rang out. The man jerked and his grip slackened.

"Get us out of here!" Duff shouted.

Natalie pushed the throttle wide-open and the little boat surged toward the capsized one.

Duff tightened his hold and dragged the man onto the boat as the craft slid to the side, nearly knocking into the doomed boat.

Flexing his arm to ease the strain of dragging a dead weight on board, Duff squatted next to the man and felt for a pulse.

Deadweight was correct. Their witness wouldn't be spilling any secrets.

Natalie glanced back. "Is he—?"

"He's dead," Duff confirmed.

"What should we do with him?"

"I don't feel like spending my vacation in a Mexican jail."

Once they were out of shooting range of the capsized vessel, Natalie slowed the fishing boat and brought it to a stop. She joined Duff, next to the body. "Should we dump him?"

Duff scratched his head. "That's my vote."

Natalie reached for her oversize purse and pulled out her cell phone. "Could you turn him over so that I can get a clear shot of his face?"

Duff did as requested. "Do you always take photos of dead men?"

"Only when I think it might help me find my sister." She snapped a few shots of his face, his profile and the tattoos on his arms. Then she texted someone.

"Did you just send those pictures to someone?"

She nodded without looking at him.

"You're not going to tell me who, are you?"

"If I did, I'd have to…you know…" She sliced a finger over her throat and glanced at him with a challenge in the lift of her brows.

Duff's mouth twisted into a wry grin. "I have a feeling you have as many secrets as I do. Do I want to know them?"

"Probably not."

"Fair enough…for now." He didn't like being in the dark with Natalie. "Promise me you'll clue me in if it means the difference between life and death."

"Deal."

Duff went through the man's pockets, searching for any form of identification. As he expected, he found none. He glanced around at the huge expanse of water surrounding them.

"All clear," Natalie said.

Duff hooked his hands beneath the man's arms and

Natalie grabbed his feet. Together they maneuvered him over the side of the boat. He landed with a small splash in the water and slowly sank.

"Let's get out of here." Duff assumed control of the helm and headed back to the shore.

When they turned in the boat, between Natalie and Duff, they gave the owner a hefty tip for the damage to his windshield and the loss of his anchor. He didn't ask questions, took the money and drove the boat out of the marina, looking right, left and over his shoulder as he left.

Natalie's gaze followed the little fishing boat out of the marina. "Do you think I'll ever find my sister?"

Duff slipped an arm around her waist. "We will," he promised.

Whether or not she'd be alive when they did find her was another question entirely.

NATALIE LET DUFF hold her hand all the way out to the main road where they flagged down a taxi and climbed in. The stress of the day weighed heavily on Natalie. As independent as she considered herself, she couldn't help the feeling of relief it was to have Duff at her side. She leaned against his muscular shoulder, absorbing some of his strength.

"What next?" he asked.

She tapped the evidence they'd wrapped in a plastic bag. "I'll get these to someone who can lift prints. But I'm worried about my sister's friends. If these guys are getting brave enough to go after me two days after nabbing my sister, who's to say they won't take one of her friends?"

"Were those the young ladies you were partying with last night?"

Natalie nodded. "Two left to go home, but the others are here for a few more days. They couldn't get their flights changed."

"Then we stick with them."

"We?"

"Okay, you. With the Navy SEALs as backup. We can hang back, but be there if you need us."

"I can't follow all of them."

"No. If one strays from the pack while you're not watching, one of us can follow and make sure they're okay."

"My sister and her friends were supposed to go to Chichén Itzá tomorrow. I think her friends were planning to cancel after losing Melody."

"Your point?"

"One of the missing women disappeared on a hike around the ruins." Natalie caught his gaze. "I could take my sister's reservation and see what happens."

"Please tell me you're not going to put yourself out there as bait again. They might think you're too much trouble and shoot you instead, since you got away twice."

She tapped a finger to her chin, thinking. "You could be right."

"And if your sister's friends decide to go on the excursion with you, they could end up as collateral damage."

"What if they decide to go anyway?"

"Then you have to go. And the SEALs will be there, as well. Only we'll follow in a rental car instead of taking the guided tour."

She stared across at him, her eyes narrowing. "Why are you so eager to help?"

"It's the right thing to do." He reached for her hand and curled his big fingers around hers. "And I like the strong, sassy type."

Again her insides warmed at his compliment and she curled her fingers around his, glad she didn't have to do this alone.

Having Lance follow her with the GPS tracking device gave her a certain sense of security. Having a Navy SEAL as her physical backup was even better. She wasn't sure she'd have made it away from the cave island alive had she gone there alone.

The taxi driver dropped them off at the entrance to the resort.

"We shouldn't be seen together any more than necessary," Natalie said.

"Why not? We've shared a breathing apparatus, a fishing boat and a taxi. That makes us practically a thing." He winked.

"Still. If there's a chance of me being taken rather than one of the other girls, I'd rather it was me."

Duff touched her cheek. "Again, they might not take you. Since we returned to the cave and those thugs fired at us, I'd say there is a strong possibility they'd shoot you rather than take you as a hostage."

"How else am I supposed to find where they hid my sister? I can almost bet they won't tell us if we ask."

"Then we have to find a way to follow them to where they are hiding your sister and the other girls."

Natalie cupped her hand over his and leaned her cheek into his palm. "The longer she's missing—"

"We'll find her." Duff tipped her chin upward and lowered his lips to hers. "I promise."

When his lips met hers, Natalie forgot what she'd

been about to say, the plastic bag she'd been carrying slipped from her hand. Electric shocks emanated from where their mouths connected and spread throughout her entire body.

She should have pushed away and run inside to the sanctuary of her room. But she couldn't. Instead she leaned up on her toes and deepened the kiss, opening her mouth to him.

His tongue swept in, claiming hers, caressing in a long, slow, slide. Duff slid his hand across her cheek, down the column of her throat and lower to the small of her back where he applied enough pressure to press her against his naked chest and snug her hips up against his. The hard evidence of his desire nudged her belly. An answering fire curled low inside her, making her ache in ways she hadn't in a very long time. Her fingers pressed into the hard plains of his muscles and she could smell the sun and salt from the ocean.

He tempted her sorely and she would have followed him to his room in a heartbeat if her sister's life wasn't hanging in the balance.

When at last he lifted his head, she dragged in a deep breath, filling her lungs. "I should go find the other girls."

"I'll see you tonight at the cabana bar?"

"If Melody's friends go there."

He nodded. "I'll find you."

Reluctantly she lifted her fingers from his chest. "If your friends discover anything…"

"I'll let you know whatever they found as soon as I can."

She took a step away and forced her hands to fall to her sides. "Thank you for saving my life twice today," she whispered. Natalie turned, scooped up the plastic bag and walked into the building, afraid if she looked back, she wouldn't go without Duff.

The man was growing on her. He had a way of being in the right place at the right time. From rescuing a drowning woman to saving her not once but twice. Her luck was bound to run out soon. She hoped she found Melody before that happened.

Natalie didn't go straight to her room. Instead she wound her way through the lobby, wandered into a lounge, bought a fruity drink and headed outside. In her roundabout way, she found her way to the bungalow where Lance was set up.

After a quick glance around she knocked on the door. It opened before she could knock more than once.

Lance grabbed her arm, dragged her in and shut the door behind her. "What the hell happened after you got on board the boat? And how did you end up with a dead guy on a scuba excursion?"

"Sorry. It's been a helluva day." She handed him the drink.

He pushed it back at her. "You look like you need it more than I do." He backed up, propping his hip on the sofa. "I got nothing on the deckhands from the boat, but the dead guy is a thug who works for a man named Carmello Devita, a well-known drug runner who likes to dabble in other dangerous and lucrative pursuits."

"Like human trafficking?"

"Like hostage ransoming."

"Why would he take Melody? She has no family other than me and I'm a long way from being rich. And the other girls who were taken weren't from rich families."

"Maybe he's diversifying into human trafficking." Lance flung out his hand. "Either way, your dead man is a known gun-for-hire working for Devita."

"Great. At least we have a starting point. Where can I find Devita?"

"That's the sixty-four-million-dollar question. The DEA has been searching for him over a year and they have no leads."

Natalie tilted her head. "And you know this how?"

"Royce is the man with the contacts."

"So what you're telling me is that we're no closer than when we got here?" Her shoulders slumped.

"I didn't say that." Lance slipped into his chair in front of the computer screen. "At least you eliminated one of his gunmen."

"We didn't eliminate him. One of his men did."

"We?"

Natalie sighed. "Duff and I."

Lance's lips curled upward. "Good news is that I did a search for him in the criminal databases and didn't find a match."

"Because he's not a criminal. Turns out my dive buddy is a Navy SEAL." She pointed to his screen. "Look up Dutton Calloway, U.S. Navy, to verify."

Lance's fingers flew over the keyboard. A minute later a screen popped up with a picture of Duff.

Natalie's chest tightened and her lips tingled. "That's him."

"Sweet," Lance said. "What's he doing here?"

Natalie filled him in on what had happened during the dive and the boat trip back to the dive location.

"You trust him?" Lance asked.

"He's saved me twice. How could I not trust him?"

"It's nice to know you have someone in the field covering your six."

"I suppose. Only I don't want anyone else to be collateral damage while I'm searching for Melody."

"Count your blessings, woman. If I weren't tethered to this computer, I'd be with you. If he offered to help, take him up on it."

Chapter Seven

Duff knocked on Sawyer's door. A moment later it opened.

Sawyer held it for him. "What did you find?"

"A cave where the attacker hid his boat and a necklace belonging to Natalie's sister. Then we were shot at, almost run over by another boat, capsized it and then hauled a man on board who was promptly shot and killed before we could question him."

Sawyer grinned and clapped him on the back. "All in a day's work." Then his smile disappeared and he grew serious. "You weren't kidding, were you?"

Duff's jaw clenched. "I wish I were."

"Wow. Pretty impressive," Quentin said. "But did you have to go and shoot the guy? We could have interrogated him, maybe gotten some useful intel from him before you killed him."

"I didn't shoot him," Duff said. "One of his own guys got him when he saw me pulling the man into our boat."

Sawyer whistled. "They didn't want him spilling the beans."

Duff nodded. "What did you learn?"

Sawyer shook his head. "Not much."

Montana sat on a couch, his long limbs stretched out

in front of him. "We followed the men from the boat and got nothing. My guy went home for lunch with his wife and five kids."

"Mine ended up in a bar," Quentin said. "He drank three Coronas and returned to the boat for the afternoon excursion."

"The captain stayed on the boat," Sawyer finished. "I went back to the booking desk here at the hotel, thinking maybe the booking agent was feeding the attackers information about the women going on the excursion. The agent had clocked out for lunch. She'll be back later this afternoon."

"So what the hell are we doing?" Quentin asked. "I thought we were here on vacation, not on a mission."

Duff shoved a hand through his hair and paced across the short length of the bungalow Sawyer had rented for his stay in Cancun. Each of the men had rented one away from the main resort hotel, preferring the isolation and the closeness to the beach. They'd secured rooms to themselves in case they did manage a little romance while there.

"I don't know much more than you. Natalie's sister disappeared two days ago on a dive trip from the same boat we went out on today. You know the rest from what happened."

"That wasn't my question." Quentin pushed to his feet. "Why are you getting involved?"

Duff stared at Quentin. "If I don't, she'll do it on her own. You heard her. She actually wanted to be captured, hoping her attacker would take her to her sister."

Sawyer whistled. "Yeah. That's insane."

"All the more reason you should step back and look

at this logically." Quentin planted himself in front of Duff, forcing him to stop pacing.

"And what?" Duff's fists clenched. "Leave her to be captured by whoever took her sister and two other women?" He shoved Quentin's chest. "Is that what you would do? Leave a woman defenseless? It would be one thing if I didn't know any better, but I do. I can't let Natalie waltz into enemy territory alone."

"Can't she take it to the authorities?" Montana suggested.

Duff snorted. "She got no help from them. You know the Mexican government isn't necessarily in control. The drug cartels have been calling the shots for so long, nobody has faith in the authorities anymore."

"We're only here for two weeks. What if you don't find the sister in that time?" Sawyer asked.

Duff crossed his arms over his chest. "All the more reason to find her and get back to that relaxing vacation we've earned. Anyone have connections in the DEA? Maybe we can get them involved."

Sawyer's jaw tightened. "I might know someone."

"Call." Duff waved a hand in his direction. "The sooner we have someone working it, the better chance we have of finding those women."

Sawyer pulled his cell phone from his pocket and stepped out of the bungalow to make his call. He was back inside a minute, his face ruddy-red and his nostrils flaring. "Sorry. My source was less than helpful."

Duff cursed beneath his breath. "Look. I'm not asking any of you to get involved in this. I'll do this on my own. You guys stay and enjoy your vacation." Duff headed for the door.

Sawyer stepped in his way. "I'm in. Just tell me what I can do to help."

"I'm in." Montana shoved to his feet and dug his hands into his pockets. "A man can only take so much sand and sea before he gets bored."

Quentin stared from one man to the next and finally shrugged. "I'm in. I could use a little excitement myself. Can't have Duff here dodging *all* the bullets."

Duff smiled at his teammates. "Thanks."

"So what's next on the agenda?" Sawyer asked.

"We go to dinner and show up at the cabana bar tonight to watch for anything strange. Natalie thinks her sister's friends might be targeted since they didn't get her."

Quentin clapped his hands. "You said the magic word. Bar. I'm there."

Montana rubbed his flat belly. "I'm for a steak and seafood, then the bar."

Duff glanced toward the door. A smart man would walk away from Natalie and let her handle her investigation on her own. But since when was he smart? He'd joined the Navy SEALs, a surefire way to end up in a body bag. Besides, his father had taught him better than that. You don't back away from a difficult situation. You meet it head-on. "I'm going for a walk, then a shower. I'll see you all in an hour for dinner. Save a place at the table for me."

Sawyer stepped out the door with Duff. "Is that it?"

"Is what it?"

"You feel like helping a stranger because it's the right thing to do?"

"Yeah. So?"

Sawyer's lips quirked. "You sure it doesn't have anything to do with the fact she's a knockout in a pink bikini?"

Duff's cheeks burned. "No, it doesn't."

Sawyer's brows climbed up his forehead.

With a sigh, Duff nodded. "Okay, maybe a little."

"She's hot."

"And smart, and not afraid of much," Duff added.

"Careful, old man. You came for fun in the sun and a fling. If you aren't watching, you'll fall for this woman and complicate the hell out of your life."

"I know." Duff sighed. "And we don't need complications."

"Not in our line of work."

Duff rocked back on his heels. "Sawyer, you ever think of doing something else besides being a SEAL?"

Sawyer's mouth tightened. "Haven't really thought about it."

Glancing away, Duff stared through the palm trees, catching glimpses of the ocean. "Do you ever want to settle down and raise a family?"

Sawyer snorted. "My family left a bitter taste in my mouth. I can't imagine me and a family being a good idea."

"You're great with your brothers in arms. Why don't you think you'd be a good father or husband?"

"My father isn't like yours. He didn't teach me to fish or ride a horse. Hell, he was never around long enough to teach me to walk. When he was, it was always to tell me everything I was doing wrong in my life." Sawyer shook his head. "If I'm anything like my father, I don't want to put that burden on any kid."

"But you're not like him. You get along with everyone. Every man on the team would take a bullet for you."

"And I would take a bullet for them. Even Quentin."
Sawyer smiled. "All of you are my real family. I don't
know what I'd do without you."

"You need to start thinking about a life after the
Navy. We won't stay young forever, and this job is hard
on a body and soul."

Sawyer stared into the distance, then shook as if to
pull himself out of his thoughts. "I think you're deflect-
ing the real issue. What's up between you and Natalia?"

"Her real name is Natalie. And nothing. I just want
to help."

"Okay. I'll take it at face value. If you need to talk
about it in the future, you know where my bungalow
is." Sawyer patted Duff on his back. "Go for your walk.
Maybe you'll run into your pretty damsel in distress."

Duff left Sawyer and headed for the beach, away
from the hotel and away from Natalie. Were his friends
right? Was he getting in over his head with something
he had no business getting into? Or was he getting in
over his head with a female who could easily derail him
with a flash of her pretty blue eyes?

Whatever it was, he couldn't leave Natalie to fend
for herself against forces much more powerful than one
lone woman. The look on her face when he'd handed
her Melody's necklace had sealed that deal. Melody was
her sister. She'd do anything to get her back.

Duff loved his biological brothers as well as his
brothers in arms. He'd do as much or more for them as
Natalie would do for her sister.

NATALIE LEFT LANCE'S BUNGALOW, careful to check for
anyone lurking in the shadows. She hurried back to her
room, stripped out of her suit and wrap and stored her

sister's necklace in her suitcase. Then she showered and changed into a soft, figure-hugging, short dress and strappy, spike-heeled sandals. After one last glance in the mirror, she went in search of Melody's remaining friends.

A knock on the door to the room a few doors down yielded Kylie, wearing her pajamas, her face lacking any makeup and her hair still crinkled from lying in bed. "Oh, Natalia, I didn't expect you."

"Did Jodie and Lisa leave this morning?" Natalie almost forgot to layer the English accent. Since she'd revealed her charade to Duff, she hadn't felt it necessary to continue. But with her sister's friends, she couldn't really let it drop yet. Not if they were being watched by potential kidnappers.

Kylie turned and padded barefoot back to the bed where she sat and pulled a pillow up to her chest in a hug. "I miss them already."

"They were your roommates?"

"And Melody." She gave Natalie a weak smile. "I'm beginning to think I'm the jinx."

Natalie sat beside her and put an arm around the young woman's shoulders. "You most certainly are not. You could not have caused this situation to happen." She tightened her hold on the girl. "When are you due to fly out?"

"Not until the day after tomorrow with the rest of the group."

"Then you have to do something to cheer yourself up."

"I wish there was something I could do to find Melody. I don't feel right going home without her." She buried her face in her hands and sobbed.

Natalie held her just as she'd held Melody when their parents had died. A lump knotted in her throat and she fought to hold back the ready tears when she thought of the horrible things that could be happening to her baby sister.

When Kylie had cried herself out, Natalie hugged her once more and gripped her shoulders, forcing the girl to look at her. "You aren't doing anyone any good holing up in your room. Your friend Melody wouldn't want you to get depressed and mope. You have to get out and at least pretend you're having a good time."

"I can't. All three of my friends are gone."

"Where is the rest of your group?"

"They came by earlier and asked if I wanted to go to dinner." Kylie rubbed a hand across her face. "I told them I didn't feel like it."

"When were they going?" Natalie asked. She didn't like the idea of the group of young women splitting up. They needed to stay together for safety's sake.

Kylie glanced at the clock. "Fifteen minutes ago."

"Get up." Natalie grabbed Kylie's hands and pulled her to her feet.

"Why?" Kylie resisted.

"You're going to dinner with your friends."

"I told you, I don't feel like it," she whined.

"Wash your face and put on a little makeup. I'll straighten your hair." She herded Kylie into the bathroom, wet a washcloth with cold water, wrung it out and handed it to the younger woman. "Get moving. Melody would want it this way."

Kylie took the cloth. "She would?"

"If you were Melody, would you want all your friends to sit around and cry over you?"

Kylie sniffed. "No." She pressed the cool cloth to her swollen, red-rimmed eyes. When she set it on the counter, Natalie slapped a concealer stick in her hand.

"That should help hide those puffy eyes." She smiled gently and plugged in the flat iron.

While Kylie applied makeup, Natalie smoothed the kinks out of her hair. A few minutes later, they left the bathroom.

Kylie had more of a bounce in her step. "I am a little hungry."

"Good, maybe we'll catch your mates in the restaurant and order something quick and easy."

Kylie hugged Natalie. "Thank you for being here for me. Somehow, I feel closer to Melody." She tilted her head. "You're a lot like her. Isn't that strange?"

Natalie smiled and resisted the urge to tell Kylie the truth. Better to find Melody first. If keeping her real identity a secret helped, then she would continue to do so.

Kylie stripped out of her pajamas and stepped into a flirty, pastel-pink dress of sheer fabric with an underslip of shiny, silky pink. She slid her feet into low-heeled sandals bejeweled in sparkling clear rhinestones. After a glance in the full-length mirror, she gave Natalie a soft smile. "I do feel better."

"Good. Then let's catch up with the others." Natalie gripped Kylie's hand and led her through the door, closing it firmly behind them. She'd have to do something about Kylie's sleeping situation. The young woman needed a friend in her room. A lone female in a foreign country would be a target to the kidnappers.

The four other young women were lingering over their meal in the resort restaurant, talking quietly, their expressions somber.

Natalie led Kylie up to the table and smiled brightly. "Do you have room for two more?"

"Of course," said an auburn-haired woman Natalie recognized as the one they called Allison as she jumped to her feet and dragged two more chairs to the small table.

It was a tight fit, but Natalie didn't care. At least she was close to them and included in their group. She'd have a better chance of keeping them safe.

"Like Kylie, are you all staying one more day before flying out?" Natalie asked.

They nodded as one.

"We were all scheduled to fly in and out on the same plane," said Brianna, a black-haired, petite beauty.

"Yeah." Chelsea, the sandy-blonde, sighed. "We even had seats all grouped together."

"It doesn't feel right without Melody, Jodie and Lisa here," Hanna said. She pushed a strand of light brown hair back behind her ear.

"You have two more nights here and one whole day." Natalie glanced around at the sullen faces. "You can't spend it in your hotel rooms moping."

"We were all supposed to go on the excursion to Chichén Itzá tomorrow," Kylie said.

"We were so looking forward to visiting the ancient Mayan pyramid. Especially Melody."

Natalie remembered how excited her sister had been. She had been working toward a minor in archeology in college. Chichén Itzá had been on her radar since she'd first read about it in a *National Geographic* magazine when she was eight years old. Their parents had promised to take them when they were older.

That dream had almost died with their parents.

Natalie had been so happy for Melody to have this opportunity. Now it seemed as though her sister would never get that chance.

The hell she wouldn't.

"Aren't you going?" Natalie asked.

"We hadn't planned on it," Chelsea said.

Kylie's lips twisted. "Although we paid for the trip in advance and they won't give us a refund."

"Then go." Natalie searched their faces. "Otherwise tomorrow will crawl by. There's no reason you shouldn't see the ruins."

"What about Melody?"

"Go for her," Natalie urged.

Kylie nodded. "I don't feel any better for having stayed in my room all day. The time dragged." She nodded toward Chelsea. "What do you think?"

Chelsea was already nodding. "We should go. It will make the day fly. Then, before we know it, we'll be on our way home."

"Without Melody…" Allison said.

"Do you think they'll ever find her…you know… body?" Brianna asked, her voice a soft whisper.

"I hope so," Chelsea said. "Her family will want closure."

"She only had a sister," Kylie said. "I can't imagine how terrible it was for her to get that call." Her eyes filled again.

Natalie fought the urge to cry with Kylie, but she wasn't ready to give up on her sister. Melody was alive and—damn it—she was going to find her, if it was the last thing she did.

Kylie sniffed and pushed away from the table. "I

don't know about the rest of you, but I could do with one more drink before we leave."

"Me, too," Chelsea said. She, Brianna, Allison and Hanna stood as one.

The six women paid for their meal and left the restaurant, walking out the back door of the hotel to the cabana. People were drifting into the bar as the sun set, cloaking the resort in semidarkness displaced by the lights from the hotel and the blue glow of the pool. Twinkling lights hung from the ceiling of the cabana, giving just enough light to see without being so bright it disturbed the ambience.

Natalie shot a glance around the bar. So far her Navy SEAL protector hadn't showed up. It was just as well. She didn't want the other men in the bar to think she was with him, in case one of them was scouting potential victims.

The music was played loud, limiting the amount of talking between the girls. They all ordered frozen strawberry margaritas and, as the night before, made a toast to their missing friend.

Natalie raised her glass to her lips, the sugar and frozen concoction melting in her mouth.

The music slowed and some of the dancers left the wooden dance floor to refresh their drinks. Others swayed to the rhythm of the band, pressing close together, hips rubbing against hips.

"Would you like to dance?" a voice said over her shoulder.

With a start Natalie turned on her chair and stared up into gray eyes. A nice-looking man with short-cropped blond hair smiled down at her.

"Excuse me?"

He chuckled. "I asked if you would like to dance."

She glanced at her sister's friends.

They all stared at the handsome man.

"Go on. We'll save your drink for you," Chelsea said.

Natalie didn't feel much like dancing with the stranger but, as last night, being out on the dance floor would put her in the line of sight of anyone scoping the crowd for likely victims.

"Okay," she said and laid her hand in his.

His grip was strong and he practically lifted her out of her chair.

Natalie followed him to the dance floor, her gaze darting toward the entrances. Where were the SEALs?

As the stranger pulled her into his embrace, Duff and his friends entered the cabana.

A thrill of recognition and anticipation zipped through Natalie. Duff's large form and broad shoulders would make any woman's heart flutter. The man was gorgeous and looking her way.

Duff's gaze found hers and he frowned.

Natalie sucked in a quick breath and stumbled.

"Careful," said the man holding her in his arms. "I've been known to be all left feet."

"No. I lost my step." She dragged her gaze from Duff's and looked up into her partner's eyes.

"I'm Rolf Schwimmer." He winked and spun her around in a fancy dance move.

"I'm Natalia."

He dipped his head. "A pretty name for a lovely woman."

"Thank you."

"Are you here on vacation?" he asked.

"I am."

He nodded toward Melody's table. "With your friends?"

She glanced toward the girls. "No, I met them when I got here. But they've been good enough to allow me to join them."

"What part of England are you from?"

"Oxford. And you?"

"I'm not from England." He smiled, his eyes twinkling.

"Obviously. Your accent is American."

"Guilty," he said. "I'm originally from Minnesota."

"A long way from home."

"As are you," he pointed out.

"Are you on vacation?" she asked.

He shrugged. "Not so much. I only wish I was here for pleasure. Alas, I'm here to conduct a little business."

"What kind of business?"

"I'm in securities and acquisitions."

"Like buying assets?" she asked, her mind going to what this man could be doing and if it had any relation to her missing sister.

"Something like that."

He didn't look down at her. Instead he danced her around the floor in a tight hold, molding his body to hers. For a while he didn't speak. When the song ended, he held on to her hand. "Stay for another? You're the only person I know."

She laughed. "I don't know you."

"Okay, so you're the only person who hasn't turned me down." He winked. "Dance with me again."

"One more time then I want to sit with my new friends."

The song was fast-paced and required skill at the

salsa. Natalie backed up a step. "I'm sorry, but I'm not good at this dance."

"Then we'll look terrible together." He swung her away from him and back into his arms. "See? You're a natural."

Natalie narrowed her eyes but didn't have time to study his face before he swung her out and back again. She laughed. "You've obviously done this before."

"Maybe." His feet kept time with the music, stepping forward and back, his hips swaying. "Don't let my blond hair fool you. I've spent a lot of time in Mexico. And when in Mexico, you learn to salsa."

By the time the song ended, Natalie was breathless. "Thank you."

"Please." He bowed over her hand. "Let me thank you." He walked her back to the table, nodded to Melody's friends and then left her to take a stool at the bar.

"Wow," Kylie said, her gaze following the man. "He was dreamy."

"You ladies should dance." Natalie took a seat and dabbed at her cheeks with a bar napkin.

"It would be nice to be asked." Chelsea looked around the bar. "Aren't those the guys from last night?" She tipped her head toward Duff and his Navy SEAL friends.

"Didn't you dance with one of them?" Kylie asked.

Natalie nodded, steeling herself from looking that way. No matter how good-looking, the man she'd just danced with didn't have the same rugged appeal as Duff with his slightly shaggy hair and tattoo-laced shoulders and arms.

Her body shivered with anticipation, hoping Duff would ask her to dance again.

"You guys, don't stare." Chelsea turned away. "You'll look pathetic and too eager."

"Here comes one of them," Hanna whispered excitedly.

Out of the corner of her eye Natalie saw a man moving toward them. Her heart skipped several beats and settled back to a normal if somewhat disappointed beat when she realized it wasn't Duff.

Sawyer walked across the barroom, stopping in front of Allison. "Wanna dance?"

Allison beamed and leaped from her seat. "Yes." She grabbed his hand and practically dragged him to the dance floor.

"So much for playing hard to get," Chelsea muttered.

One by one the young women were asked to dance.

Natalie kept a close eye on them and the men they were with. She'd be damned if her sister's friends were the next victims of the kidnappers.

"You're scaring the natives with that frown," a deep voice rumbled next to her ear.

Natalie turned to look up into green eyes and her pulse rushed. "Hi."

"The girls seem to be enjoying themselves despite missing their friend."

"I had to convince them to come out tonight."

When he held out his hand she slipped hers into it, liking how small he made her feel. Not in an intimidating way but in a way that made her feel protected. "Did your guys learn anything from the boat crew?"

"Nothing." He pulled her to her feet and led her toward the dance floor. "Who's the guy you were dancing with?"

"Rolf from Minnesota."

"What's he doing in Cancun?" Duff asked.

"He said he was here on business."

"What kind of business?"

"Securities and acquisitions." Her brow furrowed. "He's American."

"So? Our abductor could be a greedy son of a bitch looking for a quick score." Duff pulled her close and spun her around, putting her back to the man in question. His gaze swept over the top of her head. "Don't trust him."

"Got it." She rested her hand on his chest. "I'm worried."

"I know," he said, his gaze dropping to hers and softening.

"I'm no closer to finding my sister than I was when I arrived in Cancun."

"What next?"

"I don't know." As she danced in a circle, rocking back and forth, Natalie counted the five girls she felt somewhat responsible for. Three of them danced with Duff's friends, which made her feel a little better about their safety. But the other two were dancing with men she didn't know anything about.

Chelsea was dancing with Rolf, the handsome American, who'd asked Natalie to dance first.

Kylie was with a dark-haired man with an easy smile and classy clothing from his button-up starched shirt to dark, tailored trousers. Natalie watched as Kylie gazed up at him, her eyes shining despite the earlier tears.

Could he be one of the kidnappers?

Natalie glanced around the room. Men lounged with their backs to the bar, watching the action in front of the band. Were they part of the kidnapping operation?

"You're thinking too hard," Duff said, his lips so close to her ear she could feel the warmth and smell the minty freshness of his breath.

"It's my sister I'm trying to find. If it was one of your family members, what would you do?"

His grip tightened on her waist. "Probably rip the place apart until I found who was responsible."

"Right." The music came to a stop.

The band announced a short break and laid down their instruments.

Natalie scanned the room, locating each of Melody's friends heading toward their table. One, two, three, four— Where was Chelsea? Her pulse ratcheted up. "I've lost one." She stepped away from Duff, panic rising in her chest.

"Lost one what?" Duff asked, his gaze sweeping the room.

"Chelsea." Natalie hurried toward the table where the other four had congregated.

Duff followed.

"Where's Chelsea?" she asked, trying her best not to show her apprehension.

"I don't know. She was dancing when we were." Kylie glanced around. "Maybe she went for a walk with her dance partner," she offered.

Natalie stared at each of the four, quickly pinning them, one at a time, with an intent look. "Do me a favor and don't walk off with anyone other than one of your friends tonight."

"Why?" Kylie's brow dipped.

Natalie forced a smile. "You're in a foreign country known for drug wars and kidnapping. You never know if you're with a good guy or a bad one."

Allison's face blanched. "I thought Cancun was safe. Well, other than what happened on that scuba dive."

"You never know how secure you are. It's just safer in numbers."

"She's right," Hanna said. "Now you're making me worry about Chelsea. You don't suppose she went for a walk with her dance partner, do you?"

"Duff and I'll go look," Natalie offered.

Kylie stared hard at Duff. "How do you know he's one of the good guys?"

Natalie smiled. "He saved Lisa's life, didn't he?"

Kylie nodded. "I guess he is a good guy. But be careful, will ya?"

"I will." Natalie touched Kylie's arm. "Stay here with the others while we check the bathroom and the other usual places."

Damn. She'd let one of them slip out of her eyesight.

Dear God, she hoped Chelsea was okay.

Duff took her hand and led her toward the bathrooms behind the bar. "It's going to be okay."

How? She had no idea where her sister was. Now she'd lost one of Melody's friends.

Chapter Eight

Duff went with Natalie to the bathroom. When she came out, shaking her head, he took her hand and led her back into the bar.

Sawyer spotted him and raised his chin as if to ask if all was okay.

Duff gave a slight shake of his head and tipped it toward the exit, leading out to the pool and the beach beyond.

Sawyer rose from his bar stool and stretched, turning to his teammates to pass the word. One of them would stay at the bar, keeping a close watch on the four women still there.

With his friends covering his six, Duff left the bar, following Natalie out to the pool. A couple lay on one of the lounge chairs kissing, their bodies entwined, completely unaware of anything other than the pheromones and lust driving them.

Natalie hurried past and down the steps to the narrow boardwalk leading through the palms to the beach beyond.

"I think I see someone ahead," Natalie said.

A muted scream penetrated the darkness over the sound of the waves washing up on the sand.

Natalie kicked off her high heels and ran toward the sound.

A woman ran along the beach, heading toward them. A man chased after her.

When she reached Natalie, she crashed into her arms.

Natalie staggered backward, absorbing the impact. "Chelsea, honey, what's wrong?"

"I was…walking…on the beach…with Rolf…" Chelsea gulped back a sob. "And I was attacked."

Rolf ran and stumbled across the beach toward them.

Duff lunged past Natalie, fists clenched, ready to take on the man.

"Wait!" Chelsea turned toward Duff and Rolf. "What are you doing?"

"I'm going to wipe the beach with this man's face," Duff said.

Rolf ground to a stop and dropped to his knees in the sand, blood dripping down the side of his face from a gash on his cheekbone.

"*Rolf* didn't attack me. A couple of men did." Chelsea dropped to her knees beside the handsome man. "Oh, God. They hurt you." She reached out to touch his cheek.

Rolf flinched away. "I'm okay. Are you?" He rose to his feet and held out a hand to her.

She took it and let him pull her up. "I'm okay. He only knocked me down."

Sawyer and Quentin skidded to a stop on the sand, their fists raised, ready for anything.

"What's going on?" Sawyer asked.

Duff nodded toward Chelsea. "The girl was attacked."

Sawyer stepped toward Rolf. "Do we need to take care of business?"

Quentin moved up beside Sawyer.

"Not yet," Duff said. "Seems someone else did the attacking. This guy fought them off."

Sawyer and Quentin didn't back down, placing their bulk between Rolf and Chelsea.

"Chelsea, why did you leave the others?" Natalie glared at the man who'd taken her out to the beach.

"I needed some air. All of a sudden everything got to me and I had to get outside. Rolf was good enough to follow me to make sure I would be all right."

"I wasn't sure what was wrong or why Chelsea felt a need to be outside," Rolf said. "But it's not safe for a woman to walk the trails or the beach alone at night."

Duff nodded, not willing to give the man the full benefit of a doubt. For all he knew Rolf could have been part of a scheme to take Chelsea but had been bested by someone with the same idea.

"Come on, Chelsea, let's get you back to the hotel." Natalie slipped an arm around the girl. Chelsea let Natalie lead her back to the others.

The four girls waiting at the bar surrounded their friend and left for the hotel.

Natalie hesitated, her gaze swinging to Rolf. "You should have one of the hotel staff see to that cut."

"I can manage." He raised a hand to the injury and winced. He made a move to follow the five young women. "After I make sure Chelsea makes it to her room."

Duff, Quentin, Montana and Sawyer stepped in the man's way.

"We'll see to it," Duff said.

Rolf's eyes narrowed and he straightened. "Okay." Then he performed a smart about-face and marched away.

Duff's gaze followed the man for a moment. "I'm not sure I trust that man."

"Me neither." Natalie glanced up at Duff. "I'm going to follow the girls to their room."

"I'm coming."

She shook her head. "That's not necessary. We'll be in the hotel with all security cameras."

He held up a hand. "Humor me, will ya?"

She nodded, a smile slipping across her pretty lips. "Okay." She glanced around the bar, wondering if being with Duff would keep the abductor from targeting her. At the same time, she didn't care. She liked having him close.

"What do you want us to do?" Sawyer asked.

"Keep your eyes open and have another beer." Duff left his buddies in the bar and hurried after Natalie and the bevy of females. Whatever the hell was happening was getting entirely too close to Natalie and her sister's friends. He'd have to stay a lot closer to them to protect them. His bungalow was too far away. Perhaps he could have the reservation desk move him to the same floor.

Making a mental note to check on his way back to the bar, he stepped into the elevator with the women and rode up to the eighth floor.

Chelsea pulled her key card from her purse and slipped it through the lock. When she reached for the door handle, Duff brushed her hand aside. "Let me check first."

Chelsea stepped back and let Duff enter ahead of them. He walked through the small room, stepping over suitcases, discarded clothes and cosmetic cases. After he'd made certain there weren't any bogeymen hiding in the closet or bathroom, he held the door open for the women to enter, stepping outside before he was completely overwhelmed with estrogen. He held the door open a moment longer. "Do you ladies need anything before I leave you?"

Natalie nodded toward one of the girls. "We need to get Kylie's things moved in with her friends. I don't think she wants to be alone tonight."

"I don't," Kylie agreed.

Duff helped move Kylie's things into the room with the other girls. "Kylie, if you'll give me your key, I'll stay on this floor. If you need anything, I'll be less than a shout away." He held out his hand. "If you trust me."

Kylie held her key card clutched in her fingers, staring from Duff to Natalie.

Natalie nodded. "I'm on the same floor, too."

Kylie handed over the key card. "Are you going on the excursion to Chichén Itzá, tomorrow?"

Duff glanced from Natalie to Kylie and back. "What excursion?"

"Kylie and the rest of the girls had planned a visit to the Mayan ruins, before their friend went missing. Their reservations were nonrefundable." Natalie gave Duff a slight smile. "I told them they might as well go. It beats sitting in their rooms all day." She chewed on her lip. "But after what happened to Chelsea…I'm not sure it's a good idea."

"My guys mentioned wanting to see the ruins. What if we went along?"

Kylie frowned. "We have three extra paid slots from Melody, Lisa and Jodie's tickets."

"I'll go," Natalie volunteered.

"I will, too." The thought of Natalie and the other young women going off into the Mexican jungle didn't sit well with him. "If you think we can take your friends' places on the tour, I'll go, and bring one of my buddies along."

Sawyer would come. If the other two wanted to join them, they could follow in the rental car.

Kylie nodded. "Okay, then. I guess we'll go." She gave them a weak smile. "Thank you for being there for us. I can't imagine our troubles are making your vacation better."

"Don't you worry about it. We'll have a nice time seeing things we wanted to see anyway." Natalie hugged Kylie. "Only with better company."

Kylie entered the shared room with her friends and closed the door behind her.

Natalie's smile slipped from her lips. "I don't know what's going on." She glanced up at Duff. "Should I advise the girls to stay in their rooms until their flights leave the day after tomorrow?"

"They should be all right, as long as they stick together."

"You don't have to come along, you know."

He touched her cheek with the backs of his knuckles. "Neither do you."

"I couldn't stand it if something happened to them."

"In the meantime, what's your plan?"

"I'm going back to the bar. If I'm not watching out for the others, I'll have time to study the patrons."

Duff's brows knit together. "I'll go with you."

"I'm not sure that's a good idea."

"I don't care if it's a good idea. Someone tried to take you once already."

She smiled. "Under water. And I'm capable of taking care of myself."

He shrugged. "Then I'll move my things into Kylie's room, in case they need help tonight."

"Thank you."

"And about tomorrow—"

"You and your friends don't have to go," she said.

"I know. But after what happened on the dive and then the attack on Chelsea, I think those girls need all the protection they can get."

"What's in it for you?"

He chuckled and brushed her mouth with his thumb. "The pleasure of your company."

Natalie snorted softly. "Please."

"That's right. That's what I wanted to hear." He bent and brushed his lips across her. When she didn't slap his face he slipped an arm around her waist and dragged her body up against his.

If she'd pushed him away, he would have stopped immediately. Instead her fingers curled into his shirt and she leaned up on her toes to deepen the kiss.

His blood thrummed through his veins, searing his insides with a desire so potent he struggled to keep it at just a kiss. He slid his tongue across the seam of her lips.

Natalie opened to him, her tongue meeting his, twisting and gliding along the length of his. Her fingers crept upward, locking behind his neck, bringing him closer. Her breasts pressed against him and a slim leg curled around the back of his calf.

Duff's groin tightened. If he didn't break it off soon…

With herculean effort, he dragged his lips free and

rested his forehead against hers. "Definitely the pleasure of your company."

She let her hands slide away from his neck and down to his chest. "We probably shouldn't do that again."

"Why?"

Natalie sucked in a deep breath and let it out slowly. "I'm here to find my sister. You're—" her eyes narrowed as she gazed up at him "—a distraction."

He grinned and grazed her cheek with his lips. "I'll take that as a compliment. Now, I'd better get my toothbrush and shaving kit. And you'd better go check out the bar for potential kidnappers."

They stepped into the elevator at the same time and the doors closed.

If Natalie made one move toward him, Duff would be completely helpless to resist.

NATALIE WATCHED THE doors slide closed, trapping her in the small, intimate space with Duff. Her lips tingled and her core throbbed with the prospect of what could have happened had he not stopped kissing her when he did. She shifted, her shoulder bumping against his.

He reached for her hand.

She let him take it, her fingers curling around his, her pulse speeding as the elevator car started downward. "Really, we shouldn't—"

He tugged her hand and turned at the same time, his other arm slipping around her. "I know. You made that perfectly clear." With her body clamped against his, she couldn't move, was powerless to resist when his lips crashed down onto hers.

She met him with the passion roiling up inside, threatening to consume her.

When the bell dinged, indicating they'd reached the ground floor, she stepped back and dragged the back of her hand across her lips. This was not how an SOS agent acted. Twice now she'd lost control with this man.

He turned to face the doors as they slid open. "Sweetheart, you're as much of a distraction as you claim I am." He swept his hand forward. "After you. And I'll do my best to help you stay focused. I get it that you're here for your sister."

Natalie hurried past him, careful not to touch him. Afraid, if she did, they'd end up in another mind-bending, soul-stealing embrace.

He stepped out of the elevator behind her and stopped.

Natalie glanced over her shoulder, her gaze questioning.

"I'll let you have a head start." He gave her a strained smile, his trousers fitting tightly over a telltale bulge.

A surge of something akin to power burned through her. She'd had that effect on him. As she strode across the lobby, her step was lighter, her body still sizzling with the desire he'd inspired. The man was a huge distraction.

Back in the cabana bar, the crowd had thinned. Duff's friends sat at a table away from the dance floor, their heads together, each with a hand wrapped around a bottle of beer. They spotted her as she entered and turned toward her.

She dipped her head slightly and headed for the bar, slipping onto an empty stool.

Two men sat on stools farther down. One of them turned and tipped his head toward her. Natalie recognized the blond hair and the bandaged cut on his cheek.

"Is Chelsea all right?" Rolf asked.

"She's a little shaken, but fine." Natalie nodded toward his cheek. "I see you got that taken care of."

"Had bandages in my shaving kit." He stood and moved closer, taking the stool at her side. "I wouldn't have let her walk out on the beach had I known this area was that dangerous."

"She was pretty distraught. I'll bet she'd have walked out there with or without you." Natalie motioned for the bartender.

"Could I buy you a drink?" Rolf asked.

"Thank you." She ordered a glass of wine. When the bartender set it on the counter, she lifted it. "To interesting vacations."

Rolf raised his beer, touched it to the rim of her glass. Then he downed a long swallow.

"How long have you been in Cancun?" he asked.

"I got here yesterday."

He nodded. "I arrived this morning."

Natalie shook her head. "Nothing like adventure on your first day."

"I don't understand. I thought they had sufficient security at the resort. Have there been other attacks in the area?"

"I wouldn't know." She didn't tell him about the diving incident. If her attacker wanted to try again, she'd make sure it happened this time. Lance had her back with the embedded tracking device. Hopefully, Duff wouldn't interfere this time. However, Melody's friends didn't have embedded devices. Natalie needed all the help she could get to see to their safety. She'd need to be at her sharpest. One of the women who'd disappeared had been at the Mayan ruins when she'd gone missing.

"I'd better call it a night." Natalie drank the last of her wine and stood. "Thank you for the drink."

Rolf touched her arm. "Would you like for me to walk you to your room?"

She smiled. "Thanks, but the last time you walked somewhere with a woman, you got the worst end of the deal. I can get from here to the hotel by myself. But thanks." As she headed back, she cast another glance around the bar. Two couples danced to a slow song, the SEALs were scooting back their chairs and rising and no one else appeared to be prime candidates for kidnappers. Perhaps they'd moved on to another hotel.

Duff's friends exited out the opposite end of the bar, heading toward the bungalows.

Natalie considered checking in with Lance one more time, but decided a radio check in her room was good enough. As she walked through the lobby, she couldn't help but look for Duff. He should be back in Kylie's room by now. Her heart fluttered. Kylie's room was next to Natalie's. She and Duff would be sleeping only a few steps away from each other.

Out of the corner of her eye she spotted the dark-haired man Kylie had danced with earlier—the one with the button-up shirt and tailored trousers. He hurried toward an exit, his body tense, his gaze swinging side to side.

Natalie's pulse jumped. Something about the way he moved made her hackles rise and her nerves leap to attention. As he ducked through the door, Natalie altered her direction and followed.

The man entered a hallway marked Employees Only off the side of the huge lobby.

Natalie stopped short of the restricted-access hallway.

The man walked quickly to the end of the corridor and out the exit door at the end.

Natalie looked around to make sure no employees were wandering around, then jogged down the hall to the end where a large metal door with a red sign above it read *salida*. She eased through and caught a glimpse of the man.

He walked quickly through a dark alley between the main building and what appeared to be the utilities building housing the air-conditioning units. Natalie gave him time to reach the end of the building before she stepped through.

Once outside the hotel, Natalie slipped into the shadows and scanned the area for movement. For a moment she thought she'd lost track of the man.

Then she spied a trouser leg rounding the corner of the hotel toward the bungalows. Why would a man sneak through the employee-only area of the hotel and then out the employee exit? Perhaps he was one of the staff members or…he had something to hide.

With no weapon tucked beneath her minuscule dress, and her headset back in her room. She had no way to call for backup if something went south. But if Sneaky Dude was someone important to her sister's disappearance, she owed it to herself and to her sister to follow him.

She slipped out of her high heels and tiptoed to the edge of the building, wishing she had worn something dark, covering her arms and legs and hair so that she would blend better with the shadows. If the man thought someone was following him and turned, he'd see her light blue dress like a ghostly figure hovering nearby.

She stayed back far enough he wouldn't see or hear *her*, but close enough she didn't lose *him*.

He disappeared into the bushes.

Torn between running to catch up and revealing her position, Natalie moved silently in the shadows until she reached the stand of bushes.

Parting the branches, she peered through to the path leading to the bungalows.

A dark figure moved along the edge, fifty feet to her right.

Natalie eased through the branches and waited beside the bush until her quarry stopped outside the door to one of the bungalows. After a quick knock, the door opened, shedding a triangle of light onto the stoop. Slim, pale arms reached out, wrapped around the man's neck and dragged him over the threshold. The door was closed, pitching the path into darkness again.

Natalie hurried toward the bungalow so that she didn't lose track of which one it was. When she came abreast of the building, she memorized the number. She'd run it by Lance to find out who was registered there.

A tiny ray of light shone from one of the windows on the side of the bungalow. Natalie eased up to it and peered inside.

The man and woman were locked in a tight embrace. Feeling like a Peeping Tom, Natalie backed away and ran into another wall. She swallowed her gasp. Hands locked on her arms and spun her around.

Chapter Nine

Natalie stared up into Duff's smiling face. He leaned close and whispered against her ear, "We have got to stop meeting like this." He slid his fingers down her arms.

Natalie sucked in a breath and willed her heart rate to slow. "You scared a year off my life." Natalie grabbed his hand and pulled him along the path, back toward the hotel.

When they were far enough away from the bungalow with the embracing couple, he pulled her to a stop. "Why were you following that man?"

"He was acting suspicious," she said, glancing toward the bungalow.

"He might have been meeting his lover."

Natalie sighed. "You're probably right. The way they were carrying on…"

The door to the bungalow opened and light spilled out onto the stoop again.

"Damn. He's coming out." Natalie grabbed the front of Duff's shirt and rose up on her toes. "Kiss me."

He dropped his duffle bag and complied, crushing her mouth with his. Duff circled her waist with his hands and pulled her closer.

Natalie wrapped her arms around his neck and deepened the kiss, one eye open, her gaze on the man leaving the bungalow.

He stopped, hesitated and turned away, walking fast toward the beach.

Natalie really had no idea when he disappeared out of sight. The kiss that had started as a ploy to hide the fact she'd followed the guy out to his secret assignation had turned into more than subterfuge.

Duff slid his hands low on her waist.

Natalie curled her leg around his calf, leaning into him, her center rubbing against one of his thick thighs. Her short dress hiked up.

Duff cupped her bottom, his fingers digging into her.

If she hadn't been fully dressed, they might have taken it all the way.

What might only have been seconds stretched into a lifetime. Finally, Duff pulled away, his hands rising to grip her arms. "You're here for your sister."

"Right." Natalie ran her tongue across her lips, moistening them after another incredible kiss. Her head spun and her knees wobbled. "I should go to bed." *With Duff.* "Alone."

A grin spread across his face. "And here I thought you were coming around." He kissed her forehead, grabbed his duffle bag and took her hand. "Come on. I'll walk you back."

They didn't speak all the way back to the hotel, but her hand felt warm in his and she liked how work-roughened it was. This man wasn't afraid of getting his hands dirty. Hell, he probably killed people for a living. And rescued them. From what she'd read about SEALs, they did whatever task assigned: destroying enemy arsenals or strongholds, assassinating enemy leaders and rescuing hostages.

Right at that moment Natalie could have used a little rescuing from herself. With the worry of her sister's disappearance weighing heavily on her, and no clear leads, she shouldn't be thinking about getting naked with a virtual stranger. Especially one as lethal as Duff.

Strengthening her resolve to fight her desires and get a good night's sleep, she stopped at the entrance to the hotel. "Good night, Duff."

Duff was standing closer than she'd anticipated and the scent of his aftershave wafted up to her nostrils, tantalizing her, making her forget that fresh resolve, opting for immediate gratification in someone to hold her through the night.

She raised her gaze to his and fell into his green eyes.

He lifted a hand to cup her cheek and bent, capturing her mouth with his.

Natalie kissed him back, her heart pounding, sending a rush of blood through her body and heat pooling low in her belly.

"Good night, Natalie." He brushed her lips with his, this time in a feather-soft touch that left her wanting so much more.

When he straightened and opened the door to the lobby, she hurried inside and headed for the elevator bank.

Feeling as if she'd escaped what could have been a big mistake or the best decision she'd made in her life, Natalie oscillated between continuing on her march to a lonely bed and going back to invite Duff to join her.

Before she could do the latter, she stepped into the elevator and pushed the button for her floor.

The doors started to slide closed when an arm jutted between them and forced them back open.

"Did you forget we were going to the same floor?" Duff grinned and stepped into the car with her, letting the doors close behind him.

Natalie's eyes narrowed. "Then why did you let me go outside the hotel?"

He held up a hand. "You seemed in a hurry to get away from me."

"It's not you, per se."

He crossed his arms and leaned against the wall of the elevator as the doors closed, locking them into the confined space. Alone. "Not me? Then who are you trying to get away from?"

Natalie bit her bottom lip and faced the door, not Duff. "No one. Forget it." She wasn't about to tell him she was running away from the raging desire he'd inspired in her from the first time she'd seen him.

Duff's broad shoulders filled the elevator car and made Natalie's heart thump against her ribs. If he didn't know Kylie's room was beside hers before, he'd know when he walked her to her room.

They rode in silence, neither one touching the other, though Natalie had the strongest urge to reach out and grab his hand. And a lot more than his hand. The man had her tense, on edge, ready for…what? Another kiss?

A kiss didn't seem to be nearly enough where Duff was concerned.

When the elevator door slid open, Duff waited while Natalie stepped out.

In the corridor Natalie led the way, stopping in front of Kylie's room.

Duff raised his brows. "Which room is yours?"

She tipped her head toward the one next door.

The corners of Duff's lips turned upward. "Afraid I'll steal into your room while you sleep?"

"No, I'm more afraid you won't." Oh, hell, had she really said exactly what was on her mind?

He held out his hand. "Your key."

She removed it from a hidden pocket in her dress and gave it to him.

"Nothing is going to happen tonight," he said, opening the door for her.

Natalie straightened her shoulders, definitely disappointed by his announcement.

As she started past him he added, "Unless you want it to."

She stumbled. "Pardon me?"

He cupped her chin as he had downstairs. "You heard me."

Already, Natalie was lost. She leaned into his open palm. "You had to do it, didn't you?" she muttered.

He chuckled. "Do what?"

She slipped her hand in his and led him into her bedroom, closing the door behind him. "You had to make me want you."

It might be the worst decision she'd ever made on the spur of the moment, but it was the only one she could consider. She wanted him. Wanted his body next to hers, his fingers touching her in her most private places. That hard ridge beneath his jeans indicated he was as excited as she.

Duff stopped. "Are you sure?"

Natalie nodded. "I am." She reached behind her, unzipped her dress and let it fall to the floor. "Now, don't make me wish I'd had the good sense to send you away."

"Sweetheart, I'll make you wish for a lot of things…" He threaded his fingers through her hair and pulled gently, tilting her face up to receive his kiss. "But not to send me away."

With the heat of his lips on hers, she could feel the truth in his words. She opened her mouth and her body to him, refusing to back down or to second-guess her decision.

Duff ran his hands through her hair and down her naked back, flipping the hooks loose on her bra. He slid the straps down her arms and flung the garment to the side.

A shiver of anticipation rippled across Natalie's skin as Duff palmed her breasts, covering them with his big, rough hands.

She arched her back, pressing them harder into his touch.

"You're beautiful," he whispered into her ear, nipping at her earlobe.

Natalie tipped her head to the side, giving him better access to her throat and the pulse beating like a snare drum at a parade. "You're overdressed." She made quick work of loosening the buttons on his shirt and dragged it over his broad shoulders.

Ah, yes. Those shoulders were drool-worthy and shouldn't be covered. Natalie traced the tattoo on his right arm and bent to taste his skin there. Slightly salty and purely male. Sweet heaven, he was turning her inside out with the need to see all of him.

With that in mind, she jerked the button loose on his jeans and ran the zipper down. His shaft jutted out. The man went commando.

Her core melted into molten heat, making her throb

and ache for more. Natalie slid her hands over his backside, easing the jeans from his hips while clenching her fingers around his taut bottom.

Duff groaned and trailed a path of kisses down the long line of her throat, pausing at the insanely beating pulse at the base. He tongued it once, then lowered his hands, cupped her bottom and lifted her, wrapping her legs around his waist.

Three long strides brought them to the bed where he eased her onto her back. With a swift tug he removed her panties, exposing her moist entrance.

Duff's eyes and nostrils flared as he stepped between her legs. He skimmed his hands across her thighs toward the apex and the tuft of hair covering her sex. "Stop me if I'm going too fast," he said through clenched teeth.

"Please," she said. "You're going too slow."

With a soft chuckle he dropped to his knees, draped her legs over his shoulders and feathered his fingers along her inner thigh, searing a path to her core.

"Please," she moaned, digging her nails into the comforter, her body writhing. If she didn't have him soon, she'd come apart in a million pieces.

"Patience, Natalie." Duff slipped a finger between her folds and strummed the strip of flesh hidden between.

Electric shocks ripped through her, making her even more aware of the man and everything he was doing to her.

Duff dipped his finger into her channel, swirled it around and up through her folds to stroke that special bundle of nerves, igniting her in a firestorm of sensations.

Again and again he stroked her, bringing her to

the edge of sanity. When he parted her folds with his thumbs and bent to tongue her there, he took her to an entirely new dimension. He continued his assault until she thought she would die from pleasure.

Then he was on his feet, fumbling for his wallet in the back pocket of his jeans. Duff pulled out three foil packages, dropping two on the floor. Without bending to retrieve them, he ripped open the third packet and rolled the content over his pulsing shaft. He scooted her back and climbed onto the bed, parting her legs for him to slide in between.

Past her ability to control her impatience, Natalie bent her knees, locked her legs around Duff's waist and buried her heels into his bottom.

He drove into her, burying himself to the hilt. For a long moment he stayed deep inside her, giving her time to adjust to his width stretching her inside.

Natalie closed her eyes, taking all of him. She curled her fingers around his broad shoulders, digging her nails into his skin. This was what she'd been craving from their first kiss.

Duff eased out and back in, repeating his moves over and over, settling into a firm, thrusting motion, gliding in and out.

Natalie dropped her heels to the mattress and rose up to meet him, the tingling sensations returned, spreading from her center outward in waves. She rode the tide, her breath caught in her throat, her heart hammering.

Duff thrust one last time and remained buried deep inside her, his shaft throbbing, his body rigid with the extent of his release.

When at last he relaxed, he dropped down on top of

her, then rolled to the side, taking her with him, without severing their intimate connection.

Natalie rested her head in the crook of his arm and took in a ragged breath, his masculine scent filling her with intense satisfaction and the realization once would never be enough with Duff.

For a long time he held her against him, his hand drifting over her skin, stroking her in gentle tribute to what they'd just shared.

"That was incredible," she said when she could finally form thoughts in her sex-fogged brain.

"Why do I feel there's a 'but' coming?" He chuckled, his fingers curling into her bottom, pressing her closer.

She gave him a sad, halfhearted smile. "But this isn't helping me find my sister."

"Tomorrow we'll turn this resort town upside down."

She shook her head. "Whoever has her and the other women will not be that obvious. And there could be so many different places they could be hiding."

"One thing is certain," Duff said. "They tried to take you."

She nodded.

"They might try again."

Natalie shook her head, running her hand along the rigid muscle of his arm. "Not with a hulking SEAL following my every step and now sleeping in my room."

He brushed the hair out of her eyes. "I can't help it. I don't like that you're using yourself as bait."

"What other option do I have? They seem to be taking blondes."

"Surely there are other blondes they can target."

Natalie chewed on her bottom lip. "Do you think Chelsea was one of their attempts?"

"Maybe." His jaw tightened. "I'm not sure I trust the man she was with. What do we know about Rolf? What if he staged that scene to throw us off?"

Natalie had been thinking along the same lines. Now would have been a good time to tell Duff that she had a man working with her who could identify Rolf and others frequenting the resort.

She opened her mouth to admit she was not alone and had a backup plan.

A soft knock at the door made them both stiffen.

"Natalia?" a woman's voice called through the heavy door.

Natalie rolled out of the bed, grabbing for her discarded dress. "Who is it?"

"Kylie. Could I come in?"

"Just a minute. I was about to get into the shower."

"I'm sorry to disturb you. I just…just…"

"Hold on." Natalie shoved Duff's clothes at him and pushed him into the bathroom. As soon as she had the door closed, and her blue dress pulled over her body, she opened the door, shoving her hand through her tousled hair.

One glance at the girl's face and she held open her arms. "What's wrong, Kylie?"

"I couldn't sleep. The others don't know I left the room. I can't help it. I can't stop thinking about Melody."

Neither could Natalie and guilt wrapped around her heart. She'd been making love to a sexy man while her sister was being held in some godforsaken hell. Natalie hugged the girl to her chest, wishing she were Melody. Tears welled in her eyes. She blinked them back and vowed to work harder and smarter to come up with a plan to find and free her sister.

Kylie sniffed and looked up at Natalie. "Do you mind if I stay with you tonight? I don't know why, but I feel closer to Melody with you."

With a man in her bathroom, Natalie had to think fast. "You bet you can stay with me. But you'll need your own things. I'll walk you back to the others and let you gather what you'll need for the night." Natalie scooped her key card off the floor beside the door and followed Kylie out into the hallway.

By the time she and Kylie had returned to the room, Duff had cleared out, taking his clothes.

Though disappointed the night had ended the way it had, Natalie knew it was for the best. While Kylie ducked into the shower, Natalie inserted the earbud into her ear.

"About time you tuned in," Lance said.

"Sorry. I didn't take the communications equipment into the bar earlier. It's hard enough for me to think with all that's going on. I didn't need a man in my head talking to me."

"Understood," he said. "What have you got?"

She passed on the information about Rolf Schwimmer and the man she'd followed. "The man I followed might be a dead end, but I have to follow every lead."

"I'll check him out. You're right to suspect him if he was dancing with one of your sister's friends one minute and making a secret assignation the next. I'll let you know what I find."

"And you'll look into Rolf Schwimmer?"

"I'll run facial recognition software on the image I've pulled from the security cameras. I'll also run a background check on your secret lovers. Hopefully, I'll have something for you in the morning."

"Do you ever sleep?"

"Only when I don't have a case to help solve."

"Thanks, Lance," Natalie said. "You don't know how much it means to me to have your help on this case."

"If it were my sister, I'd want all the help I could get."

The shower shut off in the bathroom.

"Gotta go," Natalie whispered and turned off the headset, stashing it beneath her pillow.

A moment later Kylie entered the room, fresh-faced, with a towel wrapped around her head.

Not exactly the roommate Natalie would have preferred, but the right one to keep her on track.

DUFF LEFT THE hotel in search of his friends. He found them in Sawyer's bungalow, their voices a low murmur from outside the door. He knocked once and entered.

"Thought you were staying in the hotel tonight?" Sawyer slapped a cold beer into his hand and nodded toward an empty seat.

His body still humming from his encounter with Natalie, Duff popped the top off the bottle and downed half of the cool liquid before answering. "I am. I just wanted to give you a heads-up. If the women decide to go on an excursion tomorrow, we need to tag along to make sure they're okay."

Sawyer frowned. "What excursion?"

"Chichén Itzá. A Mayan ruin an hour away."

Quentin shook his head. "I thought we were here to enjoy the sun and sand. Not to go traipsing in the jungle. Been there, done that, could write the book."

"We might not need all of us, if Quentin wants to stay back and ogle bikini-clad women on the beach." Duff shot a glance at the other two members of his team. "What do you say?"

"I'm in," Sawyer said. "I wanted to see the ruins anyway."

"Count me in," Montana agreed. "This trip is getting more interesting by the second."

Quentin sighed. "I bet there won't be any bikinis at the ruins."

"Nope." Duff grinned. "But you'll go anyway, right?"

He nodded. "I'll go."

"We'll play it by ear in the morning. Natalie's sister's friends are only here for another day, they might decide to stay and hang out at the resort, given all that's happened."

Quentin brightened. "We can always hope. They were pretty cute in their bikinis."

"Rein it in, Romeo," Sawyer said. "They're on the young side for us."

"Each one of them is at least twenty-one, or pretty darned close, legal and single. That's only seven or eight years difference in age."

Sawyer frowned.

Quentin raised his hands, palms upward. "What?"

"They're still in college. Don't charm them into quitting." Sawyer nodded toward Duff. "We've got your six on this mission, Duff."

"Thanks. I'll be in the hotel should you need me."

"Yeah, closer to the women," Quentin grumbled.

"To sleep." Duff left the bungalow and glanced both ways along the path. A man stood outside a building near the beach, stretching his arms above his head. Since Duff had been there, he hadn't seen anyone coming or going from that particular bungalow. He turned toward the hotel and strolled along the path, glancing over his shoulder, keeping an eye on the stretching man. When the guy stepped back into the bungalow, Duff circled back. Moving silently, relying on his SEAL training, he worked his way back to the bungalow where the man had stepped inside.

In a resort environment, he found it hard to see the enemy in every person he met. Most of his targets had been pretty obvious. Here, anyone could be stalking young women. Human trafficking was a high-dollar business.

The guy he saw stretching could be the ringleader, or he could be a guy on his honeymoon, stretching after an active romp in bed with his new wife.

Duff eased up to the window of the bungalow. Only a sliver of light made it past the drawn shades. He could see the shadow of a figure moving around inside, but not much else. He circled the building to one of the other windows and found a little more of a sliver of light. Through it he noticed the bright glare of a screen. Not the blinking lights of a television screen playing different scenes. More the light of a computer monitor or a couple of monitors.

After studying the bit of an image he could see through the window, he concluded only one figure moved around. So he wasn't on his honeymoon. Perhaps he was a businessman, working remotely through a high-speed internet connection. That alone didn't make him a candidate for kidnapping.

Duff straightened, feeling a little foolish for suspecting every man he saw at the resort. For all they knew the culprit was a local making a quick buck selling females to a foreign market. Cancun was bigger than the resorts. On the other side of the resorts compound was an uglier reality of living where drug lords ran the government and the citizens answered to them. Hell, even at the resort, they were subject to the underpinnings of a corrupt government.

After leaving the bungalow, Duff stepped back onto the path, passing his bungalow and the one his friends were still inside, drinking beer and talking about women.

Duff passed the bungalow Natalie had been spying on earlier. A light still burned inside and he could hear voices. He walked on, refusing to look in another window. If the security patrol at the resort caught him, they'd throw him in jail. His commander would be livid, wanting to know what the hell he was doing.

With young women's lives on the line, he couldn't blame Natalie for following every lead. It just seemed as though they were taking shots in the dark. They needed some good, solid evidence or clues to lead them to the right party responsible.

Duff returned to the room beside Natalie's, showered and fell into bed. On the other side of the wall lay a woman who'd made him give up a perfectly good vacation to go chasing after clues that could either lead to nothing or to a huge can of worms with international implications.

And he'd come to Cancun for some much-needed rest and relaxation. He snorted in the dark. Why was it trouble found the Navy SEALs whether they were looking for it or not?

Which begged the question, why had he let himself get involved?

Hell, he couldn't picture it any other way. Natalie needed their help to find her sister and to keep her friends safe from whomever it was kidnapping young women. He couldn't ignore them.

Duff closed his eyes and willed himself to sleep. That itch he got prior to a mission made him restless. But like any other mission, he knew a well-rested body was his best defense. As he drifted to sleep, he dreamed of Natalie lying naked on the altar of a Mayan ruin. A faceless enemy dressed in ancient Mayan ceremonial garb raised a machete over her, ready to sacrifice her to a pagan god.

Duff woke with a start, shook himself, turned over and tried to go back to sleep, but he couldn't get that image out of his mind. No matter how hard he tried, he couldn't sleep.

In his gut he knew something was going to happen today, and it wasn't going to be a tour-guided picnic.

Chapter Ten

Natalie woke early the next morning. She'd been dreaming about Duff, lying naked with him in the sand, waves washing up over their bodies as they made love. The vibration of her cell phone on the nightstand beside her bed pulled her from the most glorious dream.

Natalie reached for the annoying sound and glanced at the screen. It was a text message from Lance: Got info on R and kissers, come see.

Natalie was awake immediately. She sat up and glanced across to where Kylie slept, her hand tucked beneath her cheek.

Dressing quickly, she plugged her headset into her ear and wrote a note to Kylie, saying she'd gone out for a run on the beach. The sun had yet to make its appearance, but the predawn gray light chasing the night away would make it easy to find her way to Lance's bungalow.

Dressed in shorts, a tank top and sneakers, she looked like any health-conscious runner out for a morning jog before the sun rose and heated the air.

Once outside the hotel, she jogged down the path that meandered through the bungalows until she reached Lance's. She stopped and pretended to tie her shoe, glancing around for signs of anyone watching. When she'd determined she was alone, she stepped up to the door. Lance opened it and waved her inside.

"What did you find?" she asked as soon as the door clicked closed.

"Well, actually, it's what I didn't find that had me wondering."

"Show me."

Lance sat at the computer and ran his fingers across the keyboard, then clicked the mouse, bringing up a passport image of the man Natalie followed to the bungalow the previous evening.

"Kissing guy is Frank 'Sly' Jones, former army ranger, now working in D.C. as a security consultant." He flipped to an image of a woman dressed in a skirt suit. "His girlfriend registered under the name Cassandra Teirney, real estate agent, also from D.C."

"Why was Sly dancing with one of our girls when he had a lover back in the bungalow?"

Lance shrugged. "Might be a player." He clicked the mouse and nodded toward the screen. "I'm more concerned about Rolf."

"Why?" Natalie leaned over his shoulder and stared at the monitor.

"I searched the hotel database for our friend Rolf and found Rolf Schwimmer. A quick lookup on the national passport database came up empty. None of the images matched the one you sent me via your cell phone nor of the images I was able to pull from security cameras located throughout the resort."

Natalie's belly tightened. "What *did* you find?"

"I had Royce run a facial recognition program starting with U.S. criminal databases. While he was doing that, I ran one against the U.S. military identification database and got a hit."

"He's one of our military?"

"Was." Lance brought up an image of Rolf dressed in the desert camouflage uniform of the U.S. Army Special Forces. "He left the service four years ago, after ten years and four deployments to the Middle East and two purple hearts. His legal name is Rex Masters. He was a sniper."

Natalie studied the image, recognizing the same man who called himself Rolf in Cancun. "What's he doing now?"

Lance shook his head. "That's just it. I can't find anything else on him from the past four years that he's been out of the military. No address, no tax records. Nothing."

Natalie's blood chilled in her veins. "Do you think he's hired on somewhere as a mercenary? Maybe for a foreign country or agency?"

Lance shrugged. "That's all I found. He actually arrived in this country a week ago."

"About the time the women started disappearing." Anger warmed her blood and made her want to march right out and confront the bastard. "If he's the one responsible for my sister's disappearance, I'll kill him and take great pleasure in doing so."

"We can't be certain he's involved with the missing women. However, he just left his room on the fourth floor of the hotel. If you want to get inside, I'll keep an eye on his movements and let you know when he gets close." Lance glanced at his watch. "People usually don't start stirring for another half hour."

"Then why is he?" Natalie asked.

"He's wearing running shoes, shorts and no shirt. I assume he's on his way out to run. Something I need to do."

"You got a way for me to get past his door lock?"

"I can unlock it from here." He grinned and pulled up a screen. "I'm tapped into the hotel security database. I can unlock any door anytime."

"Okay. It'll take me a couple minutes to get there. Can you block the security camera from following me to his room?"

"Got it covered. Hurry. I don't know how long the guy can run."

Natalie waited for Lance to give her the all-clear signal before she left his bungalow and jogged back to the hotel. If Rolf—Rex—got back before she was finished searching his room, she'd have a hard time justifying being there. Given that he was a highly trained military man, he might take offense to having his privacy violated. And if he was involved in the kidnapping of the women, he'd have reason to want to insure her silence on whatever she might discover.

Her heart beating fast, Natalie entered the hotel and took the stairs to the fourth floor, running all the way up. Thankfully, she stayed in good shape and wasn't that winded by the time she emerged on Rex's floor.

Lance gave her the room number. As she reached it, she noted the Do No Disturb sign hung on the handle. The indicator light blinked green as she approached. Wrapping her hand in the hem of her tank top, she twisted the door handle and pushed it inward.

Inside she found a neatly kept room with clothes hung in the closet, the shirts all facing the same direction, the trousers neatly pressed.

A suitcase sat on the luggage rack zipped closed.

Natalie checked the drawers first, finding rolled socks, T-shirts and shorts. It looked like the inside of an army recruit's footlocker. Everything was placed precisely. A drill sergeant's ace cadet.

Careful not to disturb anything, Natalie checked beneath the clothing, pulled the drawers out and looked behind each. Hating to disturb the neatly made bed, she searched beneath the pillows, mattress and the bed itself. The lock box in the closet was locked.

"I don't suppose you could get me inside the lock box?" She spoke softly.

"Sorry. It's not on the security network."

Natalie turned to the suitcase. The lightweight, black, hard-plastic case appeared like any other. She unlatched the case and peered inside. It looked empty at first glance. But as she looked closer it appeared to be shallower than the exterior would indicate. Could it have a secret panel?

Running her fingers along the inside edges, Natalie couldn't feel anything out of the ordinary. She examined the exterior and couldn't see anything that looked like a button to be pushed to reveal an inner compartment.

She took the case into the bathroom and laid it on the counter in the bright lighting and opened it. Slowly, carefully, she looked again.

There. At the inside edge, there was a slight discoloration in the plastic rim. She slid her hand over it sideways and nothing happened. Bracing her thumb on it, she pushed it upward. Something clicked and the lining of the case rose on one side. "I found a secret compartment in his suitcase."

"Yeah, find out what's in it and get the hell out. He's on his way through the side entrance."

Her heart racing, Natalie tugged at the floor of the case, trying to open it. "Can't you stall his elevator or something? I need a little more time."

"I would, but he's headed for the stairwell."

"Damn." Natalie pulled harder, forcing the bottom of the case open. She gasped.

"What's in it?" Lance's voice echoed in her ear.

"A gun and an envelope."

"You don't have time. You have to get out."

"I need to know what's in the envelope." She pulled open the envelope and photographs fell out, landing on the floor of the bathroom. All of them were of beautiful blonde women. In the middle of the photos was one of Melody—one she'd posted on her profile page of her favorite social media site.

"He's in the stairwell," Lance said, his voice urgent. "Get out, Nat."

Natalie gathered the photographs and shoved them back into the envelope, tossed it into the secret compartment and secured it in place. It didn't quite fit right, but she didn't have time to return it to its original state. Slamming the case shut, she carried it back to the room, laid it on the luggage rack and slipped out the door. With no time to spare, she ran for the elevator and punched the button.

"You don't have time to wait for the elevator." Lance's voice sounded in her ear. "The room directly behind you is vacant. Go!"

Natalie spun, grabbed the door handle and pushed it open as the stairwell door opened at the other end of the hall. She dived inside and let the door close automatically. She could hear Masters's footsteps, but the door clicked shut before he reached her position.

Her heart thundering in her chest, Natalie waited for a few seconds.

"Masters is in his room," Lance's calm voice said softly. "The elevator is at the fourth floor and is about to open…now."

Natalie pulled open the room door as the elevator bell dinged. A quick glance toward Masters's closed door and Natalie scampered across the hall into the open elevator.

"Good morning, Natalie."

DUFF SHOOK HIS head at the red flush rising in Natalie's cheeks. "You're out and about early. I take it you found out something new."

She nodded. "Let's go to your room and I'll tell you all about it."

The elevator rose to the eighth floor and Natalie stepped out.

Duff could hear the women before he actually saw them. He strode into the hallway to find Melody's friends gathered at the elevator, wearing shorts, matching T-shirts and carrying light backpacks.

"What's going on?" Natalie asked.

"We're going down for breakfast. If you still want to come along, you need to hurry, the bus leaves at eight."

"We'll be right down," Natalie said. "Don't let the bus leave without us."

The girls stepped onto the elevator and Natalie hurried toward her room.

"Are you sure it's a good idea for them to go on that tour?" Duff followed Natalie into her room.

"No. But I'm going with them. Maybe there *is* safety in numbers."

"Do you mind telling me what you were doing on the fourth floor?"

When the door closed behind Duff, Natalie turned and wrapped her arms around his neck. "I may have found our kidnapper."

He held her for a brief moment. "Tell me."

She pushed away from him, her eyes suspiciously bright. "Look, I don't have time to explain everything, but I had reason to suspect our friend Rolf."

While she spoke, she slipped out of her tank top, pulled a light, short-sleeved blouse over her sports bra and tied it around her waist, leaving a significant amount of her midriff exposed.

Duff's groin tightened, but he resisted taking her back into his arms and kissing her all the way down to that tempting display of flesh.

"Rolf isn't Rolf. He's former army sniper Rex Masters."

Natalie slipped out of her running shorts and stood in front of her suitcase in a pair of sheer pink thong panties.

Duff dragged in a deep breath and let it out slowly. "You realize you're killing me."

She cast him a weak smile. "If we only had time…"

Duff willed his body to relax. As much as he wanted to make love to Natalie, they had bigger fish to fry. "What did you find in Masters's room?"

She reached for a pair of shorts and paused. "A secret compartment in his suitcase."

"I take it you got inside." When she nodded, he asked, "What did you find?"

Natalie glanced up at him. "A gun and an envelope filled with photos of blondes. One of which was my sister." She bit her lip, her eyes pooling with tears. One slipped down her cheek. She dashed her hand across, capturing it, and straightened her shoulders. Then she pulled on a pair of denim cutoffs, frayed at the hem. In the outfit, she appeared younger, the same age as her sister's friends.

Duff's brow knit. "If he's the one, why don't we confront him?"

"I can't afford to spook him. If he disappears, my sister's location disappears with him."

"So what now?"

"We go to Chichén Itzá with Melody's friends. I can't let them go alone."

"Talk them out of it."

"I can't. There have been what appear to be two attempts to nab blondes from the patrons of this resort. If Masters is the one responsible, he might try again on the trip to Chichén Itzá. I want to be the one he goes for. You can't be around when he makes his move. He has to think I'm alone and unprotected."

Duff's gut tightened and he grabbed her arms. "The man has a gun. How will you protect yourself against bullets?"

"If he's after me to sell me, he won't want to damage the goods." Natalie stared up into his face. "And I'm not completely alone here."

"What do you mean?"

She pulled the miniature earbud from her ear. "I have someone following my movements and helping me."

Duff frowned. "What are you talking about?"

She pointed to her foot. "I have a microchip embedded between my toes, and a highly trained man on the other end of the tracking device who can locate me anywhere on earth."

"What good will that do if you're dead?"

Her lips tightened. "It's a chance I have to take to find my sister."

Duff stared at Natalie. "There seems to be a lot I don't know about you."

"And if, after this is all said and done, we are still interested in each other, I'll fill in the blanks. If anything happens to me on this excursion, my man will find you." She planted her hands on her hips. "Now, are you coming with us?"

Duff didn't like being kept in the dark, but he didn't have a choice. He couldn't let her go on her own. "I need to shower and change."

"I'll be downstairs with the others. When you get on the bus, sit with someone else."

"Won't the girls wonder why?"

"I'll sit with Kylie. I don't want whoever is abducting women to think we're together."

Duff brushes his finger across her shoulder. "I won't like it."

"Neither will I, but the longer my sister is missing, the greater the chance I won't find her. She's my only living relative. I won't let her go without a fight."

Duff circled that bare midriff and yanked Natalie close, her body pressing against his. "When we find your sister, you and I are going to have a little talk." He brushed his mouth across hers. "And then we'll talk some more." This time he claimed her lips, crushing her to him, in a desperate embrace. If his gut was right— and it always was—today would be hell.

This woman he'd only known for such a short time

had made an immediate impact on his thoughts and, he suspected, his heart.

Duff raised his head and brushed his lips across the tip of her nose "Don't do anything stupid."

"I'll do whatever it takes to free my sister," she said, her words warm against his lips.

"That's what I'm afraid of." He kissed her again and let go of her. "I'll be down before the bus leaves. Don't let it go without me on it."

Duff left her room and entered his. Dialing the number for Sawyer's bungalow, he waited while it rang.

"Yeah," Sawyer answered.

"We're going. Meet in front of the hotel at eight."

"Got it." Sawyer didn't wait for additional information, just hung up. Duff could rely on his friend to notify the other two members of his team.

Duff ducked into the shower, washing away the sweat from his run. In fewer than ten minutes he was dressed and downstairs. He met with his team at the breakfast table. They loaded up on protein and juice. Not knowing what to expect, they charged their bodies with what it took to run an extended mission.

"Keep an eye out for Rolf. He's not who he says he is and he might be armed," Duff told them, his voice low enough only they could hear.

Sawyer, Quentin and Montana nodded, finishing their meals in silence. Quentin and Montana would take the rental car and be on their way to the ruins before the bus left the hotel.

Sawyer and Duff met with the twenty-five people signed up for the tour. Natalie worked her way over to him without being too obvious. "Kylie gave the tour director your names. You're on the list in place of Lisa and Jodie."

Duff gave the slightest of nods and raised a hand when his name was called out.

Delayed several minutes by one late-riser, the bus left the hotel almost on schedule, the tour guide giving a running commentary on the rich history of the area and the Mayan culture dating back centuries earlier.

Duff sat near the back of the bus. Natalie sat toward the center with Kylie at her side. So far, he'd seen no sign of Masters. For that matter, he didn't see Loverboy from Natalie's Peeping Tom efforts the night before. Other than Sawyer, Duff and the missing Melody's young friends, the bus was filled with gray-haired senior citizens, excited to be on their way to completing items on their bucket lists.

Even if this turned out to be a nonevent, he'd be better off treating it as the most intense, focused mission he'd ever conducted. The trip seemed innocuous, but Duff had been on missions that, on the surface, should have been slam-dunks. Those had been the ones where he'd lost fellow teammates.

Chapter Eleven

Natalie sat beside Kylie, pretending to listen to what the tour guide was saying about the customs of the ancient Mayans and the importance of the temple they were about to see. All the while Natalie focused on everything around her, wishing she could have brought a gun. She felt naked and exposed in this foreign country, populated with drug lords vying for control and thugs looking for easy money.

A hundred questions roiled through her mind with each passing mile, leading them deeper into the jungle and away from the relative protection of the resort security.

Foremost in her mind was where they had hidden her sister and the other women. Who was in charge of the kidnapping ring? Was it Masters? Or was he a gun for hire? A mercenary who contracted out to the highest bidder no matter what the job entailed?

If he was a hired hand, who did he answer to?

As they rolled into the parking lot near the ruins, Natalie scanned the area. Hundreds of people came to see the ruins each day, and that day was no different. Other tour buses disgorged their passengers, the guides speaking a mix of Spanish, English, and even some Japanese or Chinese.

Natalie didn't care what language they spoke, her gaze panned the faces as she waited her turn to get off the bus. With so many people present, it was hard to pick out any one face in the crowd.

Kylie grabbed her hand and hurried her along to catch up to the other girls.

Natalie glanced back. Duff and Sawyer kept pace, staying several yards back, allowing others to come between them.

By the time they hiked from the parking area to the pyramid Castillo de Kukulcán, Natalie was perspiring in the humidity. Chelsea, Hanna, Briana, Kylie and Allison insisted on climbing to the top. "For Melody," Chelsea said.

Though not fond of heights, Natalie couldn't say no. She smiled and faked an excitement she didn't feel, hoping that from the top she might have a better chance of spotting Masters, if he was the one orchestrating the kidnappings.

Natalie brought up the rear on the long climb up the narrow steps. She didn't dare look down for fear she might freeze before she made it to the summit. No matter how much she wished she could go back, the long line of people following her wouldn't be too pleased if she made them move over to allow her to descend. So Natalie continued upward until they finally reached the top.

While the girls stood at the edge, taking pictures of the view and of themselves, Natalie hung back. She pressed a hand to her queasy stomach, petrified at the thought of going back down those narrow stairs when she couldn't even get close to the edge without hyper-ventilating.

"Are you okay?" Duff's deep voice said beside her.

Natalie shook her head.

"Afraid of heights?"

"Is it that obvious?" she said, her voice shaking more than she liked.

"You're as white as a sheet. Other than that, no, it's really not obvious." He chuckled. "Just wanted you to know my other two men are here, watching out for you and the girls."

"That's good to know." She dared a glance at the stairs leading downward and her vision blurred.

"The trick is to look at the back of the head of the person in front of you. Don't stare out at the view or look farther down than you have to. Take one step at a time."

"Thanks. But I'd prefer a rescue helicopter. I get dizzy looking down that long line of stairs. I'm not sure I can do this."

"I'll go down in front of you. If you slip and fall, I'll catch you."

"You're only making it a little better. I could have gone without the suggestion of slipping and falling."

"We're heading down." Kylie appeared in front of her. "Are you feeling okay? You look a little pale."

Natalie forced a smile. "I'm fine." *No, I'm not.* But she wasn't going to tell them that. They'd been through so much already, she didn't want to spoil their visit to the ruins by being a big baby about going down what she'd just come up.

Duff spoke to Sawyer, who managed to get in front of Chelsea before she started down.

Kylie followed the others, taking the stairs with ease.

Afraid they'd get too far ahead of her, Natalie gripped Duff's arm. "Okay, I'd like to take you up on catching me if I fall. Besides, you're tall. Even a step down from me you'll still be almost eye level."

Duff chuckled. "My pleasure." He stepped down and held out a hand to her. "Coming?"

As he made that step down, Natalie's heart stuttered, caught and held. When she placed her hand in his, her pulse raced ahead and her head spun. She stared down at the long flight of stairs to the bottom and swayed.

"Look at me," Duff commanded.

She glanced up, her gaze connecting with his. "I can't do this."

"You can, and you will," he said, his tone firm, confident.

"Easy for you to say," she quipped. "You're not the one terrified of heights."

"I was until the twentieth time I fast-roped out of a helicopter. By then I realized I was wasting a lot of energy better spent on the mission at hand." He stared into her eyes. "Your mission is to see those girls all get home safely to their parents and to find your sister. You can't do that from up here. So, are you going to stand there shaking, or are you going to follow me down off this temple?" The more he talked the stronger his voice.

Natalie straightened her shoulders and nodded. "I'm coming." Her hand in his, she took that first step down, only glancing at the steps long enough to place her foot, then focusing on the back of Duff's dark head. He really was a gorgeous man, and he was right. Her duty was to her sister and to the girls already halfway down the pyramid.

One step at a time, she placed her feet carefully, refusing to stumble, knowing she would take Duff down with her if she fell, and possibly everyone else in front of him. A domino effect of disaster.

Her breath caught in her throat and her pulse thundered in her ears.

"Breathe, Natalie," Duff said. "You've got this."

When she glanced up from the view of her feet on the stairs, she caught the intense green of Duff's eyes. "I've got this," she repeated, and took another step, then another until she settled into a rhythm that got her all the way to the bottom.

Once on the ground, her knees wobbled. She wanted to lie down spread-eagle and kiss the earth. And would have, except Duff's arm slipped around her waist and held her upright until she stopped shaking.

"Come on, Natalia," Kylie called out, fifty feet ahead of her and Duff, trailing Chelsea and her gang. "We're going to the Temple of Jaguars."

Natalie stared up into Duff's face and gave him a lopsided smile. "Thanks. I don't think I could have made it down without you."

"Glad to be of assistance." He stepped away, nodding toward the others. "You'd better get going."

Leaning up on her toes, she kissed his lips and then hurried after the young women, afraid if she stayed with him much longer, she'd make a complete fool of herself, throw her arms around his neck and promise him her firstborn child for getting her down off the sacred temple.

Natalie caught up with the others in front of the Upper Temple of the Jaguars. They spent the next thirty minutes wandering through the Ball Court where ancient Mayans had played some sort of sport with a large, heavy, rubber ball.

When they were standing in front of the Temple of the Bearded Man, Chelsea dug her hand into her small backpack. "Damn."

"What's wrong?" Natalie asked.

"I dropped my phone back on the playing field. I'll be right back."

"I'll go with you." Hanna turned around and followed Chelsea, who hadn't waited.

"My picture of the jaguar's head came out blurred. I'd like to go back and get another before we move on. I'll go with them." Allison dug her smartphone out of her pocket and hurried after them. "Wait up."

Natalie called out, "You should all stay together."

Chelsea spun, walking backward. "It's daylight and there are hundreds of people around. If something happens, we'll just yell. It will only take a few minutes."

Kylie shaded her eyes from the glare of the sun and stared after the three girls. "Should we wait here?"

"I'd rather not," Briana said. "There's no shade. We could at least wait in the Bearded Man Temple." She didn't wait for Kylie's response, moving into the shadows of the temple. Kylie followed.

Natalie paused, hoping to catch Duff's attention.

Pretending to admire one of the Ball Court's two stone rings, Duff and Sawyer stood near one of the high walls inside the Ball Court. Every so often Duff would glance in Natalie's direction, without being too noticeable.

On one such glance, Natalie caught Duff's eye and nodded toward the girls headed back to the center of Ball Court.

He gave her an imperceptible nod and nudged Sawyer.

Sawyer shot a glance toward the girls.

Duff's other two friends were standing at the entrance to the Upper Temple of the Jaguar, on standby in case Duff and Sawyer needed their help.

Natalie felt better knowing the Navy SEALs were there, guarding her back.

When she turned back to Kylie and Briana, her stomach fell.

"Natalia." Briana hurried down the stone steps, her eyes wide, her hand pressed to her chest. "I don't know what happened. One minute I was staring at some drawings with Kylie. I turned my back and the next minute she's gone."

Natalia gripped Briana's arms. "What do you mean she's gone?"

Tears ran down her cheeks. "I searched all over the temple and I can't fine Kylie. I don't know where she disappeared to." Her damp eyes widened and she pressed her knuckles to her lips.

Natalie turned Briana toward Duff and Sawyer who, by now, were watching Natalie and Briana closely from the middle of the Ball Court. "See those two men who came with us on the bus?"

Briana nodded, wiped at the tears streaming down her face. "Yes."

"Go to them, tell them what you told me and do whatever they tell you to do."

"Why?"

"Just do it." Natalie gave her a shove toward Duff. Without waiting for Briana to get across the length of the field, Natalie ran up the steps into the Temple of the Bearded Man, cursing at her stupidity. She'd taken her gaze off the girls for a moment. Now one of them was gone. The one with the lightest blond hair.

The Temple of the Bearded Man sat closest to the jungle's edge. Over the centuries trees and bushes had crept closer, a perfect place for someone to lie in wait for that perfect moment to snatch an unsuspecting young woman away from her friends.

Her heart sick for Kylie, Natalie ran around the side of the temple toward the back where the jungle's shadows were darkest.

"Kylie?" she called out, praying the young lady had only stepped around the back to study the carvings on the wall.

Near the edge of the tree line, something pink lay on the ground.

Natalie ran toward it and scooped up the bright pink beaded necklace Kylie had worn that morning. The clasp had broken and beads had spilled across the ground. Natalie flung the necklace to the side and ran toward the trees. "You want a blonde, take me!" she shouted.

As she neared the dark, overhanging vines, a shadow shifted and a Hispanic man emerged, lunged for her and pulled her into the jungle.

Not until it was too late did Natalie realize he wasn't alone. Another man with wicked dragon tattoos twisting across the skin of his arms stood beneath the branches of a tree, holding a syringe in his hand.

Natalie started to scream. The man who held her clamped his hand over her mouth.

She bit his palm and struggled, twisting and writhing, trying to avoid the syringe.

The man who'd grabbed her slammed her to the

ground on her stomach and landed on her back. His partner jammed the needle into her arm and Natalie's body went limp.

She could hear and see what was going on, but she was powerless to fight back. The two men converged on her, one grabbing her beneath the arms, the other lifting her by the ankles. They carried her along a trail, half walking and half running.

Duff. Natalie tried to shout, her mouth as paralyzed as her arms and legs. Gray clouds gathered around the edges of her vision, creeping in until she was consumed by darkness.

As soon as Duff saw the girl running toward him and Natalie racing up the steps to the Temple of the Bearded Man, he knew something was wrong.

"We got a problem." Duff backhanded Sawyer and took off at a dead run.

"What?" Sawyer caught up to him before he'd gone five yards.

"See that girl running toward us?" Duff said without slowing.

"Yeah."

"Stay with her. Natalie just ran toward that temple."

"So?"

"Just stay with her," Duff called out.

When they came abreast of the crying young lady, Sawyer ground to a stop and pulled the girl into his arms. "Hey, everything's going to be okay."

"What happened?" Duff asked, pausing long enough to hear her story.

"Kylie disappeared…" The girl hiccupped and swallowed a sob. "Natalia is going after her."

Before the last words left the girl's mouth, Duff was already racing toward the temple. He took the stone steps two at a time, ran through the columns and slipped around the back of the ancient building. He stopped, willing the blood pumping through his veins to slow enough he could hear sounds past the pounding in his ears. Nothing stirred, no one moved and he found no sign of Natalie, just the darkness of the tree line teasing him, tempting him to enter. But where?

A bright flash of color lay at the edge of the jungle. He ran toward it and bent to study the remains of a pink beaded necklace like the one Kylie had worn that morning.

Duff entered the wooded area, pushing through the brush. He found several broken branches and the ground disturbed by footprints. He bent to study them and discovered an empty syringe almost hidden by the broad leaves of a plant.

His gut clenched and he straightened. What appeared to be a narrow path, possibly used by animals, stretched ahead of him. He ran through the jungle, realizing the path circled back. Eventually he emerged in a small clearing beside the road the tour buses came in on. Tire tracks led from the clearing to the road.

Duff ran out onto the road and stared both ways. A bus carrying a group of Japanese tourists rumbled past him, heading for the temples, stirring up a cloud of dust.

They were gone.

Whoever had taken Kylie and Natalie had gotten away. With no way of catching them on foot, Duff turned toward the ceremonial ruins of Chichén Itzá and jogged back.

He'd covered half a mile when a Jeep roared up to

him. Montana slammed on the brakes and Quentin leaned out. "Get in. Maybe we can catch them."

"What about the other women?" Duff said, climbing into the backseat.

"Sawyer is taking the bus back with them. We didn't have room in the Jeep to fit all of them."

Before Duff was fully in the Jeep, Montana shifted into gear and tore out, spitting gravel up behind them.

Duff was slammed back in his seat. He didn't care. He shouldn't have given Natalie so much space. Whoever had taken the women had used drugs to subdue them.

His chest tightened as he realized Natalie had gotten her wish. She'd wanted to be taken by the kidnappers to wherever they might be hiding her sister.

Despite how fast Montana drove they never caught up to the vehicle spiriting Kylie and Natalie away. As they rounded a bend in the road they came upon a grassy clearing, the grass bent and the branches on the nearby trees waved frenetically as a helicopter rose into the sky. Below, a battered white van stood with the doors opened wide. Empty.

Duff stared up at the helicopter. "Anyone catch the lettering on the tail?"

Montana and Quentin shook their heads.

"What are the chances of tracing that helicopter?"

"Better if we were in the States," Quentin answered.

"Nil here in Mexico," Montana agreed.

Duff's fists clenched. No way he'd let Natalie disappear. She was just the kind of woman who could handle a man like him. And he liked that she wasn't completely flawless. Her fear of heights only made her more adorably human.

Quentin turned to Duff. "Where to now?"

His jaw hardened with his resolve to find her and bring her back alive. "Go back to the hotel."

Montana shot a glance over his shoulder. "You don't think they took them back there, do you?"

"No," Duff said. "But someone there will know how to find them."

Chapter Twelve

Natalie faded in and out of consciousness, fighting to remain aware but unable to stay out of the deep, dark abyss that pulled her back each time. At one point she thought she heard the thumping of rotor blades. Wind whipped her hair across her face, the strands lashing her skin.

Fade out.

How long she'd been out, she didn't know. She bounced back to a semiconscious state when her body flopped over a bony shoulder and she was jostled and flung onto a pile of what felt like rags. Still, her eyes refused to open and she slipped away.

When she finally came to she thought she'd opened her eyes, only to find more darkness. Was she awake? Her body ached and something lumpy pressed into her hip.

The lump moved and a moan sounded close by.

Natalie tried to move her body, but it was too heavy, the drug having paralyzed her muscles. It would take time to wear off. Already she could feel tingling in the tips of her fingers. One by one, she wiggled her toes. Hopefully full control of her body would return before her captors came back.

In the meantime the gray fog began clearing from her

brain. Natalie forced air past her vocal chords. "Kylie?" she said, her voice gravelly, barely recognizable to her own ears.

Another moan and the lump beneath her hip twitched.

Taking in a deeper breath, Natalie tried again. "Kylie?"

This time the moan sounded vaguely like Kylie.

A brief feeling of relief stole over Natalie. At least she and Kylie were together. If Natalie could wake her body from the pall of death the drug had induced on it, she might have a fighting chance of getting the girl out of there.

She never wanted one of Melody's friends to be caught in the same human trafficking that had taken Melody from her vacation into this new hell.

Her pulse quickened at the thought of her sister. "Melody?" she called out, her voice getting stronger.

No other sound reached her but that of Kylie breathing and occasionally moaning.

"Where are we?" Kylie mumbled. "I can't move," she added, her tone tightening, her voice rising. "Why can't I move?" She sounded as if she was about to cry.

"Keep calm," Natalie said. "We've been given some kind of paralyzing drug. I'm sure it's temporary. I'm starting to get some movement in my toes and fingers."

Soft sobs echoed through the room.

While she waited for the drug to wear off, Natalie tried to see into the darkness to get an idea of where they were being held.

The lingering, pungent scent of oil and gasoline could mean a lot of different things. They could be in an abandoned auto-repair shop or in a warehouse where they used gasoline-powered forklifts to move pallets. They could be in a completely enclosed parking garage, but it, too, would have to have been abandoned or they would have heard more noise inside.

Natalie strained her ears to pick up any sound outside the building. A low rumbling reached her, then the deep clanking sound of metal hitting concrete. Were they in a warehouse? Maybe near a shipping yard?

"I'm scared," Kylie whimpered.

"It's okay to be scared. We're in a scary situation. But there are people who will find us and get us out of here."

"Who?"

"You know those guys that were hanging out at the bar? The ones that helped save Chelsea and Lisa when they almost drowned?"

"Uh-huh."

"They're Navy SEALs."

Kylie sniffed. "They are?"

"Yes. And they're going to help us get out of this mess."

"How? They don't know where we are." Her voice shook and more sobs followed.

"Trust me," Natalie said. "They'll find us."

"When?"

"I don't know. In the meantime we have to help ourselves."

"I can't even move. How can I help myself?"

"The drug is wearing off. We have to give it time."

"What if those men come back before it wears off?"

"We'll think of something." Natalie prayed the men wouldn't return before she came up with a plan. She'd told Kylie about the SEALs to give her hope. Natalie couldn't guarantee they'd come to the rescue. A lot depended on Lance's tracking device and how quickly they were able to locate her.

In a perfect world, Natalie would let her captors take her to their ultimate destination, after she got Kylie out of whatever warehouse they were in and back to the hotel. She could be on the plane back to the States tomorrow.

In a perfect world.

Hell, in a perfect world, Melody would never have been kidnapped. She and her friends would all have been on a plane back to the States tomorrow. Happy, sunburned and innocent of the ugly truths of the world they lived in.

"I want to go home." Kylie's voice shook and the sound of her sobs made Natalie wish she could pull the girl into her arms and comfort her.

"You will, sweetie," Natalie said softly. "You will."

The sound of voices speaking Spanish outside made her stiffen. "Shh, Kylie."

"Is it the men who took us?" the younger woman whispered.

"I don't know." Natalie listened. The men who'd attacked her had muttered curses in Spanish, but she couldn't tell if they were the same voices as those outside the walls of their prison. "Pretend that you're still unconscious."

Metal on metal clanked as if someone removed a padlock from a hasp. Then a large door swung open, spilling daylight into the interior of what appeared to be a warehouse.

Natalie closed her eyes, leaving them cracked open enough to peer through her lashes.

Four Hispanic men walked in speaking Spanish so fast, Natalie, with her limited grasp on the language, only caught a few words. Women. Night. Then she heard the

Spanish words for "four hundred thousand" followed by the English word "dollars."

Her heart pounded against her ribs. She'd figured this was a human trafficking ring, selling women for money, but hearing the negotiated amount made it terribly real.

Had they already sold Melody to some rich bastard who'd carried her off to some unknown location on the other side of the world?

Hopelessness threatened to overwhelm her. With her body out of commission and her mind going through every horrible scenario, she had to get a grip or lose it entirely. Even if she never found Melody, she could help Kylie escape this nightmare. She hadn't been trained as a special agent only to end up in some sick son of a bitch's harem or sex den.

The men moved toward Natalie and Kylie. Natalie had come to realize the lump beneath her hip was Kylie's foot. No matter how much it had twitched before, Kylie lay still, not moving anything.

Natalie was closest to the door.

One of the men nudged her with the tip of his boot and laughed. He nudged her again, this time a little harder.

Natalie played dead. She wanted them to think the drug was still working and she remained unconscious. Maybe it would buy her some time without them sticking another syringe full of the same drug into her.

A cell phone rang nearby and one of the men spoke in rapid Spanish. When he ended the call, he said something to the others. They turned and walked out of the building, closing and locking the door behind them.

Natalie watched through half-closed eyes as they left, making sure all four men went through the door. The voices faded away, leaving her and Kylie alone.

"What can you move?" Natalie whispered, stretching her fingers and toes.

"Nothing."

"Give it a try," Natalie insisted.

A quiet minute passed and then Kylie said, "I think I moved my fingers."

"Good girl," Natalie said. "Now your toes."

The foot under her hip wiggled.

"I think there's something on top of one of my feet." Kylie wiggled the foot again.

Natalie chuckled. "That's me. Wiggle it and make me feel it. Kick me, if you can. I dare you."

The twitching at her hip intensified until Natalie felt a definite nudge. "That's it. The more you move, the faster the drug wears off. Keep going."

Natalie flexed her hands, exercising her fingers until her arms tingled. Then she moved her arms and bent her knees. Soon she could fling her arm to the side, her body rolling with it, freeing Kylie's foot.

"Better?"

"Yes." Kylie gasped. "I can move my entire leg now."

Natalie could move her legs a little, and the more she tried the better she got until she rolled onto her stomach and pushed to a sitting position. A few more minutes and she might be on her feet and finding a way to get Kylie out of the warehouse.

Voices sounded again outside the building. By the escalating volume, the men were excited or anxious about something.

"Quick," Natalie urged. "If you don't want them to pump you full of drugs again, pretend you're completely unconscious. No matter what, don't let them know otherwise."

DUFF BURST THROUGH the doors of the hotel lobby. Natalie had said if something happened to her, the man behind her tracking device would contact him. He assumed the man would be at the hotel, near to where Natalie was staying.

In the lobby Duff ground to a halt and stared at every man wandering through. No one made eye contact with him.

"Are you sure Natalie said someone would get in touch with you if she disappeared?" Montana asked.

"Yes." Desperate to find Natalie and Kylie, he walked up to a man who appeared reasonably intelligent and demanded, "Do you know Natalie?"

The man backed a step, shaking his head. "No. I have no idea who you're talking about."

A woman stepped up beside the man and slipped her arm through his. "Who is this man, darling?"

The man covered the woman's hand and led her away. "I haven't a clue. I think he mistook me for someone else."

"Who's Natalie?" she asked, shooting a glare over her shoulder at Duff.

"If he's here, he'd have made contact," Sawyer reasoned.

"Damn it, where is he?" Duff pushed through the back door and strode past the pool to the path leading to his bungalow. Perhaps the man would be looking for him there. Or would he look in Natalie's room?

Duff stopped so fast, Montana and Quentin plowed into him. They were on the path to the bungalows. The sun was on its way down and Duff had no idea where to look for Natalie or who her contact was. He clenched his fists, wanting to punch something or someone.

"Dutton Calloway?" A man stepped out of the bungalow farther down from his—the one Duff had peered into when he'd been searching for potential kidnappers. He was the guy with the computer setup. Duff hurried toward him. "Are you Natalie's friend?"

"I am." He held out a hand. "Lance Johnson."

Duff took the hand and gave it a brief shake. "Natalie said you could find her."

"I can, as long as the tracking device is still working and on her."

"She said you embedded it in her."

"I did. It was the safest way to keep it on her. She wouldn't have a chance of losing it or having it removed from her possession."

Lance entered his bungalow and held the door for Duff. Once Duff was inside, the man hurried toward a desk set up with two computer monitors and a keyboard. "Close the door behind you," he called out to Montana and Quentin as he sat in a rolling desk chair.

Duff followed, leaning over Lance's shoulder.

"I knew something was up when she left Chichén Itzá sooner than the tour was scheduled to depart. And when she cut across areas with no roads, I figured whoever had Natalie airlifted her."

"In a civilian helicopter," Duff confirmed. "We didn't get any identification numbers off the tail."

Lance shrugged. "Might not have done any good unless the chopper was registered in the U.S. I tracked her until she came to a stop here." He pointed to one of the screens where a green dot blinked reassuringly.

"Where is it?" Duff asked. "Do you have a coordinate?"

Lance nodded. "I used the coordinate and overlaid

it with a local map. She's in a warehouse on the south side of Cancun."

"Address?" Duff barked.

Lance wrote the address on a piece of paper and handed it to Duff.

Duff spun toward the door.

"Wait," Lance said. "Do Navy SEALs travel with their own personal arsenal?"

Duff dragged in a deep breath. "Not on vacation."

"I packed my knife," Montana offered.

"Me, too," Quentin added. "But I'd rather have my M-4 or a submachine gun."

"Even a SIG P226 would be handy," Montana noted.

"We have to use our heads," Duff reminded them. "We're not on a mission. We aren't even authorized to perform this one."

"But we're going to, aren't we?" Montana asked. "We can't leave Natalie and Kylie to whatever those nutcases have in mind."

"We're going." Duff started for the door again.

Lance stepped in front of him. "You don't have to go unarmed."

Duff fought the urge to push the man out of his way. The longer they hung around, the more chance of the kidnappers moving Natalie and Kylie. "What do you mean?"

"If you'll give me a minute…" Lance stepped to the side and unlocked what looked like a large, ordinary suitcase. He flipped a hidden latch that opened a compartment and revealed several weapons. "I don't have the P226, but I have two SIG P239s and two H&K VP9s, several spare magazines and enough bullets to keep you in business for a short amount of time."

Duff hugged the man and then shoved him to the side. He grabbed the SIG P239, two magazines and four boxes of bullets.

Lance chuckled. "Never had quite that reaction over a couple of guns." He moved to another suitcase and threw it open. Inside was an array of electronic gadgets. He shuffled through them and pulled out two-way headsets. "You can stay in contact with each other." He also handed over a handheld two-way radio. "This is so you can keep in contact with me."

Duff fitted the headset earbud into his ear, tucked the pistol into the waistband of his khaki shorts and draped his T-shirt over the bulge.

Montana and Quentin did the same.

Grabbing the larger two-way radio from Lance, Duff nodded. "Thanks."

"Thank me by getting Nat out of this alive. We'd like to have her come back to work for us."

Duff didn't hang around to find out who "us" was. He had to get to the address Lance had indicated before the kidnappers moved the women. "We have one more man traveling back on the tour bus, Sawyer Houston. Could you fill him in on the operation?"

Lance nodded and tipped his head toward the weapons they carried. "Remember, if you get caught with those weapons, the Mexican government will throw you in jail and destroy the key. And you didn't get them from me."

Duff threw open the door and hurried out, followed by Montana and Quentin.

They returned to the rented Jeep and climbed in. Montana drove while Duff pulled up the map on his smartphone.

Five minutes from their destination, Lance's voice crackled through the radio. "Natalie is on the move. How close are you?"

Duff's fist clenched around the radio. "Five minutes based on my GPS and traffic."

"You don't have five minutes. Be on the lookout for a vehicle that could be carrying them. They appear to be heading northeast."

Montana shot through a stop sign and floored the accelerator.

Quentin leaned over the back of Montana's seat, peering through the windshield.

"Turn left at the next corner," Duff said.

Montana took the corner too fast and the Jeep slid on loose gravel.

Duff hung on to the door handle and prayed they'd get there on time. "At the next street, turn right."

"Natalie is moving fast," Lance said into the hand-held radio.

His heart racing, Duff leaned forward, his gaze swinging left and right.

As they neared the next corner, a black van flew threw the intersection.

Montana stomped on the brakes. The Jeep slid toward the van, stopping in time to avoid hitting another open-topped Jeep following the van.

Four men rode in the trailing vehicle, armed with rifles. They aimed them at Montana, Duff and Quentin.

Montana swerved to the right, away from the armed men.

The rapid fire of automatic weapons screamed through the air.

Duff, Montana and Quentin ducked as bullets blasted

through the windshield of their Jeep. Montana jerked
the steering wheel in time to keep from ramming into
the corner of a building.

The vehicle trailing the van spun in a one-hundred-
eighty-degree turn and raced back toward the SEALs.

"Get out and get down!" Duff yelled.

Montana slammed on the brakes, shoved the Jeep
into park and all three men dived to the ground. Duff
rolled beneath the Jeep, pulled his weapon from the
waistband of his pants and opened fire on the oncom-
ing vehicle.

The man carrying the automatic weapon ducked but
let loose a stream of bullets, hitting the rented Jeep.

Montana, SEAL Boat Team's sniper, cursed and
opened fire with the loaned weapon. "Need my damned
rifle. This toy doesn't have the range."

Quentin waited until the vehicle was in range and
opened fire.

Duff took careful aim and hit one of the men holding an automatic rifle. The man collapsed against one
of the others, knocking his aim off, his bullets sailing
wide of their target.

Montana took out another one of the men. The driver
spun the SUV around and raced away.

Duff rolled to his feet. The van had disappeared. He
ran for the Jeep and jumped in. "Let's go!"

Montana leaped into the Jeep, shifted gears and
gunned the accelerator as Quentin threw himself into
the back.

The Jeep leaped forward, pulling hard to the left.

"What's wrong?"

Montana leaned out the window as he struggled to
keep the vehicle headed straight down the road. "We

took a hit to the left front tire." Montana shook his head, slowing to a stop. "We won't catch them on a flat tire."

"Damn!" Duff shoved open his door and leaped out.

Between the three of them they changed the flat tire almost as fast as a pit crew in a race. But by the time they climbed into the vehicle the other two were long gone. The sound of a police siren wailing in the distance made their decision for them.

"We have to get out of here. We don't have the time to answer questions that will only lead to one or all of us landing in jail."

Montana slammed the shift into drive and raced in the opposite direction of the sirens. With Duff telling him which way to turn, they managed to elude the Mexican authorities and eventually parked in a dingy alley behind a deserted building.

Duff grabbed the two-way radio. "They got away and we had to hide to avoid the Mexican authorities. Where is Natalie now?"

"You're not going to like this," Lance said.

"I don't care if I'll like it or not. Where is she?"

"So far, she's still moving. I'm working on an exact location. From what I can tell, she's somewhere off the Mexican coast headed in the direction of Cozumel."

Chapter Thirteen

The men had returned to the warehouse just when Natalie and Kylie had gotten most of the movement back in their muscles. This time eight men entered. Two women against eight men didn't stand a chance, especially when all eight of the men carried weapons.

Natalie forced her body to remain limp, her eyes almost all the way shut. She could see through her eyelashes, but not well enough to make an escape. Even if she could, she wouldn't try to make a run for it. She couldn't leave Kylie behind.

Four of the men moved toward them. One turned her onto her back and reached for her arms while another grabbed her legs. They swung her up and carried her toward the open doorway and the glaring Mexican sunlight. Though she faked being unconscious, her ears were actively listening to ensure they weren't separating her and Kylie.

A loud scream rent the air. Through the crack of her eyelids, Natalie saw Kylie struggle as two men fought to subdue her. Another man ran toward them and jabbed a needle into Kylie's arm.

Natalie's heart sank. While she might have immediate use of her arms and legs, it would be hours before Kylie regained the use of hers. She'd have to bide her time and come up with a plan to free the girl. She hoped wherever they were taking them, she'd have that opportunity.

The man carrying her tossed her into a waiting van. Natalie flopped onto the hard metal floor and lay still. Kylie's limp form landed on top of her, knocking the wind from her lungs. She refused to budge in case one of the two men who climbed into the back of the van with them noticed she wasn't actually unconscious. The driver climbed in, another man with a gun took the front passenger seat and the van lurched forward.

They hadn't gone far when the driver swerved sharply then straightened.

The man riding shotgun cursed and urged the driver to go faster. The two men in the rear of the van moved to the back window, their weapons held at the ready position.

Natalie heard the squeal of another vehicle's tires. The two men watching through the rear windows of the van cursed and shouted to the men up front. The muffled rumble of automatic weapons loosing a round of bullets reached her through the open front windows of the van.

Natalie's pulse raced. Had her Navy SEAL already caught up with them?

The driver gunned the accelerator, taking corners dangerously fast. The van slid sideways at one point, throwing her two armed guards into the side wall of the vehicle. They leaped to their feet and resumed their positions staring out the rear windows.

If the SEALs had found them, were they prepared to defend themselves against automatic weapons? She prayed they were okay and that the driver of the van they were in didn't crash into a building trying to get away from the firefight.

Soon the van slowed, entered a darkened tunnel or building and came to a stop. The driver cut off the motor. He and the other three men climbed out of the van and spoke to someone else. They sounded angry, their Spanish coming too fast for Natalie to translate.

She faced the open sliding door of the van. Through the narrow crack of her eyelids, she saw two men carrying another man. They dropped him onto the ground and straightened, their faces angry and blood-spattered.

Two more men carried another and laid him next to the first.

Natalie figured there were now six men where there had been eight. Still, six heavily armed men were overwhelming odds when it was just her and an unconscious college coed.

The loud rumble of an engine roaring to life echoed through the dark building. By the sound of it, a marine engine like one used on a high-speed jet boat. Natalie cringed. The farther away from Cancun they went, the harder it would be for Lance to track her and for anyone to come to her and Kylie's rescue. Lance would have to call in the big guns and Royce would have to mobilize more resources to free them. Natalie's Navy SEALs were on vacation. They wouldn't have the firepower to take on this elaborate human trafficking operation.

Natalie fought an overwhelming bout of dread and hopelessness. She couldn't give up. Kylie and Melody depended on her to keep a level head and to think through all her options.

The men returned to the van and one scooped Kylie off Natalie, threw her over his shoulder in a fireman's hold and carried her away.

Another man grabbed Natalie's arm and yanked her up and over his shoulder. With the man's hands holding her thigh clamped to his chest, he carried her toward a waiting boat and dumped her into the arms of another man on deck.

It took total concentration to pretend to be unconscious when the man could as easily have missed and let her crash to the deck. But he caught her, carried her down some steps into a cabin and dumped her onto a bunk. Kylie lay on the other bunk, her eyes closed.

The man left the cabin, shutting and locking the door behind him.

Natalie studied the room before moving, searching for any hidden cameras. When she determined there were none, she sat up and left her bunk to check on Kylie. She pressed her fingers to the base of the young woman's neck and felt the reassuring beat of Kylie's pulse. She lay motionless, but her chest rose and fell with each breath. She was drugged but alive.

The engines throbbed beneath Natalie's feet and the vessel jerked forward as the boat left its mooring.

Natalie rubbed the spot between her toes where Lance had injected her with the tracking device. Locked in a boat's cabin, headed out to sea, their options for escape had considerably narrowed. But, hell, they eventually had to stop somewhere to fuel up, if nothing else. She'd make her escape then. In the meantime she had to find out as much as possible about this boat, the human trafficking operation and where they were taking the women.

Natalie closed her eyes and prayed—something she hadn't done much of since her parents died.

Please let me find Melody and get her and Kylie out of this mess.

DUFF, MONTANA AND Quentin headed for the nearest marina. Ditching the bullet-pocked Jeep behind a building two blocks from their destination, they continued on foot. They stopped at a shop and purchased a straw beach bag and colorful beach towels. Wrapping their pistols in the towels, they stuffed them into the bag, along with the handheld radio. Quentin carried the bag as they approached a dive shop at the marina.

Lance had informed them Sawyer had returned with the tour bus. He'd been full of questions, wanting to know where they were and what the hell had happened. Lance had filled him in and then given Duff the location of the marina. He and Sawyer would be at the marina's dive shop before them.

Duff entered the shop at the marina, not sure what to expect.

Sawyer stood beside Lance who spoke in fluent Spanish with the owner.

Four tanks and four buoyancy control devices lay across the floor at Lance's feet and it appeared he was negotiating with the owner for more items.

Duff edged up to Sawyer. "I take it we're going on a diving excursion."

Sawyer grinned. "Yup."

"Won't we need a boat?" Duff asked.

"Lance's boss has arranged for one."

Apparently, Lance's boss had connections. "Any idea who his boss is?"

Sawyer shook his head and glanced down at Duff's skinned knees. "Looks like you took a beating."

Duff shrugged. "I've been through worse."

Lance completed his negotiations and handed the

man a wad of American bills. The owner shoved it into his pocket.

Transaction complete, Lance turned toward Duff and his team. "Let's get this gear on board and test it out before we leave."

Duff didn't ask Lance where they were going. He grabbed a mask, fins, snorkel, tank and buoyancy control vest, heavy with weights, and carried them outside the building.

Lance led the way along the dock to a beautiful forty-foot luxury yacht.

"This belongs to your boss?" Montana asked.

"No. He has friends in high places. This boat is on loan." Lance's lips twisted. "We're under orders to treat it nicely."

Quentin nodded, a smile spreading across his face. "Now this is what I call traveling in style."

They loaded the gear into the yacht and tested all the diving equipment before going any farther.

Once all the devices passed muster, Lance stepped up to the helm. "I could drive this boat, but I'll bet one of you would do a better job while I man the tracking device."

"I'll drive," Duff said. As a member of SEAL Boat Team 22, he'd been trained to operate a variety of military watercraft. Growing up near Port Aransas, he'd had the opportunity to operate a variety of fishing boats, as well. Duff knew his way around small seafaring vessels, but never anything as luxurious as this. He sat in the cushioned seat and fired up the engine. "Has Natalie's motion stopped?"

"Not yet. She appears to be heading in the general direction of Cozumel. There aren't a lot of private islands between here and there, so it might be where they're heading." Lance pulled a tracking device from a bag he'd carried on board and switched the power on.

The green blinking dot was only slightly reassuring to Duff. Not until he had Natalie alive and safe in his arms would he feel any sense of relief.

Carefully maneuvering the luxury yacht out of the port, Duff set it on course for Cozumel, following Lance's directions.

"The boss mentioned there's a safe below," Lance informed them. "He said we could find everything we might need in it. The combination is nine, one, one, two, zero, zero, one."

"I'll check it out." Montana started down the steps to the cabin below.

"I'll go with you," Quentin said. "The idea of a safe on board intrigues me." He followed Montana.

Duff, intent on navigating, didn't look away from the water in front of him. The busy port required all of his attention until he cleared the majority of the cruise ships and small touring watercraft. When he heard a whoop of excitement, he couldn't help but shoot a glance toward the cabin below.

"The last information I gave Natalie was about the identities of the kissing couple from the night before and Rolf. Did you see any of them at the ruins?"

"No. But tell me what you learned." Duff's fingers tightened on the wheel as Lance filled him in on Rex Masters and the couple Duff and Natalie saw kissing outside the bungalow, Frank "Sly" Jones and Cassandra Teirney.

When Lance finished, Duff asked, "Do you think Rex is responsible for the missing women?"

"I don't know. Why would Jones dance with other women when he had a girlfriend stashed in one of the bungalows?"

"You're not going to believe what I found." Quentin emerged carrying a submachine gun. Montana ascended carrying a black wetsuit and mask, an array of dive knives, scabbards and more.

"This isn't all of it," Quentin said. "There's also C4 and detonators."

"You're kidding," Duff said.

Montana grinned. "I'm happy to report he's not."

Sawyer lifted one of the cushioned seats at the back of the yacht and whistled. "You're not going to believe this."

"What?" Montana hurried to where Sawyer stood staring down into a large storage compartment.

Quentin joined them. "I'll be damned."

Duff, tied to his duties as helmsman, twisted in his seat. "What did you find?"

Sawyer didn't answer, but glanced at Montana. "You grab one end, I'll get the other." Together, they lifted out a long, sleek, metal device almost the length of one of the men.

Duff shot a glance toward Lance. "Who *is* your boss's friend?"

Lance chuckled. "I never know. But that's a state-of-the-art, military-grade diver propulsion device capable of propelling three or four divers at a time."

"I know what it is," Duff said. "What private citizen owns one of those?"

Looking away, Lance answered, "My boss has amazing connections all over the world."

Duff's eyes narrowed. "Who is your boss?"

Lance gave Duff a twisted grin. "Sorry. I'm not at liberty to say. I'd have to get clearance from him."

Duff snorted. "At least tell me he's not a drug lord or someone on the wrong side of the law."

Natalie's friend stared across at Duff, all humor wiped from his face. "He's one of the good guys. Our organization fights *for* justice and *against* corruption."

"Good to know." Duff accepted Lance's word at face value. He appeared to mean what he said with a passion of conviction Duff had only seen in members of the military, in particular, members of the SEALs. "From what I've seen so far, you take care of your own."

"Damn right we do. Natalie would do the same for me or anyone else on the team, even though she hasn't been an active member for the past two years. She left her mark, and it was a good one."

Duff didn't doubt that in the least. She'd been hell-bent on rescuing her sister, but when her sister's friends were in equal danger, she'd looked out for them, as well. And she wasn't afraid of anything.

His lips twitched.

Except heights.

"How much of a lead do they have on us?" Duff asked.

Lance pulled a laptop out of his satchel and fired it up. Within seconds he had the tracking blip overlaid with a satellite map. "They have a forty-five-minute lead. And they're in a fast boat equal to the speed of this one. Until they stop, we won't catch up."

"Then we'll have to hope they stop soon."

"We won't be able to overtake them in daylight," Lance commented. "They could be heavily armed."

"That's just as well. We do our best work in the dark.

And with this equipment and arsenal at our disposal, we can make a go of almost any situation."

"Even if they have an army of guards?" Lance asked.

"We won't borrow trouble." Duff stared at the ocean in front of him. "Let's get to where we're going and put eyes on the situation."

In the distance Duff could make out the thirty-mile-long island of Cozumel.

"They're slowing," Lance glanced up, his eyes wide, energy rippling off him.

"Around Cozumel?" Duff asked.

"Off the northern coastline of Cozumel."

"Isn't most of the development on the east coast?" Duff asked.

"The resorts and tourist areas are. But there are some million-dollar mansions on some of the less accessible areas. People can only reach some of these by boat."

"Will you be able to tell if she goes ashore?"

"Yes. The tracking device can track the exact location to within mere inches." Lance adjusted the screen display to enlarge the image of the island. "It appears as though they are anchoring in a private cove."

"Good. And we'll need to know if we're going to make a ship-to-ship breach or if we'll be going ashore. Either way, we'll get Natalie and Kylie out of there." Duff stared at the map. "We'll stop out of sight of the cove and go in using the diver propulsion device to recon what we can in daylight."

As they neared the island Duff aimed the yacht toward the northern tip of Cozumel, stopping short of rounding the point.

"So what's the plan?" Lance asked.

"We're going fishing." Duff hit the switch to lower the anchor, letting it fall to the ocean floor.

Lance's brows dipped. "Fishing?"

"Well, you are. Three of you will stay with the yacht and pretend to fish. Hell, if you catch anything, we can cook it for supper." Duff shut off the engine and moved toward his team. "Sawyer, you're with me."

"What do you want us to do besides fish?" Montana asked.

"Get the gear together for a night raid. We need to be prepared for climbing onto a boat or going ashore. All the while, you'll be pretending to fish, in case the people holding Natalie have a more elaborate security system that includes this side of the point."

Montana popped a salute. "Gotcha." He turned to Quentin. "Hear that? We're gonna get to do that fishing you wanted to do, after all."

Quentin grinned. "If you thought the armory was impressive, you should see the fishing gear this guy has."

The men checked serviceability and fuel levels on the diver propulsion device. Using a small boom system, they hooked up the DPD and lowered it into the water. Duff and Sawyer geared up in black wetsuits, hoods and scuba gear.

Duff stepped off the back of the boat into the water and sank several feet. The water cooled him in the thick wetsuit. Kicking his fins, he surfaced, adjusted his mask and climbed aboard the propulsion device. The engine started immediately. Duff thanked God for a fastidious yacht owner who knew his military-grade equipment and kept it in great shape.

Sawyer dropped into the water and swam over to him. "Ready?"

"Climb on." Duff stretched into the prone position, holding on to the handles. Sawyer piggybacked Duff, holding on to the side handles of the craft.

They set off. The DPD submerged and left only their heads above the water long enough for them to get around the northern tip of the island. Once around the tip, Duff weaved in and out of the rocky shoreline until they approached a cove. He slowed the craft and let it drift in the waves as they studied the water and the island terrain. Three yachts were anchored in the small bay. A white mansion dominated the hill, overlooking the white crescent of a sandy beach.

The mansion was surrounded by stucco walls, the structure rising three stories, massive windows facing the ocean. A dream house for the rich. A nightmare for anyone unlucky enough to be imprisoned within the walls. The hill surrounding the mansion was thick with short, scrubby vegetation. Not the kind they could easily push their way through in a hurry. If they wanted to gain access to the mansion, it would have to be by sea.

As Duff and Sawyer bobbed in the water, movement on one of the yachts closest to shore captured Duff's attention. Two men climbed into a dinghy at the rear of the yacht and turned to face the boat. Another man emerged on deck, carrying something large over his shoulder. A flash of hot pink made Duff's pulse ratchet up. Based on size and shape, Duff had a good idea what it was the man was carrying. Or rather who.

Kylie had been wearing a pink shirt when she'd been touring Chichén Itzá. The man carrying her dropped her into the arms of one of the men on the dinghy. He caught her and laid her out on one of the seats. Then he turned to face the yacht again.

Another man emerged from a cabin, another body thrown over his shoulder. The woman in the white blouse and cut-off shorts could be none other than Natalie.

His hand on the throttle of the DPD, Duff hesitated. As much as he wanted to rush in and rescue Natalie and Kylie, racing up to the yacht or dinghy would only get him and Sawyer killed.

As if to prove his own point, a shadow moved on the deck and a man holding a submachine gun appeared, his weapon pointing outward toward the other boats in the cove. Another thug dressed in black pants, a black shirt, a black cap and sunglasses, also carrying a submachine gun, stood against the upper railing and stared down at the operation. He lifted his head and stared out at the other yachts in the cove, his head turning as if to take in all movement.

"Going deep," Duff said. He and Sawyer sank to the bottom, directly beneath the yacht.

When he'd been down a good two minutes, he surfaced.

The man in black no longer stood on the top deck. The dinghy pulled away from the back of the yacht and motored toward the shore, with the man in the black cap sitting at the bow, facing the mansion. It didn't take long for the dinghy to run up on the sand. The women were lifted out and carried up the hill toward the mansion.

"At least we know where the women are," Duff said, his jaw hard, his gut clenched.

"I take it we'll be back after dark," Sawyer said behind him.

"Damn right we will." Once the men carrying the women disappeared behind the wall of the estate, Duff turned his attention to the other yachts in the harbor. A man stood on the deck of one, his gaze having followed the progress of the women.

He wore white slacks and a sky-blue polo shirt. He had blond hair and broad shoulders. Duff squinted against the bright sunshine. If he wasn't mistaken, the man in the blue shirt was Rex Masters, the former Army Special Forces sniper. As he stood staring out at the progress of the women being transferred to the mansion, he was joined on deck by a man wearing tailored khaki slacks, a long-sleeved, white, button-up shirt and a light-colored fedora. His facial features were indiscernible beneath the hat and mirrored sunglasses. Considerably shorter than Rex, he appeared thin and somewhat frail in comparison to the former army ranger. He spoke to Rex, waving toward the shore.

Rex nodded several times.

The man in the fedora stared toward the shore for a moment longer, then returned to the cabin.

Rex lifted a pair of binoculars and stared through them toward the mansion.

From what Duff could tell, Rex worked for the man in the fedora. Perhaps he was the scout to find the women his boss desired. Or he was security to his wealthy employer.

Duff's fists tightened around the handles of the DPD. What kind of sick bastard employed former American military to run interference for him?

If Rex was involved in trafficking those women, Duff would make certain the man paid dearly for forsaking his pledge to duty, honor and protecting the freedom of the people in his country.

"Come on, we need to get back and come up with a plan."

"I spotted a number of gunmen on each of the yachts," Sawyer said. "And that doesn't count the ones in the mansion compound itself. I might have caught glimpses of them, but not much more. I couldn't give you an accurate count."

"We'll figure it out when we get there. We'll just have to be loaded for bear." Duff swung the DPD and headed back around the point to the yacht on the other side. The sun lay low in the sky on its path toward the horizon.

Ahead, the yacht cut a long shadow across the water. Three men stood on deck, fishing poles in hand.

When Duff and Sawyer pulled up alongside the yacht, Montana and Quentin were there to tie the DPD to the back. They'd need it again later when darkness settled over the island.

"Stow your fishing gear," Duff said. "We're going hunting tonight."

Chapter Fourteen

Natalie had no idea where they'd been taken. All she knew was they were being transported from the boat to land. At least on land she might have more of a chance of escaping her captors. While waiting in the cabin belowdecks, she'd tried to wake Kylie several times. Unfortunately the dosage they'd given the girl, on top of the last dosage, had knocked her out. Natalie took comfort in the fact she was still breathing.

If Kylie had been awake and able to swim, Natalie would have attempted a get away as soon as the yacht stopped and they'd been carried out on deck and loaded into a dinghy. She could have easily overturned the dinghy with the three men on board. While they scrambled to save their own lives, Natalie would have led Kylie to shore and hidden in the vegetation.

Then again, the vegetation was thick but short. She'd have to find her way through it. To what, she didn't know. If they were on the mainland, she might be hiking a very long time before finding anyone to help them. If they were on an island, it might be a private island with nowhere to go. She'd have to stay hidden until Lance notified Royce and her old boss sent in the cavalry to rescue her.

She didn't think the Navy SEALs would have access to what they'd need to stage a rescue. They weren't on a mission. They were on vacation. Unless Royce armed them and sent them in. If that was the case, she hoped the SEALs wouldn't get in trouble for participating in an unsanctioned mission.

She mustered every ounce of self-control to give the appearance of being semiconscious as opposed to fully aware. When the men came to get her and Kylie, she'd pretended to be drugged to the point she couldn't fight back as one of the men threw her over his shoulder. Kylie didn't have to pretend; she was out.

They were loaded into a dinghy and transported to shore where they were carried up the beach to a walled compound. A white-stucco mansion towered above the walls. A gate opened as they approached and they entered the compound, passing by men with serious-looking machine guns.

"Took you long enough," a man said in English. In Spanish he told the men to follow him.

The voice sounded familiar to Natalie, but she couldn't see the man's face. With her head hanging down behind her henchman's back she could only see what they passed.

They climbed a long, wide staircase leading up to the mansion. The sun slid low in the sky. It would be dark soon. Natalie had to get her, Kylie and anyone else trapped in the mansion out. She prayed this was the place she'd find Melody. And when she did, she'd get them all out. Alive. She also prayed she'd come up with a way to do that.

Once inside the mansion they were carried down long corridors, twisting and turning into the back of the structure. They descended another set of stairs, the hall-way narrower and darker and lined with what appeared to be metal doors on both sides. Each was equipped with a heavy-duty lock requiring a key to open it from the outside.

The sound of metal scraping metal indicated their host was unlocking one of the doors.

Natalie wanted to lean around her captor to see the man with the familiar voice, but she couldn't give her-self away. Natalie and Kylie's freedom depended on her faking the extent of the drug's effect.

As she passed through the open door, she glanced up through her lashes.

The man had turned to speak to one of the other guards in Spanish. All Natalie could make out through the gaps between her eyelashes was that he had dark hair.

The man carrying Natalie let her slide off his shoulder, landing hard on her side on a concrete floor. Kylie was dropped beside her. The henchmen backed out of the room, closed the door behind them and the lock clicked in place.

The tiny room was much like a jail cell with nothing other than a sink and a toilet on one side.

Natalie stared at each corner, searching for cam-eras. Nothing indicated the room was tapped for sound or images. She could move around without worrying someone would figure out she no longer was drugged.

She rolled over to where Kylie lay sprawled on the concrete, her blond hair tangled around her face. Nata-lie pushed the hair out of her eyes and tapped the young woman's face. "Kylie. Wake up."

The girl's eyes fluttered and opened briefly, reveal-ing that they were glassy and bloodshot with dilated pupils.

"Hey, sweetie," Natalie said softly. "You need to shake it off."

"Can't move," she said.

"Start with your fingers and toes."

"Tired," she muttered, her eyelids closing. "Sleep."

"No, sweetie." Natalie shook her. "You have to wake up. We have to find a way out of here." Natalie grabbed one of her hands and slapped her palm. "Please, Kylie. I can't carry you out, and I won't leave you behind."

Kylie's eyes remained closed but her fingers moved.

"That's it. You moved them. Now, move your toes." Natalie's chest squeezed. How was she going to get them out of there when she had no way to unlock the door? And she couldn't carry Kylie. She'd never move fast enough to escape.

She rolled to her feet and stood in front of the door. Damn. There was no doorknob on the inside. Even if she had a hairpin or file, she couldn't pick the lock. She'd have to wait for someone to open the door and then make her move.

A soft sobbing sound made Natalie stop and hold her breath. It hadn't been from Kylie. It had come from outside the room they were trapped in.

Natalie pressed her ear to the door and listened.

More sobbing and a hiccup.

"Hello?" Natalie called out.

The sobbing stopped.

Natalie tried again, her heart pounding against her ribs. "Hello? Can you hear me?"

"*Ja,*" the voice sounded. "*Vem är där?*"

It was a woman's voice, but she wasn't speaking English. "My name is Natalie. Do you speak English?"

She didn't answer immediately, then she said softly, "A little."

"What's your name?" Natalie asked.

"Sigrid."

"Are you from Sweden?" Natalie asked, her breathing ragged, her eyes stinging.

"Ja."

Natalie closed her eyes to keep tears from falling. She had to swallow several times before she could speak past the knot in her throat. "Are there any other women here?"

"Ja." Sigrid sniffed. *"Två*—how you say?—two."

"Do you know their names?" Natalie braced her palm on the door, her ear pressed hard to the metal surface, straining for what she wanted to hear.

An answer came from farther down the hall. "I'm Katherine Stanton."

Her accent was decidedly Australian, if somewhat slurred.

"Is there another woman?" A tear slipped down Natalie's face.

"There was," Katherine said. "She was taken out of here just before you arrived. They said something about she was up first for sale."

"Did she tell you her name?" Natalie couldn't bear another moment.

"Melody, I think," Katherine said. "Yes, she said her name was Melody."

Natalie sank to her knees, the tears spilling down her cheek. Her sister was alive. Deep in her heart, she'd known. But hearing the other woman say she'd been there moments before filled Natalie's heart with a great joy and a profound terror.

Brushing her tears away, she rose to her feet. "Do you know why they brought you here?" Natalie asked.

Sigrid's sobs started and an answering whimper came from down the hall.

"They're going to sell us." Katherine's voice caught on the last word.

"Not if I can help it." Natalie's tone was firm and determined. "We're going to get out of here."

"How? They have guns. We're on an island. Nobody knows we're here."

Sigrid's sobs grew louder.

Katherine had already lost hope, as had Sigrid.

"Are they still drugging you?" Natalie asked. "Do you know?"

"They haven't injected anything into us since we came, but I don't feel right. I'm dizzy and tired all the time."

"Are they feeding you?" Natalie persisted.

"Yes. They usually bring food twice a day. Once in the morning and again at sunset."

"The drug might be in the food or water." Natalie leaned close to the door. "Don't eat or drink again until we get out of here."

"What are you going to do?" Katherine asked.

"I don't know yet, but you need to be ready when I figure it out."

Her opportunity came knocking with the clomping footsteps in the hallway. A key scraped in the lock.

Natalie dropped to the floor and waited as the door swung open.

THE DIVER PROPULSION device was taxed to its maximum capabilities taking all four SEALs around the point. The men hung on, knowing the DPD would get them there faster and conserve their energy for the fight ahead.

Since Duff and Sawyer had performed their reconnaissance, more yachts had arrived. Now, instead of the three that had been there before, there were eight yachts of various sizes anchored in the cove, their dinghies deployed and resting on the beach, guarded by one of their crew.

Sawyer dropped Duff near one of the larger yachts and then angled the DPD toward the shore where he and the others would wait for him. They would slip from the water, haul the DPD up on the beach and bury it in sand or hide it in the shadows of the underbrush rimming the white sandy beach. They'd wait for Duff before moving forward, needing every man to make this operation viable.

Duff dived beneath the surface and swam up to a fifty-foot luxury yacht, careful not to bump his tank against the hull. He couldn't afford to make a sound that would attract the attention of one the armed guards standing watch on the deck.

Pulling a packet of Semtex plastic explosives from inside his vest, he pressed it against the hull and jammed a detonator into the claylike mass. The charge would be a backup in case they needed a distraction. Once the charge was in place, he swam for shore and the designated landing zone where his team waited.

Sawyer, Montana and Quentin had their gear off but were still dressed in the black wetsuits and masks. They'd piled their fins, tanks and buoyancy control devices on the beach near the vegetation. For any casual observer glancing at the shoreline from a distance, the pile appeared to be just another big bush. Duff shucked his gear and added it to the pile.

"Whatever they have planned is happening tonight," Duff said, fitting the earbuds of the two-way radio headset into his ears. Lance had wrapped them carefully in a waterproof bag along with the two-way radio they would use if they needed Lance to pull a Hail Mary and drive the yacht into the cove to extract them.

Lance had passed on to his boss back in the States the location of the women and the potential of them being sold at auction that night. His boss had promised backup as soon as he could mobilize a team. In the meantime it would be up to the SEALs to stage a rescue operation to free Natalie, Kylie and any other captives.

As well as the communication equipment, they had brought along a larger waterproof bag with the submachine guns, pistols and knives.

Duff took point, followed by Sawyer, Quentin and Montana. Montana would provide cover fire if they were unable to make a silent entry.

As they neared the stuccoed eight-foot wall, Duff told himself getting into the compound would be just like scaling the mud walls of Afghan villages. They were a good seventy-five feet away from the entry gate. Unfortunately all of the visitors were apparently inside and there would be no one to distract the guards while the men slipped over the fence.

Duff glanced at the sky, eyeing a drifting cloud, heading toward the bright moon. As bright white as the walls of the compound were, their black wet suits would stand out when they breached it. Timing would be everything.

Clouds passed over the moon. Sawyer cupped his

hand. Duff stepped into it and pulled himself up to the top of the wall.

The gate guards were smoking cigarettes, their guns slung over their shoulders.

Duff dropped to the ground and rolled into the nearby shrubs. He aimed his submachine gun at the guards, ready to provide cover should they turn toward his position.

Sawyer dropped down next. Quentin stayed atop the wall long enough to haul Montana up, then the two of them landed on the ground and rolled into the brush.

The cloud cover floated away, leaving the grounds exposed to the moonlight.

One of the guards dropped his cigarette and ground it out with his foot, then turned toward where Duff and his team hid in the brush.

After a tense moment he turned back to the other guard and spoke in Spanish. They laughed and pulled out another cigarette.

Hunkered low to the ground, Duff moved toward the mansion, hugging the shadows of the bushes and palm trees. As he neared the house he paused in the shadow of a palm and studied the wide porches. Entering through the front door wasn't an option. There had to be other entrances, including a servant's entrance. He eased around the side and stepped up onto a wide porch. Hugging the shadows of the deep overhang, he slipped up to a French door that appeared to open into a study or library with shelves of books lining the walls. He tried the door handle. It was locked.

Keeping that entrance in mind, he worked his way along the porch to the rear of the building where several utility carts were parked. A door opened and two guards exited the building laughing and speaking in Spanish. Each carried rifles that appeared to be similar to the M-4s used by the American military. They split and headed in opposite directions—one away from Duff, the other toward him.

Duff shrank back against the wall of the building, pulled his knife from the scabbard on his thigh and waited for the guard to pass.

The guard didn't know what hit him. As soon as he passed the shadowed area where Duff stood, Duff slipped up behind him and dispatched him. No fuss, no cries of pain. The man slipped to the ground in a silent heap. Duff dragged him behind a bush and wiped the blood from the knife on the man's shirt.

The other guard had gone around the other end of the mansion, out of sight. Duff moved swiftly toward the back entrance the guards had come through. The door was locked.

Duff jammed his knife between the door and the frame and forced the lock. The door swung open and he slipped inside.

The room he entered appeared to be the laundry room and storage area for pantry staples and cleaning supplies.

Duff leaned out and waved the others in.

He didn't wait for them, but moved toward what smelled like the kitchen. He hovered near the half-open door and peered through the crack.

Servants hurried in and out of the room, carrying trays of drinks and hors d'oeuvres.

Duff waited until the wait staff left the room. He slipped up behind the one who appeared to be the chef and pressed his knife to the man's throat.

The spoon he'd been using to stir something on the gas stove clattered to the floor.

Duff backed him to the storage room and left him with Sawyer who, armed with a roll of duct tape, made quick work of silencing the chef.

Making his way through a swinging door, Duff entered a hallway that split in opposite directions. He could hear the sounds of voices from the left. Footsteps came from that direction. Duff slipped back into the kitchen and waited for the persons owning the feet to either pass the door or enter for more appetizers and drinks for the invited guests.

The footsteps paused on the other side of the door and then moved on.

Duff pushed the door open a crack. Two guards hurried away from the noise, speaking in Spanish. Duff understood the words *llevar las mujeres*. Bring the women. Duff motioned for the team to follow. If these guards were going to get the women to be auctioned that night, they could lead them to Natalie and Kylie.

Duff waited until the men turned a corner then he ran down the hall, careful not to make a noise. His team had his back with Sawyer following close behind, Quentin behind Sawyer, then Montana, who would back down the hallway, weapon raised.

As he neared the corner, Duff slowed. Ducking low, he peered around. The guards had disappeared but there was a staircase leading to a lower level, possibly a basement.

Pushing forward, he eased down the steps. The sounds of Spanish-speaking voices echoed off the walls at the lower level. A woman's scream made Duff abandon caution and take the rest of the stairs two at time.

He arrived at the bottom to find the guards struggling with a blonde woman Duff didn't recognize. She kicked the guard nearest to her in the shin.

He yelped and let go of her.

The woman made a run for it, but the other guard grabbed her hair and yanked her so hard she fell backward, landing on the ground, forcing the guard holding her hair to hunch over.

Duff pointed his weapon. "Let go of her." He didn't care that the guards might not know English. He didn't plan on letting them live long enough to translate.

The guards' heads jerked up at the same time as Duff fired. First one then the other slumped to the floor. The woman between them scrambled to her feet and stared at him wide-eyed.

"Please tell me you're one of the good guys Natalie was alluding to." Her voice had a pleasant Australian accent, similar but different from the one Natalie had tried to use as a disguise.

Duff nodded. "Where is Natalie?"

"She was taken away a few minutes ago." The woman bent to one of the men on the floor and dug in his pockets, unearthing a set of keys. Her hands shook so hard she couldn't push the key into the lock on the door beside her.

Quentin stepped forward. "Let me." He took the key from her. "What's your name, sweetheart?"

"Katherine Stanton." She wrapped her arms around her middle, her entire body shaking. "Are you going to get us out of here?"

"We're sure as hell gonna try." Quentin twisted the key in the door and pushed it open. "Found Kylie." He knelt on the floor and checked her pulse. "She's alive but appears to be drugged."

Duff turned to Katherine. "Do you know where they took Natalie?"

"Probably where they took Melody." Katherine bit her bottom lip, tears rushing to her eyes. "To be auctioned off like cattle."

Duff had to get to Natalie and her sister before that happened. "Sawyer, Montana, you're with me. Quentin, see to the safety of the women. Get them outside if possible. Meet at the rally point."

"How are we going to get them off the island?" Quentin asked.

"That's where Lance comes in. And if all else fails, we'll take one of the yachts anchored in the cove." Duff turned back the way they'd come. He didn't know how many more guards to expect, and being down to three men on his team didn't give him the level of confidence he preferred to have going into a mission. He had no choice. Failure wasn't an option. Natalie's and her sister's lives depended on the SEALs coming through for them. As he neared the room where the voices were getting louder, he fished in his pocket for the detonator and pressed the button.

Chapter Fifteen

The guards had dragged Natalie out of the room she'd shared with Kylie. She didn't like being split up, but then Kylie wasn't going anywhere soon. The drugs they'd given her had incapacitated her to the point she couldn't stand on her own.

Until she found Melody, Natalie couldn't fight back. She needed to save that element of surprise for when they led her into the same room with her sister. If that was their plan. She hoped the buyers weren't taking possession of their women and leaving the island immediately upon payment. The guards led her up the staircase to the main level of the mansion and turned her toward the rear of the building and a large wooden doorway.

The door opened and she was shoved into what appeared to be a large entertainment area with plush leather sofas, modern artwork and men standing, sitting and drinking. Some wore suits, others were more casual in tailored slacks and polo shirts.

All of them turned their attention from the woman at the far end of the room, positioned on a raised dais, her long blond hair brushed smooth, her body barely covered in a sexy pink corset and negligee. She crossed her arms over her breasts, her cheeks pink, her chin tilted up, her blue eyes flashing.

Melody.

Her sister's eyes were glazed and she swayed where she was standing. If not for the armed guards on either side of her, she would have fallen from her perch.

Natalie's heart pinched hard in her chest. She wanted to charge forward and stand in front of her sister, to protect her and take out every one of the sick bastards who'd come to purchase women for their own disgusting desires.

Holding back her gut instinct to barge in kicking butt, Natalie took in the occupants of the room. Eight men who appeared to be buyers. They looked as if they hailed from all over the world. When one of them turned, Natalie swallowed her gasp.

Rolf Schwimmer—or Rex Masters. By either name the man was lower than the worst form of life. He'd fooled them into thinking he was one of the good guys. She'd take him out first.

A man entered through a door at the far end of the room and walked directly across the floor to the side of the dais where a wing-backed chair sat half-facing the stage.

Frank "Sly" Jones, yet another man Natalie was determined to take down when this show got going. The only other woman in the room besides Natalie and Melody sat in a chair near the dais, her face in profile, her hand curled around the stem of a wineglass. When she turned to face Natalie, her lip curled up in a sneer.

Natalie's breath caught in her throat. The woman in front of her was Cassandra Teirney, the real-estate agent from Washington, D.C. How could Royce's data be so wrong? Real-estate agent, ha!

The woman stood without spilling a drop of the red wine. She wore a long black dress that hugged her figure and flowed with every step she took toward Natalie. "Gentlemen, let me present our second offering." She waved her hand at Natalie's figure. "We didn't have time to package her for the occasion, but you can see she is fit, beautiful and should bring top dollar. Do I hear fifty thousand?"

A man held up his hand, his gaze on Natalie's naked midriff, practically salivating.

"Perfect. Notice her long, supple legs and perky, generous breasts. Who will give me one hundred thousand for this prime specimen?"

Natalie's fingers clenched into fists, her nails digging into her palms to keep her from taking a swing at Cassandra and her sneering lip and attitude. She had to let them believe she was as drugged as her sister.

She counted the number of men she presumed were guards, some of them obviously armed, others who could be hiding a weapon beneath their jackets. In all, she counted ten. How the hell she was going to fight ten guards was beyond her. But she wouldn't let Melody leave the room without her. And she refused to let someone hurt her while she was there.

The guards led her toward the dais and pushed her to stand beside Melody.

Melody's head lolled and she glanced up at Natalie. "Nat?" she whispered.

"Shh," Natalie urged. "Don't talk."

"As you gentlemen can plainly see, these two women

are worth every penny and will bring many hours of pleasure," Cassandra continued.

Able to stand on her own, Natalie shook off the hands of the guards and stood in front of the men, trying not to glare and call every last one of them arrogant sons of bitches. These were the kinds of men who gave men of their countries bad reputations.

One of the men walked up to Melody and reached for one of her breasts.

That move broke the camel's back. Without a plan, acting on pure instinct, she cocked her leg and threw a sidekick, catching the buyer in the jaw. He stumbled backward, hit his legs against a side table and fell on his back.

The guards holding up Melody let go and lunged for Natalie. She dodged their hands, swung her leg around and caught the closest one in the nose. A loud snap sounded and blood rushed down his face. He clapped a hand to his broken nose and staggered sideways. His foot caught on the edge of the dais and he tipped over the edge, falling to the floor, landing hard.

The other guard grabbed her arm and yanked it up behind her.

"Wait." Rolf raised his hand. "Don't hurt her or the other woman. I want both of them." He turned to Cassandra. "Three hundred thousand for both."

Cassandra nodded to Frank, who scurried across to the man Natalie had first kicked. He helped him to his feet.

"She's a feisty one, which will translate to much enjoyment in bed." Cassandra turned to the others. "Do I hear a bid of four hundred thousand for the pair?"

The buyer who'd been kicked straightened and held up his hand. "Four hundred thousand."

With her hand pushed up between her shoulder blades, Natalie could barely breathe past the pain.

Rolf raised his hand. "Five hundred thousand dollars."

Natalie wanted to spit in the man's face.

"My, my, she really has your attention, doesn't she?" Cassandra crossed to Rolf and ran her fingers down his chest. "I'll bet you're pretty hot in bed, too." She stared up into his eyes. "Two women might slake your desire." Cassandra snorted softly. "But I doubt it."

Frank stood on the other side of a buyer, his face a ruddy red, his nostrils flaring. He had to be jealous of Cassandra paying too much attention to Rolf.

"Five hundred thousand dollars going once." She paused. "Going twice." Cassandra stared around the room, giving the buyers a chance to bid again. "Sold to this young man who needs two women to make him happy."

The guards shoved Natalie and Melody toward Rolf. He grabbed Natalie and pulled her against him, his hand reaching down to squeeze her bottom. "Don't say anything. I'm here to help," he whispered into her ear. Louder he said, "Nice firm bottom." He reached down and hefted a gray suitcase up onto the table. "Your money." He took Natalie's hand and turned toward the door. "Thank you for setting up this little shindig. My boss will be highly satisfied with his purchases."

Natalie hooked Melody's arm and led her along with them toward the exit. Before they could make it outside, a loud boom shook the crystal chandelier hanging from the ceiling and a shout rang out.

Everyone moved at once. The buyers ran for the exit

and the guards pulled their weapons and turned in circles, searching for the source of the sound. They didn't have long to wait.

Three men charged into the room. Dressed completely in black from the tops of their heads to the tips of their toes, they carried submachine guns. As soon as they entered the room, they dived to the sides of the door, rolled to their feet and fired at the guards holding weapons.

At first confused, Natalie didn't know whether to run for the door or to join the fight. When she caught the flash of green eyes, her heart fluttered and she warmed inside. The cavalry had arrived in the shape of three Navy SEALs.

Grabbing Melody's hand, she pulled her to the ground and shoved her behind a sofa. "Stay!" she said and rolled to her feet to assess how best to help.

DUFF REALIZED NATALIE and Melody would be in danger if they stormed the room. The explosion outside would breed chaos and hopefully Natalie would get down. First through, Duff threw himself to the side, rolled and came up on his haunches. He fired at the nearest gunman, took him down and aimed for the next.

Sawyer and Montana breached the door and performed the same maneuver, taking up positions on the other sides of sofas, dodging the bullets of the guards and returning fire.

Duff scanned the room for Natalie and her sister. His throat closed and his breathing tightened in his chest until he caught a glimpse of Natalie hiding behind a white leather couch on the other side of the room. Though her clothes were wrinkled and her hair was a mess, she appeared relatively unharmed and just as beautiful as when she'd worn the black swimsuit that first caught his attention. Behind Natalie a guard reached for her.

Duff aimed, fired and eliminated that threat. The man fell forward, landing on Natalie's back. She went down on her knees, taking the weight of the heavy man. Then she turned sideways, dumping him to the floor. Glancing across the room, she made eye contact with Duff and mouthed the words *thank you*. Her eyes widened and she yelled, "Duff, behind you!"

Duff rolled to his back. A man stood over him aiming a 9 mm pistol at his chest.

A shot rang out and the man dropped where he stood, his body landing on Duff's legs.

Duff looked around to see Rex Masters retracting his handgun. He turned and fired at a guard about to shoot Sawyer. People ran and yelled. Chaos reigned in the big room.

Kicking his feet free, Duff lurched to a standing position holding his submachine gun at the ready.

The unarmed men ran for the exit. A woman Duff recognized as the one Lance had identified as Cassandra the real-estate agent lifted her dress and raced after the men in suits.

The guards still alive were either wounded or had run out the door with the others.

Sawyer and Montana rose from their positions behind the sofa. They aimed their weapons at the wounded guards on the floor. "Throw your guns to the side."

Those who could, did.

Former army ranger, Frank "Sly" Jones, cut off from the door by Rex and Montana, ran toward Natalie where she remained hunkered down in a squatting position. He pulled a gun from the inside of his jacket and aimed it at her head. "Stop! Or I'll shoot her."

Duff stood, refusing to lower his weapon. For all he knew, Frank would kill Natalie anyway. Duff had a small chance of pulling the trigger first. God, he didn't like playing with the woman's life. But the look on Frank's face didn't bode well for Natalie.

"Throw down your weapon," Frank said. "I will not hesitate to pull the trigger and kill your girlfriend. Do it!"

"Like hell you will." Natalie rolled into the man, hitting him hard in the knees.

Frank's hand went up in the air to balance him. He squeezed the trigger as he teetered and fell backward. The shot hit the ceiling. As soon as he landed, Natalie sprang to her feet, kicked the gun from his fingers and stepped out of reach, holding out her hand. "Give me a gun. I'll kill him for what he did to my sister and the others."

Frank sneered. "You don't have the guts."

"And you are an animal." Natalie's voice shook with her anger.

Duff crossed the room and pulled her into the curve of his arm, his submachine gun aimed at Frank's chest. "It's over, Jones."

Rex Masters stepped up beside Duff. "I'll take care of him."

"Keep him alive," Duff said. "We need to find out who he's working for."

Masters jerked Jones up by the collar, spun him around and tied his wrists with zip-ties.

Duff frowned. "And when you have time, I want to

hear how you got involved in this, and why you were here as a buyer."

"I promise I'll have your answers for you. But for now, I'd like to take this man for interrogation."

Duff's eyes narrowed. "Save it for when we can all be there."

"You bet." Masters shoved Jones toward the exit.

Duff nodded toward Montana. "Stay with him. He might have saved mine and Sawyer's lives, but I still don't know that I trust him."

"You got it." Montana took off after Masters while Sawyer slipped outside to check the surrounding area for the group's escape.

Natalie pressed her face into Duff's chest. "Thank you for coming to the rescue."

Duff chuckled. "I have no doubt you would have gotten yourself out of this mess."

"I could have, but getting the others out alive was more important, and I couldn't have done it without your help." She pushed away from him and ducked behind the white leather couch. When she rose, she helped another blonde to her feet who had a slight resemblance to Natalie.

Natalie glanced up at him and beamed. "Dutton Calloway, I'd like you to meet my sister, Melody."

Melody shoved her hair out of her face and stuck out a hand. "Nice to meet you." She frowned at Natalie. "Who is this man? Are you dating and you haven't told me about it?"

Natalie hugged her sister. "Baby, I'm just glad you're going to be okay. We can catch up when we get back to civilization."

Melody pressed fingers to her temple. "What the

heck did they give me? I feel like I have a heck of a hangover and didn't have the pleasure of the buzz."

Natalie laughed.

Melody's brows puckered. "And where did you learn to kick like that. You've got to teach me that move. I might not be in this situation had I known it."

"There's a lot we need to talk about." Natalie hugged her sister.

"For now, unless we want to spend time in a Mexican jail, we need to get back to Cancun." Duff waved his weapon toward the exit.

Quentin appeared with the three blondes who'd been incarcerated in the basement. "I put in the call for our taxi service."

"Good," Duff said.

Kylie smiled at Natalie, tears trickling down her cheeks. "You were right. You got us out of there."

Natalie shook her head. "I believe our own Navy SEALs saw to that."

The Australian woman, Katherine, flung her arms around Duff's neck and laid a big kiss on both his cheeks. "Thank you so very much for coming to our rescue. Me mum will likely ask you to come visit us in Australia. You're more than welcome to stay with us."

Duff chuckled. "Thank Quentin. He kept you safe while all hell broke loose."

Katherine hugged Quentin's neck. "Already did. He promised me a date when we get back to Cancun. He also promised not to let me out of his sight." She winked at him.

"I wish we could round up the buyers and throw them in jail," Natalie said.

As they walked through the spacious marble-tiled hallway, Duff slipped an arm around Natalie's waist.

"We'd have a hard time explaining our weapons to the authorities. My bet is those men are hightailing it back to whatever country they belong to."

"What about Cassandra? We should at least take her back to the States and have her hit up with charges." They stepped outside into the clear night air.

The thumping sound of helicopter rotors sounded overhead.

Sawyer ran up to them. "The female got away. Do you want me to shoot the helicopter out of the sky?"

Duff shook his head. "No, we need to get away from here before half of the Mexican government finds us."

Already, the yachts in the cove were either backing out or turning, leaving as quickly as possible.

Rex Masters shoved Frank Jones into a dinghy and stepped in behind him. Montana climbed in, too. "I'm under orders to go with you and our interrogation subject."

Duff chuckled, certain Montana would keep anything from happening to their prize captive.

The big SEAL dwarfed the boat as they puttered out to the waiting yacht. The thin, little man with the fedora stood at the bow, watching the activity in the cove.

Lance maneuvered the yacht into the cove. Sawyer took the DPD out to the yacht and returned with a dinghy. They ferried the women to the yacht and went back to collect their gear. Duff was one of the last to leave the island, glancing back at the mansion. So much more could have gone wrong. But didn't.

He would be more than happy to return to Cancun to finish his vacation in peace. It was hard to believe he still had almost a week and a half to relax on the beach. He hoped Natalie would spend that week and a half with him. After all that had happened in just a few days, he felt he knew her better than any other woman, but he wanted to know everything about her.

He and Sawyer climbed into the dinghy and headed to the yacht.

"I have to say this has been one of the least relaxing vacations I've ever been on. And that includes the time we all went to the dude ranch with Montana and herded cattle."

"It has to get better from here. We got the women back. What else could go wrong?"

Sawyer smacked his palm to his forehead. "You had to ask."

Chapter Sixteen

"I could get used to this lifestyle very easily." Natalie stretched out in a lounge on the *Take Me Away* yacht owned by Mica Brantley, the woman Duff had mistaken for a man. As soon as they'd met up in Cancun, Mica had removed the fedora and shaken out her long, dark hair, surprising the SEALs.

She was Rex Masters's boss.

Duff, Natalie, Lance, Mica and Rex had spent the better part of the previous night interrogating Frank Jones.

Since his girlfriend had left him without batting an eyelash, Frank had been more than willing to share everything he knew about her. That wasn't much.

Cassandra Teirney wasn't even her name. She'd grown up on the streets, becoming adept at conning people. Her forte was stolen identities. One day she'd been caught stealing from someone who'd given her a choice. She either went to work for him or went to jail.

Of course she'd opted out of the jail scenario and had gone to work for the man who would become her benefactor.

Frank had snorted. "I thought she and I were a thing. I should have known better."

"Who is her benefactor?" Mica asked.

Frank shrugged. "Hell if I know. She never mentioned his name. Money showed up when we needed it along with helicopters, vehicles, vans...whatever our operation called for. The man had an entire network of drug runners at his fingertips here in Mexico."

"Why human trafficking?" Natalie asked, her voice hard, her gaze boring a hole into Frank. She still wanted to kill him, but the information he provided might help her find the people at the crux of the operation.

Frank glanced around at the people surrounding him. "You heard how much those men were willing to pay. It's insane. I never made that much in the army. Not even when I was selling guns to the enemy."

"Bastard," Rex said, between clenched teeth.

"Yeah, and you were so high and mighty?" Frank glared at Rex. "How many babies did you kill? How many innocent civilians died because you shot them or blew up their homes with them inside? What's the difference?"

Mica Brantley had stepped in. "Were there more women before these?"

Frank nodded. "They raised money on a regular basis. I came in on this operation when I met Cass in D.C. We hit it off and scored some identity theft jobs together. Being members of the real-estate community made it easy. Then she turned me on to the more high-dollar games."

Mica slapped her palm on the table in front of Frank. "The other women...where did they go?"

"I don't know. I didn't get involved until this round. You'll have to ask Cass." He smirked. "Good luck finding her. She's a master of disguises."

"We'll find her," Lance said. He'd already been on the satellite phone with Royce. If anyone could find the woman, Royce could.

Natalie wanted to be in on the raid that brought Cassandra to justice.

But she was quickly realizing it wasn't just Cassandra. Her benefactor funded her gigs. He was the one they needed to find. The sooner the better.

Frank couldn't tell them anything more about Cassandra or her benefactor. But he wasn't getting away with the part he'd played in their human-trafficking venture.

Royce had sent two of his SOS agents and the SOS plane to collect Frank late in the night. The Mexican authorities never knew and couldn't interfere in justice being served to the former army ranger who'd betrayed his country.

Lance then had turned to Mica Brantley. "Why were you here and how did you get an invitation to the auction?"

"You might have heard of my husband, Trevor Brantley."

Natalie had heard his name mentioned in the news. "Wasn't he the multimillionaire who was found dead in his mansion?"

Mica nodded and looked away, her eyes shiny with unshed tears. "My husband had connections. And enemies. The connections got me into the auction, the enemies cost my husband his life. Those same enemies took my stepdaughter. I fear she was sold at a similar auction." Mica glanced at Rex. "Rex has been helping in my effort to find her and bring her home."

Natalie had fallen silent. If she could help this woman

recover her stepdaughter, she would. If Royce would have her back, she'd ask if that could be her first assignment.

They'd split up, going their separate ways, each heading for a shower and bed. Natalie hadn't gotten the opportunity to say a proper good-night to Duff as they'd piled into taxis and returned to the resort in the early hours of the morning.

Natalie yawned in the bright light of day. None of them had had much sleep the night before. She'd been happy to sit up the rest of the night talking with Melody, bringing her up to speed on what had happened while she'd been imprisoned on Cozumel. Natalie told her sister about her former life as an agent for SOS and the role the organization had played in her rescue.

Mica Brantley had sent the invitation to join them that morning and they had been too curious to refuse, despite their lack of sleep.

"Would you like a Pain Killer?" Melody handed Natalie one of the fruity drinks packed with enough alcohol to make Natalie not care for a little while.

"I prefer beer, but thanks." Natalie took the drink and downed half of it before she laid back and smiled. "So, are you going to stay with me for the next week and have that vacation you came here to enjoy?"

Melody shook her head. "I'm going back in the morning. I've had enough of Cancun. I don't feel safe here and I need to get back to school."

Natalie sat up and leaned across, resting her hand on her sister's knee. "Do you want me to come back with you?"

Melody smiled. "No. I'll go with Kylie. We'll stick together like glue. She's as shaken as I am." She tossed back her golden-blond hair and sighed. "But you don't have to leave so soon." Her gaze shifted to the SEALs standing at the rail, staring out at the ocean, talking softly and drinking beer. "I know one person who would like you to stay."

Natalie's cheeks heated. "I have to admit, I think I could get used to him, as well."

"You know, it's about time you started living your life for yourself. In a year, I'll graduate college and move to some city where I'll live on my own. You can't always be there for me. I have to learn to live by myself."

Natalie frowned. "But you're my only living relative. I care about you and want you to be safe."

Melody crossed her arms over her chest. "And your job is all that safe?"

Natalie glanced away. "I won't go back to work for SOS if you don't want me to."

Melody leaned toward her sister. "See? You're doing it again. I want you to do what *you* want to do. Not what you think *I* need. Before you know it, life will pass you by and you'll only have regrets. If working for SOS makes you happy, do it. I'm just sorry you didn't tell me about it sooner."

Natalie stared at her sister for a long time, then nodded. "I'm glad you feel that way. I've missed the work. I like making a difference."

Melody sat straighter and gave Natalie a direct look. "Then you won't be upset when I tell you I'm applying to the FBI. I hope to get accepted and start as soon as I graduate."

Natalie's gut clenched but then she relaxed. "If it makes you happy, I say do it." They hugged and laughed.

Melody glanced toward Duff's back. "You know, if

things work out between you and Dutton, I wouldn't mind having another relative in the family."

Natalie shook her head. "We've only just met."

"Uh-huh. And I can feel the chemistry between you already." Melody held up her hands. "Just saying, you shouldn't rule out the possibilities."

Natalie's lips quirked. "Oh, I haven't." She rose from the lounge. "I just have to find a way to get him alone."

Duff turned at that moment and held out his hand.

Natalie placed her hand in his bigger one, liking the way he made her feel all soft and feminine.

He lifted her fingers to his lips and pressed a kiss to the tips. "Ready to head back? I'd like to take you out to dinner and dancing."

She let him pull her into his arms. They swayed to the rhythm of the ocean. Natalie laid her head on his chest, loving the contrast of his smooth skin and hard muscles. "I'm ready."

Ready for the infinite possibilities of what the night held in store. Ready to grab each day and live it as though it might be her last. And more than ready to let a man have a chance at stealing her heart.

"By the way, what are you doing when we get back Stateside?" Duff asked. "Two weeks with you just doesn't seem to be nearly enough. Hell, a lifetime might be too short."

Natalie's heart swelled and she wrapped her arms around his neck. "You're willing to take the risk? You know what I'll be doing for a living."

"It goes both ways, sweetheart. Until I can't do it anymore, I belong to the Navy SEALs. If you're up for the challenge of dating a SEAL, you're up for practically anything."

"Oh, I'm up for it."

Duff swung her off her feet and planted a kiss on her lips. Then he stared around. "Where's that dinghy? We have a date to get to."

* * * * *

"You know, John Blake, if you're not careful, I could really get used to having you around."

"Would that be a bad thing?"

She set the glass on the table, considering the question. "If you were going to stick around long-term, maybe not. But if you're just some stranger passing through—"

He didn't say anything, looking down at his plate of food. "I don't know what happens next," he admitted.

"Then maybe we should just keep things casual," she said, swallowing an unexpected rush of disappointment. "No strings, no expectations. No taking things too far."

He followed her to the door when she started to leave, catching her hand. "Does kissing count as taking things too far?"

STRANGER
IN COLD CREEK

BY
PAULA GRAVES

First Published in Great Britain 2016
By Mills & Boon, an imprint of HarperCollins*Publishers*
1 London Bridge Street, London, SE1 9GF

© 2016 Paula Graves

ISBN: 978-0-263-91897-7

46-0316

Our policy is to use papers that are natural, renewable and recyclable products and made from wood grown in sustainable forests. The logging and manufacturing processes conform to the legal environmental regulations of the country of origin.

Printed and bound in Spain
by CPI, Barcelona

Paula Graves, an Alabama native, wrote her first book at the age of six. A voracious reader, Paula loves books that pair tantalizing mystery with compelling romance. When she's not reading or writing, she works as a creative director for a Birmingham advertising agency and spends time with her family and friends. Paula invites readers to visit her website, www.paulagraves.com.

For my mom.
Who still makes it possible to live my dreams.

Chapter One

The tinkle of the bell attached to the front door of Duncan's Hardware heralded the arrival of a new customer, though on this frigid March day in the Texas Panhandle, the gust of icy wind blowing through the entryway would have been plenty of warning by itself.

In the fasteners aisle, John Blake winced as the cold seeped under the collar of his jacket and seemed to attach itself to his mending collarbone. The gnawing pain stole his breath for a moment before settling into a bearable ache.

The new arrival was a woman. Tall and rangy, with hair the rusty color of Georgia clay and worn in a simple ponytail, she had alert eyes the color of the gunmetal sky outside. Her rawboned features, free of makeup, were more interesting than beautiful.

She nodded at Gil Duncan, the proprietor, and scanned the shop with those sharp gray eyes, her gaze settling on John and narrowing.

He looked away, feigning a lack of interest, though every nerve in his body tingled to attention.

He felt more than saw her approaching him, but he didn't look away from the boxes of screws he was studying.

"You're new in town."

John looked up at her, finding himself the object of those smoky eyes. Close up, her gaze was sharp, her expression intelligent and curious. She also gave off an air of authority, and he thought the word *cop* even before she flipped open her jacket to reveal the six-pointed star badge of the Barstow County Sheriff's Department.

"Yes, I am," he answered with a mild smile. He was barely an inch taller than she was, and in his current condition, he was fairly sure she could take him down without much trouble. Cooperation was by far the smarter option for him, especially since he wasn't looking to draw much attention to himself during his hopefully brief stay in Cold Creek, Texas.

"You're that fellow who's renting the Merriwether place on Route 7?"

"Yes, ma'am."

Her lips twitched a bit at his polite response. "You're from…North Carolina?"

Not a bad guess, he thought. "Tennessee."

She gave a nod. "How do you like Cold Creek so far?"

"It's quiet. Been chilly since I got here."

"That won't last," she warned with a friendly smile that displayed a set of straight, white teeth. She was prettier when she smiled, he decided. "If you're plannin' on stayin' long, that is."

Was that her way of asking whether he was going to stick around? "So I hear. Hopefully it's a little less humid than where I'm from."

The musical tone of her laugh caught him by surprise. "You can bank on that. But it's windy as all get out, so you need to take care with any open flames. Doesn't take long for a fire to get out of control in these parts."

"Hey, Miranda, I got those two-by-fours you ordered

in the back," the florid-cheeked man at the front counter called out. "Wanna meet me back there with your truck?"

"Be right there, Dad," she called before turning back to John. "I'm Miranda Duncan." She grinned before adding, "Of the hardware Duncans."

He laughed. "John Blake. Of the accounting Blakes," he said in return, wondering if she could tell he was speaking the truth.

It had been a while since he'd used his real name. But Quinn had suggested it, since the people who might want to do him harm knew him by other names. Nobody he'd crossed recently would connect him to some guy named John Blake who lived in Cold Creek, Texas.

Miranda cocked her head for the briefest moment before she smiled at him again. "Welcome to Cold Creek, John Blake. Hope you'll like it here." She headed back out the door, letting in another blast of icy wind that made his bones hurt.

Damn shame, he thought, that he rather liked the red-haired deputy, because the last thing he needed to do while he was recuperating in Cold Creek was to make friends with a local cop.

He was here to stay out of sight and let his bones and muscles mend.

In that order.

Gathering up the screws and bits he'd need to repair the wind-battered storm windows of the rental house, he paid at the front counter and headed out to the old Ford pickup Alexander Quinn had purchased for his time here in Texas. The plates were from Garza County, a couple of hours south, registered in the name of a construction company called Blanchard Building. It belonged to an old friend of Quinn's, who apparently owed the man a favor.

If anyone asked, John Blake's name was on the payroll as a carpenter, and the repair work he was doing on the rental house was all part of the cover.

Quinn was nothing if not thorough.

The wind was strong and icy, hinting there was snow hiding behind the flat gray clouds that hung low over the ridgeline to the east. To the west, there was nothing but scrubland and sky as far as the eye could see.

John tugged the collar of his jacket closed and hurried to climb into the truck, grimacing at the steady drumbeat of pain in his bones. Maybe he should have checked the weather report this morning before he planned a day of manual labor.

The last thing his aching bones needed was snow.

LOOKED LIKE THE weatherman was right, Miranda thought as she gazed at the lowering gray sky overhead. They were getting snow this afternoon.

She pulled the truck into the parking lot outside the Cold Creek Municipal Complex, suppressing a smile as usual when she read the building's name on the large sign out front. The single-story rectangular brick building housed a small courtroom, the mayor's tiny office and the four-room Barstow County Sheriff's Department. There wasn't anything complex about this little dot on the sprawling Texas map, and with more and more young people leaving for the bigger towns and cities, Cold Creek might not be a dot on the map much longer.

Sheer stubbornness was all that had kept Miranda in the panhandle, herself. Stubbornness and a marrow-deep love of the land of her birth. She knew everyone in Cold Creek like old friends.

Well, almost everybody.

It was rare for Cold Creek to have new folks in town. Maybe in a bigger city, like Dallas or Houston, John Blake would blend into the crowd. He had that kind of face—pleasant features but nothing that made him stand out. His hair was neither long nor short, neither dark nor fair, and his skin tone was medium. He wasn't short, but he wasn't tall, either—only an inch or two taller than she was. He wasn't heavy or thin, neither muscle-bound nor weak.

He was simply average.

But even average stood out in Cold Creek, Texas. Because he was a newcomer in a town that didn't attract newcomers.

Settling in at her desk in the sheriff's department, she checked her messages in hopes of a new case to distract her from her inconvenient curious streak. But there was nothing waiting for her. There rarely was.

She woke her computer and grabbed a notepad from the top desk drawer. *John Blake*, she wrote at the top of the pad. He was from Tennessee—east Tennessee, she added to the notepad as she searched her memory for everything he'd told her and a few things he hadn't. His accent had definitely held a hint of the mountains.

He'd been buying nails and screws, but nothing that pegged him as any sort of builder. And he'd told her he came from a family of accountants, hadn't he?

John Blake. Accountant. Eastern Tennessee.

That should be a place to start.

Ten minutes later, she knew a good bit more—and still, a whole lot of nothing. Jonathan Eric Blake, age thirty-six, six feet tall. Until just over a year ago, he'd worked at Blake and Blake, an accounting firm in Johnson City, Tennessee, owned by his father. Before that, he'd worked for a global marketing firm in Europe for about a year, fresh out of grad school.

His current address was just off Route 7, the main north-south highway through Barstow County. He also showed up on the payroll of a construction company called Blanchard Building, Inc., in Garza County.

Working as an off-site carpenter.

What was an accountant doing working as a carpenter?

As she reached for the computer keyboard again, the desk sergeant, Coy Taylor, stuck his head through the doorway. "Duncan, we've had a call. Anonymous. Someone thought he saw Delta McGraw hitchhiking down near the Bar W."

She stood and grabbed her jacket from the back of her chair. "Was he sure it was Delta?"

"Claimed it was. You've got pictures of her plastered all over the county." Taylor gave her a sympathetic look. "You might be about the only person left in these parts who gives a damn. That girl's burned a lot of bridges in this town."

Miranda couldn't argue otherwise, but Delta had lived a hard life and maybe she had earned some of the prickliness that set most people on edge. And while this wasn't the first time Delta had gone missing for a few days, this time just felt different. She'd been gone too long, with no word to anyone, at a time when she'd seemed closer than ever to putting down permanent roots in Cold Creek.

Miranda zipped up her jacket and headed out to the fleet parking lot. The small sheriff's department had jurisdiction for the whole county, but most of the crime, such as it was, happened near the county seat of Cold Creek or along Route 7.

She turned on the cruiser's light bar but left the siren silent as she sped down Route 7 toward the sprawling Bar W Ranch, one of the largest cattle spreads in the panhandle. Despite the chilly temperatures, the Bar W Ranch kept their cattle grazing year-round through a strategic plan utilizing both warm- and cold-growth grasses. Some patches of grass were already green, despite the frigid temperatures, and several dozen head of cattle had gathered there to graze.

She peered down the highway, looking for a hitchhiker. But with the threat of snow, even traffic on the highway was nearly nonexistent. Nor could she find any sign that a vehicle had pulled over on the dusty shoulder on either side to pick up anyone thumbing for a ride.

Had it been a false report?

She called it in. "Taylor, I'm seeing no sign of a hitchhiker on Route 7. Could the call have come from a hoaxer?"

"Could have, I suppose." Taylor's gusty sigh roared through the radio. "Sorry about that, Duncan. I know you were hoping hard for some sign of the girl."

"I think while I'm down this way, I'm going to check in on Lizzie Dillard. She swears someone's been stealing eggs from her henhouse."

"A lawman's work is never done," Taylor drawled, amusement thick in his gravelly voice.

The narrow one-lane dirt road that led to Lizzie Dillard's farm, well-rutted and hell on the cruiser's shocks, had been given the dubious name Glory Road. At one point, in the area's distant past, a charismatic preacher had turned this part of the panhandle into a series of peripatetic tent revivals, and Glory Road had come into being to accommodate wagons, horses and pedestrians traveling from revival to revival.

The revivals had ended after a spectacularly messy sex scandal involving the preacher and a half dozen of his pretty young acolytes, but the name of the road had lived on to the present.

By the time she pulled into the bare yard in front of Lizzie Dillard's farmhouse, a light snow had begun to fall, whipped into icy needles by the hard north wind. Miranda tugged up the collar of her jacket and hurried up the porch steps. She knocked on the sagging screen door. "Lizzie?"

Lizzie didn't answer, even after another knock, so Miranda headed around to the chicken coop out back. "Lizzie?"

Lizzie Dillard came out of the chicken coop and looked up in surprise. "Hey there, Miranda. What're you doin' out here? You want a piece of pecan pie? It's still warm from the oven, and I could put on a pot of coffee."

Miranda ignored the answering rumble of her stomach. "No, thank you, Lizzie. I just came by to talk to you about those stolen eggs."

"Aw, honey, I didn't tell your daddy about that so you'd come out here. It's probably some wily ol' gray fox." Lizzie handed Miranda the basket full of brown eggs and turned to secure the door latch on the coop.

"A fox got in the henhouse and just stole the eggs?" Miranda tried to temper her skepticism, but Lizzie shot her a knowing look.

"I reckon I raise tough hens." Lizzie laughed at her own joke. "Sometimes, they just want the eggs. It happens. You sure you don't want to come in and warm up?"

The snowfall had started to pick up, the flakes fatter

and denser than before. The ground temperature was still above freezing, but if the snow got much heavier, it wouldn't take long to start sticking, even on the roads. "I'd better get on the move," Miranda said, not letting herself think about Lizzie's warm kitchen and hot pot of coffee. "Call us if anything else happens out here, okay?"

"Sure thing." Lizzie walked with her to the cruiser. "You be safe out there. My old bones are tellin' me this might be a big snow."

"I hope your bones are wrong," Miranda said with a smile.

Back in the cruiser, she checked in with the station. Bill Chambers was manning the front desk instead of Taylor, who'd taken a lunch break. She filled in Chambers on the call that had brought her out here. "No new calls about a hitchhiker?"

"Not a thing."

"I'm coming back in, then." At the end of Glory Road, she took a left onto Route 7, heading south toward town. Snow had limited the visibility to about fifty yards in all directions, forcing her to drive slower than she normally would. Fortunately, the snow seemed to have convinced most other drivers to stay off the road.

She was halfway to town before she saw another set of headlights in the rearview mirror, cutting through the snow fog behind her. A second glance revealed the headlights moving closer at a reckless rate of speed.

Miranda turned on the light bar and the siren, figuring that would be enough to make the car flying up behind her slow down.

She was wrong. The second vehicle whipped around the cruiser and pulled even in the passing lane. It was a Ford Taurus, she saw. Dark blue. She tried to get a look at the driver, but the dark-tinted windows, liberally frosted with a layer of snow crystals, hid the car's occupants from view.

She grabbed her radio and hit the bullhorn button. "Pull over," she commanded, easing off the gas.

The other car slowed with her but didn't pull over.

She pushed the call button and gave Chambers a description of the vehicle. "Don't know what this fellow's up to, but if there's a unit in the area, I could use backup."

"On its way," Chambers promised.

Snow was starting to dance across the road surface, collecting on the edges. If the precipitation didn't slow soon, the road would become hazardous.

"Pull over," she ordered again, but the driver of the Taurus didn't change speed at all.

What the hell was going on? Was this an ambush?

Why would someone ambush a Barstow County deputy?

With shocking suddenness, the Taurus fell back, catching Miranda off guard. She glanced in her side mirror, trying to figure out what he was doing.

The right front of the Taurus was even with the left rear panel of the cruiser. In the split second Miranda had to think, she realized the Taurus was in the perfect position for the classic police chase tactic known as the PIT maneuver.

Just as the thought flashed through her mind, the Taurus bumped the left rear panel of her car, sending the cruiser into a textbook spin.

If the road had been dry, she might have been able to recover from the PIT maneuver. But as the cruiser turned in a wild circle, the wheels hit a patch of accumulating snow and spun off the road, hitting a shallow arroyo that sent her into a roll.

Amid the shriek of crumpling metal and the blaze of fear rising in her chest, her head slammed into the side window and the whirlwind of sound and color faded into dark silence.

THE SQUEAL OF tires and the crunch of ripping metal broke through the whisper of snow falling outside the rental house, rousing John from a light doze.

His nerves rattling, he froze for a moment, his pulse hammering inside his head as he listened for a repeat of the noise.

Had he dreamed it? His house was close to Route 7, the busiest highway in Cold Creek, though so far, he hadn't seen all that much traffic on the road, certainly nothing like the busy street in front of his apartment building back in Abingdon, Virginia.

Still, it was snowing outside, and cars and snow didn't mix that well, especially in an area where there wasn't a lot of snow over the course of an average winter. Maybe he'd heard a car's tires squealing outside and in his half-dream state, imagined the rest?

His shoulder ached as he donned hiking boots and shrugged on his heavy jacket, but he ignored the pain. Pain was good. It was a reminder he'd taken three bullets and lived to tell about it.

He headed out to the porch and peered into the fog of falling snow. About fifty yards down the road, a flash of color caught his eye. Strobing color, like the light bar on the top of a police vehicle.

Except the light wasn't coming from the road. It was coming from several yards off the highway.

Patting the back pocket of his jeans to make sure he still had his phone, he left the porch and headed into the snow shower, keeping his eye on the flashing light. Within a few yards, he could see the light was coming from the light bar on the roof of a Barstow County Sheriff's Department cruiser lying on its side in a patch of scrub grass. The roof was damaged, the front windshield shattered, but the light bar continued to flash.

As he neared the cruiser, movement on the highway caught his attention. A dark-colored sedan crept along the shoulder, as if rubbernecking the accident.

John waved at the slowly passing vehicle. "I need help here!"

The sedan kept going until it disappeared into the fog of snow.

Grimacing, John headed for the cruiser. A loud creak sent John backpedaling quickly. The cruiser started to shift positions until it landed on all four wheels. Two wheels were flat, John saw, and there was significant damage to the chassis. Clearly a rollover.

Once the cruiser settled, he hurried to the driver's door and looked through the open window. The first thing he noticed was blood on the steering wheel. Then hair the color of Georgia clay.

Damn it. Could it be the deputy from the hardware store?

"Deputy Duncan?"

She didn't answer. Looking closer, he realized the window wasn't actually open. Instead, the crash had wiped out the window, showering pebbled bits of glass all over the floorboard, the seats and the injured deputy.

It was definitely Miranda Duncan, though half of her face was obscured by a sticky sheen of blood that seemed to be coming from the vicinity of her hairline. Gusts of wind carried snow flurries into the cruiser's cab to settle on the deputy's bloody face and melt into the crimson flow.

John tried the door. It resisted his attempt to open it, so he let it go and leaned into the cruiser through the window. Swallowing a lump of dread, he touched his fingers to her throat, feeling for a pulse. It was there, fast but even. He started to draw back his hand, reaching for his phone.

With shocking speed, Miranda's left hand whipped up and clamped around his wrist, while her right hand snapped up, wrapped around a Smith & Wesson M&P 40, the barrel pointed between his eyes.

"Don't move an inch," she growled.

As John sucked in a deep breath, he heard the crack of gunfire. His pulse misfired, and he grabbed the side of the window frame, pebbled glass crunching against his palm.

"Get down!" Miranda shouted as a second shot thumped against the cruiser's back door.

Chapter Two

John Blake disappeared suddenly, leaving Miranda with an unobstructed view out the cruiser window. But she could still see nothing but falling snow—the storm had reached white-out proportions.

Pain throbbed in her head as she squinted in hopes of seeing her hidden assailant, but she couldn't even see the road now. She could hear an engine, however, growling somewhere out there in the white void.

Behind her, the car door opened, and she swung around to find John Blake gazing back at her, his expression urgent. "You're a sitting duck," he warned, stretching his hand toward her.

Gunfire rang outside, the bullet hitting the front panel of the cruiser with a loud *thwack*, ending her brief hesitation. She unlatched her seat belt and scrambled toward John, taking his outstretched hand.

He pulled her out of the cruiser and pushed her gently toward the front wheel, giving her an extra layer of protection against the shooter. The movement made her feel light-headed and nauseated, and she ended up on her backside, leaning her back against the wheel as she sucked in deep draughts of icy air.

"I can try returning fire," John suggested. "I'll need your weapon—"

"Wait," she said, forcing herself to focus. Was it her imagination or was the sound of the car motor moving away?

"I think whoever's out there is leaving." John had edged closer, near enough that she could feel the heat of his body blocking the icy wind. She leaned toward him, unable to stop herself.

"I think you're right." Her chattering teeth made it difficult to speak. "I called for backup but I think the radio got smashed in the wreck."

"You could be hurt worse than you think," he warned, crouching until his gaze leveled with hers. Up close, his hazel eyes were soft with concern.

"I d-don't think I have any broken limbs," she stuttered. "B-but I'm freezing."

"My house is about forty yards in that direction." He nodded toward his right. "Want to chance a run for it?"

She nodded, realizing she was too warmly dressed to be as cold as she felt, which meant she was probably going into some level of shock. She needed to get warm and dry. "Let's do it."

He stood first. Trying to draw fire, she realized, so they'd know if the shooter was still out there. She grabbed his hand, trying to draw him back down behind the cruiser, but he shook his head. "I think the shooter's gone."

He pulled her up, wrapping one arm around her waist to help her wobbling legs hold her upright.

She drew deep on her inner resources. Forty yards. She could run forty yards on a sprained ankle if she had to, and as far as she could tell, her only injury was the pain in her head. "Let's do it."

The first few steps felt as if she was running through mud, but with John's help, she picked up speed and strength. By the time the small farmhouse loomed up out of the white fog of snow, she was feeling steadier.

John half dragged her up to the porch and inside the door. Instantly, blessed heat washed over her, and she felt her legs wobble dangerously beneath her.

"Whoa, deputy. No face-planting on my nice clean floor." John wrapped his arms around her and eased her over to the sofa that was positioned in front of a crackling fire. He sat beside her, sliding her gloves from her half-numb fingers. "Sit right here. I'll get my first-aid kit."

She held her trembling hands out in front of the fire, soaking up the warmth. She heard a cabinet opening and closing, then footsteps as John returned to the front room holding a soft-sided first-aid kit.

"You holding up?" He sat beside her and unzipped the kit.

"No face-planting yet," she answered with a lopsided grin that made her face hurt. "I need to call the station. I guess my phone's probably somewhere on the cruiser's floorboard."

"Of course." He pulled a cell phone from his pocket. "What's the number?"

She gave it to him, and he dialed the number while she looked through the first-aid kit for antiseptic wipes. She found a sealed packet and ripped it open.

"Who should I talk to?" John asked.

"Just talk to the desk sergeant," she replied, touching the antiseptic pad to the sore spot just above her hairline. It stung, making her wince. "I'm not sure who's on the desk."

While John gave his address to whoever answered

the phone, Miranda went through a handful of antiseptic wipes trying to mop up the blood from her head. It seemed to be bleeding still, though not as heavily as before. Blood stained the front of her jacket and the uniform pants she wore, enough that she no longer wondered why she felt so light-headed.

"The sergeant said backup is already headed this way, but the snow's making it slow going." John leaned forward, examining her first-aid work. "How's your head feeling?"

"Like it just rammed into a brick wall."

John's lips curved slightly. "Noted."

"I don't remember exactly what happened," she admitted, trying not to let the blank spaces in her memory freak her out. She'd probably sustained a concussion in the accident. The memories might never return. Or, conversely, they'd come seeping back bits at a time.

She wasn't sure it mattered. It clearly hadn't been a simple accident.

Not if someone had started taking potshots at her immediately afterward.

"Do you know why you were out there in a snowstorm?" John asked.

That much she could remember. "We'd gotten a call from someone who said he'd seen a woman on our missing person's list out here on Route 7, hitchhiking. I came out to check on the report, but it didn't pan out. I stopped by to talk to another constituent about a possible theft, then I headed back toward town. That's the last thing I remember before I came to in the car just before you showed up."

"The sergeant said you'd called for backup a few minutes ago. You reported a vehicle following you too closely for comfort. You seemed to think the other driver was up to something."

"Did I give a description of the vehicle?" Surely she had.

"He didn't say."

She could remember nothing about another vehicle, but something had sent her rolling off the highway and she didn't think it was the snowstorm. The visibility wasn't great, but Route 7 was about as straight as a ruler all the way into town.

"You don't remember anything about it, do you?" John asked.

"I don't," she admitted, reaching for another antiseptic wipe packet.

John covered his hand with hers, stilling her movement.

Heat rolled up her arm from where his fingers touched hers. It settled in her chest like a hot coal, warming her insides.

"Let me grab a washcloth and see if we can get that bleeding stopped for good." He was back a minute later with a wet washcloth and pulled a chair up in front of her, gazing up at her hairline with a frown between his eyes. "This may hurt."

Bracing herself, she smelled a hint of soap as the cloth passed her face, then felt the sting as John pressed the hot cloth to her head wound. She sucked in a quick breath.

"Sorry," he murmured. "At least you've stopped shivering."

So she had, she realized. She felt steadier also, her vision less off-kilter. The mental fog was starting to lift, as well.

"I don't know if I'd have survived out there without

you," she admitted, the words strangely reluctant to pass her lips. She'd been self-sufficient since she was quite young, the result of losing her mother in childhood. Her father had worked long hours, keeping the hardware business running through good times and bad. She'd learned early how to take care of herself. Accepting help from others wasn't something she'd ever done easily.

But she owed John Blake her life, even if she still had questions about what he might be doing in town. He certainly hadn't been the person firing shots at her from the highway. He'd come perilously close to getting shot himself. She'd been looking right at him when the bullet hit the back door right beside him.

A few minutes later, he withdrew the bloody washcloth from her head.

She tried not to cringe at the thought of help arriving soon. Her practical side told her she needed medical attention, especially given her memory loss. She'd have told any other accident victim to let the paramedics do their job, wouldn't she?

But she sure as hell wasn't going to enjoy her colleagues poking and prodding her as if she was an ordinary civilian involved in an MVA. She was one of them, damn it.

And she wanted to be the one who investigated what had happened.

"They're not going to let you investigate your own case, you know." The knowing look in his eyes made her feel as if she'd been laid bare, all her secret thoughts on display.

How the hell could he do that? He didn't know her.

She grimaced. "I know that."

"And while I'm sharing unwanted news with you, you should do whatever the paramedics say you should do."

"I'm fine."

"You're not." He leaned closer. She couldn't stop herself from meeting his gaze. "I spent time in the hospital not long ago. I felt like a specimen under glass. People wandering into my room all hours, poking this and drawing that. Hated every minute of it. So I know how you're feeling."

She nodded, then regretted the movement as her head spun for a couple of seconds. "They're going to want to bus me to Plainview for observation."

"Maybe you should let them do that."

"No."

"That's a pretty good knock on your head."

"I probably have a slight concussion. But I'm clear-headed now."

"Closed head injuries can be unpredictable," he warned. "You have someone who can watch you? A husband?"

"My dad," she answered. "He's probably already closed up shop and headed home. I'll get one of the guys to take me there."

"So, no husband?"

She looked up at him, surprised by the interest in his voice. "No husband."

His gaze held hers. "I'm not exactly known for my good timing."

She couldn't stop a smile, though it made her head ache. "Clearly."

"So we should probably just forget I asked that question." He looked toward the front door. "Do you hear any sirens?"

"Not yet."

"Should we?"

Good question. "How long ago did you talk to the station?"

He looked at his watch. "Twenty minutes. He said backup was already on the way, so it might be a little longer than that."

It took about ten minutes to reach this part of Route 7 under good weather conditions. "The snow's probably slowed them up."

He gave a quick nod and fell silent, his expression hard to read. She wouldn't say he looked worried, exactly. Watchful, maybe.

Silence unspooled between them as they waited, the silence of forced proximity between strangers. Normally, Miranda preferred silence to pointless chatter, but the events of the afternoon had left her nerves raw.

So when John Blake's cell phone rang, it sent a shock wave rippling up her spine. He gave a slight start and pulled the phone from his pocket. "It's the station," he murmured. He lifted the phone to his ear. "John Blake."

He listened a second, then looked at Miranda. "She's right here." He handed the phone to her.

It was Bill Chambers on the other end. "How're you holding up, Duncan?"

"I'm okay. Head's a little sore, but I'll live."

"Good to hear, because we have a problem."

JOHN LEANED AGAINST the back of his chair and tried not to eavesdrop, though there was no way to avoid hearing Miranda's end of the call without leaving the room.

She picked up the washcloth he'd laid on the coffee

table beside her and pressed it to her head wound while she listened to the caller. "How many injuries?"

Whatever answer she received made her frown.

John stopped trying to pretend he wasn't listening and met her troubled gaze. She was still pale, but her hands had stopped shaking finally and her gray-eyed gaze was clear and sharp as it rose to meet John's.

"I'm fine. The cruiser's not going anywhere, and I'm not alone. Just stay in touch, okay?" She ended the call and handed John the phone. "There's been a pileup on Highway 287. Over a dozen vehicles. Every EMS service in three counties is responding. All the deputies are out on calls, too. I guess you're stuck with me a little longer."

He nodded, but something in his gut twisted a little at the realization they were alone and more or less stranded out in here in the middle of snowy nowhere for the next while.

He had a pistol packed away in the closet. His Virginia concealed-carry license was honored in Texas—he'd made sure before he headed west to finish his recuperation in relative anonymity. But if he retrieved it now, what would Deputy Duncan think?

"What are you thinking?" she asked, apparently reading his expression.

"That we're sort of isolated out here," he answered, not seeing the point of hiding his concern. Someone had run the deputy off the road and then taken shots at her.

Would they take a chance and try again?

"You think the person who was shooting at us may come back?" She laid down the washcloth and sat up straighter, her gaze moving toward the front door.

He hurried to the door and turned the dead bolt to the locked position before moving the curtain aside to check the road. The snow had slowed finally, visibility restored to a hundred yards or more, though the highway in front of the house was covered with at least a couple of inches of the white stuff. He could probably drive to town without incident, he thought. Get her to her dad's house, at least.

He looked over his shoulder at her. "The snow has slowed. I think I could drive you back to town."

"I don't want to leave the cruiser," she answered. "If you don't mind my staying here a while longer."

Did he mind? On one level, he didn't mind a bit. She was an interesting woman, and not bad to look at, even with her hair plastered to her head with sticky blood.

But she was also a cop, and while he technically had nothing to hide from the law, he didn't want anyone looking too closely at his life. In a way, Cold Creek, Texas, was a hideout. There were people back in Virginia who'd like to get their hands on him, and he was currently in no condition to hold his own.

Soon, though, he promised himself. He'd be back in fighting form soon. And then it wouldn't matter who knew where he was.

"I don't mind," he answered.

Her eyes narrowed a notch. "Took your time answering that question."

He smiled. "I'm a bit of a loner."

"Is that why you moved out here? To be alone?"

"I guess."

"You said you were in the hospital not long ago. Car accident?"

He shook his head but didn't elaborate.

"Assault?"

He should have known silence would only pique her

curiosity. But he was tired of lying. It seemed as if he'd been lying for years, first as a CIA agent pretending to be an international finance manager, then the decade he'd pretended that he found life as an accountant satisfying.

And then, there was the past year, working undercover for Alexander Quinn. Using an alias, pretending a career that didn't exist, acting as a go-between for Quinn and another undercover operative trying to infiltrate a dangerous militia group called the Blue Ridge Infantry—

What would Miranda Duncan think if he laid out his whole deception-riddled history for her examination?

She'd probably think he was crazy. Or lying.

Or both.

"I guess you could say I was in the wrong place at the wrong time," he said finally.

"That's…cryptic."

He smiled. "Yes."

To his surprise, her lips quirked in response, a faint half smile that dimpled her cheeks. He felt a drawing sensation low in his belly that caught him by surprise.

She was so not his type. Hell, he wasn't sure he even had a type.

But damned if he wasn't sitting here, wondering what she'd look like naked. In his bed.

Her smile faded suddenly, and her head turned toward the front door. "Do you hear that?"

Listening, he realized what she was hearing.

A car engine, idling somewhere outside the house.

He crossed to the window and parted the curtains an inch. The snow was picking up again, but not enough to obscure his view of the road, where a dark blue sedan sat idling on the shoulder, directly in front of the house.

"What is it?" Miranda asked, her voice closer than he

expected. Glancing to his right, he found her beside him, trying to see out the window.

"It's a dark blue sedan," he answered, easing the curtain closed and pulling her with him deeper into the cabin.

"Is it—?"

"I don't know," he admitted. He hadn't had a chance to get a good look at the vehicle earlier while dodging bullets and trying to get Miranda to safety. "It looks similar. And it's idling outside my house, about forty yards from your wrecked cruiser."

Miranda's face went paler. "Are all your doors locked?"

He met her troubled gaze. "I don't know."

Chapter Three

While John went around the house checking the locks, Miranda pulled the M&P 40 from the holster at her hip and crossed to the front window, taking a quick look outside. The sedan remained idling at the side of the road. The windows were tinted, obscuring the occupants from view.

What do you want? she wondered.

John's footsteps drew her gaze to him. He was carrying a pistol in his right hand, barrel down, his finger safely away from the trigger. But the sight still gave her a start.

What did she know about him, really? Did he even have a license to carry that pistol?

"I have a Virginia CCW," he answered as if she'd asked the question aloud. Was she that easily read?

Up close, she saw that the pistol was a Ruger SR45. Big and black, with a brushed stainless slide. If she were the type of cop who indulged in weapon envy, she'd be indulging in it big-time.

"We need to call for backup," she said, forcing her gaze away from the big gun and back to the sedan idling outside her house.

"Already done." He nudged her away from the window. "I told the guy who answered that we needed a unit out here if they had to pull it off the pileup."

"That could take a while."

"Better late than never, right?" He glanced toward the window, his brow furrowed. "I wonder why they're just sitting out there."

"Maybe it's an intimidation tactic."

"Or maybe they want one of us to come outside to see what's going on."

"If we did that, we'd be sitting ducks."

"So we wait."

She nodded. "Whoever's out there knows I'm armed. But they can't be sure whether or not you are."

John slanted a quick look at her. His expression was neutral, unreadable, but something in those hazel-green eyes set off warning bells in her head.

Did he know something about the car outside? She had the strangest feeling he was keeping something from her.

Something important.

"The doors are locked," he said. "The windows, too."

"The windows, too?" She looked in his direction again, took in his wary expression. He was definitely keeping something from her. But what?

She didn't think he wanted to hurt her. She was vulnerable from her injury—it wouldn't take much to get the drop on her. He could have done so at almost any point since he'd dragged her inside the house.

Hell, he could have killed her out in the car, or made it possible for the shooters to do so, if he'd wanted her dead.

So maybe what he was hiding wasn't about her.

"Accounting," she said.

His gaze cut toward her. "Accounting?"

"You said you were of the accounting Blakes. When I said I was from the hardware Duncans."

"Oh, right."

"Are you taking a sabbatical from that kind of work?"

A huff of laughter escaped his throat. "No. I did that kind of work for ten years. That was ten years too many."

"Are you unemployed?" She knew the answer to that question. She might not remember what happened to send her rolling off the highway, but she remembered her computer search earlier at the station.

Even then, John Blake had piqued her curiosity.

Seeing him armed and appearing both competent and dangerous, she knew she'd been right to wonder what he was doing in a sleepy backwater town like Cold Creek.

"I'm a carpenter," he said. "I work for a construction company. Blanchard Building."

"Down in Garza County?"

His eyes narrowed slightly, and she realized she'd made a mistake. What would a Barstow County deputy know about a construction company two counties to the south?

"Have you been investigating me?" His tone wasn't threatening, but his grip on the Ruger tightened enough to make her stomach turn a flip.

She decided honesty was her best option. "We don't get a lot of strangers in Cold Creek."

"So you did a background check?"

"Not quite that drastic. I just looked up your name in the computer. With a few search parameters."

"What did you find?"

"More questions than answers."

His lips quirked at her admission. "I'm an open book." He didn't even bother to pretend he was telling the truth.

She smiled. "If you were, you wouldn't be nearly as interesting."

One of his dark eyebrows lifted, but he didn't respond.

She was starting to feel shaky again, she realized. Some of the adrenaline that had kept her on her feet and moving had begun to seep away, and her injuries were making themselves known again.

She tried not to let it show, but John's sharp gaze missed nothing. "I think that car is trying to wait us out. So maybe we should do the same. We have backup coming. So let's go sit by the fire. It's cold in here."

She let him lead her back to the fireplace and gratefully sank onto the comfortable cushions of the sofa. The heat from the fireplace felt like a living thing, wrapping around her with tendrils of warmth until some of the shivers subsided.

"You're a Cold Creek native?" John asked a few minutes later, breaking the silence that had fallen between them.

"Born and bred."

"You like it out here?"

"I do," she said with a slight lift of her chin. She saw the hint of a smile curve his lips in response and felt a little childish, as if she'd stamped her foot and dared him to disagree.

"It's not quite what I expected." He didn't sound negative, just bemused, which was a good mark in her book. She knew few people who could appreciate the flat, windblown plains and endless isolation. But at least John Blake hadn't outright dismissed the possibility of its appeal.

"What did you expect?"

"More heat, for one thing."

"You came to the wrong part of Texas at the wrong time for that."

"So I've discovered."

"Where are you from originally?" she asked, even though she knew the answer.

He shot her a look. "Didn't your background check tell you that?"

"I didn't find your birth certificate or anything."

"Johnson City, Tennessee," he said.

Where his father's accounting firm was located. "You worked for an overseas company a while back, right?"

His lips quirked again. Not quite a smile, but close. "Yeah. For about a year."

"Didn't like global marketing?"

Her question made him smile. A knowing, secret-keeping smile that made her curious streak vibrate like a tuning fork in the pit of her stomach.

"I think it's more a matter of global marketing not liking me—" He stopped short, his head cocked. "Do you hear that?"

She listened, hearing nothing. "I don't hear anything."

"Exactly." He rose and edged his way back toward the window, staying clear of the glass panes as he checked outside. His back stiffened. "The car is gone."

Miranda joined him at the window. He was right. The car was no longer idling on the highway out front. "Do you think it's a way to lure us out of the house?"

He gave her a thoughtful look. "I don't know. But I don't hear its engine running anymore. Do you?"

"No." But she did hear something else, she realized. "Sirens."

They were only faintly audible. She supposed the walls of the house muffled the sound somewhat. But whoever had been sitting in that sedan outside might have heard them coming a good bit earlier.

"Maybe the sirens scared them away," John said, reading her thoughts.

Within a couple of minutes, a sheriff's department cruiser pulled up outside the house, and the sheriff himself, Miles Randall, emerged from the cruiser, along with one of the younger deputies, Tim Robertson.

John unlocked the door and opened it before the sheriff had a chance to knock. Randall stepped back in surprise, one hand dropping to the pistol holstered at his hip.

"It's okay," Miranda said quickly, showing herself.

Randall reacted with surprise at the sight of her. "Good God, Duncan, You look like hell."

"Thanks."

Randall gave John Blake a quick, curious glance, then looked at her again. "Want to tell me what happened?"

"That," she admitted, "is a very good question."

It TURNED OUT that the deputy Sheriff Randall had brought with him had previously been a volunteer fireman with some paramedic training. Tim Robertson looked ridiculously young to John, but he assessed Miranda's condition as if he knew what he was doing, working with a skillful efficiency that set John's mind at ease.

Sheriff Miles Randall was a tall, rangy man with a drawl as big as, well, Texas. He questioned John about what he'd witnessed, asking good questions and not overplaying his suspicions. But John could tell Randall wasn't ready to trust his word completely.

John couldn't blame the sheriff. He wasn't exactly a man without secrets.

"I think we need to get you at least to the clinic in town," Randall told Miranda after Tim Robertson finished his examination. "Tim's not a doctor, and your daddy would kill me if I didn't make sure you're not going to keel over the second I leave you alone."

Miranda smiled. "I promise, I won't. But shouldn't someone stay here and protect the crime scene?"

"That's what Tim's here for."

Miranda's gray-eyed gaze slanted toward John, as if looking for his input. He straightened his spine, surprised. What did she expect him to do, back her up? Tell the sheriff he wanted her to stay?

He did, he realized. He wanted her to stay. But that was a selfish impulse, fed by his hormones and his isolation out here.

"You should do what the sheriff says, Deputy Duncan," he said, keeping his tone impersonal. Formal.

Her brow wrinkled briefly at his words, but her expression shuttered quickly. "Thank you for your help, Mr. Blake."

"Glad I was here." As she started to turn to go, he said, "Wait."

She looked at him, her expression somewhere between curious and wary.

He reached into his back pocket and pulled out his wallet. Inside, he withdrew the card he'd picked up earlier that morning at the hardware store. Her father's name was on the front. He flipped it over. "Can I borrow a pen?" he asked the sheriff.

The sheriff pulled a pen from his front breast pocket and handed it over, his expression watchful.

John jotted his cell number on the back of the card and handed it to Miranda. "If you have any more questions."

She took the card and slid it in her pants pocket. "Thanks again for everything."

She walked out with the sheriff, her gait slow but her

spine straight. She didn't look back. He told himself he never expected her to.

"I'm going to guard the wreckage until the tow truck can get here." Robertson headed out the door.

John nodded, his gaze still fixed on Miranda. The sheriff opened the passenger door of the cruiser for her, and she settled in the seat, moving gingerly. The aches and pains of the car crash were starting to catch up with her, he realized.

She'd feel like hell warmed over in the morning.

But at least she was still alive. There had been a moment, as he'd approached that crashed cruiser, when he'd been afraid he was about to unbuckle a corpse.

His cell phone rang, loud enough to jangle his nerves. He checked the display. No name or number, just the word *unknown* across the smartphone's window.

He answered. "John Blake."

"You rang?" Alexander Quinn's voice was low and smooth on the other end of the line.

He had. After calling the Barstow County Sheriff's Department to ask for backup, he'd put in a call to his boss. Quinn hadn't answered, so John had left a message for a call back.

"There's been an incident here," he said, and briefly outlined the events of the afternoon.

"Any reason to think you were the target instead of the deputy?" Quinn asked.

"I'm not sure," John admitted. "The deputy doesn't remember the crash, and I only heard it when it happened. I don't know how the other vehicle ran her off the road, so I don't know whether the location of the crash was deliberate or happenstance."

"The tri-state task force has been rolling up the remainder of the Blue Ridge Infantry over the past few weeks. Lynette Colley's been talking to the investigators. She's given them a lot of names and dates they hope to use to bring all the key leaders of the BRI to justice." Quinn didn't bother to hide the satisfaction in his voice. Bringing down the Blue Ridge Infantry had been a personal mission for Quinn since he formed The Gates. While the security agency took on plenty of well-paying cases, Quinn always kept some agents working the BRI angle.

John had asked him once why taking down the BRI was so important to him. Quinn's answer had been simple. "They're destroying these mountains, one soul at a time."

"So what you're saying is, this incident might have nothing at all to do with the bounty the BRI put on my head?"

"It's not likely that it does."

"Even with that car idling outside the house?"

"Sounds like the deputy's the one who has an enemy there in Cold Creek. Any idea why?"

"No," John admitted, walking across the front room to the side window. He parted the curtains and saw that the snow had settled to a light but steady fall. From here, he could see the wreck of the cruiser and the lanky young deputy standing guard, bundled up against the cold.

Miranda Duncan seemed an unlikely target for murder. Small-town deputy in a place with maybe three hundred residents.

Who would want a woman like that dead?

"Just keep your eyes open," Quinn said. "We've made big progress, but there are still a few members of the BRI and their ragtag crew out there, looking for a win."

"And getting to me would be a win."

"Yeah."

"I'll keep my eyes open," John answered, his tone flat.

"You should be in bed." Gil Duncan's voice rumbled from the doorway behind her, drawing Miranda's attention from the computer screen.

"I'm fine, Dad. Dr. Bennett said the concussion was mild and probably wouldn't give me any more trouble." She met her father's worried gaze and smiled. "I promise. My head isn't even hurting anymore."

Not much, anyway. Just a little ache where the doctor had sewn a couple of stitches to close up the head wound.

"What are you working on?" he asked, nodding toward the computer.

"Just some web surfing. Nothing to worry about."

"Like I'm not going to worry about my daughter rolling her cruiser in a snowstorm." Gil Duncan sighed, looking as if he'd aged a decade in the past twenty-four hours.

Miranda rose and crossed to where he stood in the doorway, wrapping her arms around his waist. "I really am okay."

He gave her a swift, fierce hug, a show of affection that he rarely displayed. "Maybe you should get yourself a different career."

She pulled back to look at him. "Maybe join you at the hardware store?"

"You worked there for years."

"Which is why I know it's not for me." She smiled to soften her words. "You know I love being a deputy."

"Rebel," he muttered, but not without affection.

"Go watch your basketball game. I'll finish up what I'm doing and I'll join you for the second half."

She watched her father walk down the narrow hall before she returned to the laptop on her bed.

She was fairly sure the blue sedan parked outside John Blake's house had been a Ford Taurus. So she'd just run the description through the Texas Department of Motor Vehicles database.

No response yet from the DMV. They'd be looking at a five-county area around Cold Creek, so it was too early to expect an answer yet.

She slumped back against the bed pillows, her gaze wandering around the bedroom that had been hers growing up. The poster of the country band Lonestar taped to the closet door was dog-eared. Softball and junior-rodeo trophies covered the top of her dresser, along with a few blue ribbons from the county fair.

In this room, she felt sixteen again.

Not a good thing.

Sheriff Randall had retrieved her cell phone from the wrecked cruiser and returned it to her at the clinic. It had survived the crash without damage, which was more than she could say for herself. She pulled her cell phone from her pocket now and called the station. The night sergeant, Jack Logan, was manning the desk. "Things still crazy from the storm?" she asked when he answered.

"Duncan, aren't you supposed to be in bed recuperating?"

"I'm in bed," she said. "Just a little bored."

"Well, everything here's settled down, so it's not like you'd be any less bored if you were here," Logan told her in a tone that reminded her of her father. Jack Logan was a thirty-year veteran, winding down his time on the force on the night shift. "Snow's stopped and the temps should be above freezing by early morning."

"How about the pileup—how many casualties?"

"No deaths. Fifteen hospitalized but none of the injuries are life threatening. Looks like we dodged a bullet."

"Some of us literally," Miranda murmured.

"Ah, hell, Mandy. I wasn't even thinking."

"Has my cruiser been towed to Lubbock for examination?"

"Yeah. We got to it by late afternoon."

Maybe they'd get something from ballistics, Miranda thought.

"They've also taped off the area and will do a grid search for more evidence after the snow melts tomorrow," Logan added.

John Blake would love that, she thought. His privacy had been well and truly invaded today. "Is Robertson still there guarding the crime scene?"

"No. The sheriff figured it was okay to just tape it off and pick up in the morning."

Miranda frowned, but she supposed the sheriff had a point. The evidence, such as they'd find, was probably in the cruiser anyway. "I'll let you go, Jack. Leave the sheriff a note—I'll be in tomorrow for a debriefing." She said goodbye and hung up before Logan could protest.

So, the crime scene was sitting there, unprotected, about forty yards from the house rented by a stranger in town.

Hmm.

When she'd first seen John Blake at the hardware store, she almost hadn't noticed him. He was that kind of guy—aggressively average, at least at first glance.

Up close and in action, however, he was anything but average.

Her uniform pants were hanging over the chair in

front of her battered old work desk. She dug in the front pocket, pulling out the card John had given her.

She checked her watch. Nine o'clock. Was it too late to call?

Before she could talk herself out of it, she dialed the number.

John answered on the second ring. "John Blake."

"It's Miranda Duncan."

His tone softened. "Still alive and kicking?"

"So far, so good."

"The lab guys came and took your cruiser a few hours ago." She could hear him moving, the faint thud of his footsteps on the hardwood floor.

"So I heard."

"Any breaks in the case?"

"Not yet." A draft was seeping into the house through the window over her bed. She pulled up the blanket and snuggled a little deeper into the mattress. "Hopefully we'll know more after the lab finishes up with the cruiser."

"I thought they'd have a crime scene crew out here this afternoon, but nobody showed."

She tried not to feel defensive. "We're a small force to begin with, we're temporarily a deputy short and we're dealing with a snowstorm—"

"Enough said." John's footsteps stopped, and she thought she heard the soft swish of fabric.

Suddenly, he uttered a low profanity.

"What?" she asked, her nerves instantly on edge.

"There's someone wandering around your crime scene," he said.

Chapter Four

The figure creeping toward the taped-off patch of frosty grass was moving with slow, measured paces. Dressed in what looked like winter camouflage, he blended into the snow-flecked scrub, only his movement giving away his position.

"He's in camo," John murmured into the phone, wishing he had his binoculars to get a better look. But he was afraid to leave the window, afraid that if he took his eyes off the creeping intruder, he'd lose sight of him altogether.

"Is he inside the tape?" Over the phone, Miranda's Texas twang had a raspy touch, reminding him that she'd already suffered through a long, stressful day. Her head was probably one big ache by now, and she had to be bruised and battered from the rollover.

"Not yet."

"I can get a cruiser over there to look around, but it will take a little while," Miranda said.

Over the phone, John heard the creak of bedsprings. Was she in bed?

He wondered whether she was a pajamas or a nightgown girl. Or, God help him, was she a woman who slept in the buff? A delicious shiver jolted through him at the vivid image that thought evoked.

He drove his imaginings firmly to the back of his head. "So far, he's just circling the taped-off area. Maybe he's just a curious hunter?"

"Is he carrying a rifle?" Miranda asked. He heard the sound of fabric rustling over the phone—was she getting dressed?

"You're not thinking of driving out here yourself, are you?" he asked.

"That's my crime scene." Her tone was full of stubborn determination. "I can get there faster than I can round up a cruiser. I'm closer."

"That's crazy—you have a concussion—"

"I'll be there in ten minutes." She hung up before John could try to talk her out of it.

He tried calling her back, but the call went straight to voice mail. Maybe she was already on the line to her office, rounding up backup.

With a sigh, he shoved his phone in his pocket and turned off the lights in the front room, plunging the house into darkness. Maybe his camo-clad visitor had been waiting for him to go to bed before he made his move.

Ball's in your court, John thought, grabbing a pair of binoculars before returning to the window. He let his eyes adjust to the change in light until he spotted the intruder again. The man was still circling the yellow crime scene tape, staying outside the perimeter.

He lifted the binoculars to his eyes and focused the lenses on the man in camo. His visitor wore a snow camouflage balaclava covering his mouth, nose and most of his forehead, leaving only a narrow strip of brow, eyes and upper cheeks uncovered. A pair of binoculars hid his eyes from view. He appeared to be using the binoculars to search the ground inside the crime scene tape, sparing him from having to trespass beyond the perimeter.

Suddenly, the man turned his face toward the window, his binoculars seeming to focus directly on John.

John took a step back from the window, but it was too late. The man in camo turned and headed into a clump of bushes north of the house.

John shrugged on his jacket, grabbed a flashlight and took a second to check the magazine of his Ruger before he headed out the door in pursuit.

He'd barely reached the taped crime scene when he heard the sound of a car engine roar to life. A moment later, the taillights of a vehicle stained the night red as a car pulled away from the shoulder of the highway about fifty yards away, heading north. John trekked toward the shoulder of the highway, watching the taillights grow smaller and smaller. About a half mile down the road, the car took a left and disappeared from view, hidden by the overgrown shrubs that lined the crossroad.

John trudged back to the crime scene and flicked on his flashlight, moving the beam over the trampled snow just outside the tape. While there were footprints visible, they were shapeless and free of identifying marks. He searched his memory for details about the man he'd seen wandering about and realized he must have been wearing some sort of boot covers with a soft sole. No wonder he hadn't worried about tracking through the snow.

He followed the tracks, using his flashlight to illuminate the snow around the crash site. He wasn't sure what the intruder had been looking for, but he could see nothing of interest. He supposed a crime scene team might be able to glean more, especially once the snow started to melt off the next day.

As he was walking back to the house, he heard the motor of another vehicle. He turned to watch its approach, soon making out the front grill of a large Ford pickup truck. The truck slowed as it neared his house, pulling onto the shoulder in front of him. The headlights dimmed and the interior light came on as the driver cut the engine. John could just make out Miranda Duncan's tousled auburn hair.

She'd made good time. Great time, actually.

She stopped a few yards away from him, squinting as he lifted the flashlight toward her. "What are you doing out here?"

"The intruder left. I was trying to see where he went, but he had a car waiting." He aimed the flashlight beam toward the ground, leading her through the snow to where he stood.

She pulled up a foot away, tugging her jacket more tightly around her as a gust of frigid wind blew across the plains, ruffling her hair. "Any idea what sort of car?"

"Too far away to be sure. It seemed to be a sedan, though. Not a truck."

"Did you see which way he went?"

"He turned left about a half mile up the road."

She nodded toward the taped-off crime scene. "Did he get inside the perimeter?"

"Not that I saw. He stayed outside the tape, but he was looking around with a pair of binoculars."

Miranda's gaze dropped to the pair of binoculars hanging around his neck.

He smiled. "I thought I'd see what he was trying to see."

Miranda frowned. "You went to the crime scene? Did you trample over his footprints?"

"He didn't leave prints." He told her about the boot covers. "He did seem to be looking for something, though."

"Like what?"

"I have no idea. I looked around after he left, but I didn't see a damn thing. I'm hoping maybe tomorrow the crime scene unit will come across something after the snow starts to melt."

"Tire prints," she said suddenly, looking up at him. A spark of excitement glittered in her eyes, lighting up her weary face. "Didn't the crew who came to tow the cruiser make imprints of the tire prints on the road out front? They were supposed to."

"I think so." He'd watched them doing something on the road and had assumed they'd been pouring molds of the prints.

"Maybe there are tire prints up the road where you saw that vehicle pull out and head down the highway."

"The temperature is supposed to be rising overnight. Those tracks—"

"May not be there tomorrow," she said, already heading for her truck.

He caught her wrist, stopping her forward motion. She looked first at his hand around her wrist, then slowly lifted her gaze to his, her expression bemused.

"You're supposed to be home in bed, getting rest," he said. "Not traipsing through the snow in search of tire prints. Besides, isn't there a unit coming from the station?"

The look of frustration in her eyes was almost comical. "They might obliterate them coming here."

"Call and warn them."

"Another vehicle could drive through—"

She wasn't going to let it go, he saw. "I don't have any way to make a mold for the tracks, Deputy," he pointed out. "And neither do you."

"We could take photographs."

"Of tire prints in the snow. At night."

Her mouth pressed to a tight line of annoyance. It was a cute look for her. In fact, his first impression that her features were more interesting than beautiful seemed, if not wrong, at least incomplete. There was an unexpected elegance to her strong bone structure, like the rugged beauty of a mountain peak or a winter-bare tree. A stripped-down sort of beauty that was all substance, all nature's bounty.

"Why don't we go inside, warm up until they get here?" he asked to distract himself from a rush of heat rising from deep in his belly. He gave a backward nod of his head, coaxing her toward the fireplace.

She gave him a reluctant look but didn't resist. It wasn't long before she was settling on the sofa and leaning toward the heat.

"How long have you been a deputy?" he asked, taking a seat beside her.

Her forehead crinkled at the question. "Almost ten years. I joined right out of college."

"Where did you go to college?"

Her slate-colored eyes narrowed slightly. "Texas Tech. You?"

"That information didn't come up in your background search?"

Her gaze narrowed. "I got a call about a missing person's case, so I didn't get to finish stripping your background bare."

The tart tone of her reply made him smile. "My bachelor's degree was from Wake Forest. My master's was from the University of Alabama."

"And now you're a carpenter?"

"After all that time and money, I realized I really hated accounting."

"Unfortunate." Her lips curved at the corners but didn't quite manage a smile. "Did you feel pressure to go into the family business anyway?"

Her tone suggested she understood that sort of pressure. "Your dad wanted you to go into the nuts-and-bolts biz?"

"I'm it for his branch of the family tree. No other kids, no living siblings. He's not that far from retiring, and I know he'd love it if I quit the sheriff's department and joined him in the sale of hardware." She laid her head against the back of the sofa, closing her eyes as she relaxed into the comfortable cushions. "Don't get me wrong. I'm so grateful for the life my dad's business gave me growing up. But I love being a cop."

"Even in a little place like Cold Creek?"

"Especially in a little place like Cold Creek." Her smile was genuine. "These are my people. I grew up with most of them. They're here in Cold Creek not because there's nowhere else they could go, but because there's nowhere else in this big, wide world they want to be. This place is in their blood, like it's in mine." She slanted a quick, sheepish look at him. "That was a little hokey, wasn't it?"

"No," he disagreed, meaning it. He had left his Tennessee roots behind a long time ago, but the pull of the mountains had never gone away. He'd felt it, a tug in the soul, during the months he'd recently spent in the Blue Ridge Mountains of southern Virginia.

He wondered if he could feel the same sort of tug from another place, especially one as flat and desolate as this part of Texas seemed to be.

Then he wondered why he was even thinking about spending more time in Texas than it took to get himself back into fighting shape, in case law enforcement couldn't round up all the stragglers left in the moribund Blue Ridge Infantry.

The sound of a car motor approaching on the highway dragged his attention away from that worrisome thought. He rose quickly and edged to the window to take a quick peek through the curtains.

A Barstow County Sheriff's Department cruiser had pulled up outside, parking next to Miranda's truck. "It's your colleague," he murmured as a tall young man stepped out of the cruiser and made his way through the crusty snow to the porch. He was the deputy who'd accompanied the sheriff earlier that day. What was his name?

Miranda followed him to the door as he opened it to the deputy's knock. "Robertson," she said briskly, joining him on the front porch rather than letting him in. She filled him in on what John had told her about the intruder. "He was wearing boot covers, so we don't have any tracks around the wreck, but Mr. Blake believes he drove away from behind that small stand of shrubs down the highway." She waved in the direction John had indicated. "He doesn't think any other vehicles have come through since then, thanks to the snow, so I thought we could get tire impressions, at least, to compare to the vehicle that took potshots at me earlier today."

Robertson took in everything she told him quietly, jotting notes. Then he looked up at Miranda, his blue eyes gentle with concern. "I thought the sheriff told you to get some rest."

John didn't miss the look of not-so-professional interest in the deputy's expression, but if Miranda was aware that the deputy had a bit of a crush on her, she didn't show it as she shrugged and said, "I was on the phone with Mr. Blake when he saw the intruder. I was at my dad's place, so I was several minutes closer than a cruiser could be."

Robertson flicked his gaze up to meet John's eyes. "I see."

"Well?" Miranda asked. "Did you bring the casting material?"

"It's out in the cruiser."

Miranda went inside to grab her jacket, zipped it up and started out the door after Robertson.

John caught up with her on the porch. "Do you think this is a good idea? It's freezing out here, and you took an awfully hard knock to the head earlier today. I'm pretty sure the EMTs told you to take it easy."

"I feel fine," she insisted, starting down the steps. But she swayed as she reached the bottom, and John hurried to give her a bracing hand before she ended up facedown in the snow.

"Yeah, I can see how fine you are," he murmured, tightening his grip around her arm to keep her from following Robertson. "Robertson strikes me as a capable guy."

"He doesn't know where to look for the tire prints."

"Neither do you, really. Come on." He tugged her arm, gently leading her back up the stairs to the house. He stopped before they entered. "Deputy Robertson?"

The deputy turned to look at him. "Yes?"

"Hold up. I'll go with you to show you where I saw the car. Let me get Deputy Duncan settled." He nudged Miranda into the house.

"You're making me look like a slacker in front of my fellow deputy," she grumbled, but she didn't fight him as he led her back to the fire and urged her to sit. "Do you know how hard it can be for a female cop to be taken seriously?"

"I do," he assured her. "But working when you've been told you have a concussion and need to rest doesn't exactly shower you with glory. It just makes you look overeager."

Her eyes narrowed. "You've been waiting to hit me with that all night, haven't you?"

He smiled. "No, but you know I'm right. What would you be thinking right now if the shoe was on the other foot, and it was Robertson out there staggering and reeling against doctor's orders, trying to prove he's a hotshot investigator?"

"I'd think he was an idiot," she conceded gruffly.

"I'll be right back." John laid his hand on her shoulder for a brief moment, his thumb brushing over her clavicle. The skin there was unexpectedly silky and delicate, an intriguing contrast to her tough, no-nonsense exterior.

He forced himself to turn and head out into the cold again, where he found Robertson waiting for him impatiently. He waved John to the passenger side and slid his own lanky body behind the steering wheel.

Robertson cranked up the heat to high as he pulled out on the highway. "Stop me short of where you saw the vehicle enter the highway," the deputy said. "Don't want to mess up the tracks."

John told him to stop about twenty yards from the

stand of shrubs that had hidden the intruder's vehicle. "It should be about thirty yards up the road. I think he must've parked his vehicle behind those shrubs because they'd block my view of the car from the house."

Robertson parked on the shoulder and pulled a flashlight from the cruiser's glove compartment. "Stay behind me," he told John.

John could have given the young deputy a few lessons on evidence retrieval, but he wasn't a cop and this wasn't his town. Plus, nobody liked a know-it-all.

The tire treads in the snow weren't hard to spot, and to John's surprise, they were nearly pristine. Apparently no other vehicles had passed on this side of the highway since the intruder drove away.

Robertson handed John the flashlight. "Can you hold this on the tracks while I get the casting material?"

John directed the beam toward the tire impressions, bending for a closer look. The treads had a pretty distinctive pattern. If the tire impressions the deputies had made earlier in the day were clear at all, they should be able to tell whether or not their intruder tonight was driving the same car.

Robertson stopped beside John. "Those are the same treads."

John looked up. "Are you sure?"

"I'm the one who took the impressions this afternoon after the tow truck hauled the cruiser away. These look like fairly new tires. Firestones, I think. The lab in Lubbock will tell us for sure."

"So I may have seen the man who shot at us this afternoon."

"Looks like."

"And we have no idea who he is or where he's gone."

"That's right."

John looked down the highway behind him, barely able to see his house, sitting small and isolated nearly a mile down the road.

And he'd left Miranda in there, alone and vulnerable, with a target on her back.

Chapter Five

She should be the one out there with Robertson. She was a deputy, damn it. A good one. And John Blake was a civilian.

Everybody was treating her as if she was made of glass, something delicate that needed to be wrapped in cotton batting and hidden away for her own protection.

She pushed to her feet, ignoring the aches and twinges in her muscles and bones, and crossed to the side window that looked out across the snowy plain between the house and the stand of shrubs where John had seen the mystery vehicle enter the highway.

The lights of Robertson's cruiser gleamed in the darkness down the road, and she could make out their silhouettes in the beams of the cruiser's headlights.

Tamping down frustration, she moved her gaze to the taped-off crime scene, wondering what the intruder had been looking for. The cruiser was already at the lab in Lubbock by now, set for examination. An attempted murder of a Texas lawman would put the case high on the list of priorities, she knew. At the very least, ballistics should give them some idea of what kind of weapon the assailant had used.

She couldn't remember how many shots had been

fired. Two had hit the cruiser for sure. And there'd been at least one other shot, hadn't there?

Could the intruder have been looking for a bullet that hadn't hit the cruiser? But why? It's not like they could keep the lab guys from finding the two slugs embedded in the cruiser.

She rubbed her aching head, wincing as her fingers brushed against the bandage covering the gash in her head. Nothing was making any sense. She wasn't likely to be on anyone's hit list. Most of the cases she investigated were minor-league domestic disturbances, drunk-and-disorderly calls and property theft, usually of animals or farming tools.

Could it have been mistaken identity?

But how could someone make a mistake about a well-marked Barstow County Sheriff's Department cruiser?

The cold night air seeped through the seams of the window, making her shiver and intensifying the ache in her battered body. She headed back to the warmth of the crackling fireplace but made herself stay on her feet. Sitting and wallowing in weariness and aching misery was not something she was going to allow herself to do.

She was young and strong. And, she reminded herself, she was all by herself in the house of a mysterious, intriguing stranger who'd just wandered into her town.

What were the odds, really, that she'd end up rolling her cruiser off the road just yards away from John Blake's house on the very day she ran into him at her father's hardware store?

Was it possible that her accident, and the subsequent assault on the two of them, was actually more about John than it was about her?

All very good questions, she had to admit. And she

might never have a better chance to take a look around John Blake's residence than right now.

The living room sprawled across the full width of the house, but there was little in it that gave her any clue about its occupant. No artwork on the walls, no personal photos on the mantel or the side tables. The lamps were simple and inexpensive, the kind she could find in any discount department store. The furniture was equally free of personality.

Average, she thought, squelching a smile. Like the man.

Except she was beginning to understand that John Blake was about as far from average as a man could get.

The bathroom revealed a few details. He liked his toothbrushes medium and his razors single bladed. He used soap, not bath gel. His medicine cabinet was stocked with both acetaminophen and ibuprofen, along with a prescription for a stronger painkiller from a pharmacy in Abingdon, Virginia. The prescription had been filled a month ago, but based on the pill count on the bottle, he hadn't taken any since the prescription had been filled.

He'd told her he'd spent some time in the hospital recently. He'd said it wasn't an accident.

Then what?

As she was heading from the bathroom toward the bedroom, she heard the rattle of keys in the door and detoured quickly toward the living room, making it to the fireplace before the door opened and John walked inside.

"Did you find anything?" she asked, trying not to sound out of breath, even though her pulse was pounding like a drum in her ears.

"Robertson is taking impressions of the tire treads."

John locked the door behind him and crossed to where she stood. "You look flushed. Feeling okay?"

"I'm fine," she assured him, swallowing her guilt. She was a cop, and John Blake was a stranger in town who had been conveniently nearby when someone tried to kill her. He wasn't at the top of her suspect list, since he'd been in the line of fire himself, but she'd be stupid not to at least take a look around and make sure he wasn't hiding some deep, dark secret.

Wouldn't she?

"Did Robertson say anything about the tire prints?" she asked as he dropped onto the sofa and stretched his hands toward the fire.

"Can't be sure until the lab takes a look, but Robertson thinks the tires are the same as the car we saw parked out front earlier today."

"But was that the car that took shots at us?"

"I think it almost had to be. Don't you?"

She frowned at the fire, wishing she could remember more about the events that had sent her and the cruiser careening off the highway. "The doctor at the clinic in town said I might never remember exactly what happened today."

"Or, in a day or two, you might remember everything." John put his hand on hers, his touch gentle. Undemanding.

But a ripple of animal awareness darted through her from the place his hand touched hers.

She didn't know whether she was relieved or disappointed when he drew his hand away and turned back to the fire. The fact that she didn't know made what she was about to say that much more difficult to utter.

"I think I should stay here tonight."

John's head snapped toward hers, a quizzical expression in his dark eyes. "I really don't know how to respond to that."

"I'm not supposed to sleep much tonight anyway," she said with what she hoped was a reassuring smile. "Because of the concussion. So I thought I could stay up, keep watch on the crime scene until morning."

"Or you could get someone from the station who hasn't been in a rollover car crash to stand watch outside," he suggested. "You should be resting, not playing cop."

"First off, I don't play cop. I am a cop."

"You know what I meant."

"Second, maybe things are different where you come from, but here in Cold Creek, we don't have many officers to spare. I'm here. I'm awake and I'm way too wired to go to sleep tonight. I can pull up a chair to that window, bundle up and keep an eye out for anybody else who might wander into the crime scene. You won't even know I'm here."

He gave a soft huff of laughter. "Believe me, Deputy, I'll know you're here."

She shot him a challenging look. "Is there some other reason you don't want me here? Do you have something to hide?"

"If I did, it's within my constitutional rights to do so, Deputy." He spoke with a firmness that tweaked her curiosity.

So he did have something to hide.

But what?

"Stay," he said after a long pause. "If that's what you want to do. I'll stay up with you. Keep you company."

"That's not necessary—"

"That's my condition for your staying in my house overnight," he said firmly. "Take it or leave it."

She looked at him through narrowed eyes, debating her options. He was right—if he had secrets, keeping them was his right unless she could prove they broke any laws within her jurisdiction. And if she wanted to stay at his house, she would simply have to abide by his rules.

No matter how much inconvenience—or temptation—they might pose.

THERE WERE THREE WOUNDS, he saw as he assessed the damage quickly from his hiding place behind a rocky outcropping near the top of the ridge. Dallas Cole and Nicki Jamison had gotten away, along with the woman and the boy they'd rescued from the cabin, but the woman's husband and his henchmen were out here in the woods somewhere, looking for him.

It was dark, so there was a chance they wouldn't be able to follow the track of blood he'd left as he ran, but if the good guys didn't show up before morning, John was going to be in a hell of a lot of trouble.

Who was he kidding? He was already in trouble. The wound in his shoulder had, at the very least, cracked his collarbone, the slightest movement of his left arm sending agony racing through his body. There was also a through-and-through wound just above his hip—that one seemed to have missed the bone, though his jeans were now soaked with blood from the wound.

The one he was worried about was the bullet in his side. It was still in there somewhere. John wasn't sure what it might have hit on its way in.

And he was starting to feel very, very woozy. Too woozy to keep his eyes open any longer.

"John?" The voice was low. Female. Faintly famil-iar. It seemed far away at first, then louder. "John, wake up..."

He snapped his eyes open, bracing for the pain. It was there, in his shoulder most strongly, but still little more than a twinge. He wasn't in the woods, he realized, as early morning sunlight angling through the window in front of him made him squint.

The voice belonged to the bleary-eyed redhead curled up in an armchair next to his, gazing at him with a faint smile on her pale lips. "You told me if you fell asleep to wake you by six."

Right. The stakeout. The deputy with the head injury had managed to stay awake, but he'd drifted off like an old man.

He stretched, grimacing at the ache in his bones. "I take it nobody wandered into your crime scene?"

She slanted a sheepish look at him. "I might have dozed off an hour or so just before dawn."

"I don't think he planned to come back. He didn't spot whatever he was looking for, so he left."

"You don't think it's because he spotted you watch-ing him?"

"I don't think he could have seen me." John stretched carefully, all too cognizant of the limitations of his re-covery. The collarbone fracture had mended, but too vi-olent an arm or shoulder movement could still make his nerves jangle. The other injuries to his side and the mus-cles over his hip were going to be painful for a while, but it was a dull ache that usually went away after the muscles warmed up.

"What kind of injuries did you have?" Miranda had turned in the armchair until she faced him, her long limbs tucked up under her and the blanket wrapped warmly around her. In the rosy light of morning, her sleepy face looked soft and young, giving her a delicate beauty he wouldn't have associated with her if he hadn't seen it for himself.

"Fractured clavicle and some muscle damage in my side," he answered vaguely.

"You said it wasn't an accident."

"No."

Her auburn eyebrows notched upward. "Okay."

Great. He'd just made her more curious, not less. "Actually, a hunting injury." And it was true, in a way.

"Deer?"

"No."

This time, her lips quirked with amused frustration. "I never could manage to enjoy hunting. I mean, I get the point of it from a conservation standpoint, and I like venison stew as much as the next person—"

He had to put her out of her misery. "Actually, I wasn't the one doing the hunting."

Her brow crinkled, but before she could say anything, her phone rang. She dug it from the pocket of her jeans and grimaced before answering. "Hi, Dad. Yes, I'm still here." She slanted a quick look at John. "I know, but—"

John walked away to give her a little privacy, but the room wasn't big enough to avoid hearing her end of what was clearly a paternal lecture. With a heavy sigh she sank deeper into the chair where she'd passed the night and settled in to listen.

John headed for the kitchen to start a pot of coffee. While he was waiting for the coffeemaker to finish, he searched his refrigerator for something that might pass for breakfast. He usually made do with coffee alone, but he'd bought a dozen eggs earlier in the week. He could make omelets. Every guy with any self-respect could make an omelet, right?

He had the eggs sizzling nicely in a skillet by the time Miranda wandered into the kitchen. "Hungry?"

She gave him an odd look but admitted she was. "May I help myself to the coffee?"

He waved his hand at the pot, and she poured a cup, stirring in a packet of sweetener from a jar sitting next to the pot. "Want a cup?" she asked as she stirred her own and gave it a sip.

"Black. One sweetener." He glanced at her over his shoulder. "What do you know? The way you like yours."

She smiled and made him a matching cup of coffee. "You didn't have to go to the trouble."

"I was hungry," he said and decided it wasn't exactly a lie. He *was* hungry, and she didn't need to know that if she wasn't there, he wouldn't have bothered cooking. "Your dad wasn't happy about your disobeying doctor's orders?"

"Not even a little. He wanted to take my keys away last night, but I threatened to arrest him." She grinned. "He didn't believe me, but at least he stopped grabbing at my keys. And he's even going to go by my house this morning on his way to work to feed my cats."

"You have cats?"

She slanted a narrow-eyed look his way. "Two. You have a problem with cats?"

"No. I like cats, actually. I just haven't been in a position to have pets in a while. What kind of cats do you have?"

"One's a silver tabby—Rex. And the other is a tortoiseshell named Ruthie." Over the cup of coffee, her eyes smiled, soft with affection. "They were litter mates I found while I was out on a call a couple of years ago. The mama cat had been hit by a car, and that had led to a drunken brawl over who had done it and—" She waved her hands. "Anyway, there were two little kittens nobody wanted, so I took 'em. And don't worry, they're neutered and spayed so I won't be having any surprise kittens."

"Good for you," he said, meaning it. Growing up, he'd seen his share of feral cats and kittens out fending for themselves and usually ending up as roadkill or coyote bait. "Nice of your dad to go feed them for you."

"I think it was his apology for being such a bear last night about my driving over here."

"He has a point, though. Beyond your very recent head injury, I mean. You're the victim. That's a pretty good reason why you really shouldn't be part of this investigation."

"I don't know if you've noticed, but this is a small town."

"No, really?"

She smiled at his tone. "We have fifteen deputies covering this whole county. And while that may seem like a lot, given the small population, we have a lot of miles to cover. I was a witness to what happened to me, even if some of the details are a little fuzzy. Who better to investigate it?"

"You still don't remember how the wreck happened?"

She shook her head. "I was out on a call—I remember that much. I talked to the sheriff, and he confirmed it. We'd gotten an anonymous call about a woman we've been trying to locate—a woman who seems to be missing."

"Seems to be?"

"Well, she's gone off without telling anyone before. She doesn't hold a steady job, so it's not like anyone's waiting for her to show up for her shift or anything. And she doesn't really have any family to keep an eye out for her anymore."

"Maybe she just moved without telling anyone."

"Except all her stuff is still at her trailer. I mean, there might be some things missing, but a lot of her clothes and all of her furniture is still there."

John could tell from the concern in Miranda's eyes that she was personally worried about the missing woman. "How long has she been missing?"

"The last anyone remembers seeing her was three weeks ago. Until yesterday, when that call came in. Someone claimed to see Delta—that's her name, Delta McGraw. Anyway, someone called and left a tip with the desk sergeant that he saw Delta hitchhiking on Route 7."

"So that's why you were out here yesterday?"

She nodded. "I drove past the place where she was supposed to have been spotted, but I didn't see anyone. I made one more stop to check on a farmer who's been complaining about someone or something stealing her eggs, then it started to snow, so I decided I'd better head back to the station before I got stuck out here."

"What happened next?"

"I don't know. I don't remember anything after I made the turn onto Route 7 heading back to town." She poked at the remainder of her omelet. "It's very strange, having this big blank place in my memory. I know something happened. I remember the aftermath. But what happened before—"

"That's not uncommon with concussions."

"That's what the doctor said. Knowing that doesn't

really help, though. I need to remember what happened. Why it happened. My roof lights were on—and apparently I made a call to the station to tell them what was happening."

"Right. I talked to the desk sergeant when I called for help. He said you'd said someone was following you."

"I don't remember that at all. But obviously, someone was. Chambers—that was the sergeant at the desk when I called it in—said I gave a description of the vehicle. Dark blue Ford Taurus."

"Same as the car we saw parked out on the highway. And apparently the car that was driving around here last night, too."

"I must not have gotten the plate number, though. Someone would have told me." She started to say something else, but the trill of her cell phone lying on the table beside her interrupted. She frowned at the display and picked up the phone, meeting John's gaze with an upward flick of her eyebrows. "Hi, Dad."

Her mild amusement disappeared almost immediately, her gray eyes darkening with anger. "How bad?"

Her father's answer made her jaw clench tightly. "Stay put, I'm on my way. I'll call the station." She hung up the phone and pushed to her feet, already halfway out of the kitchen.

"What's going on?" John asked as he caught up with her in the living room.

She grabbed her jacket and shrugged it on, turning to look at him, her eyes ablaze with fury. "Somebody tossed my house last night."

Chapter Six

Miranda came to a stop in the middle of the living room, her head aching and her stomach in knots at the sight of the mess intruders had made of her normally tidy living room. Sofa cushions had been removed from the frame and ripped apart, despite having zippered covers that could have been easily taken off. Books had been pulled from the built-in bookshelves that flanked the fireplace and left scattered on the floor beneath.

In the kitchen, the cabinets had been emptied and any open containers had been poured into the sink, creating a mess that would be a nightmare to clean up. She'd probably have to have a plumber in to clean out the pipes.

Her mattress had been stripped and cut open, just like the cushions from the sofa, and her closets emptied, the clothes left scattered on the gutted mattress and floor. The sheer level of cleanup that lay ahead of Miranda was enough to make her want to curl up in a corner and cry. Instead, she finished her circuit of the vandalized house and returned to the living room.

"What the hell were they looking for?" she asked, lifting her gaze to meet the troubled eyes of her father.

"I don't know." He made a helpless openhanded gesture toward her, and she crossed to where he stood, letting him wrap her up in a bear hug that made her feel both small and safe at the same time.

Boots on the front porch announced the return of Miles Randall, giving her time to extricate herself from her father's embrace and face the sheriff with her chin held high. Coy Taylor, who'd come on the call with the sheriff, gave her a sympathetic nod as he entered and closed out the cold behind him.

"The shed out back has been tossed, too," Randall told her, his dark eyes apologetic. "Can you tell if anything's been taken?"

She shook her head. "Anything worth any money is still here—TV, stereo equipment, appliances. I don't own any valuable jewelry, and my laptop was in my truck, locked in the chest. Was the lawn mower still in the shed? And the generator?"

Taylor nodded.

"Then they didn't take anything worth anything out of there, either."

"We can dust the place for prints," Taylor said, "but I doubt we'll get much, and all it'll do is make a bigger mess for you to clean up."

She couldn't argue with that. The destruction of property might end up being a misdemeanor, but she couldn't see that anything had been stolen. Probably a couple of kids, doped up or, hell, maybe just bored and looking for something to do. "I called my insurance man, but he's out on some weather-related calls, so he said he'd trust me to just take some photos of the destruction. Although he's not sure off the top of his head how much will be covered by my homeowner's policy."

"Have you found the cats yet?" a quiet voice asked from the corner of the room.

Miranda looked past the sheriff to lock gazes with John Blake, who'd insisted on following her to her place earlier. He'd settled there in the corner, keeping out of the way while Miranda, the sheriff and Coy Taylor had taken a look around the house.

"They're hiding under the bed," she said, blinking back hot tears that burned behind her eyes. "Once everything settles down, they'll come out."

"Honey, if you need me, I can call Mary to cover the shop—"

Miranda put her hand on her father's arm. "I'm fine. It's just a matter of cleaning everything up, and I can handle that on my own."

"I'll help," John said.

Miranda's father looked at the man in the corner, his eyes narrowed in mild speculation. Miranda tugged at his arm, drawing his attention back to her. "Go open the shop. If you leave now, you won't be late."

Gil gave her a kiss on the uninjured side of her forehead. "Don't overdo. And when you tire out, your bed's still waiting at the house." With a nod to the sheriff and Coy Taylor, he left the house, his boot thuds heavy on the wooden front porch.

Sheriff Randall gave her a thoughtful look. "I could call some of the guys off duty to come give you some help—"

She nearly recoiled at the thought. It was hard enough to be seen as an equal without having to turn to the boys for help. "I've got it covered, sir. But thanks for the offer."

"Let me know if you change your mind." Randall nodded for Coy Taylor to follow him out. The desk sergeant turned and flashed a sympathetic smile at Miranda before he left, closing the door behind him.

She let go of a deep sigh and looked at John. "You don't have to stay and help. It would be asking too much."

"You didn't ask. I offered."

"You know what I mean."

He stepped out of the corner and met her in the middle of the ravaged room. "You should be resting, but you won't. So I'm going to stick around and make sure you don't undo all my first-aid work from yesterday."

Her lips curved at his dry words. "Your work, huh?"

He just let the corners of his mouth twitch upward as he nodded at the sofa. "I think that's a loss."

"My bed, too." She quelled the urge to cry. "Just the mattress and box springs, though. I think the frame is still fine. I guess I need to make a trip to Plainview to pick up a new set." Her savings could handle replacing what she'd lost, though it would make a pretty big dent in her nest egg.

"I'm not sure you should drive to Plainview by yourself while you're still concussed, especially with the roads still messy for the next few hours. Why don't you take up your dad on his offer of a place to sleep tonight? Tomorrow, if you're feeling better, you can drive to Plainview and pick up a new mattress set."

"You have no idea how easy—" She clamped her mouth shut, appalled by how much personal information she'd almost revealed to a virtual stranger. Her relationship with her father was loving but complicated, and admitting just how complicated would make her much more vulnerable than she intended to be with anyone, especially someone she'd met only a day ago. "I just—I just need to stand on my own two feet."

"Okay." He nodded slowly. "But it's just a bed for one more night."

"There's a thrift store in Cold Creek. They might have a sofa I could buy to replace this one. I could sleep on the sofa until I have time to get a new mattress set."

His eyes narrowed as he looked at her for a long moment. "How about this? We clean up as much as we can, then I drive you to town to go sofa shopping. That way, I can help you load it in the truck and you don't have to drive while concussed. And you can sleep in your own house tonight. If that's what you want."

An odd tone to his voice gave her pause. "If it's what I want?"

He was quiet a moment, as if considering what he wanted to say. Finally, he walked over to the bookcases and started picking up books. When he spoke, his voice was deceptively casual. "Do you have any enemies?"

"Not that I know of."

"Not even someone you've arrested?"

She set another book in the bookcase next to the one he'd just restored. "Don't overestimate the number of people I've actually arrested. In a county this small, most police work is about keeping order and not much more."

He waved his arm around at the mess. "This looks personal."

Spoken like a man who knew what it was like to be a target, she realized. A dozen questions rolled through her aching head, but she had a feeling asking them outright, especially now, might send him running. If she wanted to know any of John Blake's secrets, she was going to have to be patient. Let him get used to her, feel secure enough to let down his guard.

"Well, look there," John murmured, his gaze slanting to his right.

Miranda followed his gaze and saw Ruthie creeping

slowly into the living room, her eyes wide with alarm as she scanned the room for threats.

"Hey, sweet girl," she crooned to the spooked cat.

Ruthie's ears pricked at the familiar sound of her voice, but her green-eyed gaze darted warily toward John. He ignored her, straightening the books they'd returned to the shelf with small, economical movements.

So he did understand cats, she thought.

The longer John ignored Ruthie, the bolder she became, moving slowly across the room. Her tail rose finally in a question mark, and she looked up at Miranda, her mouth forming a voiceless meow.

Miranda bent and gave Ruthie's ears a scratch. "You hungry, sweet cakes?"

"Does she usually answer you?" John asked softly without turning his head, his voice tinted with humor.

"In her own way." She led Ruthie into the kitchen, where she found that the canister of dry cat food had been dumped into the sink along with most of the other open containers.

The urge to cry overwhelmed her, and she sank into the only chair that hadn't been overturned. Ruthie jumped in her lap and rubbed her head against Miranda's chin, eliciting the tears she'd been trying to resist.

She pressed her hot face against the cat's tricolor fur. "Oh, sweetie, we're going to have to go get you some food, aren't we?"

"Your dad's shop carries pet food, doesn't it?" John's voice was a soft rumble from the doorway.

She looked up, blinking back her tears. "Yes."

"I'll run get a bag."

"He knows the brand they like." She flashed him a grateful smile. "Tell him to put it on my tab."

John gave a nod. "You sure you'll be okay here by yourself?"

She managed not to bristle at the question. "I'm armed. I'll keep cleaning up while you're gone."

He disappeared down the hall. A moment later, she heard the door open and close.

Releasing a deep sigh, she eased Ruthie from her lap and started picking up the overturned chairs around the breakfast table.

"THOSE BASTARDS." GIL DUNCAN'S voice was a deep rumble of anger as he heaved the bag of cat food over the counter and handed it to John. "She worked damn hard to make a nice home for herself. I tell you what, it was like a gut punch seein' what they'd done to her things. A real gut punch."

"Do you have any idea who'd do such a thing to Miranda?" John tucked the bag under his good arm. "I don't know her well, but everyone I've talked to seems to think the world of her."

Gil's smile was genuinely proud. "She's a good woman, like her mama was. Smart girl, too. It had to be kids, don't you think? All those hormones and restless energy just wantin' to bust out all over, but nowhere in this little town to let it rip. And these days, folks don't teach their young'uns to respect other people's things. Hell, they probably recorded what they did and put it up on YouFace or whatever you call it." Gil grinned sheepishly. "Lord, I'm soundin' just like my granddaddy, ain't I?"

John grinned back at him, deciding he liked Miranda's father. "Miranda mentioned something about a case she'd been working—a missing woman?"

"Yeah. Delta McGraw." Gil shook his head. "That

girl's had a hell of a life, and I don't reckon anybody'd blame her if she'd just picked up and left town for good. But Miranda seems to think she should've been back in town by now."

"Is she a young woman?"

"A little younger than my Mandy—maybe a couple of years younger. But in some ways, she seems a lot older. Life's been harder on her. Her mama ran off when she was real little, so it was left to that daddy of hers to raise her. All he knew how to do was make her his accomplice."

"He's a criminal?"

"Was. Con man, mainly. Small cons, get-rich-quick schemes. You know the sort. People liked him anyway, because he was that kind of fellow. Made you laugh even when he was fleecing you blind." Gil shrugged. "I reckon folks tended to give him a lot of leeway, too, because his wife ran off when his little girl was so young and he was left to take care of her."

"Is he dead or incarcerated?"

Gil gave him an odd look. "Dead. Big rig versus pickup truck. Big rig wins."

John grimaced. "So you don't think this missing girl has anything to do with your daughter's problems?"

Gill gave him a narrow-eyed look. "You seem awfully interested for someone who just met her."

"She nearly died in my side yard. We both ended up dodging bullets. I guess that makes me feel like I have a stake in her well-being," he answered truthfully.

"You a cop or something?"

"I'm a carpenter," John replied.

"Hmm." Gil didn't say anything more, turning to greet

another customer entering the store. John took the cat food and headed back to his truck.

The snow had melted off by midmorning, leaving the roads wet but clear, and traffic on the highway was starting to pick up. After John slid behind the steering wheel of his truck and buckled up, he called Miranda.

She answered on the second ring. "Checking up on me?" she asked.

"Just making sure you and the cats were still okay. Did the other one ever come out?"

"He did, and he's not very patient when he's hungry."

"I'll be there in a few minutes." He hung up and started the truck, but on second thought, he turned it off again and picked up his phone. He dialed another number and waited for the answer.

A moment later, Quinn's voice came over the line. "Marbury Motors twenty-four-hour hotline."

"It's me," John said. "Several things have happened since I talked to you last, and I guess you need to know."

Quinn was silent while John gave him a succinct but thorough recap of all that had happened since their last phone call. "Everybody swears there's no reason for anyone to target her, but—"

"But you're wondering if it has anything to do with the BRI."

"Del McClintock's still at large. He nearly killed me once—"

"He doesn't know your real identity."

"That we know of. If I've brought that mess here to Texas—"

"I really don't believe you have. But if you do something to start drawing attention to yourself there, you might."

"Fine." He made himself relax, even though he could

still feel prickles of unease running up and down the skin of his neck. "They're not after me."

"You don't sound as if you believe it."

"I don't think dropping my guard will help anyone."

"If it's not you, then it's the deputy. Are you sure there's no reason someone might want her out of the way?"

He thought about what Gil Duncan had told him about the missing person case Miranda had been investigating. "Maybe," he admitted. "And maybe you can help. Can you see if you can find me some info on a woman named Delta McGraw?"

JOHN ARRIVED WITH the cat food within ten minutes, and soon Ruthie and Rex were happily crunching their kibble while John took in the improvements she'd managed to accomplish while he was gone.

The sink was still a disaster area, but she'd picked up all the chairs and swept up the mess on the floor. In the living room, she'd finished putting the books in the shelves and piled the ripped-up cushions onto the sagging frame of the sofa.

"You've made some headway," he said, sounding impressed. But the look he shot her way made it clear that he could see right through her attempt at pretending she wasn't feeling like hell. "Why don't you rest a bit and let me catch up?"

"I'm fine."

"As fine as a concussed, sleep-deprived person could be," he agreed. "But if we're going sofa shopping in town a little later, you should rest up."

She leaned against the door frame that led into the hall

and crossed her arms, looking at him through narrowed eyes. "Why are you doing all this for me?"

"You mean helping you buy a sofa?"

She nodded. "Yeah, that. And everything else you've done to help me."

"I need another badge for my Boy Scout uniform."

She smiled. "There's a furniture-moving badge?"

"You sound skeptical."

He wasn't nearly as average as she'd originally thought, she was beginning to see. His eyes might be a muddy sort of hazel green, but they twinkled brightly when he was amused, like sunlight sparkling on a murky stream. His ordinary features seemed to come to life when he smiled, carving interesting lines in his normally unremarkable face. He wasn't ripped like a bodybuilder, but his body was well-proportioned, his muscles lean and well-defined beneath his long-sleeved T-shirt when he bent to pick up a picture frame she hadn't gotten to yet.

He looked at the photograph in the broken frame, a smile curving his lips. "Is this you and your mom?"

She pushed away from the door frame and crossed to where he stood, looking at the photo. "Yes. I was six. First day of school. My dad took that photo as Mama was walking me out the door to the bus." She'd been crying a little, the tears still sparkling on her cheeks in the photo. "She said I'd love it if I just gave it a chance."

"Was she right?"

She looked into his curious gaze. "She always was."

"She's not still around, is she." He didn't phrase it as a question.

"No. She died when I was still a kid. Hit head-on by a drunk driver over in Plainview. She was a nurse at the hospital there."

"I'm sorry."

She studied the photograph, relieved to find it hadn't been scratched by the broken glass of the frame. "Some of the photos are irreplaceable. Why would someone trash the place like this? What on earth could they have been looking for?"

John reached out for her, and to her surprise, she let him pull her into a comforting hug, feeling further evidence of his lean muscularity. He smelled good, too, she realized, despite a long night sleeping in a chair. He must have showered before she'd shown up at his place the night before.

She, however, hadn't showered since the previous morning. God only knew what she must smell like about now. With a blush, she extricated herself from his arms and flashed a sheepish smile. "Why don't we just get the sofa shopping over with now?" she suggested. "So I'll have somewhere to pass out when I finally hit the wall."

To her relief, he agreed, and she grabbed her jacket and followed him out to the truck.

John Blake was proving to be a surprising temptation, one she wasn't used to having to struggle against. Yes, she was finding him attractive, but if that had been the extent of it, she'd have been able to resist quite easily. It wasn't that she was immune to physical attraction—she'd had her share of boyfriends over the years, enjoyed their company and more—but she'd always found it easy enough to walk away when the time came for a relationship to end.

There was something about the mysterious newcomer with his murky eyes and murkier intentions that were proving to be damn near irresistible on a whole other level.

If there was anything she couldn't walk away from, it was a mystery.

And John Blake was nothing if not a mystery.

Chapter Seven

Miranda had hit the wall, as she called it, around three that afternoon, after they'd managed to clean up and bag up most of the trash in her house. It had taken a little longer than John had expected, mostly because Miranda had insisted on sifting through everything they picked up in search of trace evidence.

"Do you really think you're going to find any?" John had asked, dutifully holding the trash bag for her while she dumped a load of fiberfill stuffing from the shredded sofa.

"Probably not," she'd admitted with a grimace of a smile. "But I wouldn't be a good cop if I didn't check."

He'd talked her into leaving the bedroom for later, and she'd settled, finally, on the thrift store sofa she'd purchased in town earlier.

"It's in better shape than the original," she'd drawled upon seeing it in the previously bare spot in the middle of her living room. She'd tested it out for napping comfort and promptly fell asleep, leaving John on his own for the next couple of hours.

He was tempted to head back home to see if the crime scene unit had finished processing the scene of the wreck, but he didn't want to leave Miranda alone, asleep and vulnerable, in a house that had been ransacked in the past twenty-four hours. He settled, instead, in the only chair in the living room that hadn't been relieved of its stuffing— a wooden rocking chair that had no stuffing at all, only a slightly sagging woven cane seat that creaked a bit as he sat down.

It was solidly made, the handiwork painstaking and careful. An antique, he thought, not one of those mass-produced, overpriced jobs you could buy in almost any chain store.

He had trained as an accountant, a job he hated. He'd worked twice as an undercover agent, a job he loved, but now, as it had the first time, fate and circumstances had forced him out again, leaving his future in flux.

But carpentry was the skill he was actually good at. His grandfather on his mother's side had been a true artist with wood, and John had been the only grandchild who'd been interested enough to sit for hours at his side, watching him work and learning all the skills and tricks of the trade.

Blanchard Building was a real company that employed real craftsmen from time to time, and his cover for being in Cold Creek was a real job, using his carpentry skills to renovate the home where he was living for the next couple of months.

It was also a way to recover some of his physical strength and stamina, because carpentry could be a physically taxing skill, as he'd learned over the past week, when his rusty joints and muscles had been forced into work after almost a week in the hospital and another three weeks of physical therapy.

As he quietly rocked, the two cats wandered into the living room from somewhere in the back of the house.

They crept cautiously around the new sofa, sniffing the upholstery from end to end before they decided it was no threat. One after the other, Ruthie first, then Rex, jumped gracefully onto the sofa and settled side by side behind the crook of Miranda's knees. Ruthie gave John a wide-eyed stare for a couple of moments before she closed her eyes to nap.

John watched Miranda sleep for a little while, enjoying the view of her face soft with sleep. Awake, she was almost militantly competent, a woman of substance and power, but asleep, he saw a hint of girlish softness he suspected she tried to hide. He'd worked with female agents at The Gates, though largely from a distance, and he'd seen a similar sort of dichotomy in each of them, as well. Strength before softness, almost always. It was the only way they knew to survive in a world where men outnumbered women by a substantial degree.

He admired Miranda's strength. But it was that hint of softness that intrigued him the most, made him wonder what other secrets she hid behind that tough-girl exterior.

For one thing, despite her rangy build, she had delicious curves. He'd felt them beneath her clothes when she'd let him give her a comforting hug. Firm, round breasts and delectably flaring hips that would tempt a eunuch to let his hands wander. She'd pulled away from his embrace just in time, because John Blake was a lot of things, but a eunuch wasn't one of them.

With his mind drifting to dangerous places once more, he pushed to his feet and wandered around the house, looking for a distraction.

He found it in the back of the house.

He hadn't really noticed that the kitchen took up only half of the back part of the house. To the left of the kitchen, there was another room that hadn't been touched by the intruders, as far as John could tell. That was probably because it was nothing but a frame of a room, with no drywall or flooring. Not an addition, he decided as he took in the handiwork. Part of the framework was obviously older, the wood darkened and worn with age.

Repair work?

"Tornado damage." Miranda's voice behind him made him jump.

He turned and found her watching him with sleepy eyes the color of a stormy sky. The cats wound in complicated patterns around her legs and each other.

He remembered the order of two-by-fours she'd picked up at the hardware store the day he met her. "Are you rebuilding it yourself?"

"Slowly," she said with a rueful smile. "I wanted to do it myself. To see if I could."

"It's complicated work. Do you know what you're doing?"

"I've helped with other building jobs," she answered, not appearing to take his skeptical question personally. "My dad owns a hardware store, you know. I've grown up around builders and saved for college by working summers on building crews." She pushed her sleep-tousled hair away from her face. "I've just never been my own foreman before."

"When did the tornado hit?"

"Last November. Late in the season. I was lucky. It was a small twister and the wind only caught the edge of the house. I was working. Got home after a long day of dealing with multiple tornadoes to find the back corner of my house gone."

"How'd the cats handle that experience?"

"About like they did this time with the intruder. Hid under the bed for hours until they were convinced the freight train that hit the house was gone." She stifled a yawn.

"You should go back to sleep."

"So you can snoop around my house in peace?"

"I wasn't." He stopped before he told the easy lie. "Okay, I was snooping, a little."

"Sadly, my life is an open book." She stepped past him into the room, then turned suddenly to look at him. "Why do I get the feeling you can't say the same thing?"

Because he couldn't, he thought. His life hadn't really been an open book since his college graduation, over fifteen years earlier, when a man named Alexander Quinn had introduced himself by another name altogether and asked him to take a drive.

His CIA career had ended almost before it began, but the things he'd seen and done during that short time had changed the way he approached life. There had been no such thing as a normal life for him, even when he'd been working for his father at the accounting firm. There'd certainly been nothing ordinary about his life as Alexander Quinn's undercover operative in southern Virginia.

"Your name is John Blake. I'm pretty sure about that." She stepped closer to him, taking full advantage of her height to crowd his space. "Although you seemed to disappear for a while between your time at your family accounting firm and showing up on the payroll of Blanchard Building."

"I was finding myself."

She laughed, a deep belly laugh that made him want to laugh with her. "You know what? I'm not sure I want to know what you were doing. I have a feeling the truth wouldn't be nearly as interesting as what I'm imagining."

Damn, he wanted to kiss her. It would be so easy; she was standing there, near enough that he could reach out and pull her to him, close the space between their bodies. He remembered how her body had felt pressed to his all too briefly.

The air between them electrified, and her laughter faded until she was gazing up at him, her eyes luminous and her lips trembling apart.

So very easy to kiss her...

He pulled back, trying to remember why he was in Texas in the first place. He was here to lie low, not start an affair with a Barstow County sheriff's deputy. She was already curious about his background. She was smart and she had the resources at her command that could unravel a lot of his secrets.

He needed distance from her, not closeness.

Except someone wanted her dead. And protecting people was his business these days.

As she took a step back as well, her eyes narrowing, he said the first thing that came to mind. "Tell me about Delta McGraw."

She took another step back. "Who told you about Delta?"

"You did."

"I didn't mention her name."

"Your father told me her name."

Her brow furrowed, her eyes darkening to thunderclouds. "You talked to my dad about one of my cases?" She pushed past him and stalked down the hallway, her shoulders squared with anger.

He followed her into the living room. "Someone tried

to kill you. And me, in case you forgot. That same person came back to my house looking for God knows what. And someone also tossed this place and left no stone, canister or sofa cushion unturned."

She turned to face him. "That could have been kids."

He arched an eyebrow at her, and she sighed.

"Fine. It was probably related. But what do you think any of it has to do with Delta?"

"You said yourself it's the only real case you're investigating. And didn't you say that the call that sent you out to Route 7 in the first place was about Delta? Someone had seen her hitchhiking or something?"

"Right. But I didn't see her anywhere."

"Maybe you weren't supposed to."

Her eyes narrowed. "You mean that call was to lure me out there?"

"The weathermen were predicting snow. Hardly anyone was out on the roads by that hour because of the dire reports."

"But someone would have to know I was the one who took the call."

"It was your case. You would have been the first person the call would have gone to, right?"

She nodded, looking thoughtful. "But that still doesn't answer the question of why someone would run me off the road and try to shoot me. That's pretty drastic for a missing persons case."

"Unless she's not just missing."

"You think someone killed her." Her expression remained mostly neutral, but there was a flicker of pain in her eyes.

"How close were you and Delta?"

"Not real close. But I guess about as close as she'd let

anyone get." There was a hint of hesitation in her voice. "I tried to help her a few times. Adjusting to life without her dad was really strange for her. They had a…difficult relationship."

"Because he was a con artist?"

She frowned. "Did my dad tell you that, too?"

Busted. "I asked about her. He didn't know he was spilling state secrets or anything."

"Why didn't you just ask me?"

"Because you'd probably pull that whole police-business thing and keep it to yourself."

She shot him a look of consternation that told him his words had hit the mark. He was right and she knew it. "It *is* police business," she said weakly.

"And you weren't the only one who nearly got killed yesterday." He stepped closer to her, willing her not to back away. He needed her to understand that he had a stake in this mystery, too, because there was no way in hell he was going to let her whip out her badge and try to shut him out.

Her eyes went wide and unexpectedly soft. "I know. But you were only involved because of me."

He knew she was probably right. But there was that little sliver of possibility that he'd been the one who was the real target, wasn't there? Quinn didn't think anyone from the BRI had tracked him down to Texas, but despite his downright mythical reputation, Quinn didn't really know everything. He could be wrong.

And all it took to get a man killed was to drop his guard just once in the wrong place at the wrong time.

"You're not just a carpenter, are you?"

He snapped his focus back to her. She was looking at him with sudden understanding.

"I don't know what—"

"A year overseas working for a global marketing firm. But you're an accountant. Or a carpenter. Why doesn't that compute?"

"Miranda—"

"And there's a whole year missing more recently, until you show up a couple of weeks ago on the payroll of Blanchard Building in Garza County. But as far as I can tell, the entire time you've been on their payroll, you've been living here in Cold Creek."

"So?"

"You don't react to things like a civilian."

"I'm not a cop."

"No, you don't have that vibe," she agreed. "But I'm betting you've done some sort of intelligence work. No record of time in the military, so I'm guessing CIA or NSA. Maybe Homeland Security."

He decided to play it for a joke. "I'd tell you, but then I'd have—"

"To kill me. Right." She shook her head. "Don't worry. I'm not going to ask any more questions. Promise."

Good, he thought, though he wasn't sure it was a promise she'd be able to keep. Curiosity glittered in her eyes like diamonds, even now. How long would she be able to keep that desire to know at bay?

MIRANDA HAD MANAGED to find a bottle of bath gel that hadn't been dumped down the bathroom sink and took a long, hot soak while John went to the barbecue joint a half mile down the road to pick up takeout. By seven that evening, she was full and growing sleepy, but he showed no signs of leaving.

"You're not planning on leaving, are you?" she asked, stifling a yawn.

John met her gaze. "I'd rather not."

She leaned toward him. "Why, Mr. Blake, is that a proposition?"

He leaned toward her, as well. "Well, that depends."

"On what?"

"On whether you're being facetious or serious."

Good question. She sat back slowly. "Facetious." Sort of.

He smacked his hand against his heart, feigning pain. "Ouch. I still want to stay, though."

"You do realize I'm a well-trained law enforcement officer."

"I do."

"But you still think I need a bodyguard."

"Even a well-trained law enforcement officer sometimes needs backup."

She waved her hand toward the newly bare room. "I just have the one sofa."

"I can sleep on the floor."

"But you're still recuperating from a hunting accident."

His eyes narrowed, not missing the hint of skepticism in her voice. "Yes, but you made it plain you don't intend to share the sofa."

Before she could think up a decent comeback, headlights flashed across the front windows and she heard the rumble of a car engine rattle to a stop. Adrenaline flooded her system in a couple of heartbeats, and she reached for the holstered M&P 40 on the side table next to the sofa.

John was on her heels as she crossed to the window and looked out. "Who is it?"

She nearly crumpled with relief when she recognized her father's old Silverado. "It's my dad." She peered at the truck bed. "And I think that's a mattress set in the back of his truck.

GIL DUNCAN'S EARLIER friendliness had faded into a suspicious sort of watchfulness, John noticed as Miranda's father finished helping him position the mattress and box springs into the existing bed frame. "You're still here?"

John stifled a smile. "I am."

"Hmm." He glanced toward the open doorway, as if keeping an eye out for Miranda, who was still in the living room, checking in with the sheriff's department to see if there had been any word yet from the lab. "Any particular reason why?"

"Just keeping an eye out for her," John answered. It was mostly the truth. Even if he weren't attracted to Miranda, he'd still feel the need to be here to watch her back. The attraction was just a bonus.

"You plannin' on staying all night?"

"Dad." Miranda's firm voice from the doorway made her father close his eyes in frustration.

"Anything from the lab yet?" John asked, trying to distract Miranda from her father's nosy question.

"Not yet. I knew it would be too soon, though Bill Chambers promised me they've put a rush on it, since it was an attack on a cop."

"You need me to stick around tonight?" Gil asked. "I could sleep on that new sofa of yours."

Miranda glanced at John. He twitched his eyebrows upward, wondering how she'd answer.

"No, Daddy, I'm good. John's going to stick around a while. It'll be fine."

Gil angled a narrow-eyed look at John. "All right, then. I'll head on home, I guess."

Miranda gave him a quick hug at the front door. "Thanks for bringing the mattress set."

"It's not like you were plannin' on coming home to stay tonight," he grumbled. "So I figured you might as well have the mattress and box springs off your old bed." He gave John another speculative look and headed down the front porch step and out to his truck.

Miranda watched until his truck turned out of the driveway, then came back into the house and closed the door behind her. She looked at John. "He's overprotective sometimes."

"The best dads are."

She smiled at that. "Well, at least that solves the sleeping arrangements. You can have the sofa. Dad brought all the pillows from my old bed, so I should have plenty to spare."

"So you're not going to kick me out, then?"

"Not at the moment." She crossed to the fireplace, picked up the poker and pushed around the logs inside to stir the flames. John couldn't stop himself from moving closer, drawn by the heat.

She looked up at him, the flickering flames burnishing her skin to a soft gold and igniting the red glints in her hair. He wasn't aware of taking a step toward her, but he must have, because suddenly they were only a few inches apart, her breath mingling with his.

She was so warm, so alive. So very, very close.

All he had to do was bend his head and his mouth would cover hers.

She moved suddenly, backing away. "I'll find you those pillows."

John watched her hurry from the room, aching with frustration.

Chapter Eight

Miranda woke with the sun just after six, getting as far as the shower before she realized that, one, she wasn't expected back at the station until tomorrow, and two, she had a man sleeping in her living room, and it probably hadn't been a good idea to shed her nightclothes as she crossed the hall to the bathroom.

Wrapping herself in a towel, she tiptoed out to pick up her clothes, keeping an eye on the door to the living room.

"Hey, Miranda, I was looking at this room—"

She froze at the sound of John's voice coming from behind her.

Oh God, she thought, *please let this towel be covering everything.*

"Sorry."

She stood quickly and turned to face him, clutching the towel closed in front of her. "I thought you were still on the sofa."

"I woke early and couldn't go back to sleep, so I was looking at that room back there." He pointed his thumb toward the back of the house. "I can help you out with the repairs if you want."

"I thought you were working on your own place for your employers," she answered, acutely aware that the towel she'd chosen was entirely too short for a long conversation with a man in her hallway.

"I am, but I should be able to accomplish both in the time I have. You'll be going back to work tomorrow, right?"

She nodded.

"Then I could come over here while you're at work and start getting some of the frame repairs done, at least. And I could help you put up the drywall and lay the new floor. Those are two-person jobs."

"My dad was planning to help in the evenings."

"So there'd be three of us working. It would get done three times as quickly. What do you say?"

"I'd have to know your rates."

"I'm not talking about doing it for pay."

She cocked her head. "But we barely know each other."

He took a couple of steps closer to her, making her knees tremble. "We've spent two nights together now, haven't we? Surely that qualifies us as friends."

She tightened her grip on the edges of the towel. "You just want to keep an eye on me. You think I'm still someone's target."

"Don't you?" he asked.

She supposed she should. Someone had come close to killing her only two days ago. And someone had thoroughly searched her house with ruthless abandon—possibly the same person.

If they hadn't found what they were looking for—and how would she know, since she had no idea what that was—they might keep coming back.

So having her own personal bodyguard wasn't the dumbest idea she'd ever heard, she supposed.

"Tell you what. I'll give it some thought in the shower."

She darted back into the bathroom and closed the door, leaning against it for a moment to calm her twitchy nerves.

If being around John Blake left her this shaky after two days, what condition would she be in if he stuck around longer?

But maybe she should stop considering the question as a woman and start thinking about it with the instincts of a cop. John Blake was one big walking enigma who'd come into her life shortly before someone attempted to end it. Maybe that was a coincidence.

But what if it wasn't?

She pondered the thought while she showered, coming to the conclusion by the time she stepped out of the shower that John couldn't be the person who wanted to do her harm. She was pretty sure the accident happening in front of his house had been pure happenstance. And while there was a window of time when he could have tossed her house, it was a very narrow window.

He'd have had to rush over to her house as soon as Miles Randall drove her to the clinic for treatment, because the mess in her house hadn't been created in a short period of time.

She checked that the hallway was empty before scooting across to her bedroom, wrapped in the now-damp towel. After dressing quickly, she headed into the living room, where she found John folding up the bedding she'd provided for him the night before.

He looked up and flashed a smile that made her stomach turn a little flip. "Hey. Did you give my proposition any thought while you were in the shower?"

It was all she'd thought about. She'd spent the whole

time under the hot spray weighing the pros and cons of taking him up on his offer.

So what if he was still a bit of a mystery? He'd been nothing but helpful to her so far, and she had no reason to think that whatever he might be hiding was any danger to her. On the upside, he was apparently a good enough carpenter to get a job with a company as big as Blanchard Building. He was also pretty good to have around in a crisis.

And did it matter if she found him attractive and intriguing? She was single. So was he, according to the background check she'd run. And if she went forward without any illusions about some sort of romantic happily-ever-after, who would get hurt?

"I could use the help," she said.

His grin spread wider. "Great. So why don't we go take a look and let me catch up on what you want done?"

"Slow down, tiger. How about we go find breakfast first?" Her kitchen was a useless mess, but the plumber she'd called the previous afternoon had told her he couldn't come until this afternoon. "There's a diner in town that serves an old-fashioned country breakfast, if that's your thing."

"It's my thing," he said with a smile. "Now and then, anyway."

SHE SHOULD HAVE known better than to try to dine in at Creekside Diner, because everybody there had heard not only about her wreck, but also about the mess an intruder had made of her house. Between the hushed questions from the wide-eyed waitress and the incessant whispers of the less brave diner patrons, Miranda felt as if she was having breakfast in a fish tank, with everyone watching the show.

"Small towns," John said with a shrug when she apologized later in the truck, speaking as if from experience.

"We should probably stop by the hardware store," she said as he started to turn back toward Route 7. "To tell my dad you're going to be helping out with the repairs."

She felt more than saw John tense up. "Is that going to be an issue for him or something?"

"No." Her father wouldn't have an issue with John helping out, really. But he might find it a matter of curiosity, and that was why she needed to tell him sooner rather than later and explain it in a way that wouldn't make him run right home and start cleaning his gun.

"That doesn't sound like a very confident *no*."

She laughed. "My dad is protective of our relationship. It's been just the two of us since I was pretty young, and my dad tends to be a little overprotective."

"Too overprotective?"

"Not really—"

"I just wondered, because of something you said the other night, about wanting to stand on your own two feet." He paused a little longer than necessary at the four-way stop at Temple and Main, slanting a curious look her way. "Is your dad being overprotective what you were talking about?"

"Sort of," she admitted. She nodded toward the intersection, indicating he should keep going. The hardware store was halfway down the next block. The sooner they got this over with, the better. "I'll tell you more about it when we get back to the house."

Her father took the news better than she'd anticipated,

though the curiosity she'd seen in his eyes earlier was back. At least he didn't say anything embarrassing.

"I've got my card game tonight, but I'll be sure to come help tomorrow night," he told her with a tight smile, his gaze darting toward John, who was wandering through the power tools aisle.

"I know you will." She touched her father's hand, and his smile loosened up, growing warm.

"You sure you can trust that fella?"

"He seems to check out," she answered carefully.

"You don't think it's odd you meet him the same day someone tried to shoot you?"

"They tried to shoot him, too."

Gil looked at John, who looked up at that moment. John gave a friendly nod and went back to examining the electric sander he was holding.

"You think I'm a nosy old man."

She reached across the counter and gave his work-roughened hand a squeeze. "I think you're a hardheaded, softhearted daddy who's still having a little trouble lettin' go of his baby girl."

"You'd think after all this time I'd have it down." He put his hand over the back of hers. "Call me if you need me."

"Always do."

John approached the checkout counter with the power sander and an electronic level. "I didn't remember seeing these things among your tools." As she brought out her debit card, he shook his head. "I might need them before I'm done at my place as well, so they're on me."

As he was paying for the tools, the bell rang over the front door and Miranda turned to see Rose McAllen enter, her thin hand closed around the plump little fist of her three-year-old granddaughter. She lifted sad eyes to meet Miranda's gaze, managed a brief, unconvincing smile and headed toward the back of the store.

"Still nothing on that case?" Gil asked quietly.

Miranda shook her head. "No witnesses, no trace evidence on the body—everything seems to be a dead end."

"A murder right here in Cold Creek?" John murmured as he handed over a credit card for the purchase. "I thought this place hadn't seen a murder in years."

"Technically, it's not a murder," she explained as her father rang up John's purchase. "It was a hit-and-run accident. Rose McAllen, the lady who just walked in, lost her daughter a couple of years ago. Lindy was a teen mom, always a little on the wild side, and she'd sneaked out of the house one night to meet friends. Apparently she tried to cross the highway and misjudged the distance between her and an approaching vehicle."

"And the vehicle didn't stick around to see if she was still alive?" John frowned.

"The coroner said she was probably dead on impact. She went under the wheels and her neck snapped."

John grimaced. "Surely the driver knew he'd hit her."

"Depends. If he was drunk or high—"

"Right." John glanced behind her and lowered his voice. "She's heading this way."

"Dad, I'll call you later." Miranda turned to smile at Rose again, and crouched to look at the little girl by her side, ignoring the ache in her legs and back, remnants of her rollover crash. "Hey there, Cassie. Did you get to play in the snow the other day?"

Cassie nodded and managed a little smile.

"She helped me make a snowman," Rose McAllen said. "A little one."

Miranda stood. "She's growing up so fast."

Rose's eyes darkened with pain. "She reminds me so much of her mama."

Miranda put her hand on Rose's arm. "Mrs. McAllen, we've gone through every bit of trace evidence and put out calls for information, but nobody seems to have seen or heard anything that night. But I promise, we haven't stopped looking. If we come up with any new leads, I'll let you know."

Rose just stared at her a moment, as if she wanted to say something, but finally she just gave a nod and moved on.

"Poor woman," John murmured as they got into the truck.

Miranda buckled her seat belt. "Sometimes I wonder if that's what happened to Delta. Wherever she disappeared to, she didn't take her car, because it's parked in the yard behind her trailer with two flat tires. Which means she either got a ride or took off on foot."

"And you think she might have been hit by a car?"

"It's a possibility, but nobody's found a body. And Cold Creek isn't the kind of place where it's easy to hide a body. You can see for miles wherever you look. Even if she were hit and knocked into an arroyo, someone would have found her by now." She grimaced. "They could just follow the buzzards."

"You said she lives in a trailer."

"Not much of one. She used to live in a pretty big double-wide, but the tornado took it out last year. She stayed with me a little while, until she could sell what was left of her old trailer for scrap and scrimp together enough money to buy a smaller used trailer."

"Where did she work?"

"Here and there. She never kept a job long, although from what I hear from people, she was a pretty hard worker and she was the one who'd walk away from the job, rather than doing something to get fired."

They reached her house and entered with caution, but if there'd been an intruder while they were gone, he'd been as unobtrusive as a mouse. While John carried the new tools to the unfinished room, Miranda checked to see if anyone had left messages on her landline. There were none.

"Where did she sleep?" John asked when he returned to the living room.

It took a second to remember what they'd been talking about. "Delta? On the sofa."

"Interesting that she turned to you for a place to stay. You said you weren't that close."

"I don't think that Delta was really close to anyone, thanks to her father." She sat on the sofa and patted the cushion beside her, inviting him to sit.

He sat next to her, close enough that his comforting warmth spread over her like a cozy sweater. "Con artists don't make many friends in the long run. I guess that probably limited her options for friends."

"Hal McGraw was a charming bastard, but by the time Delta was old enough to know what was going on, he'd pretty much worn out his welcome in Cold Creek. Delta told me he'd leave town for days and weeks at a time, going to other places to pull his scams, leaving her alone to fend for herself. And I'm talking about when she was as young as twelve or thirteen."

He muttered a low profanity. "Nobody intervened?"

"From what I've heard, nobody knew. It wasn't like they mingled with a lot of other people, and Delta always got herself to school somehow, at least once she was old enough to do it. She'd learned early how to take care of herself without his help. That's why she claimed emancipated minor status as soon as she was old enough. She still lived with her dad when he was in town, but she was her own person."

"Tough girl."

"You'd think so."

"But you didn't?"

Miranda sighed, resting her head against the sofa cushion. "She was tough in a lot of ways. I guess she can thank Hal for that. But she was also sort of frozen in time. There was part of her that was still that scared little girl whose mama ran out on her when she was little and had to figure out how to keep living without any real help from her dad. That little girl didn't trust anybody. Not even me. So there was always this wall between us. I could never get over it. And she never tried."

"She must have trusted you a little, if she came to you for help after the tornado."

"She didn't come to me. I offered, and she accepted. But she got out of here as soon as she could. She liked being alone."

"Do you?" His tone was curious. "Like being alone, I mean."

"I don't know that I like it so much as I don't mind it." She turned her head to find him studying her with a thoughtful expression. "I like standing on my own two feet."

"Yeah, that reminds me, you were going to tell me why you're so determined not to stay with your dad." He arched his dark eyebrows at her.

"Right." She looked up at the ceiling, wondering

where to start. "It's nothing that big, really. You've met my dad. You know he's great."

"Seems that way, yeah."

"I love him like crazy. And he loves me the same. But…you have to know what is was like when my mom died. If you think my dad is crazy about me, you should have seen how much he loved my mom." She could smile now at the memory, though it had been years before she could remember her parents' love for each other without wanting to cry at the loss. "When she died, he was so lost. He tried to be my rock, but he was more like a sand castle, crumbling beneath each crashing wave of grief."

"And you had to be his rock."

"For a while. Until he was strong enough to be mine."

"That must have been hard. How old were you when your mom died?"

"Twelve." She wrapped her arms around herself, suddenly cold, despite the mild March temperatures outside. "I think maybe that's why Delta and I ended up being friends of a sort. Because we both knew what it was like to raise ourselves in a way."

"You're not comparing Gil to Delta's con-man father?"

"No, of course not. But he worked hard to keep us going in good economies and bad ones, and there were lots of times when I had to take care of myself. I knew he wasn't going to remarry. He still thinks of my mother as his wife. I guess he always will."

"Romantic."

She smiled. "Who knew he had it in him?"

They fell quiet for a while, but it was a comfortable silence that left her feeling drowsy and safe.

When he spoke a few moments later, his soft voice still made her nerves jangle. "Miranda?"

She opened her eyes to look at him. "Yeah?"

"Do you think it's possible the attack on you had anything to do with Delta's disappearance?"

John's question caught her by surprise. "Why would Delta's case have anything to do with the ambush?"

"You told me the other day that you were out on Route 7 that day because of a tip about Delta, right?"

"Right." She sat upright, her gaze moving suddenly around the room. "We've sort of been assuming the wreck and what happened here were connected in some way, but…"

"But what?"

She pushed to her feet and paced around her living room, looking at each empty space in the room through narrowed eyes, picturing what had been there. At first glance, the destruction had seemed almost malicious. But thinking back, the things that had been destroyed were pieces of furniture or bric-a-brac that could have hidden something else inside it. Even the mess in the kitchen had been caused by someone searching inside containers and canisters.

"Miranda?"

She turned to look at John. "If the whole point of running me off the road was to keep me away from my house long enough to search it, what exactly are they searching for?"

Chapter Nine

Before John could answer, a pounding knock on the door rattled the house and made Miranda jump. With a sheepish smile, she checked out the front window before opening the door. "The plumber," she said.

A burly man with dark skin and black hair entered, grinning at Miranda like an old friend. "Hey there, Mandy. Heard you got a mess on your hands."

"I do, Garrett. I really do."

Garrett entered and stopped briefly as if surprised to see John in the living room. "Oh, hey."

"Garrett, this is John Blake. John, this is Garrett Navarre, plumber extraordinaire."

Garrett grinned as he gripped John's hand with his massive paw. "My wife would say I'm very ordinaire indeed. Nice to meet you."

"If you can fix that mess in the kitchen, you'll go straight to the top of my superhero list," Miranda said with a laugh. "I'll show Garrett what we're up against. John, could you get a fire going? I think it's supposed to be cold again tonight."

So was she expecting him to stay again tonight? he wondered as he added kindling to the logs in the hearth.

There wasn't much reason to stoke a fire otherwise, was there?

Or was he assuming too much?

"Garrett seems to think he can fix things without forcing me to take out a second mortgage." Miranda came back into the living room as he was touching a match to the kindling.

"Good." He rose to face her and blurted out what was really on his mind. "I think I need to stay here a while longer."

Her eyes widened slightly at the abrupt change of subject, but she gave a nod. "I think maybe you should, too, actually. Because I go back to work tomorrow, and I don't want to have to clean this place up again anytime soon. Having you here might, at least, discourage someone breaking in again."

"I don't remember anyone saying—were there tool marks on either of your doors? To tell how the intruders got inside. I don't remember seeing any broken windows."

"Nobody said." Her look of consternation suggested she hadn't thought to ask. She pulled her cell phone from her pocket. "I can find out."

While she made a call to the station, John crossed to the front door and examined the lock and door handles. There were no telltale marks of anyone trying to jimmy the lock, but some locks could be conquered easily enough without leaving much sign of what had happened.

"They checked all the doors and windows. All the windows were locked, and there weren't any signs of a break-in on the front or the back doors. The shed lock had been forced, though," Miranda told him after she'd finished her call.

"Could someone have a key to your front door?"

"Obviously my dad does."

"What about Delta? You said she stayed with you a while. Did you give her a key?"

Miranda pressed her fingers to her lips briefly. "She did have a key to the house. Not the shed, though. She didn't have a reason to need one."

"Did you get it back from her?"

She looked up at him. "Are you suggesting Delta did this?"

He almost wished it was what he was suggesting. "Actually, I was thinking about the fact that she's gone missing."

Miranda's face went pale.

Garrett came into the living room, carrying a large plastic bag. "Here's the stuff from the sink and drain. Can I just dispose of it, or is there any reason you'd need to keep it?"

Miranda glanced at John. "Could be trace evidence, I guess."

He grimaced. "I'm not volunteering to go through it."

A smile touched the corners of her mouth but got no farther. "Put it on the front porch," she told Garrett. "I'll take care of disposing of it."

Garrett complied with a cheerful nod and returned to the kitchen.

Miranda stepped closer to John, keeping her voice low. "You think maybe whoever trashed this place got the key from Delta, don't you?"

"It's possible, isn't it?"

"Probable, even." Using her fingers as a comb, she pushed her hair away from her face, wincing when her fingertips brushed against the bandage on her forehead.

"I don't think she'd have given the key to someone will-ingly."

"Your dad made her sound a little on the flaky side."

"Flaky doesn't mean traitorous."

"I know. But could she have been duped into doing it?"

Miranda appeared to give the question a moment's thought before shaking her head. "No. She was really savvy. Really cynical, I guess. She wouldn't have fallen for it. If someone else has the key I gave her, I think they took it against her will."

She didn't finish that thought, but the conclusion was hard to miss. If someone took the key from Delta by force, what else had they done by force?

"You think she may be dead, don't you?" Miranda's pained question broke the silence.

"It's been a possibility from the beginning, hasn't it?"

"A possibility, yes. But she's gone off before."

"You said this was the longest time she's been away."

Miranda sighed and paced over to the fire, gazing into the flames. The firelight seemed to deepen the sad-ness in her expression, giving her a tragic sort of beauty. "I wanted this case to have a happy ending. I wanted to see Delta come wandering back to town, surprised by all the fuss."

"It might still happen."

She turned her back to the fire and looked at him. "I don't think it will this time. I can't shake the feeling that something bad has happened to her."

"Did Delta have any enemies?"

"I don't know. I was probably the closest thing she had to a friend, but even I didn't know much about her life beyond what little bit she decided to share with me." She crossed to the sofa and sat beside him again, a little closer this time, her warmth washing over him. She smelled good, he thought, a fresh earthy scent like garden herbs warming in the sunshine.

"Could Delta be the one who broke in?"

She shook her head. "I thought about that, but why would she? She knows I'd let her in. And she'd know there's nothing hidden in this house that she'd have to rip things apart to find."

"So maybe it's someone looking for something Delta left here."

"I don't think she left anything, though."

Garrett came out of the kitchen again, carrying his tool bag. "All done, Mandy. You paying with cash or credit today?"

"I'll give you a check." Miranda pushed to her feet and grabbed her purse from the shelf by the door. She followed Garrett outside.

John pulled his phone from the pocket of his jeans and called Quinn to catch him up on the events of the past day.

"So, you've moved in with this woman?" Quinn couldn't quite keep the amusement out of his voice.

"Just for a while, until we can figure out what's going on and who might be gunning for her."

"Well, I have an update on someone who might be gunning for you," Quinn said. "The FBI thinks Del McClintock may have headed west to hide out with family in Oklahoma."

Too close, John thought. "What part of Oklahoma?"

"His cousins live in Altus. Not that far from Cold Creek, really. A little over two hours by car."

Damn it. "You think that's a coincidence? Or do you think he has a bead on my location?"

"It's hard to say. The FBI isn't a hundred percent sure he's in Oklahoma at all. It's just a place to look. But I think it's best if you keep your eyes open. Have you told anyone there why you're in Texas?"

"Of course not."

"Do you trust the deputy?"

He thought about it. "I think so. I think she's one of the good guys. But I'm not sure I want to tell anyone about John Bartholomew and what he was doing for the past year in Virginia." He heard footsteps on the porch outside. "I've got to go. I'll be in touch."

He pocketed the phone just before the door opened and Miranda came back in, holding a yellow receipt, looking exasperated. "Whoever made this mess in my place has cost me an arm and a leg. Most of the damage isn't going to be covered by my homeowner's policy, and now I have to worry about getting new furniture and canisters and—" She flung her hands wide. "I don't even know how much I'm going to have to replace."

"Well, your sink is working again, at least. Maybe we can make a grocery run and replace some of the stuff that got dumped down the drain."

"Probably going to have to wait until I get paid again now." She waved the yellow receipt at him. "Know what I need? Something to take my mind off my troubles. Why don't we go take a look at the back room and see what needs to be done next?"

John followed Miranda to the unfinished room and listened to her description of what she wanted to accomplish. "This was originally a second bedroom, and I don't want to lose that function, but I'd also like for it to be a little more versatile than just another bedroom. It's large enough that I think I could fit a desk in here as well, and maybe build in some shelves for books and file boxes. The sheriff's department is willing to pay my tuition for some continuing education courses and seminars in law enforcement, and I want to have a place to keep my books and notes from those courses."

He could picture it. The room was situated in the back corner of the house, with four windows offering a vista of the plains that seemed to stretch into infinity. A different sort of beauty than the hills and valleys of his Tennessee home, but beautiful nonetheless. She could work here, surrounded by the place she loved, improving her skills at protecting the community she served. It was a very Miranda thing to want.

At least, he thought it was. How much could he really know about a woman he'd met only three days before?

"I love this room. It's a little smaller than my bedroom, but I was considering changing rooms just for this view. And then the tornado hit and practically demolished it." Her eyes darkened with remembered pain. "It took out half of each corner wall and the rain ruined the floor and the other walls. We had to strip up the floors and take down all the drywall and the ceiling."

He looked up at the exposed wood of the frame. "You and your dad did the reframing?"

"Yeah, and we got the siding put up on the outside to protect it from the elements. But I haven't had a ton of time to get the interior fixed up the way I want it. I've had to do it a little at a time during my off-hours."

"I can help speed that up while you're at work. Looks like you're ready to put the walls in next."

She nodded at the sheets of drywall lined up on one side of the room. "I thought I'd try to tackle that when I got home from work tomorrow."

"I can get it started for you first thing in the morning. Do you have a basic floor plan for the room? Where you want the various elements to go?"

"Do I ever." With a grin, she motioned for him to follow her.

They made a quick stop in her bedroom for her to grab a notebook from the bedside table, then settled on the sofa in the living room, spreading the notebook open on the coffee table in front of them.

"I'm looking at a couple of different plans. I just can't decide which way I want to go." She pointed to the first page, where in neat pen strokes, she'd sketched out a simple floor plan featuring a bed, a single piece of furniture she'd labeled "highboy" and a desk against one wall between two windows. "This is the more traditional route," she said. "The bed is against one wall, the desk at its foot. Shelves would go on the wall opposite the bed, ending at the closet door."

He pointed to the opposite page. "And this?"

"I'd have to go with a daybed in this scenario, because more focus is on the corner desk and the shelves. This layout makes the room more of a study with a sleeping area. The other one is more a bedroom with a desk and bookshelves."

"What do you anticipate using the room for?"

"A study," she said.

"I think you've made your choice, then."

The smile she flashed at him made his whole body go hot. "My dad thinks it's crazy. He thinks I should be adding bedrooms to the house, not converting one to a study."

"Adding bedrooms?"

She rolled her eyes. "You know, for when I get married and start having babies. He keeps sending me clippings from the newspaper whenever one of my friends from high school gets married or has a baby."

"And, of course, this being a small town, those events all get big write-ups in the local weekly."

"Exactly." She laughed. "I make it sound like he's a terrible nag. He's not. I think he just worries that I'm alone here with no husband or babies in sight."

"Wants to get you settled so he can stop worrying."

She shot him a narrow-eyed look. "This sound familiar to you, too?"

"A little. My father wanted me to join the family business from the time I graduated college. I just—" He shook his head. "I wanted something more than a corner office in a Johnson City accounting firm."

"So you joined the Foreign Legion?"

What would it hurt to tell her about his work with the CIA? He hadn't lasted long, and everything he'd been dealing with had ended up being declassified or scrapped in the end. "I worked as a CIA liaison in Athens, Greece, for a year after college."

Her eyes widened. "I know I joked about that, but—"

"It wasn't nearly as interesting as it sounds. And I sort of blew my one and only assignment, so—"

"How'd you blow it? Or is that classified information?"

"Not classified. Just embarrassing." He rose and crossed to the fireplace, gazing into the flickering flames. "Athens was always volatile politically. Lots of protests— antiglobalization, anarchists, black bloc, you name it. About a week earlier, Athens cops had killed an unarmed teenager and things were really hot in the city. I was living in a hotel that offered long-term rentals, and that morning, I apparently walked right out of the hotel into the middle of a violent protest. I took a chunk of concrete to the head and woke up three weeks later in an Athens hospital with no memory of the event."

"My God."

"Needless to say, everything I had on me that might be considered sensitive information was gone. My hotel room had been searched and cleaned out. My cover was more or less blown and I wasn't any use to the CIA any longer."

"So they fired you? Because you got hurt?"

"Because I was compromised. It wasn't personal." He shrugged. He'd known the stakes, known how easily a career in the CIA could end. "At least I'm still alive. I've been told it was touch and go for several days."

"So then you went back to Johnson City and spent some time in that corner office?"

He laughed. "Not exactly. By then, my cousin Pete had earned the corner office. I had to start at the bottom. I figure I got maybe midway in ten years, at which point I realized being a decent accountant wasn't the same as wanting to be an accountant."

"So what did you do between the time you left the accounting firm and the time you showed up on the Blanchard Building payroll?"

"I worked for a company called The Gates. Ever heard of it?"

She shook her head. "No. Strange name."

"It's a security agency. Based in a little town called Purgatory, Tennessee, down in the Smokies. The boss is a guy named Alexander Quinn. Former CIA—legendary at the company, but most of what he's done in his life is so classified I'm not sure even the presidents he served knew some of it." John poked at the waning fire, stirring up embers. "Seems that Quinn came from money, and when he came in to a big inheritance, he left the CIA and started his own agency."

"What kind of security work?"

"All kinds, really. Some investigation, some bodyguard work, some security analysis and threat assessment."

"In an agency working out of a little town in the Smokies?"

"That's the base. But he has people working for him all over the place. If you talked to the agents currently working for Quinn at the main office in Purgatory, they probably wouldn't recognize my name. I was working for him out of Abingdon, Virginia."

"Doing what?"

"Well, I was officially a freelance security consultant. I did some jobs consulting with companies in Abingdon that were looking to improve all areas of their security. But what I was really doing was helping an undercover agent Quinn had in place in a little town called River's End, in the Blue Ridge Mountains not far from Abingdon. She was trying to infiltrate a militia group—"

"The Blue Ridge Infantry," Miranda interrupted, her brow furrowed. "I've heard of them. But didn't I read that the FBI had finally had a big break in the case that's allowing them to round up everyone involved?"

"It wasn't the FBI who made that break happen. It was a tough lady named Nicki Jamison. I might have helped a little, too."

Miranda crossed to where he stood, meeting his gaze. "You weren't hurt in a hunting accident, were you?"

"No. I mean, I was being hunted, but—"

She closed her eyes. "Is that why you're here? Recuperating?"

"That, and lying low."

"So John Blake isn't really your name."

"No, it really is my name. But nobody in Abingdon— or River's End—ever knew it. I was known as John Bartholomew there."

"But you said you're lying low."

"I am. Just because John Blake isn't the name I used doesn't mean that someone with some computer savvy couldn't eventually figure it out. And the BRI had some pretty nasty hackers working for them."

"So maybe I need to be watching *your* back."

"Maybe you should. Because the FBI believes one of the guys who might be looking for me is somewhere in Altus, Oklahoma."

Her eyes widened even more. "That close?"

"They're not sure he's there. But he has family in Altus."

Before Miranda could respond, her cell phone trilled. "Hold that thought," she said before she answered. "Duncan."

As she listened, her gaze snapped up to his, her eyes looking huge and dark in her suddenly pale face. "When?"

Whatever she was hearing on the other end of the call, it was bad news, he saw. Her free hand rose to her mouth as she listened with increasing distress. "And she's sure?"

The other caller must have answered in the affirmative, for Miranda gave a brief nod and said, "I'm on my way."

"What is it?" he asked as she put her phone away and looked around for her jacket, spotting it on the back of the chair by the door.

She shrugged the jacket on. "A woman who lives off

Route 7 had some chickens escape their coop this afternoon. When she chased them down, she stumbled on the body of a woman." She lifted her troubled gaze to John. "They think it's Delta McGraw."

Chapter Ten

The dead woman lying in the shallow arroyo behind Lizzie Dillard's chicken coop was definitely Delta Mc-Graw. And she'd been dead for at least a couple of days.

The sight of her friend's body, cold and mottled with cyanosis and in the early stages of decomposition, seemed unreal somehow. She knew the full emotional impact would hit her soon enough. But right now, she had to be a cop first.

"She definitely wasn't out here the day of my wreck," Miranda told Sheriff Randall as they stood looking down at Delta's cold body. "I was out here and I had a pretty good look around."

"She's been dead longer than that," Randall said. He looked toward the road, where John Blake sat in his truck, watching them work. "I see you brought your new friend."

"He's watching my back."

"You think we don't?" The sheriff's voice held an oddly defensive tone she hadn't expected.

"No, of course not. But we're a small agency. If John Blake has the time and wants to watch my back—"

"Didn't you say he's a carpenter or something?"

"He has some law enforcement training in his past."

"A wannabe." His tone was dismissive.

"No, more like a once was." She glanced at the truck, not wanting to reveal too much to the sheriff, even though she'd trust Randall with her life. If John was telling the truth, and she had no reason at this point to believe he wasn't, his life was in as much danger as hers. She was watching his back, as well. "He's nice and he saved me the other day. If he wants to use his off time to make sure I don't get ambushed alone again, I'm not going to complain."

"Fair enough." He looked down at Delta's body. "Poor girl. She had one hell of a rough life."

"I had such a sick feeling this time when she disappeared. She was finally starting to put down roots, I thought." Tears stung her eyes, but she blinked them away. Not now. She couldn't fall apart now.

Randall caught Miranda's arm and pulled her back as two more deputies arrived, armed with crime scene kits to gather trace evidence and secure the scene. "Putting down roots?"

Miranda nodded. "I put it in my first report on the case. When we asked people around town if anyone had seen her, Luis Gomez from High Plains Realty contacted me, said that he'd been talking to Delta about looking for a house to buy."

"She had that kind of money?"

"I didn't think so, but honestly, there's a lot about Delta I didn't know."

The sheriff was silent for a moment, then tilted his head toward the house. "You need to talk to Lizzie, see if she saw or heard anything. She was too rattled earlier for Jenkins to get anything out of her."

With a nod, Miranda headed across the yard to where

Lizzie sat on the top step of her front porch, her head down and her shoulders hunched. When she looked up at Miranda's approach, her normally ruddy face was sickly pale, and her eyes were red rimmed and puffy.

"I gave up smokin' ten years ago. I've never regretted it until now." Lizzie held her shaking hands out in front of her. "I'd sell this whole damn farm for a cigarette right about now."

Miranda sat on the step next to her. "It must've been a real shock to find her out there like that."

"I'm a farm girl. I see death all the time. It's part of raisin' animals for the market, you know? But that poor girl—" Lizzie buried her face in her hands. "I know she wasn't here yesterday evening when I went out to feed the chickens, because I walked out to the road to talk to Coy when he drove by on his way home and I went right by that arroyo."

Miranda made a mental note to check with the desk sergeant. Maybe he'd seen something on his drive home that might be helpful. "You don't remember hearing anything last night?"

"Not a thing." Lizzie scraped her graying hair away from her weathered face. "I work hard and I sleep hard. You know what it's like. Now, if old Rocket was still alive, he'd have barked his head off if there was anybody out there, but I had to have him put down last month, and I haven't had the heart to get me a new dog. Though Coy said his neighbor's hound mix just had puppies. Said he'd probably be happy to save one out of the litter for me."

So anyone could have come along this road and dumped Delta's body out during the night, Miranda thought, without anyone seeing it happen.

But who would know that?

Almost anyone, she supposed, when she thought about it. She herself knew about Lizzie having to have old Rocket put to sleep the previous month. She'd heard it from Tina Shire, who worked at the vet clinic in town. And anyone who'd ever driven down Glory Road would know there wasn't another house within almost two miles of Lizzie's farm.

In some ways, it was the ideal place to dump a body, as long as you didn't care if it was found sooner rather than later.

"Lizzie, if you think of anything you might have seen or heard last night, even if it seems unimportant, you'll let us know, right?"

"Of course." Lizzie patted Miranda's hand. "You must be sick about it. I know you two girls were friends."

"I'm not sure Delta ever felt as if she had any friends," Miranda said sadly, looking across the farmyard to where Sheriff Randall and the rest of the deputies had started processing the crime scene. Despite the warm sunlight beating down on the scene, Miranda still felt a bleak chill in the air.

Maybe it was coming from inside her.

"That's the fellow who moved into the old Merri-wether place out on Route 7, ain't it?" Lizzie nodded toward John, who was watching Miranda rather than the deputies at the scene. "Hear tell he saved your life the other day durin' the snowstorm."

"He did," Miranda admitted. The cause of the crash was being kept secret at the sheriff's department, for now, but the crash itself was all over the town grapevine. Neighbors had been calling her father's store for a couple of days, asking if she needed anything and offering to bring food to her house.

If her place hadn't been trashed by the intruder search, she might have taken a few of them up on the offer.

"Heard he's some sort of builder or something," Lizzie said.

"Something like that. He's actually going to be helping me finish repairing the tornado damage on my place."

"Mighty kind of him."

"Yes." Miranda pushed to her feet, ignoring a symphony of aches and pains. The knocks and dings from the rollover wreck, combined with the strain of all the bending, lifting and carrying she'd done cleaning up her trashed house, had taken a toll on her body.

But you're still alive, she reminded herself as she headed back to where the coroner's truck had arrived to pick up Delta's body. Things could have been so much worse.

She could have been zipped up in a body bag just like Delta.

"Mandy, go home," Sheriff Randall told her.

"What? This is my case."

"You're still on medical leave until tomorrow. And even then, I saw the way you looked at Delta's body. You're too close to the case. We've got other people who can investigate. Take the rest of the week off and get your head straight. Then we'll talk."

"Damn it, sir, that's not fair."

"You still believe life is fair?" Randall's expression was set in stone. There would be no changing his mind, Miranda knew.

"Fine. Will you at least let me call in for updates on the case?"

Randall's expression softened just a notch. "Sure. But I'm serious about taking the rest of the week off. You could easily have been killed in that wreck the other day, and I can see you're still sore. Take these days to get some rest and clear your head." He nodded toward the coroner assistants, who were placing the body bag on a gurney to slide it in the back of a truck. "Since Delta didn't have any family left, she needs someone to handle her funeral. I don't know if she had any money stashed away anywhere or any sort of burial policy, but..."

Miranda doubted it. She hadn't been able to find any sort of bank account for Delta when she'd first taken on the missing person case, so it wasn't likely she had bothered with anything like life insurance. "Can I at least be the one to take another look at her place? I knew her better than anyone else on the force. There might be something there that'll mean more to me than another investigator."

Randall looked as if he wanted to say no, but finally he gave a gruff nod. "I'll want another deputy with you."

She bit back a protest and nodded. "Tell me when to be there."

"I'll get with Robertson and give you a call."

"Thanks." She returned to the truck and climbed into the passenger seat. John watched her in silence, waiting for her to speak.

"It was Delta."

He let out a slow breath. "I'm sorry. Are you okay?"

She buckled her seat belt and leaned her head against the backrest. "I don't know. I feel kind of like I'm in limbo. Waiting for it to hit me."

He reached across the cab and put his hand over hers where it lay on the seat beside her. "What happens next?"

"I have to look into a few things. See if she had any sort of will or plans for what would happen in the case of her death." She shook her head. "She was twenty-seven years old. Who plans their own funeral at that age?"

"Is there anything you can do right now?"

She looked across the cab to find him watching her with a gentle expression that made tears prick her eyes. She blinked them back. "I would really like to go home now. Can we just go home?"

JOHN PULLED HIS truck up next to Miranda's on the concrete driveway and cut the engine, waiting for her to move.

She sat in the passenger seat and was very still for a long moment before she slowly reached for the seat belt buckle and released herself from the harness. "I should call my dad and let him know." She sighed. "Although as fast as news travels in this town, he probably knows already."

Before she could move, her cell phone trilled, harsh in the silence of the truck cab. She pulled it from her pocket and checked the display. "Can I call it or what?" She got out of the truck and started toward the house, lifting the phone to her ear as she walked. "Hi, Dad."

John followed more slowly, giving her a little privacy to talk to her father about her friend's death. By the time he reached the porch, she had hung up the phone and was unlocking the door.

"The sheriff took me off the case," she said as she locked the door behind them. When she lifted her gaze to meet his, she looked more hurt than angry.

"Because you're too close to the case?"

"Yeah. And he's making me take the rest of the week off, too. I think it's just to keep me from nosing around the case, although he says it's because I need to take more time to recover from my injuries."

"Maybe that's a good idea."

The look she gave him was sharp enough to cut. "Et tu, Brute?"

He crossed to where she stood, arms folded, her brow furrowed. "I know you're tough. Hell, you were in a roll-over accident three days ago, and I just watched you clean up a wrecked house and work a crime scene without even dragging your heels. But maybe it's time to give yourself a break."

"I'm not fragile."

"I know that." He put his hands on her shoulders, running his thumbs lightly over the curve of her collarbones.

She opened her mouth as if to argue, then closed her eyes, taking a shaky breath. Slowly, she dropped her arms, her hands coming to rest on his sides, just below his rib cage. She took a step closer, the delicious heat of her body sliding over him until he felt as if he was on fire inside.

"I'm glad you're here." Her voice was barely a whisper, her breath soft and hot against his chin. He bent his head until their foreheads touched, and he drank in her sweet herb scent.

"I'm glad I'm here, too." He brushed his lips against her forehead. "I'll stay as long as you want me to."

She lifted her gaze to his. "Don't make promises. It's way too early for promises."

"Okay. No promises." He was crazy to make promises, anyway, given how up-in-the-air his life was at the moment. "Why don't you lie down a while? I could figure out something for supper."

"I couldn't sleep." She moved away from him in restless strides, coming to a stop at the window. She gazed out at the dying daylight for a moment, her face tinged rose by the setting sun, before turning to look at him. "I wouldn't mind supper, though. What do you have in mind?"

"I thought I'd run to that little store down the road and pick up some groceries. Maybe grill a couple of steaks and bake a potato?"

"Sounds good." She pulled her keys from her pocket and handed them to him. "The house key is the silver one there on the end. Pick up some vegetables, too, and I'll whip up a salad."

"Okay, you're on." He smiled at her as he unlocked the door. "Lock up behind me. I'll be right back."

He hurried through his shopping, not liking the idea of leaving her alone for long. Delta McGraw clearly hadn't died of natural causes. And if the attack on Miranda was connected, the stakes had just gotten a lot higher.

"I haven't found much of anything on Delta McGraw," Quinn told John when he checked in with his boss. "I have found a few things on her father, Hal, however."

"Anything that could help us figure out who killed his daughter?"

"I'm not sure. The one thing I've learned is that he was charged with extortion by an oilman in Plainview shortly before his death. Apparently he tried to blackmail the man over something the oilman's son had done—selling drugs or something. The report I got had been redacted in places. Anyway, the oilman told Hal to go do something anatomically impossible and called the cops on him for his attempted extortion."

"What happened?"

"Hal died before it ever got to court."

"Is that the only thing?" John asked.

"The only thing I've found," Quinn replied. "But if he blackmailed one person…"

"He might have blackmailed several," John added. "But I'm not sure how that relates to his daughter's death."

"Maybe the apple didn't fall far from the tree. Ask around. Stay in touch." Quinn ended the call.

Pocketing his phone, John pondered his boss's suggestion as he carried his basket of groceries to the checkout stand. The teenage boy at the cash register rang up the purchase with amusing enthusiasm, keeping up a stream of friendly chatter until John paid the bill. "You have a nice evening," he said with a grin, displaying a mouth full of metal.

He let himself in at Miranda's with the house key, expecting to find her waiting for him in the living room, where he'd left her.

But the living room was empty.

He started to call her name but stopped himself, standing still and listening instead. He heard a soft hitching sound coming from somewhere in the back of the house.

The sound went silent as he moved through the house, his footsteps on the hardwood floor seeming loud to his own ears.

The bedroom door was open, the room empty. The bathroom was empty, as well. He found no one in the kitchen, either, but he could almost feel a presence nearby. Waiting.

He set the bag of groceries on the kitchen table and eased over to the door to the unfinished room. It was only halfway open, obscuring his view of all but a sliver of the room. Reaching behind his back, he grabbed the butt of the Ruger hidden in a holster clipped to his jeans and drew it.

Slowly, he pushed open the door. It creaked, the loud sound jangling his taut nerves.

"Don't move." Miranda's voice sounded thick and hoarse, but there was no mistaking the tone of command.

He went very still. "Are you alone?"

"Are you?"

"Yes."

"Come in."

He found her sitting under one of the windows, her knees tucked up near her chest and her head leaning back against the wall. She still held her M&P 40, but the barrel was pointed toward the ground.

She'd been crying.

As he walked slowly into the room, she set it on the floor beside her. "Sorry about that."

"No worries." He nodded his head back toward the kitchen. "I brought the groceries. You still hungry?"

"I will be. Just give me a few minutes." She spoke as if she wanted him to go. But when she lifted her damp eyes to his again, he could see she really didn't want to be left alone.

He reholstered his own pistol and crossed to where she sat, easing himself into a sitting position next to her.

"What did you buy?" she asked, sniffling a little.

"Two nice sirloin steaks, two enormous baking potatoes—plus sour cream and butter, because this is no time for watching our weight. And I wasn't sure what kind of salad stuff you liked, so I might have bought out half the produce section at the grocery store. Didn't know what kind of salad dressing you'd want, so I bought small bottles of several to choose from."

She managed a watery laugh. "I'm sure I'll find exactly what I want."

"Listen, before we start supper—I need to ask you something about Hal McGraw. Did you know he was arrested for extortion shortly before his death?"

She looked up at him. "Of course. But how do you know?"

"My boss told me."

One of her eyebrows lifted. "And why would he know anything about Hal McGraw?"

"I asked him to do some research on Delta."

"Without asking me?"

He shrugged. "Do you want to know what else he said or not?"

She was quiet for a moment, then gave a brief nod.

"Well, he asked a really good question. I was wondering if you might know the answer. Do you think Hal McGraw might have been blackmailing anyone else?"

"We always figured he must have been. But once he died, it wasn't likely anybody was going to come forward to tell us about it. We figured most of the offenses were probably personal problems, not legal ones, and none of our business."

He didn't like asking the next question, considering the tear tracks still staining Miranda's cheeks. But it had to be asked. "What about Delta? Do you think she knew about her father's extortion plots?"

Her brow furrowed as she gave the question some thought. "I don't know," she admitted finally. "I guess she might have."

"Then that brings up another question, doesn't it? Did Delta pick up where her father left off?"

She turned her gaze to him again, her expression troubled. "And is that why she ended up dead?"

Chapter Eleven

"If she was blackmailing anyone, I never heard about it." Miranda poked at the remains of her baked potato, scooping out one last buttery morsel. She popped it in her mouth.

"Well, you wouldn't, would you? The whole idea of extortion is to pay for the blackmailer's silence. You done?" John reached across the kitchen table for her plate.

She pushed it toward him and sat back, feeling comfortably full. "You're not a bad cook, John Blake."

"A man's gotta know how to grill." He flashed her a smile that made her heart give a little flip. She was beginning to wonder how she'd ever thought of him as average or ordinary.

"The only wine I had in the house went down the drain," she said as she pushed to her feet and joined him at the dishwasher. "But I saw you picked up a bag of coffee. I could brew a pot if you like."

He shook his head. "I'm fine. Why don't I go start another fire while you get the dishes going, and we can just try to relax for a while? You've had a stressful day."

Stressful and upsetting, she thought, adding the word he was kind enough not to say. She'd felt a little embarrassed when he'd found her crying in the back room, but he hadn't made things worse by trying to comfort her with awkward words of sympathy. He couldn't know how she was feeling, and he knew it.

To be honest, she wasn't sure herself how she was feeling. Grief of a sort, she supposed, but Delta had never really let her get close enough for her to think of the other woman as a true friend. Still, the sight of her lying dead in the bottom of a shallow arroyo had been deeply disturbing on a number of levels, some of them personal.

She finished loading the dishwasher and set it to run, then joined John in the living room. The fire had reached a crackling blaze, helping to fend off the gathering chill of the evening, and John had moved the sofa so that it faced the fireplace.

"Hope you don't mind." As she approached the sofa, he smiled up at her, sliding one arm over the back of the sofa. "Didn't want to waste a nice fire by sitting halfway across the room."

She hesitated.

"I don't bite," he murmured in a tone that made the words sound like a lie. There was a challenge in his expression, as tempting and dangerous as the firelight reflected in his eyes.

Come on, Mandy. You're not a sixteen-year-old virgin faced with your first bad boy. He's a tax accountant. You've dated bull riders before.

She sat beside him, daringly close, her hip snugged against his. For a few moments, they sat in silence broken only by the crackle of the fire and the distant hum of the dishwasher at work.

"Tell me about Delta," he murmured a few moments later. She felt his fingers play in her hair. Lightly. Undemanding.

"She was a couple of years younger than I am. Three years behind in school because she failed a year early on, thanks to her dad dragging her all over Texas for a while. She couldn't keep up with her schoolwork as she went from town to town, so she had to start over fresh the next year, somewhere down near Abilene, I think." Delta had told the story so matter-of-factly, without a hint of how she'd felt about her rambling lifestyle with her father. "I think that wasn't long after her mother left them."

"So they weren't from here originally."

She shook her head. "You're probably wondering why they settled in a little place like this."

"The question did cross my mind."

"Mine, too. Delta never really said what made them stay, but if I had to guess? I think she told her daddy to settle down or she'd call the cops on him."

"Really. How old was she then?"

"Twelve."

"Tough little girl." John's voice held a touch of admiration.

"She was. It's so hard to think she's gone now. She endured so much. Overcame so much." Grief tangled around her heart, squeezing hard. She took a deep breath, attempting to relieve the sudden sharp stab of pain.

"I was hoping for a better ending," he murmured, his fingers warm against her cheek. He pressed his lips to her temple, a brief, uncomplicated caress.

Except her reaction to his touch was anything but uncomplicated. Her heart skipped a beat before shifting into a higher gear, and her skin prickled hot beneath his fingers.

"I wanted to believe we'd find her alive, but—"

"But you didn't really think you would?"

She let herself relax, resting her head against his jaw. "She kept a lot of things to herself, but she'd have told me if she was leaving for this long."

With a soft *prrrup* sound, Ruthie jumped up on the sofa next to her, her tail forming a question mark. She wasn't hungry, Miranda knew, because she'd fed the cats before John had returned from the grocery store.

"Hey there, Ruthie," John said in a soft voice.

The cat's ears twitched, and slowly, she turned her green eyes to look at him with a quizzical expression.

"I had a cat when I was in Johnson City," John said. "Well, sort of. He was a stray who took up with me. He'd been someone's cat before—he was tame and had already been neutered. The vet said someone might have accidentally let him out of the car on a trip or something— he was too well behaved to have lived his life outdoors for long. He wasn't microchipped, though, and my 'lost cat' ads didn't bring his real owners around, so I took him in. Let him live with me until he died."

All the while John had been speaking, Ruthie had been watching him, her ears perked as if listening. When he stopped, the tortoiseshell cat walked over Miranda's lap and reached up, claws sheathed, to touch his mouth.

"Well, then. Ruthie must like the sound of your voice."

"Or maybe she's trying to make sure I stop talking."

Miranda watched with amusement as Ruthie settled in his lap, a low purr rumbling from her throat. "That's the Ruthie seal of approval."

"She must have low standards." He scratched behind her ears, then under her chin, each stroke earning him a blissful stretch from Ruthie.

"Not at all. But if you can get Rex to sit in your lap like that, you're a miracle worker."

John stroked the fingers of his other hand lightly over the skin behind Miranda's ear, sending a ripple of pure pleasure darting down her spine. If she wasn't careful, she'd end up purring like a kitten herself.

"Miranda?"

"Hmm?" She turned her head and found his face inches from hers, his eyes gleaming with desire and intent. But he remained perfectly still, giving her the chance to make the final move.

Toward him or away from him? It was her choice.

And then, suddenly, it wasn't her choice any longer.

He leaned in and pressed his mouth to hers, his lips somehow both firm and soft. With soft, nipping movements, his kiss deepened, urging her lips apart until his tongue brushed lightly against hers. Lightly at first, then with dark seduction, making her head swirl until she found herself clinging to him just to remain upright.

His fingers threaded through her hair, holding her in place while he slowly, thoroughly kissed her until she couldn't find her breath.

Suddenly, his breath caught and he drew back, hissing with pain. A flash of fur darted from between their bodies.

John looked down at the three scratches turning red down his wrist. "I don't think Ruthie approved."

"I'm so sorry." Miranda winced as the scratch marks started to ooze blood. "She likes you, I swear."

"Yeah, I know." John stood up and started toward the hallway. Miranda followed quickly, wondering what he was going to do to poor Ruthie.

"She was just scared," she said quickly.

In the hallway, he turned to look at her, his expression

quizzical. "I know that. What do you think I'm going to do, go wring her neck?"

"I didn't know. Some people freak out when they're scratched, and—"

"I had a cat. Scratches happen." He went into the bathroom and looked around. "Where do you keep your first-aid supplies?"

"There's a kit in the cabinet under the sink."

John found the kit, a small metal box full of adhesive bandages, individual packets of antiseptic pads, antibiotic ointments and pain reliever tablets. He selected the antiseptic, ripping the packet open and dabbing the antiseptic on the three scratches. "All better now."

She was relieved that he'd handled Ruthie's reaction with such levelheadedness. She'd dated a tough cowboy once who'd nearly cried when Rex had reacted to his relentless teasing with a claws-extended swipe, despite Miranda's warnings to stop. She'd had to restrain the idiot from going after her cat, and that had been the end of that relationship.

Of course, she and John weren't really dating, were they? They were just temporarily sharing a house. With kissing benefits included, apparently.

"I'd better go apologize to Ruthie," he said after he'd finished treating the scratch. "Don't want to get on her bad side."

She watched him head down the hall in search of her miffed cat, trying to ignore the melty feeling in the center of her chest.

"CAN YOU TELL if anything looks any different?" Tim Robertson had remained in the doorway while Miranda took a slow circuit of Delta McGraw's tiny trailer. She'd been there a few times over the past few months since the tornado had wiped out Delta's previous home.

"Someone's been here," she said, taking in the disturbed places in the dust that lay in a thin layer over everything in the trailer. "They took their time, though. Nothing like the search at my place."

"Wonder why they didn't just toss this place like they tossed yours?"

"Maybe because they had more time," she suggested. "There was a narrow window of time at my place to do any sort of search. Even if I'd died in the wreck, someone would have been there within a few hours to check on the cats."

Tim nodded. "You have any idea what they were looking for at your place?"

She thought about what she and John had agreed to earlier that morning over a breakfast of instant oatmeal and the fresh strawberries he'd bought at the market the night before.

"I'm not going to tell the others at the cop shop about our suspicions that Delta's death and the attack on me might be connected," she'd told him. "Because the last thing I want is to be put on leave for my own safety. I need access to the department's resources."

"Don't you think they might figure it out on their own?" John had asked.

Miranda looked at Tim, who remained near the doorway, leaning against the wall with his arms folded over his chest. He was a good deputy, she knew. Smart and resourceful.

Would he figure it out on his own?

Maybe. But she wasn't going to help him put her own

investigation in cold storage, which would surely happen if the sheriff thought her life might be in danger.

"I don't know what they were looking for," she told Tim. That much, at least, was true. She might have a pretty good idea why they'd been searching her house, but she had no idea, yet, what they'd been looking for.

On closer inspection, she found plenty of signs that the place had been carefully searched, but if they'd taken anything, she had no way of knowing what it was. Even if she'd been Delta's closest friend, she couldn't pretend she knew that much about Delta's life outside their limited interactions. The handful of times she'd been in this trailer had been brief, usually when she stopped by to say hello after too many days, even weeks, of not hearing from Delta.

The woman had been a loner at heart. Probably the result of the kind of life she'd had with her pariah of a father.

In the end, she found the money by accident. As she walked into the kitchen one last time to make sure she hadn't missed anything, her foot caught on the edge of the linoleum in the door, sending her sprawling forward. She caught herself on the edge of the narrow counter inside the tiny kitchenette and felt it give.

Regaining her footing, she gave the counter an upward tug, and that small section of the counter lifted up on a hinge.

Underneath, a shallow square space was empty except for a thick manila envelope bound shut by a couple of rubber bands. She opened the envelope and sucked in a sharp breath.

Inside the envelope were several fat stacks of plastic-wrapped one-hundred-dollar bills.

THE FLOOR OF the unfinished room had been framed atop the existing concrete foundation, sheathed in plywood awaiting the installation of final flooring. Miranda and her father had framed the floor and the walls, she'd told John earlier that morning when they'd been discussing the next part of the building project, but they'd had professional builders handle the roofing, siding and insulation. Heating, ventilation and air-conditioning ductwork had also been added by the pros, but the rest of the work Miranda intended to do herself, with help from her father and now from John, as well.

Next job up—installing the drywall. Sheets of the plasterboard stood against one of the walls, ready to go. Miranda had already measured and cut the boards to fit the walls, helpfully marking each one with a corresponding framing board in the wall. She'd left him with her power screwdriver, a bucket of drywall screws and the smiling admonition to avoid screwing any body parts to the wall.

He started installing the drywall top to bottom, working up a nice sweat despite the mild day. Within an hour, he'd managed to screw up an entire wall and had started the next when something in the fiberglass insulation near the floor caught his eye.

Was that a split in the fiberglass batting?

He found a pair of work gloves in the toolbox in the corner. They were snug but covered his hands, protecting them from the scratchy fibers of the insulation batting as he pushed his fingers inside the split.

There was something in there. Hard and rectangular, like a box. Or a book? It moved a little when he touched it, though it seemed to fit snugly into its hiding place. He didn't want to make the slit in the fiberglass any worse, but being too careful wasn't going to make it possible to get the mystery item out of the recess.

Removing his hand, he sat back, trying to figure out if the rectangular object might have something to do with the wiring or the HVAC system. After reassuring himself it couldn't be, he pushed his hand through the opening in the insulation and tried to grab the object again.

This time, he caught it firmly between two fingers and wiggled it until it popped free. Turning it sideways, he pulled it out through the fiberglass and dusted strands of the glass fiber away from it.

It was a small, hard-backed book, wrapped in clear plastic, the end pieces of the wrap taped together at the back side of the thin book. It wasn't a novel or anything like that; the dark blue cover was made of fabric and had no title or any writing at all on the front or back.

The sound of keys rattling in the door sent a light shock through his system, and he almost lost his grip on the book. He pushed quickly to his feet, bracing himself until he heard Miranda's voice down the hall. "John?"

"In here," he called.

Miranda's footsteps rang down the hallway, moving at a fast clip. She stopped in the doorway for a second, taking in the newly installed drywall. "Wow. You've been busy."

"I have," he said, "and I may have—"

"Guess what I found at Delta's trailer this morning." If she noticed the book in his hands, she didn't give any sign.

"What did you find?"

"Ten thousand dollars in one-hundred-dollar bills." She looked both excited and troubled, and she walked back and forth in front of him, the emotions warring in her storm cloud eyes. "I have no idea where she could get her hands on that much cash, but there it was, hidden in a secret compartment in her kitchen counter, of all places."

Hidden, John thought, glancing at the book dangling from his gloved hand. "Wrapped in plastic?" he asked.

She stopped her restless pacing and turned to look at him. "Yes. How did you know?"

He lifted the book in his gloved hand and motioned toward the partially finished wall. "I was putting in the drywall and noticed there was a split in the insulation. I reached inside and found this."

Miranda took a couple of steps closer to get a better look at the book. "It looks like a journal or a diary. Maybe a ledger?"

"I didn't want to touch it with my bare hands, in case you need to process it for fingerprints."

"Good idea." She reached into her pocket and pulled out a pair of latex gloves, probably spares from her search of Delta's trailer earlier that morning. She donned them quickly and took the book from his hands. Carefully she unstuck the tape holding the plastic wrap in place. "Can you go to the kitchen and get me a gallon bag out of the box over the stove? Bring the whole box."

He retrieved the box of gallon-sized resealable bags and handed her one. "Here you go."

She passed him the book. "Gloved hands only. And try not to touch it much. I'm not sure we can get prints off that fabric surface, but you never know."

As he balanced the book flat on his gloved palm, she carefully folded the plastic wrap she'd removed from the book and slipped it inside the gallon bag he'd supplied, sealing it up and setting it on the top of the toolbox by the door. "Now let's take a look at that book."

He handed over the small blue book. She took it in her gloved hands, trying to touch only the edges and the corners as she opened it. John moved to look at the contents over her shoulder.

Small, neat writing filled the pages, but they didn't form any sort of journalistic narrative. Instead, they were line after line of notes. Names. Places. Short commentary on one or both. *Never pull a con in Vegas. Everybody already knows all the tricks.*

"This must have belonged to Delta's father," John said.

Miranda nodded, flipping through the pages slowly, giving him time to make out the neat writing. "It's almost like a how-to book on pulling cons."

As they neared the later pages of the book, some of the notes changed. Still names and places, but now notes such as "Does his wife know he's bedding boys?" and "One more DUI and he loses his license."

"And now we have blackmail," John murmured.

About ten pages from the back of the book, the writing changed abruptly from the neat, almost printlike writing to a larger, more looping cursive. "That's Delta's writing," Miranda said.

John looked down at the book. "So you're saying…"

"I'm saying Delta McGraw was following in her father's footsteps." Miranda looked down at the journal. "And this may be what got her killed."

Chapter Twelve

One of the small back rooms at Duncan Hardware served as Gil Duncan's office. Inside, he'd crammed filing cabinets, a computer and a multifunction printer. One of those functions was copying, and Miranda spent a couple of hours that afternoon making two sets of copies from Delta McGraw's journal.

"I have to take this book to the sheriff's department," she'd told John earlier, after a second read through had convinced her that the journal might contain a clue that would help the department solve Delta's murder.

"Don't you want to go back through it again a few times first?" John had asked. He'd sat quietly enough across the table from her while she gave all the journal pages a more thorough reading, but she hadn't missed the impatience creasing his forehead and feathering fine lines from the corners of his eyes.

He was right. She did want to go back through it a few more times. Once the book was in the hands of the sheriff's department, it would be off-limits to her, since Miles Randall had made it clear he wasn't going to let her be part of the investigation.

So she'd just have to run her own investigation on the

side, and to do so, she was going to need the information in that journal.

She finished copying the last page and slipped the journal back into the plastic bag. After removing her latex gloves, she took the paper from the copier and bumped the stack against the top of the copier a few times to straighten the pages into a neat sheaf. She bound them together with a couple of rubber bands.

"Here." John handed her the canvas shopping tote she'd brought with her to conceal the copied pages. She shoved the bound pages inside, and John tucked the whole thing under one arm.

They headed out the back door to the employee parking area, where she'd parked her truck.

"Do you think the sheriff will suspect you've kept a copy?" John asked as he buckled his seat belt.

"I don't know. Maybe. I don't think he's going to make a stink about it, though, unless I get in the way of his investigation."

"And will you? Get in the way, I mean."

"I'll do my best not to."

She could see suspicion in Miles Randall's eyes when she handed over the two bags of evidence, but he didn't comment as she told him where the book had been hidden and how she'd done her best to maintain any potential evidence. "I'm not sure you'll be able to get any prints off the journal. And even if you could, I'm pretty sure the prints will be either Hal McGraw's or Delta's. I think Delta must have hidden the book when she was staying at my place for a couple of weeks."

"The room was already up that soon?"

"Oh, yeah. We had the builders reframe everything and get the siding and roof up as soon as we could after the tornado. We've just been taking our time with the rest of it, working when we could. But Dad's been swamped with all the orders from other people trying to rebuild, and you know you've been keeping me busy here at the station."

Randall was silent for another moment. Miranda realized she was holding her breath and let it go in a quiet sigh.

"Okay," Randall said finally. "But you're still off this case, Duncan. Understood?"

"Understood."

Randall frowned at the plastic-encased journal. "We'll dust the outside for prints. Nobody touched this at all?"

"John Blake found it, but he was wearing gloves because it was hidden in fiberglass insulation. I wore latex gloves when I held the book. Nobody touched it without a glove."

"But you looked through it?"

"Of course."

"What's inside?"

She described what she'd read, being as truthful and complete as she could.

Randall was a good man. A smart man. He knew as soon as she began talking what they were dealing with. The disappointment in his eyes echoed the sadness in her own heart. "She'd taken up her father's work."

"Looks like it." Miranda had hoped after Hal's death, Delta would finally be free of his legacy.

Instead, it looked as if she'd chosen to embrace it.

"Guess that explains that ten grand you found at her house this morning." Randall rubbed his chin thoughtfully. "Is there anything in that book that's actionable?"

"I don't know. She made notes about things she believed to be true. But if she had any actual evidence hidden anywhere, I don't know where she hid it. All that's in there right now are leads to go on but nothing we could take to court."

"Well, we'll see what we can track down from it." As Miranda rose to go, the sheriff asked, "How're you feeling?"

"A little tired. But improving." She could probably go to work right now and be fine, but since the sheriff wasn't going to let her anywhere near the Delta McGraw case while she was wearing the uniform, it had occurred to her that having the next few days free to work the case informally might be in her favor. "I'll be fine by Monday."

"Take care to get some rest, Deputy." Randall softened the stern tone of his voice with a slight smile.

"Thanks. I'll do that." She left the sheriff's office and headed for the front exit.

Coy Taylor was just coming on duty when she passed the sergeant's desk. He flashed her a smile. "You back yet?"

"Not until Monday," she said with an exaggerated sigh. "You're on afternoon duty this week?"

"Yeah. Chambers is covering mornings for the next couple of weeks. His kid starts his first varsity spring practice at the high school this week, and I guess Chambers wanted to be there to watch." Taylor settled behind the desk. "Heard you went to Delta's place this morning. Find anything?"

"You know I can't say, Sarge. But I'm hopeful we'll get a break in the case soon, and then you'll know all the details." As a desk sergeant, Taylor wasn't given details on every case they worked, only the parts that had been released to the press. Everything else stayed strictly between the deputies investigating the case.

In fact, she shouldn't be sharing any of the stuff she'd learned with John Blake at all. But since he'd almost been a victim of the same mystery gunman who had gone after her the other day, she figured she owed him the chance to get in on the investigation.

And she could use his help, since the sheriff had more or less banned her from her own case.

"Real shame about Delta." Taylor shook his head. "She had a real rough life."

Miranda nodded. "Yes, she did."

The phone rang, and Taylor shot her a look of apology as he answered. Miranda continued out the door to where John was waiting patiently in the passenger seat of her truck.

"How did it go?" he asked as she belted herself in behind the steering wheel.

"If he knew I was not only investigating this case on my own, but bringing a civilian in on it as well, I think I'd be in serious trouble."

"So don't let him find out."

Easy to say, she thought. But maybe not so easy to do.

"I THINK WE can probably set aside anything that wasn't from the last couple of years." Miranda looked up from one set of the journal pages she'd copied at her father's store. She looked tired, John thought. Probably should be getting some rest rather than diving headfirst into the blackmail journal. But she'd rebuffed the suggestion when he brought it up.

"I don't know—Delta might have kept up some of her father's blackmail schemes."

"Yeah, but I'm not seeing anything in Hal's notes that would be worth ten thousand dollars in hush money. Are you?"

John looked at the notes he'd taken from the early set of pages. Most of the crimes Hal McGraw had chronicled in his journal might be worth a couple of thousand dollars to keep them from coming out, but ten grand?

"Of course, I suppose it's possible that money I found came from multiple sources," Miranda added.

John shook his head. "I don't think so. Not the way you described those packets of bills. It seems as if it all came from the same place."

"True." She rested her chin on her folded hands and looked at him across the kitchen table. "So what kind of crime would be worth paying a blackmailer ten grand to cover it up?"

He dropped his pen and mimicked her position. "More to the point, what kind of crime would be worth killing for?"

"Very good point." Miranda picked up her pen and started marking through a few of the listings in her notes. "By the way, did you notice that a few of Delta's last entries looked as if they were written in code?"

"I did." He looked down at his own notes and marked through a few that didn't seem likely to stir up a murderous rage. "It looks like some sort of cipher. Did Delta like things like puzzles and ciphers?"

Miranda frowned. "I don't know. She never let me that far into her life, you know?"

"Well, if her father was a con man, she probably had at least a passing knowledge of ciphers and tricks. I'm surprised Hal didn't keep his own book in code."

"I'm surprised he kept a book at all," Miranda said. "He never seemed to be the organized sort."

"Does the first entry date mean anything?" John flipped back to the first page of his copy of the journal. "Looks like the first entry was about eleven years ago. January 12. Does that mean anything?"

"That's Delta's birthday. She would have turned sixteen that year."

"Sweet sixteen."

"Actually, on her sixteenth birthday, she was declared an emancipated minor by the courts. I don't remember much about it—I was in my senior year of high school and Delta McGraw wasn't really on my mind at the time. I do know that Hal McGraw didn't try to stop her. I think he knew he wasn't exactly a great dad."

John tried to put himself in Hal McGraw's shoes. His wife long gone, his own life a series of scams and cons, the law dogging his heels and his daughter officially declaring her independence from him—would that situation make him do a little soul-searching?

Not a guy like Hal McGraw. He'd try to do something to win back his daughter.

"What if that's why he started keeping this journal?" he asked. "What if this was meant to lure Delta back all along?"

"Lure her back?"

"She declared her independence from him right about the time these entries started. Maybe he tried to buy her affection and loyalty. Made a big push to earn more money, give her a reason to stick around."

Miranda frowned thoughtfully. "Maybe. I do remember some of the girls at school talking about how she was suddenly dressing nicer and wondered how come she suddenly had money after ditching her daddy."

"He might have been trying to impress her."

"Could she have known all along what Hal was doing?"

"You tell me. You knew Delta. Do you think she knew?"

"I don't know. But clearly she knew what that book meant, and rather than destroy it, she tried to protect it." Miranda rose from the table, revealing in her restless movements the troubled state of her mind. She paced to the window and looked outside at a landscape bathed in the ruby glow of the setting sun. "She must have hidden it here when she was staying with me. She was here alone a lot."

"You said her father had made her his accomplice, right?"

She nodded, still looking out the window.

"So she'd know how to run an extortion scheme."

"Yes. She would." Miranda turned slowly to face him. "I just wanted to believe she'd put that kind of life behind her."

"She didn't have a job, did she?"

"Not recently." Miranda closed her eyes. "I should have spent a little more time trying to figure out where she was getting the money to live on if she wasn't working a job."

"But you didn't."

She shook her head. "I can be as much a loner as Delta was. I get really wrapped up in what I'm doing in my own life and I sometimes forget to touch base with people."

He could sympathize. "You can't fix what you didn't

do. Not at this point. But you can find justice for her. Right?"

"Right." She pushed her fingers through her hair like a comb, shoving the mass of auburn waves away from her face. "We had some leftovers from yesterday's barbecue. Want me to heat them up for us for dinner?"

"You sit. I'll get the leftovers."

She didn't argue, sliding back into the chair she'd vacated a few minutes earlier, then straightening the scattered pages before her into a neat stack. John retrieved the leftover steaks and baked potatoes from the refrigerator and piled them onto plates to heat in the microwave. He also grabbed the remaining salad and placed it on the table.

"Hmm," Miranda murmured as he pulled glasses from the cabinet.

"Hmm what?"

"This entry. It's in Delta's handwriting, and I don't think this notation is code, but I'm not quite sure what it means." She turned the page around so he could read it, pointing to the note in question.

Hef. Co. clerk—Rem. Alamo Fund. 50K missing?

"Heflin County is the next county over," Miranda explained. "And there's a Texas-based charity for wounded Texas soldiers called the Remember the Alamo Fund. But I haven't heard anything about missing money."

"Maybe it hasn't been discovered yet. Or someone managed to pay it all back after getting a note from Delta."

"So her blackmail was altruistic?" He tried not to scoff, but there had been several packets of hundred-dollar bills hidden in Delta's kitchen counter that would suggest otherwise.

"No, of course not." Miranda sighed. "I just mean, maybe that was the response to Delta's blackmail rather than paying the money to her."

"Paying it back would have been about covering his tracks."

"Or hers. I don't know who the Heflin county clerk is."

"Or hers," John conceded. "But if he or she was willing to go to the lengths of coming up with fifty thousand to pay back the charity—"

"He or she might have gone even further."

"Having that hanging over your head would be a nightmare. Even if the money was refunded, you'd have to worry that what you did would come out. Forget about your position with the charity. Even being accused of that sort of transgression could put your job in jeopardy."

"Especially in Texas. County clerks here oversee elections. Imagine the kind of election shenanigans a blackmailer could cause holding something over the head of the county clerk. And you know, if something like that came out and your spouse didn't know about it, it could wreak havoc on your personal life, too."

John nodded. "A person might be willing to kill to make it all go away."

"So we need to find out who the Heflin county clerk is and if he or she has any connection to the Remember the Alamo Fund." She pushed away from the table and headed down the hall to her bedroom.

John followed, stopping in the doorway while she grabbed her laptop computer from a drawer beside her bed. She plugged it in and sat on the edge of her bed, glancing at him over her shoulder. "You can come in."

He sat on the bed beside her, trying to ignore the little shiver of animal awareness that rippled through him. So many other things he'd like to do in this room besides surf the internet…

"Here we go. Jasper Layton is the Heflin county clerk." She pulled up a search engine page and entered the name. Several links came up, most of them connected to his position as county clerk.

She made a sound, and he found himself edging closer to read the screen over her shoulder.

She clicked a link and a page came up, an article from the Heflin County newspaper. "'Liver transplant miracle not without its downside—recipient and family find themselves deep in debt.'"

"His wife needed a liver transplant," John murmured, scanning the article. "Guess that might explain why he was willing to risk everything to skim money out of the charity fund."

"But how did he pay it back?"

"Good question."

Miranda picked up her cell phone and brought up the previous tab from the Heflin County website. She punched in a number. "Jasper Layton, please." Listening for a second, she frowned. "Oh. I'm sorry to hear that. Thank you."

"Sorry to hear what?" John asked as she ended the call and set the phone on the bed beside her.

She turned her head to look at him, her expression troubled. "Jasper Layton is dead."

Chapter Thirteen

"He ran his car off Wildcat Ridge. There was no evidence that he hit the brakes." Sheriff Paul Leonardi leaned back in his chair, steepling his hands over his flat stomach as he looked across the desk at Miranda and John. "What's your interest in Jasper Layton, if I may ask, Deputy Duncan?"

Miranda had anticipated the question, and she had her answer ready. "We're investigating a murder in Barstow County, and Mr. Layton's name showed up in some of the victim's personal effects. When we learned that Mr. Layton was deceased—"

"You thought you'd come talk to me."

"You said there was no evidence he hit the brakes," John said. "Do you think he intentionally ran his car off the road?"

Leonardi gave John a long, narrow-eyed look of speculation. "You're not a deputy."

"No, sir."

The sheriff flicked his gaze toward Miranda. "You bring a civilian along to all your meetings with fellow law enforcement agents?"

"Mr. Blake is a consultant," she said, as if dismissing the question. "Do you think Mr. Layton's accident was intentional?"

"Let's put it this way. The autopsy determined that cause of death was blunt-force trauma to the head. Layton went through the windshield and landed under the car. There were no signs of alcohol or drugs in his system. It was in the middle of the afternoon, so it's not likely he fell asleep at the wheel."

"But you seem reluctant to call it suicide."

"I didn't see the point of multiplying the tragedies Mrs. Layton and her children had to face." Leonardi shrugged. "It wouldn't have made any difference. He was past the two-year exception in his life insurance. They were going to get the money regardless."

Miranda glanced at John. He looked back at her, his dark eyebrows twitching upward in response.

"The article I read said this happened three weeks ago?"

"Yes."

So, she thought, soon after Delta disappeared. But quite possibly before she had died and definitely before her body was dumped on Lizzie Dillard's farm. And that meant even if Jasper Layton had been one of Delta's blackmail victims, he wasn't likely to have been her killer.

"Is there anything else I can help you with?"

"Just one thing, and I don't think you're going to like it."

Leonardi sat forward, leaning his forearms on his desk blotter. "You want to talk to Angela, don't you?"

"I do."

Leonardi's lips pressed to a thin line. "Is that really necessary?"

"I'm afraid it is."

"I'd like to be with you when you talk to her."

"If you're worried I'll tell her something about her husband's mode of death, rest assured, I won't."

"Then what's left to ask her?"

She glanced at John again. He sent back a meaningful look.

"I'd like to ask her about her husband's involvement in the Remember the Alamo Fund."

One twitch of the muscle in Leonardi's lean jaw was the sheriff's only visible reaction, but it was enough. "What about it?"

"Did you know at least fifty thousand dollars went missing from the fund earlier this year?"

"You're mistaken." His tone was dismissive.

"Are you involved with the fund?" she asked bluntly.

Leonardi rose to his feet, towering over them. "I'm a busy man, Deputy Duncan. I've answered all the pertinent questions about Jasper Layton's unfortunate accident. If you have any further enquiries, you can have your boss contact me."

"You hit a sore spot back there," John murmured a few moments later as they left the Heflin County Hall and stepped into the mild afternoon sunlight. "I think he knows the money is missing."

"Or was," she said as she unlocked the door of her truck. The interior had heated up beneath the warm Texas sun, coaxing a trickle of perspiration down her temple as she started the truck and headed its wide nose out of the parking lot.

"You think Layton paid the money back."

"If he stole fifty grand from the charity, it would come out unless it somehow got paid back before anyone figured it out."

"But how could he have paid it back?" John asked. "You saw that article about his wife. Her transplant left them in serious debt."

"That's why I wanted to talk to Angela Layton."

"You think she knows what her husband did?"

"I think if anyone would know, it's probably her." Miranda pulled the truck into a small shopping strip just off the highway, parking in front of a diner that occupied one of the glass-front shops at the nearest end. "So we need to talk to her."

"But first, we're going to have a late lunch?" He followed her as she got out of the truck and headed for the door of the diner.

"I don't know how much you know about life in a small town," she said as they neared the front door of the diner, "but if you want to know anything about anyone in town, a town diner is the place to start."

At a little after two in the afternoon, the diner was sparsely occupied. Miranda headed for the counter at the back. Within a few seconds, a pleasantly plump, motherly waitress appeared from the back and put menus on the counter in front of them. With a smile, she welcomed them to the diner.

"I'd like a cup of coffee—black, one sweetener—and a slice of your double chocolate cake," Miranda ordered with a smile.

"Same," John said.

"I've heard such good things about your chocolate cake," Miranda added, taking a chance.

"Really?" The waitress smiled with pleasure at the compliment. The rectangular name badge pinned to her light blue dress said "Vicki" in neat embossed letters. "Heard from who?" she asked, as Miranda had hoped.

"Angela Layton, for one."

Immediately Vicki's expression faltered. "That poor woman."

"These past few months have been so hard on her."

"Just when she was finally starting to see a little light at the end of the tunnel." Vicki shook her head. "Did you make it to the funeral?"

"We were still at the hospital," John said, slanting a quick glance at Miranda. "My mother was still recovering from her transplant."

"That's where we met Angela and Jasper," Miranda said. "John's mother was having a kidney transplant when Angela was in the hospital. We met Jasper in the cafeteria and, well—"

"We clicked, you know?" John flashed Vicki a smile that seemed to charm the waitress into a broad, answering smile.

"I know what you mean," Vicki said as she poured coffee for both of them. "Did you come to town just to see Angela?"

"Actually, no," Miranda answered, "we're just passing through on our way to Amarillo, but we thought we'd at least stop in here at the Lone Star Diner to try a slice of that cake."

"We had hoped maybe Angela might be feeling well enough to be here, too," John admitted. "But that was probably hoping too much."

"She hasn't felt a lot like getting out and about," Vicki said as she served them slices of the chocolate cake. "But maybe you could give her a call. I'm sure she could use some cheering up."

"That's the thing," Miranda said with a slight shake of her head. "Jasper gave John their phone number, but somewhere between the hospital and the motel where we were staying, he lost it. We were lucky to remember Heflin County."

"She's probably not in the mood for visitors anyway," John said after swallowing a bite of cake.

"Not so sure about that. She'd probably appreciate a friendly face right about now." Vicki reached under the counter and pulled out a thin phone directory. "I think they're listed."

While Vicki went to wait on a couple of customers who had just entered and taken one of the tables near the front window, Miranda quickly looked up the listing for Jasper and Angela Layton. She jotted the number and address to her phone.

"Are we really going to invade that poor woman's privacy?" John asked quietly.

"I don't want to, but if anybody's going to be able to tell us why Delta had that notation about Jasper Layton in her blackmail diary—"

"What if Jasper didn't tell his wife anything?"

"We won't know unless we ask."

Still, she had to give herself a mental pep talk during the mile-and-a-half drive from the diner to the small ranch-style house on Prescott Road, including most of the walk up the flagstone path to the front door, before she found the courage to knock.

The woman who answered was plump and cheerful, and definitely not the woman whose photo had been part of the online article Miranda had found during her internet search for Jasper Layton. She introduced herself as Angela's aunt Laura.

"Angela's resting in the sunroom," Laura told them when they asked. "Are you friends?"

"We actually knew Jasper," John lied. "Through his work with the Remember the Alamo Fund."

Laura's expression fell. "Poor Jasper. Poor Angela, for that matter. Finally starting to feel better, a whole new future ahead of her, and then this."

"We wanted to see if she needed anything. If there was anything we could do for her," Miranda said, and meant it. She might have questions for the woman, but maybe if she could find the answers about what really happened to Jasper, it would give Angela Layton some comfort.

At least, she hoped it would. She hoped she wasn't about to make everything worse.

"I'll ask if she's up to having visitors." Laura disappeared down a hall, returning a few moments later. "She'll see you. Down the hall, first room on the left."

Miranda and John followed the directions and found a slim, blonde woman sitting on a colorful sofa in front of a wall full of curtainless windows. Bright sunlight and warmth flowed into the room through the wall of glass, bathing the blonde in golden light.

Angela Layton looked considerably better than she'd appeared shortly after her liver transplant surgery, but beneath the glow of improving health was the pallor of grief. She rose to greet them as they entered the sunroom, extending a slim hand. "Aunt Laura said you knew Jasper?"

Miranda felt like a creep. "Actually, we didn't. Not personally."

Angela sank to the sofa again, looking at them through narrowed eyes. "Are you reporters?"

"No." Miranda gestured at the round ottoman sitting in front of the sofa. "May I?"

"Who are you?"

"My name is Miranda Duncan. I'm a deputy sheriff with the Barstow County Sheriff's Department."

Angela's expression went from wary to confused. "Barstow County?"

"Did you know anyone named Delta McGraw?"

Something shifted subtly in Angela Layton's eyes. "Should I?"

"I believe she might have been blackmailing your husband."

For a moment, Angela looked as if she was about to order them to leave. But after a second of tension, she slumped back against the sofa cushions and closed her eyes. "He paid it all back."

"To the Remember the Alamo Fund?"

Angela nodded, her eyes still closed. "We were so desperate for money. All of our savings were gone. Jasper had borrowed all he could against his 401K and it just wasn't enough. One of the doctors at the hospital in Dallas was making a big stink about getting his fees, and I was still feeling so sick, I couldn't even go to work part-time to try to pick up the slack."

"And there were the funds at the charity, so easy to get his hands on," John murmured.

"It wasn't easy for him," Angela snapped, anger flashing in her blue eyes. "It broke him. Do you really think that accident that killed him was an accident?"

Miranda glanced at John, whose expression was carefully neutral. But she was beginning to be able to read the subtle clues to the emotions he kept in check. There was a grim cast to his hazel eyes that echoed the dismay burning in her own chest.

"He held onto the funds for a long time. I think maybe he was hoping something would happen to save us." Angela passed a thin hand over her face. "Then one day, he told me someone knew what he'd done."

"Delta."

Angela nodded. "Delta."

"How did Jasper know Delta? Or did he?"

"He told me he knew her through his job as county clerk. Apparently her father had owned some property here in Heflin County and she'd come here after his death to deal with some probate issues. He wasn't sure how she figured out what he'd done, but the next thing he knew, she called him and told him she knew he'd skimmed the funds from the charity and if he wanted her silence, he had to pay her ten thousand dollars."

Miranda's heart sank. Intellectually, she knew that Delta had to be involved in extortion, but hearing it laid out so baldly was a blow.

"What did Jasper do?" John asked.

"He couldn't pay her. He hadn't even really decided whether he could keep the money to pay our bills. So he told Delta why he'd taken the money and told her he would put it back."

"What did she say?"

"She said if he did, she wouldn't tell anyone what she knew."

"For a price?"

Angela looked up at them. "Jasper said no. That once she heard why he'd taken the money in the first place, she backed off. She just said she'd know if he put it back or not, and if he didn't, she'd double her price."

"So he put it back?" John asked.

"Yes. And then three weeks later he drove off Wildcat Ridge." Tears glittered in Angela's eyes, but they didn't fall.

"I'm so sorry." Miranda started to reach across the

space between them to touch Angela's hand, but the expression on the woman's face stopped her. She dropped her hand back to her lap. "You clearly don't think it was an accident."

"It wasn't. He left the life insurance policy sitting on the desk in his study. I found it there before I even heard about the crash." She brushed away the tears welling on her lower eyelids. "He'd left a sticky note on top."

"What did it say?" Miranda asked.

"It said the two years were up."

"The suicide clause," John murmured.

Angela nodded. "He took the policy out four years ago, when I was first diagnosed with liver failure. I'd contracted hepatitis B when I was working as a nurse at a clinic down on the border a few years ago. I got over it quickly enough and didn't really think anything more about it, until my liver started failing." She shook her head. "Jasper went out and bought a life insurance policy that day. Until then, I guess we thought we were invincible."

"His insurance will cover your bills, won't it?"

This time, Angela didn't stop the tears. "There'll even be some left over so I can keep the house until I'm recovered enough to go back to work."

Miranda looked at John. He gave a slight nod, and she stood. "Mrs. Layton, I really am very sorry for your loss. And I'm sorry I had to bother you this way."

Angela didn't rise to see them out, but she did speak as they were turning to go. "Did you find out what you wanted to know?"

Miranda turned back to look at her. "Yes. Your husband was a good man. Don't ever let anyone make you think otherwise."

For the first time since they'd entered the room, Angela managed a faint smile. "I know."

Back in the hot truck cab, Miranda leaned against the headrest and closed her eyes. "I wish we hadn't done that."

"It answered a few questions."

"At what price?" She opened her eyes and looked at John. "There's no way Jasper Layton killed Delta."

"But we couldn't really know until we talked to her whether Angela Layton might have done it."

"We're back to square one."

John held up the bundle of copied pages he'd brought with them. "We still have these."

"Well, then, you look through those pages and see what you can find while I hunt down a gas station."

John flipped through the pages while she navigated the side streets until she found a gas station near the highway that would take them back to Barstow County. When Miranda got back into the truck after pumping the gas, he looked up at her with a slight smile.

"Does this mean anything to you?" he asked, looking down at the page he was holding. "'Jarrod Whitmore. Trainor and 7,'" he said. "Why does the name Jarrod Whitmore sound familiar?"

"Ever heard of the Bar W Ranch?"

"Of course. It's just a couple of miles down the highway from where I'm staying. I pass the place all the time."

"Bar W is owned by Cal Whitmore. Jarrod is his youngest son. He's always been a little on the wild side."

"What about the rest of it? 'Trainor and 7'?"

"I'm not sure. Trainor is a road that crosses Route 7 about five miles south of the ranch, but I don't know…" She froze in the middle of putting her key in the ignition as the answer hit her like a hammer blow. "Oh, my God. Trainor Road and Route 7."

"What is it?" John asked.

She turned to look at John, hear stomach roiling. "Do you remember that lady you met at my dad's place the other day? Rose McAllen?"

He frowned. "You mean the one with the little girl?"

"Right, her granddaughter, Cassie. Rose's daughter, Lindy—Cassie's mother—was killed in a hit-and-run on Route 7. To be more specific, she was killed on Route 7 right at the Trainor Road crossing. About a year after Hal McGraw's death. She was walking on the highway and a vehicle struck her and kept going. We've never found the person responsible."

John looked down at the page he was holding. "This is Delta's handwriting, isn't it?" He showed her the copy.

Miranda nodded.

"So Delta—"

"She knew," Miranda interjected. "She knew that Jarrod Whitmore was the one who hit Lindy McAllen and left her to die. In fact, she was blackmailing him about it."

"We *were* looking for a crime someone might be willing to kill for," John murmured.

Miranda met his troubled gaze, her stomach in knots. "I think we just may have found it."

Chapter Fourteen

By the time they arrived back in Cold Creek, the sun was already dipping well toward the western horizon. Miranda pulled into the parking lot of the hardware store and shut off the engine to make a phone call to the Bar W Ranch, while John ran into the store to pick up some paint he was going to need when he got back to the work on his own place.

By the time he returned to the truck with his purchase, Miranda was off the phone, sitting with both hands tightly gripping the steering wheel and a frustrated look in her gray eyes.

She turned her head to look at him as he climbed into the passenger seat. "Got Mr. Whitmore's housekeeper. She said the Whitmores are in Montana looking at a couple of bulls for sale and won't be back until Monday. And Jarrod's in Ireland."

"Ireland?" John asked, surprised. "What's he doing in Ireland?"

"The housekeeper didn't offer any other information."

"Well, at least we have an extradition treaty with Ireland."

"First we have to figure out if he was the person driving the vehicle that killed Lindy McAllen."

"You'd have access to the case files, wouldn't you?"

Miranda started the truck and pulled out of the parking lot. "Yeah. I should be able to access them from my laptop at home, though. I noticed Sheriff Randall's truck was still at the station when we drove by. I don't want him asking questions about why I keep showing up at the station when I'm supposed to be on medical leave."

"So let's pick up dinner somewhere, go back to your place and try to relax a little," John suggested. He was beginning to think she was overtaxing herself so soon after the crash. She'd been rubbing her head for most of the drive back to Cold Creek, as if she was trying to ward off a headache, and her pale face and the dark circles under her eyes were starting to concern him.

"We have so many more pages to work through," she protested.

"And they can wait until tomorrow," he told her firmly. "Right now, you need some food, a nice hot bath and a good night's sleep. In that order."

She slanted a look at him but didn't say anything else until they reached the small roadside barbecue stand near her house. They picked up barbecue brisket, baked beans and tangy vinegar slaw to share and were back at Miranda's house by five thirty.

Rex and Ruthie both greeted them at the front door when they entered, as good a sign as they were likely to get that nobody had tried to break into the house while they were gone.

John fed the cats in the kitchen while Miranda pulled an old folding card table and two chairs onto the front porch. By the time John went outside, she'd already laid out their meal on the table and had kicked back, her feet propped on the porch railing, sipping iced tea through a straw while she watched the ruby sunset sinking into the western horizon.

"Every time I wonder why I haven't moved out of this little bitty town, I look at one of those sunsets, breathe in the clean air and listen to the killdeer calling and I remember why I'm still here."

"It's very different than where I'm from." He took a sip of his own tea and followed her gaze toward the sunset. "But just as beautiful in its own way."

"Miss the mountains?" She dropped her feet to the porch floor and turned to spoon a couple of slabs of brisket onto her plate.

"Some. Not as much as I would've thought." There was a wild beauty in the flat scrubby plains of the panhandle that spoke to something inside him he hadn't even realized existed, a hunger for wide open spaces and endless horizons that couldn't be found in the hills of home.

"I used to think of this place as untouchable." She added beans and slaw to her plate and poked a fork into a piece of brisket. "Crime didn't really exist here, you know? Not like in the bigger cities. I could count on my hand the number of serious crimes in the past ten years. Until now."

"Can't keep the world out forever."

"No." She dropped her fork. "Now we have a murder, and an unsolved hit-and-run and God knows what else we're going to find once we figure out what kind of code Delta was using—"

"You can't keep the world out forever," he repeated, reaching across the table and closing his hand over hers. "But maybe we should try to keep it out for tonight?"

She looked at him for a long, tense moment, then

turned her hand so that her palm touched his. "Do you think we can really do that?"

"We could try."

She gave him a narrow-eyed look for a second, then smiled. "Okay. No shoptalk for the rest of the evening."

They settled in to a comfortable silence as they ate, but soon, with their stomachs full, the leftovers put up in the refrigerator and the card table restored to the hall closet, Miranda sat on the sofa across from John and shot him a questioning look. "What now?"

"What do you usually do when you have men over?"

Her gaze skittered away. "I don't usually have men over."

"Ever?"

"I don't have a lot of time to date these days," she said, sounding mildly defensive. "And when I do, we generally drive in to Plainview or Lubbock for dinner and maybe a movie, and then it's late, so I have to come home so I can get a decent night's sleep before work in the morning." She pressed her face into her hands. "God, that sounds pathetic."

"Yeah, well, the last woman I went out with didn't even know my real name, so I don't exactly have room to judge."

She managed a smile. "I don't think this is what you had in mind when we agreed to no shoptalk."

"Relax. I don't have anything in particular in mind." He joined her on the sofa, sitting close enough that he could touch her if he liked, but not so close he would send her nervously skittering into the next zip code.

"Maybe we could ask each other questions," she suggested. "You know, getting-to-know-you kind of questions."

"Sure. You want to start?"

"Okay." Her smile was a little nervous, but she turned her body toward him, giving him a nice view of her long neck and the ripe curves of her breasts beneath her thin blue T-shirt.

Progress, he thought, trying not to stare too obviously.

He must have failed, he realized a moment later when a look of amusement lightened her gray eyes and her nerves seemed to settle in a heartbeat. "I've already done a background check on you, so no easy questions from me," she warned with a widening smile. "Let's start with a hard one. Ever milked a cow?"

He laughed. "Yes, actually. On my granddaddy's farm. He had a place west of the mountains, where he raised chickens and pigs and he had a milk cow and a couple of swayback mares he'd let us ride until we got too heavy for them."

"You and your brother and sister?"

"Yeah. Josh, Julie and me."

"All your names started with *J*?"

"Not one of my parents' better decisions. My poor mom went through the whole list every time she was trying to call any one of us."

Miranda laughed, the sound warm and inviting, drawing him closer despite his intention to keep his distance. "My dad just had me, but when he gets mad, he uses my full name."

He leaned even closer. "Which is?"

"Miranda Crockett Duncan."

"Crockett? As in Davy?"

"Remember the Alamo," she said with a sheepish laugh. "My dad tells me it was a compromise. He wanted to name me after his mother, Geraldine, and my mother wanted to name me after her best friend in grammar school, Mercedes Gonzales."

"Miranda Mercedes Duncan?" He couldn't hold back a wince. "Yeah, I think Crockett was definitely the way to go."

"You'd think. But there was this one kid in summer camp who found out my middle name and kept singing the Davy Crockett TV show theme whenever he saw me."

"Summer camp where?"

"Down near San Antonio. Of course."

"And you went to college at Texas Tech."

"Wreck 'em, Tech!" she said with a big grin.

"So, have you ever actually left Texas?"

"Of course. I drove across the state line into Oklahoma once. Quickly." She shot him a big grin. "Seriously, of course I've been other places. I went to Spain for a semester my junior year of college. I've seen Notre Dame in Paris and once talked my way onto a sculling crew practicing on the Thames."

"What did a girl from Cold Creek, Texas, know about sculling?"

"Not a damn thing." She laughed. "But the guys thought I was cute, so they nearly capsized the boat trying to teach me how it worked."

He could picture the scene all too easily. There was something about Miranda Crockett Duncan that made a man want to do things he never realized he could. Or should.

He touched her cheek because it was there, softly curved and tempting, within his reach. Her smile faded and her gray eyes grew large and luminous as she gazed back at him in breathless anticipation.

He kissed her. Her response was swift and fierce, her

hands threading through his hair and drawing him closer. Her lips parted, inviting him in, and before he knew quite how they got there, she was lying on her back beneath him, her hands sliding under his shirt until they touched his skin, her fingertips leaving a shivery trail of need the farther they traveled.

Suddenly, her fingers pressed against a tender place above his shoulder, and he couldn't quite swallow the hiss of pain it evoked.

She went still, drawing her head back to look at him. "Did I hurt you?"

"No," he lied, dipping his head toward her again.

But she wriggled out from beneath him, pushing him back into a sitting position. "That was a bullet-wound scar."

"I told you about that."

"You said they were hunting you, but I didn't realize they actually shot you. I thought maybe you just got assaulted or something." She reached for the collar of his shirt, tugging it aside until she found the corresponding entry wound scar. "How many other scars like this do you have?"

He nudged the waistband of his jeans down to show her where he'd taken a bullet just above his hip. "That wasn't much more than a flesh wound."

"Is that it?"

He let the jeans fall back into place and lifted the bottom of his shirt to bare his right side. The wound there was the worst of his scars because it had taken surgery to remove the bullet lodged a few inches away from his hepatic artery. It had nicked his liver, but the damage to that organ had been minimal and it had healed on its own, once the surgeon had removed the bullet from its dangerous hiding place.

"How much damage did it do?" she asked quietly, her eyes wide with dismay.

"Not as much as it could have."

"What did you do that made the Blue Ridge Infantry put you on their most-wanted list?"

He frowned. The night wasn't going the way he'd hoped at all. "I thought we weren't going to talk shop."

"I don't consider this talking shop," she said with a frown. "What did you do to cross them, exactly?"

"Remember I told you about that tough lady named Nicki who helped bring down the Virginia branch of the militia?"

Miranda nodded.

"Nicki was deep undercover. She had no contact with our boss, Alexander Quinn, except through me. I guess you could say I was sort of her handler."

"And the BRI found out what you were doing?"

"Not exactly. What put me on their radar was my part in helping Nicki sneak their top man's wife and kid out of their cabin in the woods."

Miranda's eyes narrowed. "Were they being held hostage?"

"Not exactly." He settled back against the sofa cushions with a sigh. "Nicki had been trying to get close enough to find out the identity of the militia leader. People talked about him in hushed, almost reverent tones, but they never called him by name. The only thing she'd learned was that he had a medical condition that needed nursing care, and she made it her goal to be chosen as his medical caretaker."

"What kind of condition?"

"Diabetes. The story was, he was having trouble stabilizing his blood sugar and he didn't trust doctors or hospitals."

"And Nicki was a nurse?"

"She had paramedic training."

"So she managed to get them to trust her?"

"We thought they did. One day, they told her she was in and arranged for her to go meet the leader." There were some fuzzy places in his memory of what had happened next, but one thing he'd never forgotten was the gutting fear that had come over him when he'd realized the Blue Ridge Infantry was on to Nicki's scheme. "It turned out, Nicki had been working for the leader of the Virginia BRI the whole time she was in River's End. He was her boss at the diner where she'd worked as a fry cook."

"My God. And she never had a clue? What about the diabetes—if he was having so much trouble getting his blood sugar regulated, didn't he show signs of it?"

"That's the thing. It was never Trevor Colley who was sick. It was his little boy."

Miranda lifted her hand to her mouth. "Juvenile diabetes?"

He nodded. "The kid was really sick, and Colley let his fear of doctors and hospitals put that kid in danger. They took Nicki hostage and made her try to help the little boy while they waited for Nicki's backup to arrive so they could take them out."

"Which is where you and your bullet wounds come in."

"More or less. Nicki had gotten involved with someone else, someone in nearly as much trouble as she was, and he helped me get to her once the operation went crossways. Nicki convinced Colley's wife that they needed to get the little boy to a real doctor. That if they didn't do something soon, he'd die. Nicki's friend, Dallas, helped her get the woman and the boy to safety."

"While you were doing what, offering a diversion for Colley and his men?"

He didn't answer. He didn't have to.

"My God, you let them shoot at you so the others could get to safety?"

"I didn't know what else to do. I'd had one job—keeping Nicki as safe as possible while she did her very dangerous job. I had to see it through."

She just stared at him for a moment, her heart in her eyes. Then she reached out and caught his face between her long-fingered hands. "You crazy, amazing man." Bending, she kissed him firmly, not resisting when he pulled her into his arms.

The kiss deepened, but only so far. He didn't know if he was the one keeping things in check or if it was Miranda, but in the end, he didn't suppose it mattered. They ended up holding each other quietly, the fire of desired tamped down beneath an odd sort of survivor's communion.

"I was serious when I said you should take a hot bath and get a good night's sleep," he said a while later, long after the lingering light of day had disappeared into cool, blue night.

"But then I'd have to move," she grumbled against his throat. "And I'm so comfortable."

"I might be persuaded to give you a back rub once you got out of the bath."

She leaned her head back and looked up at him. "You're playing with my emotions now."

As he opened his mouth to respond, her cell phone

rang, the sound muted where her hip pressed against his side. She wriggled out of his grasp and pulled out the phone. "It's a local number," she murmured, pushing the button to answer. "Miranda Duncan."

He saw her brow furrow as she listened to whoever was on the other end of the line. "I see," she said finally. "Okay, I understand." She hung up the phone, her expression still troubled.

"Who was that?" John asked when she didn't say anything else.

"It was Rose McAllen." She leaned forward, resting her elbows on her knees. "She told me to stop looking into her daughter's death."

"Why?" he asked.

She turned her head to look at him. "She didn't say, but I could tell she was worried. Maybe even scared."

"Do you think someone's threatened her?"

"I don't know." She rubbed her chin with her fingertips before she turned to look at him. "It's odd, don't you think, that I make a call to the Bar W Ranch, wanting to talk to Jarrod Whitmore about Lindy McAllen's death, and a couple of hours later, Rose calls and asks me to stop looking into her daughter's case?"

"You think Whitmore threatened her?"

She frowned, as if giving the question real thought. "I don't know. Honestly, it doesn't sound like Cal Whitmore's style."

"He's a wealthy, ruthless cattleman, and you don't think threats seem like his style?"

"He's a wealthy, successful cattleman," she amended. "And most people around here like him. They don't fear him."

"Maybe because they've never had to cross him."

"He tends to grease the skids with money, not threats." She looked at him, still frowning. "Do you remember when we saw Rose and Cassie the other day at the hardware store? I told her then that we'd never stop looking for the person who killed Lindy. And she gave me the strangest look, as if she wanted to say something. But then she just turned away."

"And you think it's because she doesn't want you to keep looking?"

"I think she already knows that Jarrod Whitmore was the one who did it. And I think Cal Whitmore has paid her for her silence."

"But how could she have known it was Jarrod? Did she witness it?"

"No," Miranda answered, an odd look in her eyes.

"Then how?"

Miranda pushed to her feet, pacing toward the fireplace. The afternoon had been warm, so they hadn't bothered with a fire, but now that night had fallen, there was a definite chill in the air, and John could see her looking with almost wistful longing at the cold hearth before she turned to face him, wrapping her arms around herself.

"Remember earlier today, when Angela Layton told us that after Jasper met with Delta, he decided to pay the money back to the charity?"

"Yes."

"Doesn't that seem like a strange thing for someone to do in response to a blackmailer's demands?"

"It could have been the only way to make her go away."

"Or maybe it's what she wanted from him all along." She rubbed her hands up and down her arms as if fighting off a chill. "Maybe it's what she demanded from Jarrod Whitmore, too."

He stood up to face her, finally understanding what she was getting at. "You think Delta—"

"Wasn't blackmailing people for money," she elaborated. "I think she was trying to make them do the right thing."

Chapter Fifteen

Miranda's cell phone rang shortly after six the next morning. She grabbed it from the bedside table, rubbed her eyes and checked the display. It was the station. "Duncan," she answered, her voice hoarse with sleep.

It was Sheriff Randall. "Waller and Mendoza are both in the hospital in Lubbock. They took their wives into town for dinner and got broadsided by a dump truck on the way home."

She sat up quickly, her stomach knotting with anxiety. "How bad?"

"Broken bones, shaken up, but everybody's going to recover."

"Thank God."

"But we're shorthanded now."

"No worries. I'll be right in." She hung up the phone, grabbed her robe and headed for the bathroom to shower.

By the time she finished dressing, she could smell bacon frying in the kitchen. She secured her hair in a ponytail and followed the aroma down the hall, where John stood at the stove, flipping strips of bacon. "You're up early."

He looked at her. "And you're dressed for work."

"Two of our deputies were in a car accident last night.

They're going to be all right, but they're still in the hospital, which means we're shorthanded at the station. So I'm going in this morning." She eyed the bacon. "Once I eat, that is."

While she poured orange juice for both of them, he whipped up a quick batch of scrambled eggs, added them to the bacon and buttered toast on a couple of plates and joined her at the table. "You sure you're ready to go back to work?"

"I was ready two days ago," she said, dismissing his worries with a wave of her hand. "But that means you're on your own with Delta's journal. I can't be caught with my copy of the pages at work."

"I was already planning to try to figure out what kind of cipher she used on the last few pages of the book," he told her. "So I'll work on that and maybe by the time you get home, I'll have figured some of it out."

"That would be great." She smiled at him over her glass of orange juice, keeping her tone light. "You know, John Blake, if you're not careful, I could really get used to having you around."

"Would that be a bad thing?" He sounded serious.

She set the glass on the table, considering the question. "If you were going to stick around long-term, maybe not. But if you're just some stranger passing through—"

He didn't say anything, looking down at his plate of food. "I don't know what happens next," he admitted.

She swallowed an unexpected rush of disappointment. "Then maybe we should just keep things casual. No strings, no expectations. No taking things too far."

He followed her to the door when she started to leave, catching her hand as she was about to step through the doorway. "Does kissing count as taking things too far?"

She turned to look at him, torn between amusement at the hopeful look on his face and uncertainty about the wisdom of continuing to tempt fate when neither of them could make any promises. But amusement, and the delectable memory of his kisses, won out. "Kisses are okay."

"Good." He leaned forward and pressed a sweet, hot kiss against her lips. "I'll try to have a breakthrough on the code by the time you get home."

"You do that." She gave him another swift kiss and headed out to her truck.

All the talk at the station was about Wallace and Mendoza, with photos of the horrific crash scene already floating around from deputy to deputy. "Amazing they survived at all," Tim Robertson told Miranda as he passed her the photos the Lubbock Police Department had emailed over.

The twisted, crumpled metal that had been Mendoza's SUV looked as if it couldn't possibly have protected the occupants from mortal injuries, but when Randall stopped by the bullpen around midmorning, he told them that both Wallace and Mendoza were expected to be released from the hospital the next day. "They'll both be out a while until their broken bones heal, but everybody's going to recover sooner or later. Thank God."

He stopped by Miranda's desk on his way out. "Sorry I had to call you in. I know you could have used a little more recovery time yourself."

"I'm fine," she assured him. But after he left, she took another look at the crash photo and felt a little shudder run through her.

Her cruiser hadn't looked nearly as bad as Mendoza's SUV, but something about the photo triggered a brief memory of the day of the crash, an image of a dark blue sedan coming up quickly behind her cruiser as she was heading back to the station.

She'd tried to see through the windows, but they were darkly tinted, only the reflection of the snowfall and her own cruiser, with its flashing blue and cherry lights, visible in the opaque glass.

She handed the photo back to Tim Robertson and rubbed her gritty eyes. In some ways, the wreck seemed as fresh in her mind as the kiss John had planted on her lips that morning as she headed out to work.

But in other ways, it seemed more like some misty, mysterious dream.

By ten that morning, most of the other deputies were out on calls that Bill Chambers seemed to make sure went through to any phone but hers. Only Tim Robertson remained, poring over some photos spread out on his desk. He looked up briefly from the photos and smiled at her. She managed to smile back, but she wasn't sure if she had been able to cover her growing sense of annoyance.

She was on glorified desk duty, it appeared. The orders had probably come straight from Miles Randall himself. She might as well have stayed home and helped John with the ciphers.

"What're you looking at?" she asked Robertson.

"Photos from Delta McGraw's trailer."

She got up and crossed to his desk, looking over his shoulder. "And what are you looking for?"

Robertson gave her a doubtful look. "I thought the sheriff took you off this case."

"What's it going to hurt for me to take a look? I knew Delta. I might see something in those photos that you wouldn't even notice." She leaned closer to look at the photo he held. It was a close-up of Delta's bed, which was slightly rumpled but clearly not slept in. One edge of the bedside table was also in the photo, the round base of a lamp and the corner of a book just visible near the image edge. She couldn't make out much about the book cover, except the little triangle she could see appeared to have what looked like a series of numbers and letters on it.

"Do you have a full shot of the bedside table?" she asked.

Robertson flipped through the photos until he came across a close-up of the bedside table. The book cover was indeed covered by numbers and letters. The title *Ciphers and Code Made Easy* filled the top half of the book in bright blue letters.

Robertson looked up at her, his eyes slightly narrowed. She could tell he understood the significance of the book, but he wasn't going to share what he knew with her, thanks to Randall's insistence that she not be involved in the investigation.

"Hmm," she said. "Not what I thought." She handed the photo back to Robertson and returned to her desk. She pulled up a search engine and typed in the name of the book. It came up in several links, including an online bookstore that included a preview of the book's table of contents. As she hoped, the chapter listings were essentially the names of the codes included in the book. One of them, surely, would be the code or cipher Delta had used to encrypt the last few pages of the journal.

But she didn't have a copy of the pages with her, not wanting to risk getting caught with them at the station.

She grabbed her cell phone and called John.

He answered on the second ring. "Miss me already?"

"Maybe a little," she said with a smile. "I may have a shortcut for you and your deciphering." She told him about the book and gave him the website address for the online bookstore. "You can probably look up the types of ciphers and codes listed in the table of contents and compare them to what Delta was using in the journal."

"It's really killing you that you can't do this for yourself, isn't it?" he asked.

"Yes."

"I'll figure it out for you. Promise." He lowered his voice, even though there was nobody else to hear him. "I miss you already, too."

"You're just trying to torment me," she murmured.

"How's the first day back at the station?"

"Boring." Almost as soon as the words escaped her mouth, the phone on her desk rang. "But maybe it's about to pick up. Talk to you later." Pocketing her cell phone, she picked up the desk phone receiver, wondering who'd call her direct number. "Deputy Duncan."

"Deputy, it's Phil Neiman from the old Westlake Refinery. You helped me out a few months ago when I had some break-ins, remember?"

"I do. How are you?" The refinery had long since ceased operation, but it was something of a historic site from the early Texas oil boom days and Phil Neiman had bought the place to keep it from being bulldozed, determined to keep it viable as a tourist attraction.

"I've been better. There's been another break-in. I was hoping you could come on out here and write me up a report for my insurance."

"Of course," she said. "I'll be there in a few minutes."

She grabbed her jacket and headed for the fleet parking lot to grab a cruiser, telling Bill Chambers at the front desk where she was going. It wasn't exactly an exciting call, she thought as she drove up the highway to-ward the Westlake Refinery, but it was good to be in the saddle again.

JOHN HIT PAY dirt on Chapter Seven of *Cyphers and Code Made Easy*, titled "Vigenère." He was familiar with Vigenère, a fairly simple cipher built off a keyword. Delta McGraw's scribblings looked as if they might be encrypted using a Vigenère table.

The hard part would be figuring out the keyword. He knew next to nothing about Delta McGraw's life, except that her father had been a con man. He supposed that was a place to start.

He had actually been trained how to decrypt Vigenère ciphers algebraically, but he had a hunch that there was probably somewhere on the internet where he could simply enter the cipher and try decrypting it automatically by guessing at the keyword.

He found just such a page on the first page of his search list. Starting with the last entry in the journal, he typed in the cipher:

Oicl Tlrx ulrqhr, Btriayiqe. Eoihmnmi 3. Cbb Tmg-coe ln Btriayiqe jazh dmg. Tayo Guzc's suiqvus fdip rfha zae i toc.

Now to figure out the keyword.

He started with the most obvious: *HalMcGraw*. The result was more gibberish. He then tried variations on the name—first name, last name, Harold spelled out, on the assumption that Hal was short for Harold, and the last name, McGraw by itself, as well. All to no avail.

He was pondering other options when his cell phone rang. It was Miranda.

"I'm out on a call, but I thought I'd see if you've had any luck."

"Maybe." He told her his theory about the cipher being a Vigenère cipher. "But I don't know much about Delta, so it's hard to guess at her keyword."

"I'm not sure I knew her well enough for that," Miranda admitted ruefully. "Like I told you, Delta didn't have friends. I was probably as close as she got." Her last few words crackled through the phone line, as if she was driving through an area where the cell service was spotty.

"You're breaking up," John told her.

"I...can't... I'll call...back." The call ended abruptly.

John laid his phone on the table and went back to his laptop. She hadn't used her father's name. He didn't know her birth date or where she'd been born. He didn't even know her mother's name, although he supposed he could do a search of her name and see if there was any sort of internet trail he could follow.

He sat back in the kitchen chair, his gaze wandering to the doorway to the unfinished room, where he'd found the journal in the first place.

Why had she left the book here? She obviously hadn't wanted it found, but why leave it here in Miranda's house? Had she felt threatened in some way? Was Miranda the only person she felt she could trust?

Miranda.

He scratched his chin and looked at the blank box for the keyword. With a little shrug, he typed in the word *Miranda*.

A readable set of words appeared in the decryption

box. With a flood of satisfaction, he read Delta McGraw's last journal entry.

> Call Girl murder, Plainview. November 3. Coy Taylor in Plainview same day. Call Girl's friends said john was a cop.

Coy Taylor. A niggle of recognition tickled his brain. Why did the name Coy Taylor sound so familiar?

THE WESTLAKE REFINERY was a shell of its former self, little more than a long, rectangular corrugated steel building surrounded by the rusting remains of tanks. Miranda pulled up in front of the main building, surprised not to see Phil Neiman's old yellow Cadillac convertible parked near the door. She pulled out her cell phone to give him another call, but once again, she had no signal.

Frowning, she gazed down the highway at the tall cell tower only a mile away. Why didn't she have a signal?

She radioed to the station as she approached the silent building. "I'm at Westlake Refinery," she told Bill Chambers when he responded. "Can't see Neiman anywhere, but I'm heading inside."

She tried the door, half expecting to find it locked. But the handle turned easily in her hand.

"Mr. Neiman?"

There was no answer.

Frowning, she eased inside the open door and looked around. The place was quiet and still, though she spotted smudges in the dust on the floor that might have been footprints. No sign of tread marks, though. She started to crouch to take a closer look when she heard footsteps behind her.

"Hey there, Deputy." Phil Neiman's voice echoed faintly in the cavernous building.

She rose and turned around with a smile. "Hey, Phil, I was wondering where you…" Her voice faltered as she saw the man standing behind her. "What the hell?"

Coy Taylor stood behind her, holding a large Smith & Wesson pointed at her heart. "I thought you'd never get here."

MIRANDA WASN'T ANSWERING her phone. In fact, it seemed to be going straight to voice mail. John left his third message in the last fifteen minutes, not sure whether he was more frustrated or worried.

Someone needed to see what he'd found. It was possible, he supposed, that the sheriff's department had already decoded the entries themselves, but what if they hadn't? If Miranda was available, he'd ask her who Coy Taylor was, but since she wasn't answering, what was he supposed to do now?

He needed to find out who Coy Taylor was, for starters. And if he couldn't ask Miranda, maybe her father would know.

Gil Duncan answered on the third ring. "Duncan Hardware."

"Mr. Duncan, it's John Blake."

"Hey, John. What can I do for you?"

"Can you tell me who Coy Taylor is?"

There was a brief pause on Duncan's end of the call. "You haven't asked Miranda?"

"She's back on duty today and out on a call. I haven't been able to reach her, and I just needed to know why the name sounds so familiar."

"Oh. Well, easy enough. He's one of the desk sergeants at the sheriff's department."

John's blood iced over. "I see. I guess that's why it's familiar. Thanks."

There was an odd tone to Duncan's voice when he replied, "Anytime."

John hung up and stared at the deciphered note from Delta McGraw's journal.

> Call Girl murder, Plainview. November 3. Coy Taylor in Plainview same day. Call Girl's friends said john was a cop.

Did Coy Taylor know that Miranda had found Delta's journal? And if so, what was he planning to do about it?

He retrieved his wallet and pulled Miranda's business card out of one of the pockets. Besides her personal phone number, the card also listed the sheriff's department main number.

Would Coy Taylor answer?

"Barstow County Sheriff's Department."

"Is this Coy Taylor?"

"No, sir," the voice on the other end replied. "He comes in after three. You want to leave a message for him?"

"No. Is Sheriff Randall available?"

John's question seemed to catch the other man by surprise. "Who's calling?"

"John Blake. I'm the man who helped Deputy Duncan the other day after her crash."

"Right. Okay. I'll see if the sheriff has time to talk to you."

After a brief pause, a different voice answered. "Mr. Blake, what can I do for you?"

"Sheriff, have you had a chance to examine that journal Delta McGraw left at Miranda's house?"

"I'm looking at it now."

"Then you've seen the ciphers."

There was a long pause on the other end of the line. "Ciphers?"

"The last two pages of the journal were written in cipher form." He'd spent the last few minutes testing the rest of the encrypted entries using the Vigenère decryption website and the keyword *Miranda*. The rest of the entries had been about petty crimes like shoplifting, theft and another embezzlement case similar to the one involving the late Jasper Layton.

"These don't look like ciphers," Randall disagreed.

John flipped back a couple of pages. "What's the last entry in the journal?"

"I can't share that with a civilian."

"Sheriff, I'm looking at a copy of the journal."

"You're what?"

"What's the last entry in the journal?"

After a tense pause, Randall said, "It's about a ranch hand at the Bar W who's been stealing money from the ranch's petty cash."

John found the entry. It was on the last page before the encrypted entries started about halfway down the next page.

"Look at the journal—can you see any signs that pages have been removed?"

After a brief pause, Randall's voice rumbled over the phone. "You're telling me someone tampered with this journal?"

"Who entered the journal into evidence?"

"What kind of question—"

"Who?"

There was a rustling noise as the sheriff apparently checked the label on the evidence bag the journal was probably kept in when it wasn't being used. "Coy Taylor."

Son of a bitch, John thought. "Sheriff, I think we have a big problem."

Chapter Sixteen

"What the hell's going on, Taylor?" Miranda dragged her gaze from the barrel of Taylor's Smith & Wesson to his face. "Where's Phil Neiman?"

"At home, I suppose." Taylor gave a slight shrug. "How'd you like my Phil Neiman impression?"

"Not much."

"It got you here." Despite his smug tone, Taylor's gun hand shook a little, making Miranda's heart skip a beat, but he got the twitching under control. "Did you make copies of the journal?"

"What?"

"The journal." His voice rose with tension. "Did you make any copies before you turned it in?"

Miranda's initial confusion and alarm had settled into a sort of alert tension. If she lied and told him no, what would keep him from shooting her on the spot?

Nothing.

"Yes," she answered.

"Where are they?"

"If I tell you, you'll shoot me."

"I'm going to shoot you anyway." Taylor's tone remained calm, but she saw a hint of unease behind his dark eyes. "But if you'll tell me where to find the copies, at least your daddy might be spared."

"Coy, this isn't you."

His expression flattened. "Miranda, you don't know me. Nobody in this town really knows me. Nobody's ever really bothered to."

Anger flared hot in her belly. "So that's why you're pointing a gun at me? Because you're so misunderstood?"

"Where are the copies of the journal? How many did you make?"

"Why does that matter?"

"How many did you make?" Taylor's voice rose, his face reddening.

"One. I made one." She let her gaze fall back on his gun hand, trying to gauge her chances of disarming him. It would have helped a lot if she'd already drawn her gun before entering the building, but she hadn't suspected she'd be facing an armed man with murder on his mind. "You know the sheriff has the journal already. Whatever you're hoping to hide—it's too late."

"He has part of the journal. He doesn't have all of it." Taylor's lips curved in a nasty smile. "One of the perks of being the person who enters evidence into the properties room."

"What did you do? Tear out the incriminating page?"

"Pages," he said with a little shrug of his shoulders. "She put it in some sort of code. I removed the two coded pages."

Why was he telling her this? Why hadn't he just shot her already? Because she had copies of the pages where his name was mentioned?

"How do you even know you're mentioned in that journal, then?"

"Because Delta tried to blackmail me, the stupid little bitch!" The last words came out in a spittle-flecked rage. "Did she think I'd do what she wanted because she had the goods on me? I'm not some sniveling little coward she could manipulate."

"What did she want?"

"Money. She wanted money for that stupid whore's kids." He shook his head. "She didn't know who she was messing with."

"You killed her."

Taylor looked at her as if she was an idiot. "Of course I did."

"You're the one who drove me off the road."

He didn't answer.

"Why? What did I do?" She looked at him through narrowed eyes. "Or was it that you needed to get into my house and poke around a while?"

"I couldn't risk your coming back home before I had a chance to find it." For a moment, Taylor almost looked troubled. "It's not what I wanted. I just didn't have any choice."

"You knew about the journal already."

He looked at her for a long moment. "Remove the mike."

"What?"

"Your shoulder mike. Detach it from the receiver." As she reached for it, he added, "Slow. No sudden movements."

She unplugged the mike from the unit and held it out.

"Toss it on the floor in front of me."

She did as he asked. He stomped on it with the heel of his boot. The plastic mike crunched under the blow, splitting apart. He gave it another hard stomp, mangling the wires inside.

"Phone?"

"It's not getting any reception."

"I know. I'm blocking it." He held out his free hand. "Hand it over."

She pulled her phone from the pocket of her uniform pants and handed it to him.

He shoved it in his back pocket. "Now your weapon. Remove your utility belt. Don't touch the pistol."

She unbuckled her belt and held it in front of her. He took it with his free hand and nodded toward her feet. "You packing an extra?"

"No."

"Lie to me again and I'll call your daddy down here to join us."

Biting back a furious retort, she pulled up the leg of her trousers and removed the ankle holster holding her spare pistol. She handed over the second holster, as well.

"Other leg?"

She lifted the pants leg to show him there wasn't another weapon.

"All right. We're getting in my car and we're going wherever you've got that copy of the journal hidden."

"I'd be stupid to do that. You'd kill me the second I handed it over."

"Don't you get it, Mandy? You're dead either way."

"Then why should I help you?"

"Because I know where your daddy lives. And that might be the very next place I go to look for those pages if you don't lead me to them right now."

She looked at Taylor, took in the ruddy cheeks, sandy

hair and brown eyes she'd seen nearly every day for most of her life and realized she didn't even know who he was.

"What did you do? What did she have on you?"

He laughed. "Get moving. Out the back."

She turned around slowly, her mind racing to piece together the fragments of the puzzle Coy Taylor's treachery had just presented. What had he said before? *She wanted money for that stupid whore's kids.*

What kids? What woman?

"Who else did you kill?" she asked as she moved slowly toward the refinery building's back exit.

He didn't answer.

"You said Delta wanted money for someone's kids. Did you kill a woman?"

"She tried to roll me."

"A prostitute?"

"Keep moving."

The murder of a prostitute would be a big deal in Cold Creek. Not that they were exactly flush with prostitution in a town that size, where everybody knew everybody else's business.

But maybe Plainview. Or even Lubbock. He could have killed someone there.

"Was it an accident?" She tried to infuse her voice with sympathy. "Things just got out of hand?"

"Don't try to play me, Mandy."

She was getting close to the door. Her options for escape were pretty slim at this point and getting slimmer all the time.

"Open the door," Taylor ordered. "Slow."

She opened the door slowly and started outside. Then, with a sharp spurt of action, she slammed the door shut behind her and started running for the front of the building.

She heard the door whip open behind her, the crack of Taylor's pistol and the ringing clang as the round hit the building only a couple of feet from her. She increased her speed, running all out, her long legs eating up big chunks of real estate.

She just had to get to the cruiser. The keys were still in her pocket and the car radio should still work.

It was her only chance at escape.

She skidded in the gravel as she took the corner and reached the front of the building, where her cruiser was parked. She had already made it to the front door when she realized something wasn't right.

Both tires on the driver's side were flat.

"Nowhere to run, Miranda!" Taylor called as he came around the building, laughter in his voice.

There was a shotgun in the trunk of the cruiser, but she'd never reach it before he ran her down and killed her.

To hell with that, she thought, and jerked open the car door. Scrambling inside, she ducked instinctively when she heard the next shot, though by that time, the bullet had already hit the back door with a hard thump.

Please start, she begged the cruiser as she stuck the key in the ignition and turned.

It rumbled to life, and a bubble of bleak laughter escaped her lips as she jerked it into gear and started driving.

The flat tires were less of a problem than they might have been, since the cruiser had been equipped with run-flat tires. But when she reached for the dash-mounted radio, she saw that Taylor hadn't settled for simply slashing her tires. The mike was missing on the dash unit, as well.

She looked around frantically in the seat and on the

floorboards in the futile hope that he might have left the mike in the car. But it wasn't anywhere in sight, rending her radio useless.

And her phone was with Taylor.

Drive, she thought. *Just drive. You may be miles from the next outpost of civilization, but you still have a chance. And make it harder for him to kill you without getting caught.*

Make it harder for him.

Lifting her chin and gritting her teeth, she hit the siren switch.

"WHERE DID YOU get these?" Miles Randall frowned at the pages John laid on the desk in front of him.

There was no point in trying to cover for Miranda. "She made copies before she turned it in. She didn't want to be left off the Delta McGraw case."

Randall's frown deepened, but John thought he spotted a hint of admiration in the sheriff's blue eyes, as well. "You deciphered this gibberish?" he asked, eyeing the ciphers Delta had used to encode the latter entries of the journal.

"I've had some experience dealing with ciphers." John showed him the translation of Delta's notes about Coy Taylor. "Does this make sense to you?"

Putting on a pair of bifocals, Randall took a closer look at John's decryption. "Plainview, November 3?"

"Delta seemed to think it was significant that Taylor was in Plainview the same day as the hooker murder."

"Seems pretty slim evidence."

"Have you heard anything from Miranda yet?"

"No," he admitted. "We tried radioing her a few minutes ago, but she's not answering. We also tried calling

Phil Neiman, the man she was supposed to meet at the refinery, but he hasn't answered his phone yet."

"Maybe that call she got wasn't legit."

Randall frowned. "I can try Neiman again."

John paced impatiently while the sheriff picked up his phone and made a call. After a moment, Randall spoke. "Phil? This is Miles Randall. We got a call from you earlier today about a break-in at the refinery?" As the sheriff listened to Neiman's response, his frown deepened to a scowl. "So, you didn't call? And there hasn't been a break-in?"

No, John thought, his chest tightening with fear. God, no.

"Thanks." Randall hung up the phone and looked intently at John before he pushed the intercom button. "Bill, radio all available units. We need everyone we've got at the Westlake Refinery immediately." He turned and grabbed the jacket hanging on his chair.

"I'm going, too," John said as the sheriff tried to brush past him.

"Let us do our job."

"I'm going," John insisted, falling into step with Randall. "I can come along with you or I can go myself, but I'm going."

Randall looked as if he would argue, but finally he gave a nod of defeat. "You ride with me."

IT HADN'T TAKEN long for Taylor's blue Ford Taurus to catch up with the crippled cruiser, since the run-flat tires couldn't easily handle speeds above fifty miles per hour. Once she spotted the Taurus coming up fast behind her, however, she took the risk, pushing the speedometer needle over sixty-five.

At the higher speed, the cruiser shimmied and shook, forcing her to muscle the steering wheel to keep the cruiser on the road. But the alternative was to let him catch up with her. And if that happened, she wasn't sure she'd live through whatever he had planned for her.

But if she could hold on a little longer, there was a chance to get out of this mess alive. For the past few minutes, her dashboard radio had squawked with calls from the sheriff's department, trying to find her. She'd also heard a call to all available units to converge on the Westlake Refinery.

There were only so many ways to get to the refinery from Cold Creek, and she was driving down one of the main roads that led there. Sooner or later, one of those units would find her.

She just hoped it wouldn't be too late.

She passed a turnoff, tempted to take it, but she knew there wasn't an occupied dwelling down that road for another two miles. The road was bumpier and would be that much harder to navigate with the ruined tires, too. And it wasn't one of the main ways to reach the refinery.

She forced herself to keep going, focused on keeping the cruiser from spinning off the highway.

How could the killer be Taylor? She'd worked with him at the sheriff's department for the past six years. She'd known him a lot longer than that; he was a frequent patron of her father's hardware store. How could he be a cold-blooded killer and nobody realize it?

She didn't know much about his background, she realized. He wasn't a Cold Creek native; he'd moved there more than twenty years ago, when he was in his early twenties. He'd married a local girl, but the marriage hadn't lasted more than a year. His ex-wife was living somewhere in Dallas, Miranda thought. Or at least, that was the last thing she'd heard.

Was that when he'd started frequenting hookers?

Behind her, the sedan was moving closer, but she'd gotten a decent head start back at the refinery. Taylor had been forced to run back to retrieve his vehicle, a familiar-looking blue sedan with tinted windows that brought nerve-rattling memories of the day of her crash rushing back to her, including a few images she hadn't remembered before.

The Taurus had pulled even with her, a hulking, mysterious presence in the driving snow. She'd tried to pull him over, she remembered, but he'd responded by falling back to perform a PIT maneuver that had driven her off the road.

He could have killed her. It had probably been his intention. He just hadn't planned for John Blake to come to her rescue, had he?

Oh, John. She longed to talk to him now, the urge so powerful it felt like an ache in the center of her chest. Just to hear his voice, to somehow find words to tell him—

What? What did she want to tell him? That in the past few days, he'd made her feel more vibrant, more whole, than she'd ever felt before? That her life would feel empty without him?

That was crazy thinking. She barely knew him.

But crazy or not, it was true.

The cruiser gave a hard lurch and she forced herself to pay attention to the road ahead. She was coming up on another crossroad, but again, there was little hope for help down the road in either direction, so she stayed on the highway, pressing her foot on the accelerator when she saw that her speed had begun to drop.

She had to stay alive.

She had to see John again.

In the rearview mirror, the Taurus had almost caught up with her. And the odds were good that he'd make the same move here he'd made the day of the snowstorm, weren't they?

People were, after all, creatures of habit.

Come on, Taylor. Make your move.

I'll be ready.

"IS THAT A cruiser ahead?" John peered down the dusty road, certain he was seeing a flicker of red and blue lights somewhere in the hazy distance.

"I think it is." Sheriff Randall gestured toward the cruiser's glove box. "There's a set of binoculars in there. See what you can make out."

He found the binoculars and lifted them to his eyes, adjusting the dials until he got a clear look at the vehicle moving toward them. It was probably four miles down the road, which meant they'd intercept it in a couple of minutes at their current speed.

Was it Miranda? Or one of the other units the sheriff's department had called to action?

"Could that be one of the other responding units?" he asked the sheriff.

"If so, he's going the wrong direction. The Westlake Refinery is about five miles farther down this road."

"If it's Miranda, why isn't she answering your radio calls?" John tried to get a better look at the cruiser's driver, but the sun glinted off the windshield, obscuring any view of the driver. He shifted the binoculars down to see the license plate, reading off the numbers and letters. "Is that the cruiser Miranda was driving?"

"I don't have it memorized," Randall growled, but he radioed the number to his dispatcher, who came back a few seconds later with confirmation.

"It's the cruiser Duncan signed out."

"Something's wrong with the tires," John said, trying to get a better look through the binoculars. "They look flat."

Randall muttered a profanity.

John dropped the binoculars to his lap and looked up. A dark-colored sedan pulled up next to the cruiser, edging closer in an apparent attempt to drive her off the road.

Suddenly the cruiser slowed, letting the other car move ahead. Then the cruiser made a sharp inward turn, hitting the other car on the rear panel.

The darker car went into a 360-degree spin, ending up off the road.

Unfortunately, so did the cruiser, sliding sideways into a shallow arroyo on the other side of the road.

The sheriff's cruiser was closing in on the scene fast, close enough that John spotted the driver's door of the blue sedan opening. A dark-clad figure emerged from the car, one arm outstretched. Sunlight glinted on something he held in his hand.

"No!" John shouted, but it was already too late.

The man fired on the wrecked cruiser.

Chapter Seventeen

The cruiser hadn't rolled. But the crack of gunfire and the crunch of the cruiser's back driver's side window shattering were stark reminders that Miranda was still in grave danger.

At least this time, help was on its way. She'd seen another cruiser heading her way at a fast clip, less than a mile down the road now, before she pulled the PIT maneuver to drive Coy Taylor's car off the road. But she hadn't managed to wreck him.

And she was still unarmed.

She slid into the passenger seat and opened the door, swearing when the bottom of the door caught on the edge of the arroyo the cruiser had slid into. The opening was far too small for her to escape through.

Damn it!

Another shot fired, this one zinging through the driver's side window. If she hadn't moved, she'd have taken the bullet in the head. A hard shudder raced through her as she squeezed herself into a tight crouch in the passenger floorboard. It wouldn't be enough, she knew. Not if he kept firing.

Where the hell was that other cruiser?

There was the sudden boom of a shotgun, and she

heard a cry of pain from somewhere outside the cruiser. Seconds later, she heard the cruiser's door creak open.

"Miranda?"

She lifted her head and met the frightened hazel eyes of John Blake. He crouched in the doorway, his gaze shifting to look her over, as if searching for signs of injury.

"I'm fine," she told him quickly, pushing herself up into the passenger seat. She stayed there a few seconds, catching her breath as her pulse galloped like a thoroughbred in her chest. "Taylor?"

"He took some buckshot. The sheriff's got him cuffed and disarmed." John held his hand out to her. "You sure you're not hurt?"

"I'm sure." She took his hand. A spark of heat and energy seemed to flow from his fingers into hers, bolstering her strength. She slid up the slight incline of the cruiser's bench seat and let John help her out onto the shoulder of the road.

A few yards down the highway, the sheriff was shoving Taylor into the back of his cruiser, ignoring the injured man's groans. Randall turned and gave Miranda a nod. "You okay?" he called.

"Fine," she answered, no longer certain she was telling the truth. Now that the danger had passed, her limbs had started trembling wildly and she felt as if the world beneath her feet had begun to shift like quicksand.

She caught John's arm, and he turned to look at her in alarm. "Miranda?"

"I'm okay," she said through chattering teeth.

"No, you're not." He put his arm around her and led her over to the sheriff's cruiser. She bumped gazes with Miles Randall, who stood in the cruiser's open door, talking on the dashboard radio. "Suspect in custody. All units to—" Here he stopped and looked around him before continuing. "West Highway, north of mile marker 210."

John had his arms wrapped tightly around her waist, holding her as the tremors dashing through her slowly started to dissipate. "You're okay," he murmured in her ear.

Finally, she started to feel it.

"PLAINVIEW IS GOING to look into a series of unsolved prostitute murders, but we're not even sure we can tie Taylor to the one Delta mentioned in her journal." Miles Randall leaned back in his desk chair and looked briefly at John before his gaze settled on Miranda, who sat straight backed in the armchair next to John's. Over an hour had passed since they'd arrived at the sheriff's department in Tim Robertson's car and went their separate ways for a formal debriefing.

During their time apart, Miranda's condition had improved considerably, John noted. She had stopped shaking altogether and her color had returned. She'd also been reunited with her utility belt, extra weapon and cell phone, retrieved by one of the deputies processing the crime scene at the old refinery. She'd already strapped on the belt and her service weapon again, as if donning armor. "It's possible Delta had more evidence hidden somewhere. Or maybe when we track down the dead prostitute's friends, they can help us figure out what Delta knew and how she knew it," Miranda suggested. "Is Plainview going to allow us to aid in the investigation?"

"I've talked to the Plainview chief of police. He's agreed to combine our resources in the investigation,"

Randall said. "But you're not going to be on the case, Duncan."

"What?"

"Taylor tried to make you his victim. Twice. Like it or not, that makes you entirely too close to the case to be objective."

The muscle in Miranda's jaw worked violently, but she managed to keep her mouth shut, John saw. He couldn't blame her for her frustration, however. He hated like hell being left out of the final roundup of the Blue Ridge Infantry's straggling holdouts.

He needed to call Quinn, he reminded himself as he listened to Randall tell Miranda what her new assignment would be.

"Even decrypted, some of Delta's notes are a little hard to figure out," the sheriff told her. "She seems to have chronicled a few serious crimes and we need to determine if any of her allegations are actionable. I'm putting you and Tim Robertson on working those leads."

Miranda's tension seemed to ease a bit, though John's own level of annoyance rose considerably at the thought of Miranda working closely with tall, good-looking and clearly smitten Deputy Robertson.

What right do you have to care? You're out of town as soon as Quinn gives you the all clear, aren't you?

"Take the rest of the day off," Randall told Miranda, slanting a look at John. "Get some rest and be ready to start fresh in the morning."

John half expected Miranda to protest, but she merely stood and gave the sheriff a businesslike nod of agreement. She headed out of the sheriff's office with a glance at John.

He rose and started to follow, but the sheriff called his name. "A moment, please?"

John glanced back at Miranda, who was standing in the doorway, looking at him. "I'll catch up," he told her. "Meet you at your place?"

"See you there." She inclined her head briefly and closed the door behind her.

John sat again in the chair across from the sheriff. "Is something wrong?"

"I'm not sure," Randall admitted. "First, I guess I need to tell you that I've done a little bit of investigation myself. Of you."

John managed not to bristle. He couldn't fault the sheriff for wanting to know whether the stranger in town playing bodyguard to one of his deputies was on the up-and-up. "And what did you learn?"

"I know you were working for a man in Tennessee named Alexander Quinn." At the slight narrowing of John's eyes, Randall smiled. "I may look like a small-town hick sheriff, Mr. Blake, but I assure you I'm not."

"Don't suppose you tried calling Quinn?" John asked, faintly amused at the thought.

Randall laughed softly. "I did. Not exactly a success."

"I don't imagine so."

"But there were other ways to find out some of the things I wanted to know. Tennessee law enforcement, for example. And I had an interesting discussion with the Dudley County sheriff."

John sat up a little straighter. Dudley County included River's End, Virginia, the tiny mountain town where he'd nearly met his maker at the end of Del McClintock's Remington 700.

"It seems you were known by a different name when you were in that area. John Bartholomew, I believe?"

"I was undercover."

"Indeed." Randall leaned forward. "I'll just get to the point. I know there's a dangerous man looking for you. A man named Delbert McClintock. And that McClintock is believed to be somewhere near Altus, Oklahoma, at the moment."

"So I hear."

Randall's expression darkened. "Then you need to know what we found on Coy Taylor's cell phone."

MIRANDA UNLOCKED THE front door of her house and entered, realizing for the first time in days she didn't feel as if she had to go in low, weapon drawn, looking for trouble in every corner.

It was nice to feel as if she finally had her house back. Her haven.

And John would be here soon.

The thought should have warmed her, but something she'd seen in John's eyes earlier had left her feeling unsettled. A reminder that as close as they'd become over the past few days, he was still little more than a stranger in Cold Creek. Like so many, he was just passing through.

Unless she could give him a reason to stay.

She slumped on her sofa and leaned forward, pressing her hands to her face. How, exactly, did she plan to give him a reason to stay? Seduction? Sex might hold him in place a day or two longer, but it wasn't enough to keep a man around indefinitely.

She'd tried a couple of times before to hold on to a man who already had one foot out of town, and both relationships had fallen apart sooner rather than later.

Maybe she had to face the idea of leaving Cold Creek and following John wherever he wanted to go.

Could she do that?

Her head said no. But her heart whispered yes.

If John wanted her to go with him, she could do it. Couldn't she?

"If he even wants you," she muttered.

Frustrated and anxious, she pushed to her feet and stripped off her utility belt, removing all the tools and storing them in the locked drawer in the corner, where she kept them when she was off duty. She left the service pistol in the drawer of the side table next to the sofa and headed into her bedroom to change clothes.

She looked at her undressed body in the mirror on her closet door. Not too bad, she had to admit. She might be a little on the big-boned side, and she'd never have a tiny waist or delicate arms and legs, but she was lean and toned, with curves in the right places. And, okay, there were a few fresh new bruises here and there on top of the fading bruises from her earlier crash, but those would fade.

Besides, John had scars from his own brush with death. She'd felt them beneath her fingertips while they were kissing—

She finished dressing, slipping on her most flattering sweater and her favorite pair of jeans, grinning a little sheepishly at her unaccustomed spurt of vanity. She checked her reflection and noticed with dismay that she'd lost her ponytail holder at some point during her escape from Taylor. As a result, her hair was tangled and wild.

Definitely not seduction material.

She gave her hair a brisk, ruthless brushing, saw it wasn't going to be tamed without washing it and starting over, so she settled for pulling it back into a neat pony-tail. She even grabbed a tube of lipstick from the back of her sorely neglected makeup drawer and dabbed a bit of the warm peach tint on her lips. Fortunately, she'd inherited her father's dark eyelashes and could skip mascara.

Taking a deep breath, she looked at her reflection. "You can convince a man to stick around a little Texas town, Miranda Duncan," she murmured to the woman in the mirror. "Oh, yes, you can."

Then, laughing at the absurdity of her self-directed pep talk, she walked out of her bedroom and straight into a bearded stranger.

With a gasp, she tried to run down the hall to where she'd left her pistol, but the intruder's hands curled around her arms with cruel strength, jerking her back against his hard body.

A voice rumbled in her ear, deep and thick with a mountain drawl. "Uh-uh, darlin'. You ain't goin' any-where. You're going to help me find somebody I've spent months lookin' for."

As cold fear washed over her, she realized her cap-tor's identity.

"You're Del McClintock," she said, barely keeping her voice steady.

"That I am," he said with a low laugh. "And you're the woman who's going to bring John Blake to me with-out a fight."

"He's not here." John and the sheriff had walked a thor-ough circuit of his rental house twice now, finding no sign that Del McClintock had ever been there. He was on the phone with Alexander Quinn now, relaying the news that Randall had shared with him back at the sheriff's department.

"Maybe he just hasn't arrived yet," Quinn suggested.

"No way. Taylor's phone call to Altus was hours ago," John disagreed. "It's a two-hour drive. He'd be here by now."

"What if Taylor didn't send McClintock to you?" Quinn asked quietly.

The question struck John like a thunderbolt. "Miranda—"

Across the living room, Randall looked up from his phone, his expression instantly worried.

"Is she with you?" Quinn asked.

"No." John passed a shaking hand over his mouth and chin. "I haven't even told her yet—"

"On it," Randall murmured, dialing his phone.

"She went home," John told Quinn. "I was supposed to meet her there, but what the sheriff told me about Taylor's call—"

"Understandable," Quinn said quickly. "But you need to make sure she's okay. You know the BRI will use people as pawns to get what they want."

"At least she's armed," John said.

Except she was at home, finally free of the fear that had come with Coy Taylor's first attack on her. With no reason to think she wasn't alone.

Or that she needed to be armed.

"I've got to go, Quinn. I'll be in touch." He hung up and looked at Randall, who met his gaze darkly and shook his head.

Damn it.

"I can have backup at Miranda's place in minutes."

"No," John said, unlocking the chest where he kept his Ruger. He checked the magazine, chambered a round and grabbed a second magazine in case he needed it. He clipped the holster to his waistband and secured the pistol in place. "We don't want an armed standoff. Get them there, but make them stay back. No lights, no sirens. And we'll take my truck."

Randall nodded and made the call on the way out of John's house.

As John locked up behind him, his cell phone rang. A shudder of relief ran through him as he saw Miranda's name on the display. "Miranda," he answered. "I'm so glad—"

"I know," she interrupted quickly, her voice cheerful. "I know we agreed to meet at your place, but I've gotten sidetracked here at the house."

John froze on the top step of the porch. They certainly had not agreed to meet at his place.

But before he could respond, she continued in the same overly bright tone. "Could you come here instead?"

"Of course." He tamped down the flood of dread washing over him and tried to keep his voice normal, in case someone else was listening on her end of the line. "I can be there in five minutes or so."

"I'll be waiting." She hung up without saying goodbye.

John forced his shaky legs down the steps and across the yard to where Randall was waiting by the truck. The sheriff took one look at John's face and asked, "What's happened?"

"Miranda just called," John said bleakly. "And I'm pretty sure she's not home alone."

"GOOD JOB, SUGAR." Del McClintock's deceptively friendly drawl sent ripples of revulsion down Miranda's spine, but she made sure it didn't show. "He's on his way?"

"Should be here soon." She was sitting beside him on

the sofa, trying to look anywhere but at the side table just a foot away from her, where her M&P 40 was currently hidden from view.

McClintock had traded out his rifle, which now lay propped against the wall by the fireplace within easy reach, for a large deer-hunting knife that looked lethally sharp. Could she get to the pistol before he could sink the knife into her back and give it a fatal twist?

She wasn't ready to risk finding out. Not yet, anyway.

She'd given John a clue that everything wasn't normal, but had he understood her? His voice had sounded a little tight at the end, but not so strange that she could be certain he'd gotten the message.

"Why is this so important to you?" Miranda asked as the silence in the room stretched painfully tight. "From what John told me, you did a real number on him, not the other way around."

"He told you about Nicki Jamison, didn't he?"

"No," she lied.

"Sure he did. How else would your buddy Coy have known to give me a ring when he figured out who your boyfriend really was?"

"He's not my boyfriend. And Coy's not my buddy. And I don't know how he figured out who John really was."

"Not really of that much interest to me, to tell you the truth," Del said with a shrug. "All I care about is finding him. So I owe ol' Coy a big thank-you."

"I can take you to him and you can thank him in person."

"No, that's all right." He flashed a mean smile at her. "He sure ain't real fond of you, though, sugar. What did you do to get on his bad side?"

"Well, today I arrested him for murder," she answered flatly.

The sound of a vehicle slowing on the highway outside broke through the tension, and Del rose to his feet, grabbing Miranda's arm. He tugged her with him, and she went without a struggle, dropping her hand to the side-table drawer pull as she trailed behind him. The drawer opened just wide enough to reach her hand inside if she got the chance.

But Del didn't allow her the chance, giving her a sharp tug as her feet tangled in the throw rug. "Watch it," he warned, shoving the tip of his knife blade under her nose.

She got her feet under control and stayed close as he flicked the front window curtains open just far enough to see the dark blue Ford pickup truck pulling into the driveway to park next to Miranda's truck.

Beside her, Del McClintock laughed softly, excitement bright in his eyes.

"Showtime, sugar," he said.

Chapter Eighteen

"He's in there," John said quietly. "He's at the front window and I'd bet he has Miranda with him."

Randall looked up at him from the floorboard of the truck cab, grimacing. "I'm too old to stay in this position long."

"I know. Just let me get inside and I can distract him." John opened the truck door, leaving his keys in the ignition. The truck's rhythmic warning bell grated on his nerves and he closed the door quickly behind him to stop the noise.

There was a chance Del McClintock would take a shot at him as soon as he opened the door. That's why he'd agreed to don the lightweight Kevlar vest the sheriff had offered him before they left John's house. It might not save him, but it could keep him on his feet long enough to save Miranda.

At least, he hoped so.

He took the porch steps two at a time and knocked on the door, trying to anticipate what would happen.

McClintock would send Miranda to the door. Could he pull her out and shield her with his body until Randall could get out of the truck?

No. Too big a risk. Miranda could be caught in the cross fire too easily.

The door opened. As he expected, Miranda stood in the doorway. "Hey, there," she said with a weak smile. "I thought you'd never get here."

"You know me. Can't keep me away."

Her smile faded, and she took a step backward, her eyes shifting hard to her left, where the open door must be shielding McClintock from sight. "Come in."

She stepped back as he entered, and he grabbed her, giving her a hard shove away from the door with his left hand as he grabbed his Ruger from the holster at his waist, slamming the door with his elbow to reveal McClintock hiding behind the door.

The other man was caught off guard, but only for a second. As John brought up his pistol, Del swept his hand up toward John's hand. John caught a glint of metal just before the blade sliced into his arm above his wrist, sending pain shrieking up to his shoulder. His grip on the Ruger went slack and the pistol fell to the floor with a clatter.

A second wave of agony raced through his rattled nervous system when McClintock pulled out the knife and dove for the Ruger. John forced his sluggish reflexes into action and he drove his knee into McClintock's chin, sending his head snapping back before he could reach the errant pistol.

He kicked the pistol out of reach and dodged McClintock's furious swipe of the knife toward his leg.

"Back away, John!" Miranda's voice broke through the cacophony of pain and adrenaline raging in his brain, and he stumbled backward, looking for her.

She stood a few feet away, holding her M&P 40 aimed

at McClintock's heart. "Drop the knife," she said in a low, deadly voice.

McClintock looked up at her, his shaggy hair in his eyes. A slow smile spread across his face, half hidden by his beard. "I do like a lady who knows how to handle a gun," he said, letting the knife fall to the floor in front of him with a clatter.

"Kick it over here," she ordered.

"Do it," John growled as McClintock hesitated. He didn't know if he could be much good to her if McClintock made a move. His right arm was nearly useless. Blood had already soaked most of the bottom half of his sweater sleeve and was dripping into a puddle at his feet.

McClintock had risen to a crouch and gave the knife a sideways kick. Then, suddenly, he grabbed John by the bad arm and dug his fingers into the wound, driving John to his knees.

John took a swing at him with his good hand, but McClintock had already moved, diving for the Ruger.

He came up with it before John could tackle him, swinging the barrel toward Miranda.

Instinct made John want to grapple with him, but he ignored it and fell back, out of the cross fire.

A gun barked. He wasn't sure, at first, which of them had fired, until McClintock hit the floor face-first. The Ruger fell to the floor again and skittered away.

John turned to look at Miranda, terror squeezing the breath from his lungs. Only when he saw her standing tall, her pistol still aimed at McClintock's prone body, could he breathe again.

He heard footsteps on the porch outside. At the same moment, Miranda swung her pistol toward the door.

"Don't!" John held up his hands. "It's the sheriff."

He pushed to his feet and opened the door with the only hand that still worked. "Situation under control," he said quickly as the sheriff looked ready to enter with his gun drawn.

Randall looked around quickly, assessing the situation with one sweep of his sharp eyes. He holstered his pistol and nodded at John's bloody arm. "Gunshot?"

"Stab wound." His legs were starting to feel rubbery, he realized.

Randall radioed in the situation and called for paramedics as Miranda hurried to John's side and led him over to the closest armchair.

"I'm bleeding on your rug," he said. His tongue felt thick and his head was starting to swim.

"I can get a new rug," she said and started to cry.

"It looks worse than it really is," the doctor told Miranda a couple of hours later in the waiting room of the Plainview Memorial ER. "It missed any major veins or arteries, and the nerve damage appears minimal. He might have minor numbness in his fingers for a month or two, but everything should return to normal after that."

She took a deep breath. "Good. Thank you."

"It didn't require surgery. We just stitched him up and bandaged the wound. I told him he should keep it in a sling for at least a week. Two would be better. He doesn't need to use it much for eight to ten days, and frankly, he's not going to want to."

"Is he in a lot of pain?" she asked, afraid to hear the answer.

"More than he needs to be. He's refusing anything but ibuprofen."

Of course he was. "Can I see him?"

"We tried to talk him into staying overnight, just because he lost a decent amount of blood and his blood pressure is a little low, but he declined, so we're letting him go. He's being checked out right now, and an orderly will bring him out in a wheelchair in just a moment."

"Thank you." She smiled at the doctor as he walked away.

Her father had been waiting with her. He held out his hand to her as she returned to the seat beside him. "Good news?"

She nodded. "He's going to be okay. They're about to release him."

"He's going home with you?"

"My place is a crime scene. I'll take him to his place and stay with him there instead." She smiled at the look in her father's eyes. "If I can convince him to let me."

Gil smiled. "Piece of cake."

"I need to check in with the sheriff." Eyeing the no–cell phones sign on the wall, she headed for the nearby exit and made her call from outside.

Randall answered on the first ring. "What's the news?"

She told him what the ER doctor had said. "I'm going to try to talk him in to letting me stay with him, at least until we can give our formal statements."

"I've been getting calls from his boss since I got back into the office, wanting an update. Apparently Blake's not answering his phone."

That was because it was out in her truck, locked in the glove compartment. "Tell him what I told you. I'm sure John will call him back as soon as he gets settled at home."

"You've had a hell of a day today, Duncan. I think you ought to take another couple of days off, let all the dust settle. We're going to be dealing with the fallout from Coy's mess anyway. Better for you to stay clear of that until it's sorted out."

"I'm not going to argue this time," she said. Movement out of the corner of her eye caught her attention, and she turned to see a female orderly pushing John into the waiting room in a wheelchair. "John's coming out now. I'll be in touch."

John pushed himself up as soon as the wheelchair rolled to a stop, swaying a little but regaining his balance before Miranda reached his side. His right arm was in a sling, and he looked a little pale and glassy-eyed with pain, but he managed a slight smile as she wrapped her arm around his waist and draped his left arm over her shoulder. "Hey, there."

She smiled back at him. "'Hey, there' to you, too."

"Mr. Duncan." He nodded at Miranda's father.

"Gil," her father said firmly. "Seeing as how you've saved my girl's life three times now."

"She saved me," John said firmly, giving Miranda a look that turned her insides to fire.

"She's got a way of doin' that," her father agreed, giving her a different sort of look but one that left her feeling nearly as warm. "She wants to stay with you at your place, and I reckon you ought to let her, because if you don't, she'll just park outside your house and sleep in her truck."

"Daddy."

He grinned at her. "Reckon he ought to know who he's dealing with."

He stayed with John while she went to the parking lot for her truck. After helping John into the passenger seat and closing the door, he gave a wave and a smile, patting the side of the truck to tell her it was safe to go.

"He's a good man," John murmured.

"I know."

"I'm not going to argue if you want to stay at my place for a few days." His voice softened. "Or weeks."

She glanced at him, but his eyes were closed and his head lolled against the headrest as if he had already fallen asleep.

"I thought they didn't give you the good drugs," she murmured.

He didn't answer.

He woke quickly enough when she got him back to his place, however, and managed to unbuckle his seat belt on his own by the time she opened the passenger door. He stumbled a little getting out but made it into the house without having to lean on her.

"Oh, I forgot." She got him safely seated on his sofa and went back outside, returning a few minutes later with his phone. "Sheriff Randall said your boss has been trying to call you."

John groaned and took the phone, checking the missed calls. "Guess I should call him."

While he was talking to Alexander Quinn, Miranda went into the kitchen in search of some fluids. Even without hitting any major veins or arteries, he'd bled enough to deplete some of the fluids in his body. Rehydration would make him feel better quickly.

She returned to the living room with a large glass of apple juice from his refrigerator. She gave it to him after he laid his phone on the coffee table in front of him. "Did you get everything settled with Quinn?"

"Not everything," he said, taking a couple of big gulps of the apple juice. "Thanks. I needed that."

"What do you mean, not everything?" She sat next to him.

"Well, he was very happy about McClintock, but the sheriff had already caught him up on all of that." John winced as he shifted his injured arm so that he could turn to face her. "But he was a little surprised when I told him I might not be heading back east, even though it should be safe for me to do so now."

"Oh? You're not going back there?" She tried to not read anything into his words, but her heart had started pounding like a jackhammer.

"I'm not."

"Why's that?"

He tipped up her chin, forcing her to look at him. What she saw in his warm hazel eyes did nothing to slow her racing heart. "I guess maybe I'm in a Texas state of mind these days."

"The ol' Lone Star worked its magic?" she asked with a smile.

"*You* worked your magic." He bent until his forehead touched hers. "If you want to tell me I'm crazy, I wouldn't blame you. I know you're a practical kind of woman, and I swear, I usually am a practical kind of guy, too." His eyes closed and his voice softened to a murmur. "But I don't think I can leave you."

Tears stung her eyes, but she blinked them away. "Good. Because I'm not against using force to keep you here."

His eyes snapped open and he laughed. "So you don't think I'm crazy?"

"Oh, no, I never said that." She grinned at him, feeling about a thousand pounds lighter. Her heart was still beating wildly, but it was joy, not fear, that drove its cadence. "I think we're both crazy. Because if you hadn't wanted to stay here, I was going to do my damnedest to talk you in to taking me with you."

He kissed her, lightly at first, then with a fierce hunger that made her head swim. When he pulled away, she had to hold on to his good arm to keep from sliding to the floor.

"You wouldn't have had to work very hard," he said with a laugh.

"I should warn you, despite my considerable skills as a law enforcement officer, I'm not exactly known for my feminine wiles."

"I think your feminine wiles are outstanding," he murmured as he slid his hand over the curve of her hip and bent to kiss the side of her neck. She tugged him closer but made the mistake of clutching his injured arm. He made a hissing sound against her throat and she drew back, horrified.

"I'm so sorry! See what I mean?"

He touched her face. "I'm not exactly known for my way with women, either, so clearly, we're made for each other."

She smiled. "Clearly."

"Of course, you're going to have to teach me a few things about living in Texas," he warned, threading his fingers through her hair and drawing her close again.

"Such as what?"

"Such as how to deal with all this flat land as far as the eye can see."

"It grows on you."

"And where I'm going to find a job to support us and our eight children."

She drew back in horror. "Eight?"

"Not enough?" he asked with a laugh.

"We'll negotiate that point later. And as for a job—there's always the hardware store. Dad's been wanting to hire someone to take over for him when he retires, you know."

"And if I offer myself as a sacrifice, he'll quit bugging you?"

She grinned. "Well, I wasn't going to put it that way."

"I thought you might suggest I take a job with the sheriff's department instead," he said thoughtfully. "Any reason you didn't?"

"Is that what you want to do?" She had come entirely too close to losing him that afternoon to feel sanguine about the idea of his wearing a badge and a gun daily, but with time, she supposed, she could deal with it. "Because if that's what you want—"

"I'm not sure it is," he said seriously. "I'm not sure what I want yet, to tell the truth. I've spent a lot of my life trying to figure out my place in this world, and while I'm not saying working as a deputy definitely isn't that place, I'm not ready to say it is, either."

"I get that."

"I know you do." He caressed her face. "You get me in a way nobody ever has. Which is why the one thing I'm starting to believe is that whatever else I'm supposed to be doing with my life, my place in this world is with you."

Tears pricked her eyes again, and this time she couldn't stop them from falling. "I feel the same way."

He traced the track of her tears with his thumb, kissing her eyelids. "Yup. Two of a kind, you and me. Crazy as coots."

Crazy in love, she corrected silently as she lifted her face for his kiss.

Her favorite kind of crazy.

* * * * *

MILLS & BOON®

Let us take you back in time with our Medieval Brides...

The Novice Bride – Carol Townend

The Dumont Bride – Terri Brisbin

The Lord's Forced Bride – Anne Herries

The Warrior's Princess Bride – Meriel Fuller

The Overlord's Bride – Margaret Moore

Templar Knight, Forbidden Bride – Lynna Banning

Order yours at
www.millsandboon.co.uk/medievalbrides